Praise for *The Vanishing at Castle Moreau*

"In *The Vanishing at Castle Moreau*, Wright pens an imaginative and mysterious tale that is both haunting and heartwarming."

New York Times bestselling author Rachel Hauck

"Jaime Jo Wright never disappoints, and *The Vanishing at Castle Moreau* is no exception. With real, flawed characters who grapple with real-life struggles, this gripping suspense novel will draw readers in from the very first page. Good luck putting it down. I couldn't."

Lynette Eason, bestselling, award-winning author of the EXTREME MEASURES series

"Tucked between the haunting pages is a story that will quickly draw you into a chilling legend you won't be able to escape until the very end. Fear might keep you turning pages, but it's Jaime Jo Wright's ability to radiate beauty in the dark places that make this story unforgettable and prove again and again why she is a master of her craft."

Natalie Walters, award-winning author of *Lights Out*, the SNAP AGENCY series, and the HARBORED SECRETS series

"Jaime Jo Wright, a pioneer of Gothic inspirational romance, is in her prime! Filled to the brim with atmospheric romance, *The Vanishing at Castle Moreau* is not only a chilling and resonant exploration of grief, love, and abuse, but also a welcome piece of wonderfully researched Americana. This all-too-real story, underscored by fairy-tale motifs, will leave readers spellbound until the last page."

Rachel McMillan, author of *The Mozart Code*

T0000059

The
VANISHING
at
CASTLE
MOREAU

Books by Jaime Jo Wright

The
VANISHING
at
CASTLE
MOREAU

JAIME JO WRIGHT

BETHANYHOUSE

a division of Baker Publishing Group

Minneapolis, Minnesota

© 2023 by Jaime Sundsmo

Published by Bethany House Publishers
Minneapolis, Minnesota
www.bethanyhouse.com

Bethany House Publishers is a division of
Baker Publishing Group, Grand Rapids, Michigan

Printed in the United States of America

Library of Congress Cataloging-in-Publication Data
Names: Wright, Jaime Jo, author.
Title: The vanishing at Castle Moreau / Jaime Jo Wright.
Description: Minneapolis, Minnesota : Bethany House Publishers, a division
    of Baker Publishing Group, [2023]
Identifiers: LCCN 2022047542 | ISBN 9780764238345 (paperback) | ISBN
    9780764241291 (casebound) | ISBN 9781493440603 (ebook)
Classification: LCC PS3623.R5388 V36 2023 | DDC 813/.6—dc23
LC record available at https://lccn.loc.gov/2022047542

Scripture quotations are from the King James Version of the Bible.

This is a work of fiction. Names, characters, incidents, and dialogues are products of the author's imagination and are not to be construed as real. Any resemblance to actual events or persons, living or dead, is entirely coincidental.

Cover design by Jennifer Parker

Author is represented by Books & Such Literary Agency.

Baker Publishing Group publications use paper produced from sustainable forestry practices and post-consumer waste whenever possible.

23 24 25 26 27 28 29   7 6 5 4 3 2 1

To my other mom,
Joanne

The one who rescues,
who loves,
and who stands in the gap.

God knew I needed you.

The Girl

MAY 8, 1801

When I was a little girl, my father would often come to my bedside after my screams wakened him in the night. He would smooth back my damp ringlets, the mere feel of his callused and strong hand inspiring an instantaneous calm.

"What is it, little one?" he would ask me.

Every night, the same question. Every night, I would give the same answer.

"It is *her* again, Papa."

"Her?" He would tilt his head, giving credence to my words and refraining from scolding or mockery.

"Yes." I would nod, my head brushing the clean cotton of my pillowcase. "The woman with the crooked hand."

"Crooked hand, hmm?" His query only increased my adamant insistence.

"Yes. She has a nub with two fingers." A tear would often trail down my six-year-old cheek.

My father would smile with a soothing calm. "You are dreaming again, *mon chéri.*"

"No. She was here." He must believe me!

"Shhh." Another gentle stroke of his hand across my forehead. "She is the voice of the mistress of your dreams. We all have one, you know. Only yours needs extra-special care because she isn't beautiful like the rest. She is the one who brings the nightmares, but she doesn't mean to harm you. She is only doing her best with what she has been given, and what she has been given are her own horrors."

"Her hand?" I would reply, even though we repeated this explanation many nights in a row.

"Yes," my father would nod. "Her hand is a reflection of the ugliness in her stories. Stories she tells to you at night when all is quiet and your eyes are closed."

"But they were open," I would insist.

"No. You only *think* they were open."

"I am afraid of the ghost, Papa," I urge.

His eyes smile. "*Oui*. And yet there are no spirits to haunt you. Only the dream mistress. Shoo her away and she will flee. She is a mist. She is not real. See?" And he would wave his hand in the air. "Shoo, mistress. Away and be gone!"

We would survey the dark bedroom then, and, seeing nothing, my father would lean over and press his lips to my cheek. "Now sleep. I will send your mother's dream mistress to you. Her imaginings are pleasant ones."

"Thank you," I would whisper.

Another kiss. The bed would rise a bit as he lifted his weight from the mattress. His nightshirt would hang around his shins, and he would pause at the doorway of my room where I slept. An only child, in a home filled with the fineries of a Frenchman's success of trade. "Sleep, *mon chéri*."

"Yes, Papa."

The door would close.

My eyes would stay open.

I would stare at the woman with the crooked hand, who hovered in the shadows where the door had just closed. I would stare at her and know what my father never would.

She existed.

She was not a dream.

one

Daisy François

APRIL 1870

The castle cast its hypnotic pull over any passerby who happened along to find it, tucked deep in the woods in a place where no one would build a castle, let alone live in one. It served no purpose there. No strategy of war, no boast of wealth, no respite for a tired soul. Instead, it simply existed. Tugging. Coercing. Entrapping. Its two turrets mimicked bookends, and if removed, one would fear the entire castle would collapse like a row of standing volumes. Windows covered the façade above a stone archway, which drew her eyes to the heavy wooden door with its iron hinges, the bushes along the foundation, and the stone steps leading to the mouth of the edifice. Beyond it was a small orchard of apple trees, their tiny pink blossoms serving as a delicate backdrop for the magnificent property.

Castle Moreau.

Home to an orphan. Or it would be.

Daisy clutched the handles of her carpetbag until her

knuckles were sure to be white beneath her threadbare gloves. She stood in the castle's shadow, staring at its immense size. Who had built such an imposing thing? Here, in the northern territory, where America boasted its own mansions but still rejected any mimicking of the old country. Castles were supposed to stare over their fiefdoms, house lords and ladies, gentry, noblemen, and summon the days of yore when knights rescued fair maidens. Castles were not supposed to center themselves inside a forest, on the shore of a lake, a mile from the nearest town.

This made Castle Moreau a mystery. No one knew why Tobias Moreau had built it decades before. Today the castle held but one occupant: Tobias's daughter, Ora Moreau, who was eighty-six years old. She was rarely ever seen, and even more rarely, ever heard from. Still, Ora's words had graced most households in the region, printed between the covers of books with embossed golden titles. Her horror stories had thrilled many readers, and over the years, the books helped in making an enigma of the reclusive old woman.

When the newspaper had advertised a need for a housemaid—preferably one without a home or ties to distract her from her duties—it was sheer coincidence that Daisy had seen it, even more of a coincidence that she fit the requirements. And so it was a surprise she was hired after only a brief letter inquiring after the position.

Now she stood before the castle, her pulse thrumming with the question *why?* Why had she accepted the position? Why would she allow herself to be swallowed up by this castle? The stories were bold, active. Women disappeared here. It was said that Castle Moreau was a place that consumed the vulnerable. Welcoming them in but never giving them back.

Daisy stiffened her shoulders. Swallowed. Tilted her chin

upward in determination. She had marched into hell before—many times, in fact. Castle Moreau couldn't possibly be much worse than that.

Cleo Clemmons

Two Years before Present Day

They had buried most souvenirs of the dead with the traditions of old, and yet what a person didn't understand before death, they would certainly comprehend after. The need for that ribbon-tied lock of hair, the *memento mori* photograph of the deceased, a bone fragment, a capsule of the loved one's ashes—morbid to those who had not lost, but understandable to those who had.

Needing to touch the tangible was a fatal flaw in humanity. Faith comforted only so far until the gasping panic overcame the grieving like a tsunami, stealing oxygen, with the only cure being something tangible. Something to touch. To hold. To be held. It was in these times the symbolism attached to an item became pivotal to the grieving. A lifeline of sorts.

For Cleo, it was a thumbprint. Her grandfather's thumbprint. Inked after death, digitized into a .png file, uploaded to a jewelry maker, and etched into sterling silver. It hung around her neck, settling between her breasts, just left of her heart. No one would know it was there, and if they did, they wouldn't ask. A person didn't ask about what was held closest to another's heart. That was information that must be offered, and Cleo had no intention of doing so. To anyone. Her grandfather was her memory alone—the good and the bad. What he'd left behind in the form of Cleo's broken insides were Cleo's to disguise. Faith held her hand, or rather, she clenched hands with faith, but in the darkness, when no one was watching, Cleo fit her thumb to her grandfather's print and attempted to feel the actual warmth of his hand, to infuse all the cracks and offer momentary refuge from the ache.

Funny how this was what she thought of. Now. With what was left of her world crashing down around her like shrapnel pieces, blazing lava-orange and deadly.

"Pick up, pick up, pick up," Cleo muttered into her phone, pressing it harder against her ear than she needed to. She huddled in the driver's seat of her small car, all of her worldly possessions packed into the trunk and the back seat. She could hear the ringing on the other end. She owed it to Riley. One call. One last goodbye.

"Hey."

"Riley!" Cleo stiffened in anticipation.

". . . you've reached Riley . . ." the voice message continued, and Cleo laid her head back against the seat. The recording finished, and Cleo squeezed her eyes shut against the world outside of her car, against the darkness, the fear, the grief. This was goodbye. It had to be.

The voicemail *beep* was Cleo's cue. She swallowed, then spoke, her words shivering with compressed emotion. What did a person say in a last farewell?

"Riley, it's me. Cleo. I—" she bit her lip, tasting blood— "I-I won't be calling again. This is it. You know. It's what I hoped would never happen. I am so, so sorry this happened to you! Just know I tried to protect you. But now—" her breath caught as tears clogged her throat—"this is the only way I can. Whatever happens now, just know I love you. I will *always* love you." Desperation warred with practicality.

Shut off the phone.

There was no explaining this.

There never would be.

"Goodbye, Ladybug." Cleo thumbed the end button, then threw the phone against the car's dashboard. A guttural scream curled up her throat and split her ears as the inside of the vehicle absorbed the sound.

Then it was silent.

That dreadful, agonizing silence that came with the burgeoning, unknown abyss of a new start. Cleo stared at her phone lying on the passenger-side floor. She lunged for it, fumbling with a tiny tool until she popped open the slot on its side. Pulling out the SIM card, Cleo bent it back and forth until it snapped. Determined, she pushed open the car door and stepped out.

The road was heavily wooded on both sides. Nature was her only observer.

She flung the broken SIM card into the ditch, marched to the front of the car, and wedged the phone under the front tire. She'd roll over it when she left, crush it, and leave nothing to be traced.

Cleo took a moment to look around her. Oak forest, heavy undergrowth of brush, wild rosebushes whose thorns would take your skin off, and a heap of dead trees and branches from the tornado that had ravaged these woods decades prior. The rotting wood was all that remained to tell the tale now, but it was so like her life. Rotting pieces that never went away. Ever.

She climbed back into the car and twisted the key, revving the engine to life. Cleo felt her grandfather's thumbprint until it turned her skin hot with the memories. Memories of what had set into motion a series of frightful events. Events that were her responsibility to protect her sister from.

Goodbye, Ladybug.

There was no explaining in a voicemail to a twelve-year-old girl that her older sister was abandoning her in order to save her. Cleo knew from this moment on, Riley would play that message, and slowly resentment would seep in as she grew older. Resentment that Cleo had left and would never come back.

But she couldn't go back. Not if she loved Riley. Sometimes love required the ultimate sacrifice. Sometimes love required death. Death to all they knew, all they had known. If Cleo disappeared, then Riley would be left alone. Riley would be safe. She could grow up as innocent as possible.

So long as Cleo Clemmons no longer existed.

two

Cleo

PRESENT DAY

I s that it?"

The pointed question came from a young woman, her nasal septum pierced with a ring, her nose studded, and her left eyebrow sporting a row of rings that, if Cleo was honest, looked painful.

"Umm . . ." Cleo swept her gaze over the gas station's counter. She had gum, a candy bar, a bag of chips.

Don't do it. Don't. Do. It.

"Do you have whiskey?"

The attendant raised her ringed eyebrow with a hint of bored curiosity. "Take your pick." She pointed to the shelves on the wall behind her and the rows of alcoholic beverages lining them. "And welcome to Wisconsin."

Cleo offered a nervous laugh. Wisconsin. She hadn't ever been here. Once, her grandfather had taken her to Missouri. Until now, that was as close to Wisconsin as she'd been. "I'll take that one." She pointed to a bottle of whiskey in a locked glass-case display.

The girl raised her eyebrow again. "You sure?"

"Yes." Was she supposed to opt for the shot-sized bottles not being kept under lock and key? Cleo tapped her foot impatiently. Biting back the words that made her grab at her necklace for comfort. The ridges of her grandfather's thumbprint rubbed against her own. She caught strength from it—strength and guilt. Awful, consuming guilt.

And quick, before I change my mind. Cleo was breaking her New Year's resolution.

"That'll be one hundred and forty-two bucks and eighty-one cents." The attendant sniffed, and Cleo briefly wondered how a person blew their nose with a ring stuck through the middle part of its cartilage.

"My truck is a gas guzzler." Cleo swiped her card, making small talk.

"Yeah, and whiskey isn't cheap," the attendant muttered.

Cleo reached for the paper-bagged whiskey and her snacks that had been tossed into a plastic bag. "Thanks." She threw a lopsided smile toward the beringed woman, who stared after her without saying a word.

Cleo pushed on the door that led outside, then quickly shuffled to her right as an older woman stepped through the same door.

"I'm sorry," the woman mumbled.

"No worries," Cleo responded.

"Hey!"

Cleo paused and looked over her shoulder, not sure if the "hey" was directed at her or the woman who was headed toward the aisle of bagged junk food. The attendant was eyeing Cleo, leaning on the counter, her elbows propping her upper body. "I'm Stasia."

Cleo stared at the young woman for a moment, trying to compute the reason behind the sudden personal introduction.

Stasia's smile slanted, but her dark eyes sparkled and changed the sullen appearance of her face into someone quite pretty. "I noticed your out-of-state plates. You going to be in town for a while or just passing through?"

Cleo adjusted the bag on her arm, shooting a quick glance at the other woman, whose head was bent over a bag of Doritos, apparently to find out their caloric count. *Just buy them and to heck with the calories.*

She shifted her attention back to Stasia. "Umm . . ." Stasia's sudden interest was unsettling. "I'll be in Needle Creek for a bit." She hesitated to explain further but did anyway. "At Castle Moreau."

"Castle Moreau?" Stasia's eyes sharpened. "Really?"

"Yes?" It was a question in return for Stasia.

Stasia chewed her bottom lip, flicking the lip ring against her teeth. "Well, it's Castle Moreau." She held her hands up as though Cleo should just naturally know what she meant. "A landmark of Needle Creek. Mysterious and delectable with its—" Stasia paused for effect, waggling her eyebrows—"its deadly charm," she concluded.

The explanation did nothing to assuage Cleo's nerves.

"Okay." Stasia waved her off with a once-again serious face. "Be safe." With that, she slid backward and off the counter, picking up her phone to stare at its screen.

Be safe.

The words ripped through Cleo with the solemnity of what they implied. To be safe meant danger loomed. She'd been dodging that for the last two years. Two years. Cleo Clemmons was no longer; she was Cleo *Carpenter* now. Better to keep her first name or she'd completely mess up her cover. One would think she was running from the mob and not a twelve-year-old girl.

Actually, Riley would be fourteen now.

Cleo opened the back hatch of her black Suburban and set the whiskey in a plastic crate so it wouldn't tip over or slide around as she drove. She wasn't sure what Wisconsin's alcohol laws were for transporting it, but Cleo figured it was better to have the whiskey well away from the front seat if she happened to get stopped by a patrol officer.

Settling in behind the steering wheel, Cleo reached out and scratched the furry forehead of her long-haired tabby cat. He was various shades of gray and black tipped with brown, with eyes a luminescent yellow. Murphy had found Cleo one morning near her car. He'd been sitting on the pavement just outside the driver's door with an anticipatory expression, his delicate nose tilted upward and his tufted ears at attention.

Murphy had been Cleo's sidekick ever since. She'd put little effort into finding his original owner. He was just too cute, and although Cleo had been raised to have integrity, she figured checking to see if Murphy was microchipped was effort enough. He hadn't been. No tags. No phone number. So, Murphy was hers from day one.

Pulling out of the gas station, Cleo glanced at the phone that was positioned on the dash. It wasn't hers. It'd been supplied to her and the very presence of it made her nervous. All phones had GPS in them now, right? Granted, who would know she carried a phone that had been prepaid and purchased by her long-distance employer? No one. It was why she'd agreed. She could maintain her anonymity from her old life while still being able to communicate with her current one.

The phone pealed, startling Cleo enough to make Murphy

trill deep in his throat. A questioning sound the cat was prone to make anytime Cleo gave off the aura of discomfort.

Cleo jabbed the Bluetooth button on the steering wheel. "Hello?"

"Cleo Carpenter?" Deacon Tremblay had the voice of a radio DJ.

"Yes, it is."

"Good. I was hoping to hear from you today."

Don't gaslight me into feeling guilty for not calling. Her defenses rose instantaneously. "I haven't arrived at your grandmother's yet," she said instead.

Although it couldn't be that far away now. She'd already left the small town behind and was traversing the back roads that dragged her deeper into the wooded acreage of rural Wisconsin. She still didn't quite believe any of this was happening. It felt . . . risky. The Tremblay family was well known, influential. They were American aristocracy. But desperate times called for desperate measures. Granted, it'd been desperation the past two years, and frankly, she was tired. Tired of odd jobs, of waitressing, of cleaning toilets at gas stations for cash under the table. The advertisement had been enticing with wages that would pay for her gas, her groceries, and, well, the bottle of whiskey. She'd found out it was *that* Tremblay family later—after she'd pursued the advertisement. Deacon Tremblay, however, had made it clear he was managing it all from New York. The idea he'd show up in Podunk, Wisconsin, wasn't much of a concern.

"I wanted to give you a few pointers." Deacon's voice jerked Cleo back to the conversation at hand. "Grandmother can be . . . well, she won't be thrilled about this."

"They never are." Cleo applied pressure to the brakes as a stop sign approached. She winced at her dry comment. How would she know?

"Yeah, well . . ." There was a moment of awkward silence, and Cleo was quick to catch on.

She tapped the steering wheel as she looked both ways at the four-way stop. Woods, woods, and more woods. A soul could get lost here.

"Your grandmother doesn't know I'm coming, does she?" Cleo was going to have to keep careful track of the broad picture and make sure the major pieces didn't crash and make it all fall apart.

Deacon cleared his throat, and it reverberated through the vehicle's stereo system. "No. She isn't aware of your arrival."

"I'm sure one more person won't upset things too much." Cleo fixed a smile on her face so it would somehow translate through the phone and make her sound more optimistic than she felt. Maintain professionalism, even with rich people like Deacon Tremblay. Although she had to hand it to him. At least he was personally invested in his grandmother's situation versus having an assistant make all the calls.

"One more person?" he asked.

There was silence.

Tires crunched on the asphalt road that was barely compressed gravel and strewn with sticks from a recent windstorm.

"Well, I mean . . ." Cleo fumbled for words. She really didn't have to explain what she meant, did she? "Her family . . . they're there, right?"

More silence.

Deacon cleared his throat again.

"Mr. Tremblay?" Cleo slowed down and pulled onto the side of the road beneath a canopy of oak trees. She needed to focus.

"*I* am her family. Grandmother lives alone. I thought I'd made that clear."

Cleo stared at her phone as if she could see Deacon through it. She was glad this wasn't a video chat. She had a weird thing about talking to drop-dead gorgeous men, and she'd seen enough of him on celebrity sites to know what he looked like. Famous like an American Kennedy, loaded like a Kardashian, and having dated a few celebrity women, Deacon Tremblay was the epitome of desirable. Desirable men made her nervous and shattered her confidence.

She tempered her breathing as she pondered her next words. "Well, that's fine then." Really, the less people the better. It just seemed weird that Deacon Tremblay would pick an obscure, no-name like her to dig into the privacy of his grandmother's belongings. There were companies designed to do that sort of work. Large ones. Professionals.

"My grandmother's residence needs organization, as we discussed, but you are on your own as far as coordinating what you'll need. I want this done quietly, efficiently, and no talking to the press."

That last part was no problem. "Sir, I'm an expert at keeping things quiet."

"My grandmother is a hoarder. The public would have a field day with that information. It's why I hired *you*." Deacon Tremblay's tone had grown sterner.

The emphasis brooked no assumptions. The online advertisement had been basic. Home organizer needed for elderly woman. Cleo had responded to the employer, who'd listed themselves as D. R. Brown. It wasn't until later that she found out it was the infamous multimillionaire playboy from New York City and the heir to the American Tremblay fortune built during the post-Revolutionary War era. The Tremblays were one of the best-known original American families still to exist. Deacon had been flying low under the radar in his job posting. Obviously, anonymity and obscurity were important to him—as they were to her—yet Cleo couldn't dispel the anxious panic that rode just beneath the surface. Someone as careful as Deacon Tremblay would *not* hire a person equally obscure with no visible past. Cleo Carpenter did not exist. A simple background check would give her away. He *had* to have figured that out.

"Ms. Carpenter?" Deacon's deep voice snapped her back to the conversation. "Is this job going to be too large for you?"

She could picture it now. Boxes stacked to the ceiling and falling over. Garbage rotting in corners. Mounds of clothing. Crates filled with collectibles and junk simultaneously. Rat skeletons buried under ten years' worth of newspapers. She did *not* want to clean out dead rats for a living, but she also didn't have the option to be finicky.

"No, no, I can do it." Cleo mustered as much patience as she could. "But what if I need outside help? Like a dumpster or something?"

"Then arrange it," Deacon replied.

"Arrange it?" With what money? Did she call Deacon? Were they doing this project under the Moreau-Tremblay estate or under an assumed name to avoid nosy reporters and paparazzi?

"Yes, arrange for whatever you need to get the job done," Deacon added in a tone that implied it was the most logical next step. "That's what I hired you for."

"No." Cleo couldn't help the irritation that leaked into her voice. "No, you hired me to help organize your grand-mother's home."

"Isn't cleaning up a part of organizing?"

"Well, yes, but—"

"And you're an organizer?"

"Well—"

"So, *organize* whatever help is needed. I'm paying for it.

You and I will work on this and no one else. If you need money, let me know. I can't manage the project, though. That's what you're for."

"I'm not a project manager!"

"Ms. Carpenter." Deacon Tremblay was all business now. "Do you or do you not want the job?"

"I do, but—"

"Great," Deacon said, cutting her off. "Now, back to my purpose in calling you. Like I said, Grand-mère is not aware of your arrival. When you pull into the property, you'll want to go to the side entrance. You can ring her there, and when she comes, make sure you immediately tell her I sent you."

"You sent me." Cleo felt like a parrot. She also felt her self-confidence draining away.

"Yes. Let her know I'm covering all the expenses—that will be her first concern 'cause she's stingy with family money. And let her know that if she bars you out, I'll give you the authority to break in."

"Break into her house?"

"The castle." It was no-nonsense, the way Deacon Tremblay declared it.

"A castle?" Cleo met Murphy's gold eyes in an exchange of doubt and concern. She had visions of King Arthur's Court and that old movie starring Sean Connery and Richard Gere.

"No one ever said my family was conventional. Neither are our homes."

Deacon's admission might have warmed Cleo on another day. It might have given her that slow-nod moment where she admired his veiled apology for flaunting their wealth. It was a rich man's attempt at humility. But it did not impress her now. She was stupefied.

"A castle," she repeated, tapping her fingers against the steering wheel.

"Built in the early eighteen hundreds. Apparently, my great-great-whatever-grandfather missed his homeland."

"He was English?" Cleo assumed without thinking.

"French actually. You've seen the photographs of French châteaus?"

"No." Or maybe she had and just hadn't paid attention.

"Oh. Anyway, we French have a rich history in them alongside the proverbial English domination of the architecture."

Cleo waited because she really had nothing to add. Not a thing. She drummed her fingers on the steering wheel while Murphy perched on the seat next to her, his tail slapping the leather.

Deacon cleared his throat. "Nevertheless, my grandmother lives in Castle Moreau, and I expect she'll insist you breach the walls in order to deal with her toxic mess."

"Why is it called 'Castle Moreau' if your last name is Tremblay?" Cleo asked.

Deacon chuckled at her question. "My great-great-great-grandfather's surname was Moreau. He had a daughter. She married. Names shifted. But the castle retains the original name."

"Ah." Cleo nodded.

Murphy uttered a little *meow* in his throat, pushing up to all fours and stretching. Cleo gave the cat a comforting pat on his head. She wished someone was in the car to do the same for her.

three

Daisy

She wondered if all castles were like this. Dark hues of navy blue in the corners where stone walls met mahogany floors, no windows in the hallways, only niches that created arched hollows in the walls, with cast-iron arms bearing kerosene lamps. It was cool but not damp. In fact, contrary to what Daisy had imagined when she'd stood outside the castle, the wind didn't infiltrate the place. The elements were blocked by the castle's thick walls.

"The castle is small iffen you compare it to the ones of the old world." The stoop-shouldered, elderly man shuffled ahead of Daisy, lofting a lamp to help light the way. It had been evening when Daisy stood in the castle's shadow, dusk when she'd mustered the nerve to lift the heavy knocker forged in the shape of a dragon's head, and now it was nighttime. "There's the south wing where'n you first comes in." His grammar was awful, but Daisy hadn't the heart to judge him. He seemed as uneducated as she was, so in a way, he made her feel a warmth that otherwise didn't exist here at

Castle Moreau. "South wing has them rooms that Madame Tremblay uses—like'n her study, and a place with stuffed, fancy chairs to drink yer tea, a library, another fancy place iffen visitors come—which they don't—an' so on. The east wing is the family wing. You won't go there. Rooms bein' private and all, you'd more'n like get sent to the dungeon for trespass."

"There's a dungeon?" Daisy's breath hitched as the heels of her worn shoes made echoing footsteps on the floor.

A chuckle rumbled in the man's chest. "Wouldn't surprise me in this place." It was a cryptic response and a non-answer to her genuine curiosity. "Yer room is here—in the north wing."

"Is it where all the servants live?" Daisy adjusted the weight of her carpetbag on her elbow. The bag held all her belongings, and its well-worn and faded rust velvet had seen far better days.

The old man paused and lifted the lamp, which illuminated the drooping skin beneath his eyes, his jowls, and the long lobes of his ears. His face reminded Daisy of a beagle, and the floppy-eared dog reminded her of melted candle wax. So did Festus. At least that was what he'd called himself when she arrived. Festus. No surname or anything else to signify his position at the castle.

He stared at her now, and in the low light, Daisy couldn't tell if his eyes were gray, or if they were so clouded with age that what had once been brilliant blue irises had through the years undergone a transformation of sorts.

"Other servants?" he rasped. "Ain't none more than you."

"Oh." Daisy couldn't hide the look of consternation that crossed her features. Who was going to show her what her duties were? Festus?

He shuffled forward again without offering further explanation as to the abysmal lack of staff. "You gets the north wing to yerself." Festus announced this as if it were grand news and she the lucky recipient of some unexpected fortune. But as he rounded a corner that led to yet another lonely hallway, Daisy could barely swallow her anxiety.

Alone.

In the north wing.

Festus stopped before a door that was the same dark wood as the flooring. He twisted the heavy knob, and the door opened slowly with the eerie squeaking of old hinges.

"Here you be." He stepped aside for Daisy to move past him.

She stared at the room with a mixture of amazement and utter horror. It was far larger than she'd expected. It was obvious that this was not a servant's quarters, but an actual room probably used at one point for esteemed guests of the Moreau family. The room was indeed spacious, yet the luxury ended there.

The bed was canopied and covered in sheets that hung off the top frame, shielding the mattress from view. Spiderwebs swooped in the top corners of the room, decorating the crown molding with lacy strands of very-much-alive arachnids. A window at the far wall was void of its drapery. There was a wardrobe with a skeleton key sticking out from its lock. An Oriental rug stretched across the floor in faded hues of blue and yellow, which seemed to mock the rest of the dark room's aged elegance.

"It's like Miss Havisham's house," Daisy muttered to herself.

"Pardon?" Festus barked.

Daisy startled and turned her gaze on him. "Oh. Well, she's from a book I read—*Great Expectations* by Mr. Dickens. Miss Havisham lives in an old mansion draped in cobwebs."

Festus waved her off with a meaty hand and a grunt. "No time for books, me. Can't read no how."

Daisy had also been barely able to read. But fictional friends had offered her companionship, and so at thirteen she'd striven and labored until she could piece together language on paper and enter worlds that offered her escape from her own.

She allowed Festus to dismiss her observation. Comparing Castle Moreau to Miss Havisham's thwarted wedding and rotting cake and horrific home conditions would be insulting, and she was a bit glad Festus didn't know the novel she'd referred to.

"Right then," Festus said. "Rest now. You can do yer things in the morning."

"How . . . I mean, who . . . ?" Daisy was suddenly flustered. "Who should I look for in the morning?"

At Festus's blank look, she tried again.

"To receive directions for my tasks, who should I find?"

Festus's eyes widened in utter ignorance. "Iffen I knew that, we wouldn't need you." Then he closed the door with a thud, leaving Daisy to stand there alone, without guidance or direction, in the middle of a room that promised the appearance of ghostly apparitions as soon as the clock struck midnight.

Daisy shivered.

She had never appreciated spirits, and she much preferred that Festus would have brought her to a less lofty abode. One with a cot, a small dresser, a black-scarred mirror, and maybe, for a bit of luxury, a pillow.

But he hadn't.

Tonight she would sleep with spiders and spirits, the visions of Miss Havisham, and the terrors of echoing castle walls. All in the woods, in a place where a castle didn't belong.

She'd slept on the floor last night because she had no desire to snuggle beneath the dusty coverings on the canopy bed. When Daisy inspected the mattress, it seemed comfortable enough, but the layer of dinge was enough to curl her lip—and she wasn't spoiled or snooty like Estella, the girl in Dickens's novel. She just appreciated not feeling like her skin was crawling, or that during the deep hours of sleep, a spider was caressing her cheek while cackling under its breath to itself. Spiders were, after all, the worst of God's creations. Daisy had said as much to the orphanage mistress whom she'd lived under from ages seven to ten, and she'd received ten whacks with a switch and an hour-long bonding moment with the corner of the room for her sacrilege and ungratefulness to God for His creation.

Daisy hadn't blamed God. She believed He understood her repulsion to the eight-legged terrors, also her repulsion to the mistress. They were most likely from the same family, spiders and orphanage mistresses—and God, according to the reverend at the small church they attended, was there to rescue her.

And He *had* rescued her from the orphanage mistress when the Greenbergs took her in as their daughter—as a replacement for their dead daughter. Cursing the fever that had taken her, Daisy had slipped into the deceased girl's position, yet she had never actually measured up to the girl's legacy. She had the scars to prove it.

Still, God, in Daisy's opinion, was a rescuer, and all the others were the evil ones from which she needed rescuing. Including, but not limited to, spiders.

Daisy tied the strings of her apron around her waist,

assuming she would need to wear one. It was yellow and had a small patch of violets embroidered at the bottom. The apron had been Mrs. Greenberg's, but Daisy had stolen it the night she'd abandoned her guardians once and for all. Castle Moreau might not provide uniforms, and Daisy wanted to be outfitted as appropriately as possible. While God was her rescuer, He didn't rain down aprons on escaped orphans who had barely reached the age of twenty and one, but He did promise forgiveness. So Daisy took comfort in the thought God forgave her as she ran her hands down the stolen apron to smooth its wrinkles.

Without a mirror of any sort, Daisy could only hope that her hair, which rivaled strawberries with its color, was tucked into its bun as well as it could be. That it was curly was an understatement. Usually it was fuzzy.

She was still concerned over Festus's declaration last night that if they had someone for her to report to for duties, they wouldn't have needed *her*. It seemed, aside from Festus, she was all on her own, the sole member of Castle Moreau's staff. Surely there had to be a cook! She felt a deep pit of dread in her stomach at the idea that she might have to cook and clean as well as pretend to know what she was doing for the rest of it. Daisy was woefully unprepared to clean an entire castle with a feather duster, let alone manage the place. In fact, she didn't know the first thing about being a housekeeper, or a maid, or whatever fell below a maid on the household scale of servants.

"These aren't the days of Charles Dickens," Daisy told herself, her voice splitting the dank silence of the massive bedroom. "This is the late end of the century, and it is America." The castle was wreaking havoc on her imagination. If she didn't remind herself, one look at the woods outside the window would convince her she had traveled back in time to the days of knights and chivalry, and that the old woman who occupied the castle was a countess, not a writer of novels that would make even the likes of Mary Shelley wince in fear.

Thinking of Shelley's novel *Frankenstein*, Daisy squeezed her eyes shut. Oh, to curl up with a book—it was a luxury she'd always had to sneak and steal time for.

"Stiff upper lip," Daisy mumbled to herself. Mr. Greenberg used to say those three words through gritted teeth just before whipping her backside with the strap. He probably meant it to intimidate her, but Daisy found it was quite useful in shutting out the evil world around her.

Daisy made her way into the maze of hallways, surprised at how dramatically the lighting had changed in the morning hours. The castle was a bit brighter and felt more appealing the closer she got to the south wing, where the bulk of daily activities took place. She was thankful she had an excellent memory and could find her way without too much trouble. As for Festus, the man was nowhere to be seen this morning.

Her footsteps echoed on the dull wood floors that once had to have been richly polished. The hallway opened onto a balcony that overlooked the main hall. A large chandelier hung from the center of the ceiling at eye level with the balcony, though its crystal pendants no longer dazzled due to dust and time, the candles cold and unlit.

Daisy moved to the banister of scrolled wood, thicker than the circumference of her hands as she gripped it to peer over the edge. Below, in the hall, the floors were tiled in an intricate design that reminded Daisy of a peacock in full pride. Deep blues and emerald green with scattered hues of gray created a burst of color, muted only by what had to be months of grime being tracked through the great hall.

Two tall windows flanked the main entrance, their stained glass of blues and greens matching the tile floor. Daisy could imagine a fine masquerade or promenade taking place here, with guests arriving in full regalia with pompadours and wigs, silks and satins, buttons of brass and cravats of crimson. Today, though, the hall's beauty and color had been dimmed by age and lack of care. The castle was shrouded now in something dark, like a cloak that had fallen over its glory days long, long ago . . .

Shaking herself from her musings, Daisy drew a deep breath and moved to the stairway that wound its way to the floor below and the rooms where, according to Festus, Daisy would find some form of humanity. More than likely the castle's only occupant, Ora Tremblay, the authoress of horror.

A door to her left at the far end of the balcony caught Daisy's eye as she prepared to descend. She hadn't noticed the door until now, as its molding blended with the pattern on the wall. If it wasn't for the brass doorknob, she would have missed it altogether.

Distracted, she abandoned the stairs and tiptoed toward the mystery door. Curiosity was a dreadful thing, and she'd been filled with it for as long as she could remember. A wayward curl of red frizz dangled over her right eye, and Daisy pushed it aside as she twisted the knob.

The seal between the door and its frame groaned stubbornly, making her think it had been a long time since this door had been opened. She hesitated. Servants shouldn't snoop. Most definitely not. Mrs. Greenberg would be swatting her at this very moment in rebuke. *"Young ladies do not go where they are not invited!"* Mrs. Greenberg would snap.

Daisy had to admit she hadn't been invited anywhere in Castle Moreau—except for being invited to care for it. If

Festus's implication was correct, then she was the only house servant, which meant it was within her rights to investigate the various rooms . . . wasn't it?

The room beyond the door was silent, minus the agonizing whine of the hinges as it protested being opened. Daisy poked her head in, then entered entirely. Her eyes took a moment to adjust to the room. It was vast and oppressive. The walls were paneled in dark mahogany to match the flooring. The windows on the opposite wall were covered with heavy green draperies, pulled shut, canceling out any light that might otherwise make the room cheery.

A large stone fireplace with a majestic mantel stood cold and empty of coals. It didn't appear to have been lit for some time, and the stuffed chairs forming a semicircle in front of the fireplace were covered with dust cloths. Bookshelves lined the wall from floor to ceiling on her right. The shelves were filled with thick tomes, and for a brief second, Daisy had a euphoric rush of delight.

"Do you always enter a room unannounced?"

A gravelly male voice shattered Daisy's calm. She shrieked, jolted backward, and rammed her elbow against the edge of the solid door.

Rubbing her elbow, she squinted toward the shadows to her left. The form of an imposing desk came into view, with little to adorn it but a lamp that remained dark. A man sat behind the desk, his hands folded and resting on the desktop.

Daisy realized then that he'd been silently observing her from his place behind the desk. She couldn't make out all his features, but what she could see caught her breath in her chest. Deep-set eyes. Rakish dark hair. A sharp jawline. Black shirt buttoned to his neck but with no tie.

Daisy could feel his eyes on her. Penetrating. Judging. Drawing conclusions about her . . .

"I'm so sorry?" Her words slipped out as a question and gave away her nerves that made Daisy's voice quaver beneath his assessment.

He didn't respond. Staring seemed to be his action of choice, and that was more unsettling than if he'd launched into an angry fit at her interruption.

Needing to fill the silence, Daisy fumbled for words. "I-I'm Daisy, the new housemaid. I was merely trying to find . . . well, I thought it best if I . . . I mean, everything is so dusty and needs attention, I thought . . . Would you like some tea?"

He stared a moment longer and then responded, "No."

"No?" Daisy squeaked. "Well then, coffee perhaps?" She prayed there was coffee, and someone in the kitchen who would have already made it.

"No."

"No," Daisy repeated.

He continued with his staring.

"Can I . . . do you need anything? Sir," she added quickly.

This time he bent his head down to look at whatever he had been reading. It was a blatant dismissal, and Daisy took the opportunity it afforded and made her escape. She shut the door with a firm thud behind her, leaning back against it, tilting her head until it rested against the door.

That had been unexpected.

Very unexpected.

It was so, so *Wuthering Heights.* Or worse, perhaps he was a male Mrs. Havisham, doomed to abiding in a locked room, harboring a broken heart from thwarted love.

Footsteps on the stairs caused Daisy to jerk her attention toward the sound. Festus stepped onto the top stair, his eyes shifting between her and the door. Awareness crept over his face as he took in what had to be Daisy's bewildered expression and the fact that her hand was still on the knob.

Festus cleared his throat. "I shoulda told you night before. Leave the room at the far end of the balcony alone."

"Who is he?" Daisy breathed, unable to squelch her horrified curiosity.

Festus's brows drew together, and his "harrumph" was loud enough that Daisy was certain the man behind the door would have heard it.

"*He* is Lincoln Tremblay." Festus rammed his hands deep into the pockets of his trousers. "Madame Tremblay's grandson. She calls him *mon chéri* sometimes."

"*Mon chéri?*" The French words on her tongue felt strange and unfamiliar.

"*You* don't call him that," Festus warned, shaking his head. He motioned with his knobby hand for her to follow him back down the stairs.

Daisy hurried after him. "What do I call him then?" She had to know since she would more than likely be helping to serve him.

Festus grunted and didn't bother to give her his attention as he descended the stairs. "You don't call him nothing."

"But what if I need to get his attention?" Daisy frowned, hurrying after the exceptionally spry old man.

"You won't." Festus reached the bottom of the stairs and turned to level a stern glare on her. "*He* speaks only to Madame Tremblay."

"But I spoke to him."

"Did you?" Festus's voice held a hint of wry teasing and deep warning.

"I thought—"

"Thoughts are deceivin'."

With that, Festus was obviously finished discussing

Lincoln Tremblay. Daisy glanced up the stairs one last time. But she wasn't sure she was finished. The haunted visage of the man sequestered in his study stayed with her. She wasn't certain if he was a man to be pitied or to be terrified of.

Perhaps he was a bit of both.

four

Cleo

It was definitely a castle, though nothing close to the massive, imposing quality of Neuschwanstein Castle that Cleo had seen pictures of and what Cinderella's castle at the popular theme park was modeled after. It had three stories, turrets at both ends, and was completely made of stone and it was square in the middle.

Cleo shut the car door after giving Murphy a nervous glance. She had bit off way more than she could chew. This was obvious. Deacon Tremblay had magnanimous ideas that she could organize his grandmother's home, and she had no idea what questions to ask before accepting a job that paid well and had stipulations about being discreet and confidential. That last part she could do—she *had* been doing—but she probably should have asked how big the task was *and* clarified it wasn't a hoarder's paradise—or a flipping castle.

Cleo surveyed the open space before the castle. It was apparent that historically the winding drive had once served carriages, which were welcome to pull up and stop before the grand entrance that boasted large timber doors. At present, weeds grew in patches throughout the driveway. The lawn on either side was either dead, yellow, or still green but struggling. A sprinkler system would do wonders.

Cleo shook the random thoughts from her mind. Squirrels ran rampant in her head, always taking her thoughts places other than where they were supposed to be. If she'd had a caring set of parents as a child, she might have had the benefit of being identified as having ADHD and being given measures to help manage it. Of course, she could only assume that was her issue. Which made this job even more ironic. What right-minded consumer would hire someone with self-diagnosed ADHD to *organize* anything?

Yep. She'd bit off *way* more than she could chew, let alone swallow.

Cleo appreciated the woods that bordered the expansive but dying lawn. Their presence created a hemisphere of oak and maple sentinels that seemed to guard Castle Moreau. In front of them stood a smaller army of apple trees. Their scraggly branches were leafed, and the blossoms had died off in exchange for tiny hints of fruit.

"Go away!" The reedy voice startled Cleo to a complete halt. She glanced every which way to identify where it had accosted her from, but she saw no one. Cleo took another step toward the front doors.

"I said, *get!*"

Cleo lifted her gaze to the second-story window at the western end of the castle. A wiry-haired, old woman leaned so far out of it, it petrified Cleo that she'd flip right over the sill and land headfirst into the bushes below.

"I know who sent you and I want nothing to do with anything that grandson of mine dreams up in his pretty little head!" The woman flailed her left arm out the window as if to shoo Cleo away.

Cleo stood her ground for no other reason than she needed Deacon Tremblay's money to survive. She could not go back. Ever.

"Mrs. Tremblay?" She offered the moniker as a pathetic peace offering.

"Don't *Mrs. Tremblay* me!" The elderly woman's hair was as white as Albert Einstein's and about the same style. As best as Cleo could tell from her position on the ground, the woman had on black circular glasses that were reminiscent of Harry Potter's, only chunkier. "You tell my grandson he can wave his money anywhere he wants, but I'm a Tremblay, and a Tremblay does as a Tremblay wants!"

They certainly did.

Cleo recalled the images of Deacon Tremblay plastered on magazines in stores, on the internet, and even on his own book cover. Who wrote an autobiography at just shy of forty years old? It wasn't like he hadn't much life left to live. But Deacon Tremblay—at least according to the tabloids and media outlets—was a reformed playboy turned business executive after he inherited the lion's share of the Tremblay fortune in America. Nothing stopped a Tremblay. That there hadn't been a Tremblay to hold office at the White House was a bit of a shock.

"Do you have weeds in your brain?" Mrs. Tremblay howled at Cleo, once again jerking Cleo from her mental wandering.

"No!" Cleo retorted defensively before realizing she was snapping back at the Tremblay matriarch. "No." She softened her tone.

Mrs. Tremblay pulled back from the window and disappeared.

Great.

Cleo shot a desperate look at Murphy, who lounged on the passenger seat of the car, staring at her with eyes that seemed amused by her predicament.

Now what?

Should she just stand out here or force her way into the castle under the name and authority of Deacon Tremblay? Definitely not the latter. She wasn't aggressive by nature—or even assertive. She could be when needed, but . . . *sheesh*, a job serving fast food would be so much simpler!

"I said to shoo, and I meant it." Mrs. Tremblay appeared at the front entrance. The timber door was partially open, just enough for the older woman's foot, hip, and profile to be seen by Cleo.

"Actually, you said to go away." Cleo bit her tongue the instant the words escaped her lips.

Mrs. Tremblay stepped out, squeezing through the gap in the door as if she couldn't open it all the way. She eyed Cleo up and down, surveying her as if she were an alien. Her brown eyes were sharp behind her round glasses. Wrinkles pulled at her lips, reddened with lipstick that had seeped into the wrinkles, making her look a bit like an elderly female Joker from one of the Batman movies.

"You're sassy." Mrs. Tremblay's observation did nothing for Cleo's confidence.

Yes. She was sassy. She'd spent the last several years dampening the sass into submission. But sass didn't equal confidence, and right now she had about as much gumption as a mouse stuck in a trap.

Mrs. Tremblay's gray eyebrow perked up. "My grandson thinks he knows what's what. He's a Tremblay, and all Tremblay men masquerade around with their charm and *ils vous séduisent*. Are you his lover or his assistant?"

Cleo drew back, her eyes rounding and her body stiffening.

This would probably be the only time in her life someone would accuse her of being a multimillionaire's mistress, and she wasn't even flattered.

"I-I . . ." She also wished for her sass to return to wherever it had suddenly fled. Flustered, Cleo searched for words.

Mrs. Tremblay gave a delicate snort through her delicate nose. "You're not his lover, then. I can tell that by the look in those pretty blue eyes. He would have snuffed out that anxiousness and you'd be more like a cat. Victorious that you'd snared the neighborhood tom."

"Okay, that's *enough*." Cleo found her voice again. The woman was anything but grandmotherly, and if she wanted to talk about cats, she was plenty catty—although Cleo found offense to that on behalf of Murphy, who was now perched on the car's dash, staring at Mrs. Tremblay with an aura of censure.

Censure away, Murphy. The woman deserves it.

Cleo sucked in a deep breath and found some fortitude deep within. She raised her index finger and leveled a gaze on Mrs. Tremblay that she hoped was both respectful yet drew boundaries. If she'd learned one thing in the past few years, it was that boundaries were critical.

"Mrs. Tremblay, I've never met your grandson. We've only spoken on the phone. I'm here to help you organize your home and get things into a more livable condition so that you can be healthy and content, and so your grandson doesn't need to worry."

Another snort. "Worry? He doesn't worry, Mona Lisa!" The nickname slipped from the old woman's mouth as though half insult, half compliment. "Deacon is only concerned with perception. The media loves to chat about his grandmother when they get bored, and Deacon, frankly, has done an abysmal job of late to feed them any gossip. So, here they are, focusing on *my* home as if it's some landmark being ruined by a crusty old woman with a penchant for collections."

"You like to collect things?" Cleo tried a different tack, born out of her own personal interest. "When I was little, I used to collect stuffed animals."

Mrs. Tremblay's mouth quirked. "I collect . . . a variety of things."

"Such as?"

Mrs. Tremblay pursed her lips for a long moment, then answered, "Well, I would invite you in, but—"

"I'm all right with a little mess," Cleo interrupted, hoping to squelch the woman's reticence before it grew any more. "My mother—she wasn't a great homemaker, so I'm used to messes."

Mrs. Tremblay responded with another snort. "Mona Lisa, your *maman's* messes are foothills to my Everest."

She'd seen the reality TV shows about hoarders, their addictions, and the baggage—literally—that went along with it. Cleo quickly determined that *hoarder* was an inadequate term for describing Virgie Tremblay and her centuries-old American castle.

Cleo followed the stoop-shouldered woman through a maze of boxes that were stacked at least six high and five deep in the main entrance of the castle. The stacks spanned a floor that appeared to be inlaid wood in an intricate pattern but was now covered in years of grime.

Cleo lifted her eyes to take in the vaulted ceiling. The stairwell reminded her of the movie *Titanic* and its iconic stairway scene. Only this set of stairs led up to a balcony and was marred by rows upon rows of boxes and crates, books strewn about, and a variety of old clothes hanging over the banister.

No. Mrs. Tremblay was a *collector* who hoarded—everything collectible—but she wasn't unclean. There were no cat carcasses, no rat droppings, and thankfully no cockroaches scurrying around. It was just a mass collection of *things*, yet all was being kept as neatly as an old lady could keep them.

Mrs. Tremblay gave Cleo a sidelong glance, wary and obviously distrustful of Cleo's reaction.

Cleo offered a small smile that wasn't so exuberant as to appear manufactured to cover the real emotion she hid inside: absolute petrified terror at the idea of having to organize it all. How? How did one even begin to dig through piles of collections and sort them? Certainly not everything could be kept, and if that was the objective—getting rid of things—how did she convince this stubborn woman that it was time to part with the bulk of her things?

"Worse than you thought?" Mrs. Tremblay's chuckle held an edge of challenge.

Cleo shrugged, hoping she came across nonchalant. "I've seen worse." She hadn't, of course, but lying was coming more naturally to her as the years passed.

Mrs. Tremblay narrowed her eyes. "No, you haven't."

Cleo diverted by pointing to an open box at the base of the stairs. "I see you collect books?"

"Who doesn't?" Mrs. Tremblay waddled toward the box and kicked it lightly with the toe of her orthopedic shoe. "I snagged these at a garage sale last week."

"Are they good ones?" Cleo attempted to continue the conversation.

Mrs. Tremblay gave her a snort. "How would I know? I haven't read them—probably never will."

"Oh." Of course. Cleo was finding Mrs. Tremblay's communication style was marked by logic, taking a realistic view of things. Very literal.

"I suppose you want to get started." Mrs. Tremblay eyed her, assessing her like a surveyor with high-end equipment judging boundary lines on property.

Cleo swallowed hard. They hadn't moved from the center of the room, which looked less like a grand entrance and more like a museum's warehouse.

Mrs. Tremblay cleared her throat, phlegm rattling in her chest. She pursed her lips to the side, then offered Cleo a grimace mixed with a sigh of resignation and some other undefinable emotion Cleo couldn't quite put her finger on.

"I'll show you to your room."

"My room?" Cleo couldn't help the squeak in her voice. This was beyond unexpected. It was unexplainable. Just moments before, Mrs. Tremblay had wanted to throw her out. Unsettled, Cleo was positive the last place she wished to stay was at Castle Moreau. "No. I mean . . . I was going to get a hotel room." If she could find a place that took cash.

Mrs. Tremblay placed her arthritically bent hands on her hips. She was about four inches shorter than Cleo. She blinked behind her Harry Potter spectacles, then smiled thinly. "You're worse off than I thought," she said after studying Cleo. "I'll bet your name isn't even Cleo."

Cleo choked. "Excuse me?"

Mrs. Tremblay waved her off. "It's all right. I'm not new to this."

"New to what?"

Mrs. Tremblay shook her head. "There you go again. You may have pulled the wool over my grandson's eyes—seeing as he's probably desperate for anyone to help who *doesn't* want media attention—but you've not pulled it over mine.

My eyes are wide open." Her smile was unnerving, and her stare didn't falter.

Cleo swallowed. This was a bad idea. A very, very bad idea.

Mrs. Tremblay spoke before Cleo found the words to politely decline the offer of employment, the offer to stay in the castle and cohabitate with this woman whose ancestry was built on the golden foundation of American dreams.

"You can call me Virgie. I much prefer that over anything 'Mrs.'" The woman crooked her finger at Cleo and beckoned her to follow. "You'll have to clean it, but there's a room for you in the north wing." She quirked an eyebrow. "And when you chat with my grandson, you can tell him that next time, if he thinks he can outsmart me, he's sorely mistaken. I gave him the Tremblay name. I can take it away."

With that, Mrs. Tremblay—Virgie—withdrew her sharp attention from Cleo and pushed her way up the stairs.

five

Daisy

It was as she'd feared. There was no other staff to care for the castle. This was made more apparent when she entered the kitchen. The chill was stark, the stove cold, the hearth dark, and it was void of the smells that should accompany the room.

Hungry, Daisy poked in cupboards and in an icebox. Aside from a stale loaf of half-eaten bread, there was not even a crumb. What the occupants of Castle Moreau ate was befuddling! Daisy crept to a doorway and opened it, staring down at a flight of stairs that disappeared beneath the earth into a cellar. Even that looked abandoned, as spiderwebs cascaded along the walls in swoops and swags. A chill blew up the wooden steps, causing Daisy to shiver and shut the door. She could explore the dark beyond of the castle another time. The idea that food would be stored down there was not enough of a motivation for her to risk her life against arachnids and rats and other creatures that had enough fortitude to create a home in the darkness. Not to mention, she'd read in a novel once that a man had buried a peddler in his cellar after he'd rammed a pitchfork into the man's back. All because the peddler stole an apple from his tree. No. No cellars today— even if novels were known for being more gruesome than real life. The perversion of an author's mind.

From what she'd heard, Madame Tremblay was not far off. Madame Moreau-Tremblay. The authoress who gloried in the gory and Gothic storytelling. The authoress who was now Daisy's employer.

Leaving the kitchen, Daisy spent time meandering hallways, looking out arched windows, and surveying the green, well-manicured yard. Bushes bordered the castle, a few blossoming with flowers she didn't know the names of. Woods crowded the property as if guarding it, and Daisy wondered what the castle possibly needed guarding from.

She peeked into a parlor and noted the layer of dust collecting on the end tables, the fireplace mantel, the windowsills. Closing the door, she moved to the large dining room with its buffet of ornately carved wood and mirror backdrop. Unfortunately, she saw no food here, which was no real surprise but still made Daisy's stomach rumble. The table was covered in a sheet that had turned gray with time and lack of use. It appeared no one at Castle Moreau ever ate.

How depressing. A death sentence in a way. She shivered involuntarily. Castle Moreau was living up to its reputation for not being welcoming.

Daisy's feet echoed through the hallway as she made her way to another room. This room's door was partly open, and she caught a faint scent of perfume.

"Finally." A woman's voice greeted her. It was deep, almost manly, with an undertone of lofty superiority.

Daisy hesitated in the doorway, trying to determine the source of the voice. Her eyes rested on a lean woman with high cheekbones, a head of gray hair, slashes of black for eyebrows, and eyes so blue that age would never make them dull.

"Madame Tremblay?" Daisy managed.

The woman stood by the window at the far end of the sitting room. Her blue eyes raked over Daisy with censure, coming to a stop at the top of Daisy's fuzzy red hair that was so red, the brightest apple held nothing by comparison.

"Are you Irish?" The woman moved toward her, her dark-navy skirts rustling against the wood floor.

"I . . ." Daisy fumbled for an adequate response. "I don't know, Madame Tremblay."

"You don't know?"

"I'm sorry, Madame." Daisy offered a quick, awkward curtsy. That's what servants were supposed to do, wasn't it?

"I suppose Festus told you that your position was my grandson's idea?"

Daisy froze.

"No?" Madame eyed her, then gave a smile that was neither warm nor cold. It was simply devoid of temperature. "Apparently he is lonely."

Daisy had so many questions.

Madame ran her finger across a table as she moved in Daisy's direction. "Occasionally, I've hired out to have help with upkeep, but I prefer not to have staff living on the premises—specifically, inside of Moreau."

Daisy waited, a heaviness hovering in the air that caught her breath and left her feeling suffocated. She clasped her hands together as Madame neared her. She stood over Daisy by a good three inches, her height only adding to the curious sensation that Madame floated instead of walked. Like an apparition would. Only Madame Tremblay was very much alive.

"I will expect you to stay out of sight. The library is off-limits. You may clean as necessary, but don't bother with afternoon tea and all the snobbery. I spend most of my time here, writing. You've read my novels, yes?"

"No."

"Mm." A thinning of the lips as Madame eyed her for a moment before adding, "If you frighten easily, continue to refrain."

"Yes, ma'am." Daisy gave an obedient nod, having every intention of finding a Madame Tremblay novel as soon as possible. She'd heard so many things about the woman, but now, having met her, having seen the wrinkles at the woman's eyes, the long fingers dotted with ink stains, Daisy wondered what horrors really lay behind those frigid blue eyes. Horrors that still hatcheted away at the woman's mind to get out and write themselves on her paper.

Madame Tremblay stopped her slow glide toward Daisy with mere inches between them. She reached out with her index finger, tilting Daisy's chin up, her fingernail grazing Daisy's skin. "You're alone in the world?"

Daisy was afraid to look away from Madame. "Yes."

"Good." A tap of the fingernail to Daisy's chin. "Keep it that way." With a sweeping turn, Madame moved to a delicately spindled desk. "I must return to my writing." Her fingertips brushed the top of a wooden box that graced the right side of the desk. "You may go."

When Daisy hesitated, Madame Tremblay raised her brows. "Yes?"

Dare she ask about food? Daisy knew she must. If she didn't, they'd all starve, and if she was required to cook, well, they'd all still starve. "About meals . . ."

Madame waved her away. "Meals. Festus's wife prepares them in their home, and Festus delivers them at mealtimes.

As I said, I'm not keen on having staff roaming the hallways of Moreau. You are an exception, to spare myself from listening to my grandson complain about the lack of assistance in this place."

Daisy gave a brief nod. When she didn't move, Madame tilted her head. "Yes?"

"Nothing, Madame." Daisy swallowed back the impulse to inquire about Lincoln.

"Mmm, well then. Be off now."

Daisy turned toward the door to leave, but Madame's voice stopped her.

"And, Daisy? Be aware. There are moments you may . . . *hear* things. Do not be alarmed. With a house this old, this *riddled* with history, it's bound to be haunted."

Daisy looked over her shoulder at Madame, but the woman had her head down and was scribbling something on paper. Haunted? She'd stated it so nonchalantly, it was difficult to fathom whether Madame was being serious.

Daisy closed the door behind her and released the breath she'd been holding. It was all a conundrum of eerie revelations. An almost empty three-story castle with turrets that hid hauntings, a library that hid a recluse, and a woman who wrote novels that made the faint of heart grapple with terror.

She leaned against the door and stared up at the balcony and the library door beyond.

Castle Moreau was hers now. Hers to care for anyway. She had secrets and shadows to corral here.

Drawing in a deep, shuddering breath, Daisy mustered courage. She would need it. Especially if she also had to tame ghosts.

She'd discovered the servants' quarters. Most of them were empty, tomblike, without furniture or anything to inspire occupancy. It was a wonder that Festus had given Daisy a room that was meant for someone with much more affluence than she had. She hardly deserved to be given a fine room when there were these unused ones more suitable for her station. Daisy turned in the small room and looked across the hall toward the other room. There was a panel of bells on the wall just outside, labeled with room names. It would make sense to be stationed down here at night. What if Madame needed her? How would she be summoned while in a room that was located in a wing far from the Tremblay family quarters?

Daisy had been snooping all afternoon. The castle—or rather the extremely large mansion meant to imitate a castle—had a ballroom on the third floor, boasted suites of rooms meant for guests, a music room with a piano shrouded in tarps, as well as what appeared to be a harp in the corner, also covered in a white sheet that made it look like a misshapen ghost.

But it was the lower level, the servants' quarters, that disturbed Daisy more than anything. It was so hollow, so empty. It gave her the feeling that one day the entire staff had simply vanished and left no trace of themselves behind.

Daisy tiptoed from the empty room and peered into another, smaller room that had a desk at the far end as if waiting for the housekeeper or butler or someone in charge to occupy it. A narrow window edged the top of the ceiling, where the earth split and became even with the lawn. Daisy crept toward it and tilted her head back, attempting to see out. She could only see forest and grass and nothing more. The window was too small to crawl through. Had there been a fire and she were trapped here, it would have taunted her as she burned to death. The window was only large enough for perhaps her head and one shoulder and arm to fit through.

Shaking the macabre thought from her head, Daisy spun and hurried from the room. Her footsteps were echoes of emptiness pounding along the floorboards where, at some point, servants *had* to have once walked. It was almost laughable that she was here, hired as a housemaid. To do what exactly? Dust the mantels? Clean the floors? Bring coal to the bedroom fireplaces?

Castle Moreau might be the residence of Madame Tremblay and her grandson Lincoln, but it was not a home. It was a void. Like a person without a heartbeat. A corpse that lay lifeless with no spirit to inhabit it.

Daisy shivered and hurried down the corridor. If it weren't daylight, she knew she wouldn't have ventured down here alone. It reminded Daisy of the Greenbergs' house, though far more superior. It reminded her of the dark room . . . the chair, the place where—

She sucked in a sob, pushing back the thoughts that threatened to be remembered. Memories buried under layers of the dirt of life, grinding them into the ground and determining to lock them in a coffin that shouldn't ever be exhumed. Daisy hurried up a narrow flight of stairs that led into the kitchen. She grappled for the wall, her fingers brushing across the bricks. She was short of breath. At the mere hint of the memory, she was short of breath! Daisy loathed the idea that one empty room could carry her off to a place she never wished to visit again. She had left her guardians for a reason. To shut the door and never return.

God save her and pray they didn't follow. They shouldn't follow. They had Patty now, and Rose. Daisy leaned over the sink as her breath came in short gasps, and she felt as though she might vomit. She shouldn't have run. Not without the girls. Not without Patty and Rose. They were so young. Twelve and fourteen. The Greenbergs would ruin them under the guise of Christian charity.

Daisy gagged, choking on the bile in her throat. Feeling like she might faint, she gripped the edge of the porcelain sink. This was not how it was supposed to be. She was free now. Free and alone. Castle Moreau was a veritable fortress in the woods. The mere name of Tremblay would keep danger away simply because of the rumors and the lore surrounding it.

A writer of such horror that most believed to be based on truth. How could one woman have stories so debased by deadly themes without having exposed herself to them? It wasn't becoming of a woman, young or old, to write of such violence. And Madame Tremblay? Her words, or so Daisy had heard, were practically written in blood itself.

Daisy sank slowly to the floor, wiping her mouth with the back of her hand, noting how viciously her fingers shook. She was safe now. She *was*! She had escaped the place she feared the most. Or perhaps she'd removed herself from one danger only to put herself into another place just as dangerous. Still, Daisy would quickly assure anyone who dared challenge her decision, that if it were true and Madame Tremblay was an equal to the words on the pages she penned, that murder itself—death— was far more favorable than from where she had come. There were times Daisy had begged death to visit her in the lonesome room under the guardianship of the Greenbergs. But death had avoided her, while life itself had extended a hand and insisted there was purpose. There was refuge.

So, if it turned out she didn't survive here at Castle Moreau, it would be no worse an outcome than had she remained a ward under caregivers who gave anything but care. They did not pen their horrors on the page. They were real horrors, and they were terrifying.

Daisy would rather welcome ghosts and shadows, lore and rumor. She could still see a small crack of hope between these castle walls. And it would remain there, within her sight, until someone snuffed it out.

The Girl

C'est ma poupée," I replied to the woman with the crooked hand. She watched me, hugging the wall, her eyes dull and vacant. I assumed she had asked me what I was playing with, but the woman never actually spoke.

Because I was the only girl—the only child—of Tobias Moreau, I often found myself in my nursery alone. Playing with dolls was my favorite pastime, and my papa spoiled me with pretty ones dressed in lace and frills, with painted red lips and rosy cheeks, with blue eyes and hair the color of flax.

But I was lonely. At six years old, the hours alone left me talking to imaginary people—or so my father believed. The woman with the crooked hand was always there. During the daytime, I could abide her. She did not seem as frightening then. Rather, as a child, I believe I pitied her. It was at night that she turned into a nightmare, pacing my room, hiding from my papa's inspection, and standing over me while I slept.

My *maman* was a precious woman but unable to care for me as she wasted away in her bed. I saw her coughing red spittle into her handkerchief. I knew it was blood—was it wrong that it fascinated me? *Maman* was dying, Papa said, but he issued it with a sad smile.

"Your *maman* goes to a better place, *mon chéri*. God will create for her a castle much larger and more magnificent than the one I created for her."

"Will it have flowers, Papa?" I asked.

"*Oui*. Many flowers."

"Yellow ones?"

"Of course."

"And pink?"

"How could God not give your *maman* pink flowers? Like the blossoms in the orchard in spring. They are her favorites, *oui*?"

But for now, I played with my dolls, waiting. Waiting for the woman with the crooked hand to vanish behind the walls. Waiting for my *maman* to die.

six

Cleo

She had escaped Castle Moreau. Her car jostled over the unkempt driveway, tufts of weeds scraping its underbody as she left. Murphy curled on the passenger seat without sharing her sense of urgency. A glance in the rearview mirror, and for a brief moment, Cleo could have sworn she saw the castle shift as it heaved a deep breath, beckoning her to return. One of the turrets looked forlorn, but the window in its side appeared to wink at her with an evil glint that dared her to try to flee its pull.

She was losing her mind.

Cleo gripped the steering wheel, directing her gaze on the road ahead.

Well, she knew that already. Knew she was losing her mind long before she ever came here to Castle Moreau. Even before she'd abandoned Riley—

She cut off her thoughts as tears were quick to spill over. Oh, that she wasn't so emotionally inclined to tears. Cleo

swiped them away with the back of her hand before returning it to the steering wheel and focusing on the here and now.

Virgie Tremblay had shown Cleo to her bedroom—one
she'd not technically agreed to occupy yet. The very sight of
the antique furniture, the stacks of boxes with narrow aisles
between them in which to walk, and the thick aura of time
trapped inside with the closing of the bedroom door had
worked together in making Cleo feel suffocated. Claustro-
phobia was real, especially when her background lent itself
to making it worse.

Cleo fingered the chain around her neck bearing her
grandfather's thumbprint. She managed the steering with
her left hand, reaching over with her right to scratch Murphy's ear.

"We had to get out of there. Clear our minds, right?"

Murphy's whiskers twitched in response as Castle Moreau
disappeared from the rearview mirror as they rounded a corner. Cleo's excuse to leave the castle was leading the mistress
of the castle to believe that she would bring back dinner.
Apparently, Virgie was used to TV dinners and so a catered
meal sounded delicious. Cleo admitted to herself, with a pang
of guilt, that it was more of a lie than a promise. There had
been a brief glimmer of light in the old woman's jaded eyes
when Cleo had mentioned food.

In minutes she'd breached the edge of town, and maybe
it was guilt, maybe it was her own hunger that made Cleo
drive to the nearest grocery store. She needed time to think.
Thinking required chocolate. Dinner required groceries. She
could put it on Deacon Tremblay's tab if she decided to return
to Castle Moreau, but in the meantime, she'd have to front
the cash—she hadn't used a credit card in years.

Too many obstacles.

Too many reasons to just stay in the car and drive straight

out of town. She'd done it once before and under far more wrenching circumstances.

Still.

Chocolate.

Once Cleo locked Murphy safely in the car with a window cracked, she made her way into the store, grabbing a cart to wheel ahead of her. She fully intended to go down every aisle in the small market. That would buy her some time to calm her tumultuous emotions and conjure some common sense.

She had no obligation to stay, outside of an ethical commitment to a job she'd accepted. Ethical commitment hadn't been her strong suit in the past. Cleo eyed the grocery aisles.

Breakfast Foods.

Coffee/Tea/Cookies.

Canned Goods.

To the left of the canned-goods aisle was the liquor area near the front of the store. Liquor was so easy to shop for in Wisconsin.

"You made it out alive?"

Cleo was startled out of her vacant stare at the rows of alcohol that lined the wall from floor to ceiling.

Stasia, the girl from the gas station, stood beside her, a bag of corn chips in one hand and a bunch of bananas propped between her elbow and side. Her dark-lined eyes were frank and bold, unapologetic for scaring Cleo out of her thoughts.

Cleo managed a wobbly smile. "I'm not sure Castle Moreau is life-threatening."

Stasia's eyes narrowed. "Yeah, until you learn all about it. *The* most haunted castle in the Midwest, they say."

"Haunted?" Cleo echoed. "There's more than one Midwestern castle?" she added with a bit of skepticism.

Stasia shrugged. "Unless you count White Castle and their hamburger sliders, there are a few. 'Castle' is a loose term for a mansion *pretending* to be a castle. It's not like we have Neuschwanstein around here."

"But Moreau is haunted?" Cleo looked over Stasia's shoulder at the coffee-and-tea aisle. Coffee would be good. Coffee and chocolate.

"Depends on what you believe." Stasia adjusted the bananas. "They say women vanish there. As in disappear, never to be seen again. *Poof!*" Stasia tucked her short, black hair behind her ear, and Cleo counted five rings on her upper ear, one of them a shimmering blue. "Moreau, the guy who built the castle at the beginning of the nineteenth century, built it for his wife. But she died shortly after. That's when others began to vanish. It's like a *Star Trek* vortex. Sucks in women and never spits them back out."

"That's morbid," Cleo said.

Stasia waved her off. "So is crime TV, but I watch it all the time. You don't?"

"No."

"That sucks." Stasia shrugged again, her mouth twisting in a look of pitiful apology. "Crime TV prepares you. Like, you'll *never* vanish if you know how a killer thinks. You'll be ready for them. True preparedness and survival skills."

"Interesting theory." Cleo managed a smile.

Stasia nodded. "If you're like me, then you assume every stranger you meet is planning to kill you. That way you won't be taken by surprise."

"So, I'm a killer?" Cleo couldn't hide her sarcasm any longer.

Stasia gave a wry grin. "Aren't you?"

Cleo had no reply to that.

Stasia studied her a moment with those frank brown eyes that gave Cleo the feeling the younger woman was sizing up her soul.

"Oh well." Stasia's eyelid dipped in a half wink. "Here I am. Making my mother proud every day." She raised her chin in a quick motion. "That's what you get for being home-schooled. Unsocialized for hours, I became besties with lore and lurid facts. Not every homeschooler's experience, *but* apparently my senior thesis on Jeffrey Dahmer solidified the fact that I *am* the stereotype for the weird homeschooled kid all grown up."

"I should go." Cleo cleared her throat and did the whole polite smile plus brief nod of dismissal.

"You're going back?" Stasia's voice rose a bit, yet she seemed to bite back surprise and instead hid it with a thin smile. "God go with you."

"He always does," Cleo quipped before she realized what she'd said.

A shadow crossed Stasia's face, and she nodded. "You'll need Him."

"What am I doing?" Cleo asked Murphy as she shoved three plastic bags of groceries into the car's back seat. The cat lifted his head, yawned, then settled back into his curled position on the front seat. "For real, Murphy, what *am* I doing?"

Cleo had picked up two frozen pizzas and a loaf of garlic bread to add to the carb dinner. A bag of apples because it seemed appropriate if she considered Castle Moreau the home of Snow White's witchy stepmother. And finally a bag of chocolates. She'd spent one of her hard-saved fifties and now Cleo was sure she'd lost her mind. Between the whiskey at the gas station, which she'd bought earlier in the day from Stasia, to these groceries that somehow communicated her subliminal intent to return to the castle of horrors—according to Stasia—Cleo was almost out of funds.

Which meant she needed this job.

Cleo shut the door and leaned her forehead on the frame of the vehicle. Her eyes glimpsed the baseball cap in the back seat. It was pink with sequins on the front in the shape of a unicorn. Tears sprang unbidden, out of nowhere.

She tore her focus away from the cap. She should've left it on the road that day along with her crushed phone. But she couldn't do it. It had been sitting there on the seat for the last two years, as if somehow it would return home one day. Return to *her*.

But Cleo had no intention of bringing danger back into the world she'd abandoned. She would rather face whatever lay ahead for her at Castle Moreau. In fact, if Stasia was right, maybe she *would* disappear—vanish—inside the castle, never to be seen again. It would serve at least one purpose. She wouldn't be a threat anymore. Not to herself, and not to the one who'd worn the pink cap.

Riley.

Cussing under her breath, Cleo bit the inside of her bottom lip until she could taste blood. She was far too emotional of a person to succeed at this flying-under-the-radar thing. Too often she missed details or made errors in judgment, and her inability to stay focused on a plan was like trying to capture lightning in a jar. Which meant they either had stopped looking for her or they'd never started. That last part hurt, maybe worse than if they'd stopped looking. Yet it would've been for the best. For everyone. For Grandma, for Riley . . .

Either way, it was still too dangerous to change course now. No matter how shattered she was inside. People survived a lifetime as fragments of themselves, didn't they? Looking all right on the outside, but crushed on the inside? It was possible.

Cleo would do what she had to do.

Rounding the vehicle, she yanked open the driver's door, then stilled when she saw an object perched on the hood. Rolling her eyes at the random person who'd left their garbage there, Cleo moved to the hood to retrieve the item.

She lifted it, her fingers connecting with the hard plastic square. It was clear plastic, its contents making Cleo wrinkle her brow and resort to her pastime of talking to her cat. She slipped into the driver's seat and held it out for Murphy's uninterested focus.

"A cassette tape?" Cleo shook it to grab Murphy's attention. The tape rattled in its case. An unmarked case and an unmarked tape. "That's so nineties." Her curiosity was piqued. Murphy's was not. Instead, the cat trilled a little noise in his throat to acknowledge Cleo was talking to him and nothing more. "Who even owns a tape player anymore?" Cleo eyed the grocery store's parking lot. There wasn't anyone parked near her to even ask if the tape belonged to them. No garbage can to dispose of it either. So she tossed it onto the passenger-side floor.

Not yet ready to return to the castle, and ignoring that the frozen pizzas were going to start thawing, Cleo started the engine and drove off lost in her thoughts. She felt aimless. She had no mission or purpose other than to remain obscure. What better place to do that than at a castle? And really, outside of it being a collector's garbage pit, what made her so wary of the place? Deacon Tremblay? He wanted to stay as obscure as she did, but for totally different reasons. Cleo could only imagine the field day the media would have if they saw the true condition of the old castle, not to mention Virgie's compulsion to collect everything under the sun.

Stasia hadn't helped in making the castle less creepy. At the same time, her admission of being a crime-TV fanatic put her in the category of paranoid conspiracy theorist, making the gas station girl's eerie insinuations seem quite far out.

It was a castle for Pete's sake, not a crypt of terror. Cleo drove down a side street lined with retail shops. She was making this whole situation into way bigger of a deal than was necessary and . . .

A store boasting a retro boombox on its sign snagged Cleo's attention. Without thinking, she swung into an open parking spot alongside the store. Cleo shot a glance at the cassette tape lying on the floor. What was on it anyway?

She reached down and grabbed the tape. "Be right back, Murphy." The feline didn't blink but seemed to melt further into the seat as the sun cast a warm ray over him.

Cleo cracked a window, shut the door, and locked the car.

As she entered the shop, a tin bell announced her arrival. A man behind the counter, with no hair to speak of and a handlebar mustache that framed his chin, lifted his head. His eyes were friendly. Blue but not cold, the same shade as his *Sesame Street* T-shirt.

He smiled. "Hey. Can I help you?"

Cleo avoided staring at Big Bird's beaky smile on the man's shirt and instead held up the tape. "Hi. I was wondering if maybe you have something I could play this on?"

"You bet I do." His smile stretched wider as he rounded the counter. "I'm Dave. I grew up simultaneously pressing play and record on my tape player just so I could record the hit songs on the radio."

At his expectant look, Cleo winced in apology. "I'm younger." A lame response, she knew, and immediately she felt her anxiety start to creep up. It seemed in social situations with others, she always found a way to make herself sound naïve and a bit childish. She wasn't. She just wasn't sure how to communicate well with people, especially strangers. Life had yet to teach her that one.

Dave laughed despite her silence "You're the era of CD players, aren't you?"

Cleo shrugged. "I had an iPod?"

"Ahh." Dave tugged at his T-shirt. "You're of *that* era. Got it. It's okay. No worries." His eyes twinkled.

Cleo managed a smile.

Dave stepped around the counter. "As for a used tape player, I have one over here. Were you looking to buy one or just play the tape?"

Cleo followed Dave through the store's tight rows of product—shelves holding vinyl records, CDs, cassette tapes, VHS and Beta tapes. She wasn't sure what Beta tapes were, but from the looks of it, she had a feeling they were the extinct precursor to VHS.

"I'd like to just play the tape and see what's on it . . . but if I need to, I can buy the player." She couldn't. Not really. What had made her offer to buy one was just another example of her acting before thinking. Cleo grimaced behind Dave's back, but his next words rescued her.

"Eh, no worries. If you're just wanting to hear what's on the tape, I'd feel like a jerk selling you something you're never going to use." He reached for a silver dual-deck cassette player, unwinding its cord. "I have an outlet right here," he said and plugged in the player.

"Thank you." Cleo handed him the tape, grateful she didn't have to buy the electronic device. "I found the tape on the hood of my car outside a grocery store. I don't know why I have the compulsion to find out what's on it."

"On the hood of your car? That's weird. But I get it. I'd want to play it too. Curiosity kills the cat and all." Dave removed the tape from its case. He shot Cleo a look of understanding. "It's humanity's demise, I swear."

Popping the tape in, he shut the tape deck and hit the rewind button. Just seconds later, the tape was back to the starting point.

"Annnnd here we go!" Dave pressed play.

They stood as the tape played. There was a scratchy sound, the clarity being anything but digital and fuzzy as the audio was captured on a magnetic ribbon.

"*This is . . . February ninth, nineteen eighty-one.*" Part of the words cut out, but the date was clear as a man spoke. There was a scraping sound, like someone had pulled out a chair. "*Tell me . . . circumstances around your . . . how'd you escape?*"

Cleo grew serious, exchanging a look with Dave, whose brow furrowed. She stepped closer to the tape player, and Dave stretched an arm out, casually leaning on the table.

A woman's voice replied, "*It was dark . . . cold outside, and I . . . no shoes on, but I didn't stop.*"

"*And?*" the man on the tape prompted.

"*I don't remember.*"

"*What did you see?*" Another question from the interviewer.

The girl coughed. "*Just . . . darkness.*"

"*And what about Anne?*"

Silence.

A fuzzy air played on the tape, as there was no answer.

"*What about Anne?*" The man's voice grew insistent.

"*She . . . I don't know. She vanished.*"

"*Vanished?*" Doubt laced the interrogator's tone.

Then came sniffles. The sound of soft weeping.

Cleo's skin was growing cold. She looked at Dave, who was staring intently at the tape as it slowly turned in the player.

"*We need to know where Anne is,*" the man said.

"I told you . . . she . . . isn't anymore." The girl was sobbing now.

"Isn't anymore?" The demand was not gentle, but urgent.

"She . . ." A long pause, another sniff. Then it was as if the girl on the tape leaned in so the mic would catch her words clearly. *"Anne Joplin* isn't *anymore. She's gone."*

Dave jammed his finger on the stop button. His eyes were intense as he turned to level a look at Cleo. "Tell me *where* again you got this tape?" He stepped closer, his expression tight.

Cleo fumbled for words. "I-I told you. It was on the hood of my car." She watched Dave as he turned back to the player and popped the tape out, slipping it back in its case. "Why?" she asked, wondering if it would be smarter to leave the tape behind and just leave.

When Dave shifted his attention back to her, he didn't seem threatening so much as startled—and determined.

"Anne Joplin." He shook the tape at Cleo. "She was the last woman to disappear at Castle Moreau. In 1981."

A sickening nausea swept up from Cleo's stomach into her throat. "What?" It was rhetorical. A whimper of stunned disbelief.

Dave answered anyway, his countenance shadowed. "Anne was my cousin. Who gave you the tape? I've never heard it before!"

"I told you." Cleo took a step back.

"No one just leaves a tape like this on the hood of someone's car!" Dave shook it again until it rattled in its case.

With her heart officially in her throat, Cleo did what she did best—abandon the situation. She spun on her heel and made for the door.

Dave shouted after her, desperation in his voice. "I'm sorry! *Please!* Don't go!"

71

Cleo hesitated only because he wasn't chasing after her and his voice sounded watery with despair.

"Please," he begged.

Their eyes met.

Dave's blues were cooler now, worried and chilling at the same time. "My cousin Anne disappeared when I was six. This girl? On the tape? It's the girl who last saw Anne. I need to know where this came from. I *really* need to know." His desperation was palpable now.

Cleo wished she'd tossed the tape into the parking lot. Wished she'd never come into Dave's store. Wished she didn't have thawing pizzas in the car that she wouldn't be able to cook now.

There was *no way* she was returning to Castle Moreau.

Cleo had gone with her gut in the past and it had spared others from harm. This time she'd go with her gut to spare herself.

seven

Daisy

1871

Daisy hadn't been able to find Festus. Madame was sequestered in her room and hadn't come out for over
forty-eight hours. Since Lincoln Tremblay "didn't exist,"
Daisy ignored him as well. She'd put in a solitary effort to
clean, focusing on her own bedroom because it didn't seem
anyone was terribly concerned with any other room. And if
they had hired her to assist Festus, he was a horrible com-
municator, as Daisy hadn't seen him since her first day at
Castle Moreau.

Meals had magically appeared in the kitchen and just as
magically disappeared. Daisy assumed she would have to
serve them, but each meal she went to plate was already
mostly eaten with just enough left for her. This meant, at
some point, Castle Moreau's occupants were feeding themselves. Under the cloak of secrecy. Moving about the castle
like wraiths on a mission never to be seen.

Daisy had since determined that she needed a few things

if she was going to succeed and be an asset to the castle. She had a few coins and wanted to spend them on a block of cheese—she missed cheese and hadn't had it for years—and some sturdy cotton to sew new pillowcases for her bed. Did the castle have its own linens somewhere? More than likely. But who did she ask? Daisy trembled at the idea of knocking on Madame's door to ask for clean pillowcases. The other bed coverings were washable and clean now, whereas the pillowcases had been moth-eaten. Although Daisy had seen worse in her life, she still preferred new ones if possible.

Daisy trudged down the main street, dodging wagons and horses as she crossed. A woman pushing a pram offered her a small smile, and Daisy returned it. Everyone seemed to belong, to have a purpose and a mission. Envious, Daisy opened the door to the mercantile and entered. After a bit, she'd found what she was looking for.

"Where do you hail from?" The mercantile owner summed her up with a raking of his gaze.

It was difficult to remain subtle when your hair announced your coming from a mile away. Daisy tried not to reach up and pat it self-consciously.

"Castle Moreau," she replied with no intention to engage the mercantile owner further. She could sense herself withdrawing under the man's stare. A familiar feeling she was fine to avoid forever.

The owner halted, and a fellow female customer spun from her position in front of a bolt of calico. "Castle Moreau?" she gasped.

"That's what she said, Mrs. Beacon," the owner stated while continuing to leer at Daisy. "How did you come from there?" he pressed.

"Richard," a woman's voice scolded as she breezed into the room from the back. His wife? "Leave the poor girl alone."

There was a slight trace of warning in her voice. She seemed aware of her husband's wandering eye.

"She's from Castle Moreau, Tabitha," Mrs. Beacon breathed, not even trying to be subtle in her gossip. As if Daisy weren't standing there, her gaze shifting from person to person.

"Oh." Tabitha's face pulled taut. She patted the side of her dark hair streaked with gray as concern etched into the corners of her eyes. "Dear girl. We can find a place for you to stay here in town. There's no need to return there."

Richard's smile became thin. Wanting.

Daisy's skin crawled. "I'm fine, but thank you."

"Fine at Castle Moreau?" Mrs. Beacon abandoned the calico and gave Daisy all her unwanted attention. "With Madame Tremblay? Have you read her novels?"

Daisy didn't have time to respond, as Mrs. Beacon continued with her appalled expression: "Gory and outright scandalous. She writes of a female killer—of course she sets that woman killer and her despicable acts in London. But, bringing such horror here? Even in the form of a novel, to our small town? Why? Who glories in reading stories of women being slaughtered? Madame Tremblay makes the murderers *women*. Women! And why? Her mind concocts these creatures of the night that are monsters!"

"You seem remarkably familiar with her writings." Tabitha smirked.

Mrs. Beacon shot her a perturbed glance. "I'm merely stating what we all know. Besides, how many now?"

"How many what?" Daisy interjected, finding her voice.

"How many have disappeared there?" Mrs. Beacon raised black eyebrows, staring down her shrewish nose.

Richard shifted uncomfortably behind the counter.

Daisy looked at Tabitha, whose pallor was fading again.

"How many what?" Daisy insisted.

"Women have been known to visit Castle Moreau." Mrs. Beacon leaned in as if revealing the world's most sinister secret. "They do not return."

"We don't know that," Tabitha spat, wanting to dispel the frightening thought with denial.

"Hester May was last seen a mile from Castle Moreau," Mrs. Beacon stated. "Just last January. Where is she now? Hmm? No one has seen her for months. Not a trace of her. Not a shred of material, a bonnet, a shoe—"

"An entrail," Richard said, relishing the shocked expression on Mrs. Beacon's face.

The woman quickly gathered herself and nodded vehemently. "Precisely. Madame Tremblay writes of violent murder and brutality and then women vanish? It cannot be a coincidence."

"One woman, though?" Daisy couldn't help but see a thousand ways they could explain the story of the missing Hester May outside of Castle Moreau and the Tremblays.

"That was only Hester May." Tabitha offered Mrs. Beacon a look of understanding. "Before Hester, there was the butcher's daughter, Elizabeth."

"Pretty thing," Mrs. Beacon murmured.

"And before Elizabeth, there was the . . ."

The three paused, with Richard becoming suddenly preoccupied with his inventory ledger on the counter.

Mrs. Beacon leaned in and spoke behind her hand to Daisy. "Several of the, you know, *unseemly* women have gone missing as well."

"They probably wandered off," Richard muttered.

Tabitha skewered her husband with a look that would brook no further argument.

"Didn't one of the traveling salespeople who came through

here just a month ago mention his niece had gone missing?" Mrs. Beacon mused.

"At Castle Moreau?" Tabitha asked.

"Hmm, I'm uncertain about that one." Mrs. Beacon shifted her attention fully on Daisy. "Do be careful if you insist on returning. No good comes from that place. Not since the moment Monsieur Moreau had it constructed seventy years ago."

"Poor woman, may she rest in peace," Tabitha added.

"Woman?" Daisy said weakly. She wanted to run more from these townspeople and their slander than she did from Castle Moreau.

"Madame Moreau," said Tabitha, "was the first mistress of the castle. She passed not long after they built it. She left behind a little girl and her husband."

"As well as her spirit," Mrs. Beacon inserted. Her tiny eyes grew wider, and Daisy was certain her narrow nose grew longer. "At night, if you pass by the castle, you can sometimes hear Madame Moreau's wails. They waft from the upper turret of the castle over the treetops until they float away on the river just beyond."

Silence met them all.

Finally.

Daisy reached for her package of cotton and cheese that had long since been wrapped and prepared for her. She set the coins she owed on the counter and took a step toward the door.

"No one ever discovered what happened to the Moreaus' little girl either," Mrs. Beacon said. "There were rumors Monsieur Moreau murdered his daughter after he succumbed to maniacal grief."

Without a farewell, Daisy spun on her heel and hurried from the mercantile. She welcomed the lonely walk back toward Castle Moreau, but she didn't welcome the stories that had been planted in her mind.

Just stories. They were just stories.

Stories of murdered children, dead wives, missing women, all centered around Daisy's new employer, Madame Tremblay— the Gothic authoress who seemed to delight in murderous things.

She slowed her pace as she walked along the road leading to Castle Moreau. Why return? Because it was return there or return to the Greenbergs'. Though neither was preferable, her needing to choose one was unavoidable. Otherwise she feared that she would become one of those "unseemly women" Mrs. Beacon looked down upon. It was the natural progression of things. An orphan, without a guardian or benefactor, without a position of service, would likely find herself on the street. Or boarding a train with the promise of a future out west. In her imagination, that option was tempting, but deep in her soul, Daisy knew the outcome of such an adventure would not be falling into the arms of a handsome cavalry soldier or rancher, or one of those romanticized mail-order-bride stories she'd heard about. No. More than likely she'd end up in a boardinghouse as a girl with a mission that had nothing to do with boarders of the proper kind.

Daisy was young, but she wasn't ignorant. She knew what most men wanted. She knew what lingered behind Richard the mercantile owner's eyes. She knew what it was like to be in the closed room at the Greenberg home. A guardian was meant to protect, but that had not been Daisy's experience.

A carriage rolled behind her, and Daisy stepped into the long spring grasses on the side of the road to let it pass. The driver, his hat tilted back on his head, lifted his hand in a friendly wave. A woman sat beside him, wearing a pretty dress of green

Daisy returned the wave. She noted her shoes crunching against the earth as she watched the carriage move into the distance. The road was lined by woods on each side, creating a picture-perfect canopy of branches curving overhead. Green buds promised the blessing of a leafy overhang in a few weeks. Daisy paused in her walk to draw in a deep breath. The fresh air filled her lungs, and she reveled in the freedom of being alone. The freedom of no longer having to duck around corners to avoid Mr. Greenberg's animosity or Mrs. Greenberg's jealous abuse.

Castle Moreau may be rife with morbid rumors and secrecy, but as far as she knew, there was no proof any of it was true. She had slept there for two nights now and she'd had no interaction with spirits of any kind. No wailing of ghosts or the feeling of being watched. If women had disappeared there, it was ludicrous to blame a castle for it. Or the Tremblays. Or—

Daisy jerked her head toward the forest at her right. A low moan drifted through the empty branches, then dissipated. She held her breath, thankful it was daylight, and squinted into the shadows.

"Hello?" Daisy wasn't afraid of ghosts. Not here. Not on a road at least a mile from the castle. It was most likely an animal. Wounded perhaps? The idea made her quaver inwardly with sympathy.

She took a tentative step toward the woods.

A whimper.

She strained to hear.

Another whimper.

"Hello?" Daisy pushed into the woods, her bundle of

cheese and cloth tucked into a basket that hung from her elbow. She moved a branch away so it didn't slap at her face and simultaneously stepped over a log. "It's all right," she called out in hopes that if it was a wounded animal, it wouldn't startle and try to run. Of course, an animal wouldn't understand her words, but hopefully her tone of voice would communicate kindness and caring.

A high-pitched moan urged Daisy to pick up her speed. The moan sounded human, most definitely human! Dropping her basket, she pushed her way through the brambles and underbrush, maneuvering through the woods toward the sound. She could still see the road behind her through the trees, which comforted her and reminded her of civilization, while the woods ahead resembled a darkening abyss.

"Stay right there!" Daisy instructed. "I'm coming."

What if this was how it happened? The thought came to her unbidden as she ducked under a tree branch—how the women had disappeared from what was assumed to be Castle Moreau. They were lured into the woods by the sounds of someone injured, only to be taken by the gruff and greedy hands of—

"Help me . . ."

The voice was definitely and thankfully female. Daisy stifled her fears and stilled, scanning the terrain until she saw a glimpse of rust-colored material on the ground just beyond a large oak tree.

"I'm coming!" Daisy assured.

Within seconds she neared the tree, where she noted a pair of brown leather shoes, worn and split along the seams. The body was petite, young, and terribly thin. Daisy's eyes connected with the large blue ones of a girl she guessed to be just a few years younger than herself. Perhaps fifteen. Dark circles made her eyes appear as if they were sinking into her skull. Her lips were pale, almost gray, and her skin was so white that it almost seemed to Daisy it was translucent. She could see the blue veins running down the girl's bare arms. Her dress was torn, without sleeves, and the bodice lay open, revealing a dirty chemise underneath.

Daisy dropped to her knees beside the girl. "What happened?" she breathed.

The girl trembled but didn't shrink away. She blinked and whined in her throat, pointing to her leg. Daisy followed the aim of the girl's finger, and it was then she noticed the metal-toothed trap that had latched around the girl's foot. It was half covered by leaves, and the skin just below the monstrous device was black.

"We've got to free you of that thing." Daisy began to push the leaves and debris aside gently but swiftly. "Are you hurt anywhere else?"

"N-not really," the girl replied, her breath catching.

"How long have you been here?" Daisy asked while assessing the trap to determine how to force it open.

"I d-don't know." The girl's face was streaked with tears.

"Shhh," Daisy said, feeling downright motherly toward the girl. She reminded Daisy of the ones she'd left behind at the Greenbergs', and a sudden sense of remorse over leaving them, coupled with the need to help this girl, boiled within her. "What is your name?" Daisy adjusted her position closer to the girl's feet.

"Elsie. Elsie Stockley."

"Well, Elsie Stockley, how *did* you find yourself here?" Daisy offered a smile, but Elsie didn't return it. "We need to get your foot out of this trap." Daisy stated the obvious as she peered through the trees toward the road. It was quiet, outside of a chickadee somewhere calling its name in a gentle cadence.

"I tried." Elsie winced as she tried to sit up straighter. "It won't budge."

"Well, it's a hefty trap," Daisy acknowledged. She ran a hand over the contraption. It wasn't rusted, which was good. That meant it wasn't old, and the springs shouldn't be bound due to dampness and age. "It's probably meant for a small animal. Fox or coyote or raccoon." She knew this because Mr. Greenberg had trapped animals.

Daisy leaned back on her haunches and leveled a frank look at Elsie. "It's going to hurt, but I think I can release the trap and get you free."

Elsie nodded urgently, her eyes reflecting both fear and determination.

Daisy positioned herself over the trapped foot. "Now, when I pull open the trap, remove your foot as fast as you can. I can't lift it or the trap will spring shut again." She patted Elsie's knee, then drew a deep breath. "It'll be all right. Ready?"

Elsie nodded again, bracing her palms against the forest floor.

Mustering all her strength, Daisy pulled the jaws of the trap open. Once the gap became wide enough, Elsie dragged her foot out with a shriek of pain that echoed through the woods.

The second the girl was free, Daisy let go of the trap, its springs snapping the teeth shut once again. She shoved the trap aside.

Elsie sobbed, grabbing her calf above the injured ankle, rocking back and forth.

Daisy lifted her dress and grappled for her underskirt, ripping the hemline into a strip. "This will help stop the bleeding." She tied it tight around Elsie's ankle while the girl's cries rose in volume at the touch.

Once the bandage was applied, Daisy said, "Let's get you to a safe place. Then we'll fetch a doctor to tend your wound."

Elsie shook her head. "No doctor. I got no money!"

"Where's your family?" Daisy pressed.

Elsie winced. "My brother left to take a shipment south on the Mississippi by steamer. Our parents are both gone. I was going to stay with my aunt over in Trempealeau County, but she took ill."

"Well, you can come with me then." Daisy didn't bother to ask how Elsie came to be stuck in a trap in the woods. But the girl's story made sense as far as having no one to help pay a medical bill. Daisy only hoped Madame Tremblay didn't have an apoplectic fit when she showed up with an injured stranger.

"Come with you? Where?" Elsie furrowed her brow. "I-I need to get to my aunt's home."

"I live just a mile from here. At Castle Moreau."

Elsie's reaction startled Daisy. The girl scurried backward, dragging her injured leg, distancing herself from Daisy. She shook her head vehemently and said, "I ain't going there! No way, no how."

Daisy considered taking a moment to beg the good Lord for patience, but after Mrs. Beacon's unsettling gossip, she couldn't blame Elsie for her fear. "I know the rumors about Castle Moreau, but—"

"Then ya heard about Hester May. She was my best friend Addie's sister!" Elsie continued as though Daisy would be familiar with Hester May simply by reputation of her having gone missing. "We may be a small town, but we know. We *know* what Castle Moreau is. No way am I going there."

"Then what about your friend Addie? Why don't I take you there? Where does she live?" Surely, if Elsie had a best friend, the family would assist her.

"No." Elsie blanched. "They left after Hester May wasn't found."

"So you've nowhere to go," Daisy concluded, though she wasn't sure she fully believed Elsie's story.

Elsie bit her lip.

Daisy leaned toward her. Their eyes met. "I'll protect you," Daisy promised. And she would. She looked at Elsie and saw Patty and Rose, whom she'd abandoned to the Greenbergs. Never again. She would never be so selfish as to leave someone in need ever again. This was her vow to herself as well as to Elsie.

Yet her earnest devotion didn't seem to sway the girl. Elsie issued a little snort laced with pain. "You can't protect me from the Moreau curse."

Daisy stilled, the dissidence in Elsie's voice chilling her.

"That place sucks you in and never spits you out. We'll be nothing but two more names on a list of the vanished," Elsie sobbed. "I don't want to *vanish!*"

Daisy reached out her hand, trying to still the trembling of her fingers. "We'll stick together, and we won't vanish. I promise."

She didn't bother reminding herself that some promises were impossible to keep.

eight

Cleo

She'd returned to Castle Moreau. Like a vulture to a dead animal, only she had no intention of feeding off Moreau's sordid history that grew at a disturbing rate.

Cleo stared up at the imposing third floor of the castle, then slowly lowered her gaze to the flight of stairs leading to the heavy, arched entryway. The turrets, the windows, the stonework, the carved lions bordering the stairs—the massive structure was a cross between *Harry Potter*'s Hogwarts and the iconic castle in *Downton Abbey*. Or maybe it was more like the one in *Jurassic World*. Cleo would prefer a rampage of carnivorous reptiles to the ghosts of Moreau. And what sort of disturbed person would leave a cassette tape on the hood of someone's car, with voices on it linked to a cold case from forty-some years ago?

She'd come back to deliver the pizzas. She'd come back because she had nowhere else to go. She'd come back because—

85

and Cleo hated herself for this—Deacon Tremblay was a multi-millionaire, and she was almost out of money.

The town of Needle Creek had zero help-wanted posters, not to mention they would all want Social Security numbers, tax papers filled out, legal-employment formalities.

Deacon Tremblay paid in cash. Off the books. Anonymity. Cleo couldn't put a price on anonymity, and considering the last female to disappear here was way back in 1981, she had to assume that whatever had cursed the women before her now lay dormant.

Cleo jogged up the broad steps to the front door. She pushed on it, and it opened with a creak straight out of a horror film. She poked her head into the vaulted foyer. Dust motes danced in a shaft of sunlight while a single fly buzzed around a pile of cardboard boxes. The place was empty.

"Mrs. Tremblay?" Cleo called. She entered hesitantly, then jumped when the front door thudded shut with a firm *You're never leaving here again* sound.

Cleo adjusted her grip on the plastic grocery bag and tiptoed around the boxes and crates. A pile of winter coats was in the way, and Cleo nudged them off the path leading through the collections.

"Mrs. Tremblay?" she called again. There was a large arched opening into a sitting room to the left. Cobwebs laced its corners. A distinct smell of sour milk irritated Cleo's nose, and she cleared her throat to avoid gagging.

She peeked into the sitting room. Evidence of wealth was everywhere. Luxe tones of reds and violets, gold tassels on draperies, gilded-framed portraits, and a marble statue of a dog in one corner. But colliding with all the richness was the daunting elements of time and corrosion. A water stain on the ceiling stretched from the western corner toward the fireplace. Among the various piles in the room, she saw more boxes of books and clothes, their cardboard flaps left open. An outdoor plastic wastebin sat in front of one of the tall windows, filled to the rim with paper and soda cans.

Time had not been a friend to Castle Moreau. Its occupant, a lonely old woman, had marred its beauty with her hoarding.

"Mrs. Tremblay!" Cleo spotted the older woman amid a covey of boxes. The sight reminded Cleo of a child's play fort.

Mrs. Tremblay was perched at the end of a battered settee, her sweater-clad shoulders stooped in a posture of defeat. She stared vacantly at a banana box that screamed its brand name in red block letters but was loaded with magazines instead of fruit.

Cleo approached Mrs. Tremblay. "I-I brought some pizzas," she offered, "and garlic bread."

There was no response.

The sassy elderly woman from before was now a pitiful shell of no response.

"Mrs. Tremblay?" Cleo lowered the bag of frozen food to the floor and crouched in front of the woman. "Virgie?" She tried the first name in hopes it would snap her to attention.

It didn't work.

Yellow-gray hair was pinned behind Virgie's ears. Her eyebrows needed trimming, and her shoulders were flecked with dandruff.

"Virgie?" Cleo reached out, her hand hovering over the frail one before finally lowering and covering it. Virgie's hand was cold, the skin papery.

"I loved him." Virgie's whisper was hoarse.

"Who?" Cleo tried to capture Virgie's gaze.

"I loved him," Virgie said again.

Cleo waited.

Virgie's eyes shifted to rest on Cleo's face. Her brows pulled together in concern. "Did you know him?"

"No." Cleo shook her head, hoping Virgie would enlighten her.

Virgie's eyes filled with tears. "'Blessed are the meek: for they shall inherit the earth.'" She turned her hand and gripped Cleo's painfully. "But who would want to inherit this?" Her fingers pressed around Cleo's, pinching them. "Inherit a curse? A place of damnation? No. A pit of hell. That's what the earth is. A taste of sulfur and I gnash my teeth." Virgie ground her teeth together, her jaw working back and forth.

Cleo winced at the awful sound. "Virgie, stop," she said urgently, attempting to dislodge her hand from the old woman's.

Virgie tightened her grasp.

"I saw him once." Her pale-blue eyes grew wide.

"Who?" Cleo couldn't help but ask.

"The devil. The devil himself." Virgie's words trailed down Cleo's spine. "He's never let me out of his sight since." Virgie leaned forward, close to Cleo's face. Her rancid breath raked across Cleo. "He's watching you."

Cleo shivered.

"He's. Watching. *You.*"

Virgie released Cleo and fell back against the settee. The frozen pizzas in the bag on the floor might have thawed, but Cleo kneeled frigidly in place beside Virgie.

The woman knew.

She knew the devil had been chasing Cleo since the day she was born, and somehow Virgie knew he'd chased her all the way to Castle Moreau.

Curse her overinflated sense of needing to help. It mocked her that she'd run from the one who'd needed her the most, yet it also made abandoning anyone else an utter impossibility.

Cleo sat on the top step of the castle's front entrance, her tennis-shoe-clad feet perched on the step below. Leaves and dirt had settled in the corners of the stairs, but all was dry, the air here fresh. Tree branches blew in the breeze, their newly budded leaves green and fluttering. The forest seemed to creep closer to the castle by the minute, reaching for it with bony arms. The sun seemed unfriendly with its golden haze, a deceptive beauty in a place of ugly rot.

Cleo held her burner phone to her ear, listening as it rang through.

"Tremblay."

Deacon Tremblay's baritone voice sent an unwarranted shiver through her.

"It's me." Cleo cleared her throat. "Cleo Carpenter."

"I figured as much. You're the only one who calls me from this number. So, is my grandmother causing issues?"

"Not particularly." How to tell the man that she thought his grandmother was acting nonsensical? It didn't sound very kind. But Cleo was concerned, and concern trumped her struggling with trying to find the proper words. "Your grandmother gave me a little trouble when I first arrived, but now she's . . ." Cleo searched for the right words.

"Being a sass?"

Cleo choked. "Um. No. She's more . . . catatonic."

"Catatonic?" There was disbelief in his voice now.

"Does your grandmother have dementia?" Cleo tried to calm her nerves. Tried to be direct. To be a functional adult instead of a bumbling girl on the run. "Alzheimer's maybe?"

"No," Deacon snapped. "Nothing like that. Why?"

"Because she seems confused," Cleo added, "and frightened."

"Frightened? She's got nothing to be frightened of, and my grandmother could win a war against Attila the Hun if she wanted to. There's also no Alzheimer's. She saw a doctor just last month—they sent me her medical records. A clean bill of health."

"Well, she's talking about the devil," said Cleo. "And hell."

"The devil and hell," he clarified.

"Then she said she 'loved him.'"

"Loved who?" Deacon asked.

"She didn't say. But I'm a little worried. I haven't been here long, and I've seen two completely different sides to Virgie." There. She'd said it. Not using the word *crazy* so she didn't sound rude, and not outright stating the woman acted as though she had a split personality.

A few moments passed in silence. Cleo assumed Deacon was considering his options. Finally he confirmed her suspicions.

"If you need to take her to the doctor, then take her. But keep it on the down-low."

"Will they let me? I mean, I'm not her legal caregiver." Cleo wasn't fond of the way Deacon seemed to brush his grandmother under the proverbial rug, not to mention she was feeling less self-confident by the minute.

"I'll pay you extra."

"Pay me triple." The instant the words escaped Cleo's lips, she clapped a hand over her mouth.

"Not fond of the castle?" There was a hint of humor in his question.

"I-I'm not fond of the stories I'm hearing about the castle," she admitted. *"Stick to the truth as much as possible."* An old homeless man had told her that once when she'd had coffee with him at a shelter. She remembered it even now.

Deacon Tremblay was chuckling in her ear. "It's all stories. Legends. It's a castle. What did you expect?" He paused, then cleared his throat. "As for my grandmother, she'll be fine. She always is."

"She's eighty years old." Cleo couldn't help but argue on behalf of the elderly woman. It wasn't fair for Virgie to be alone, to be abandoned with the exception of a long-distance relative in the form of her grandson. Not that she was one to talk about abandoning people.

"She's infallible," Deacon stated emphatically.

"But she thinks the devil is watching her." Not to mention watching Cleo too.

"Tremblay women live to be well into their nineties. I'm not concerned."

"You should be." Darn it. Cleo bit her tongue.

"Oh, I should?" An edge to his voice.

"Yes! I mean, no. I just—"

"You're planning to go to the press, aren't you?"

Cleo's eyes widened at his accusation. "I—"

"That's low," Deacon growled over the phone. "She's an old woman. Leave her alone." He then muttered under his breath, something about how he should've known better than to hire a stranger.

"I'm not—" Cleo began, hoping to reassure him, but Deacon interrupted.

"Leave my grandmother alone, Carpenter, or you'll have the entire Moreau-Tremblay estate coming down on your head."

Cleo nodded. She was wordless. Petrified. She hadn't intended to come across as threatening, but now she knew what would happen to anyone who was disloyal to Deacon

Tremblay. The steel in his voice belied any nonchalant care he seemed to show for his grandmother. The Moreau name—the Tremblay name—was coated in layers of armor, and he would dare anyone to try to bust through it.

nine

Sleeping in the room that Virgie Tremblay had designated for her was out of the question. The last thing Cleo wanted was to leave Virgie huddled in her cardboard-box fort in the castle's first-floor sitting room and hike her way to the west wing on the second floor and sleep in an abandoned suite that screamed of being haunted.

Instead, Cleo decided to sleep in her car. Murphy lay next to her on the back seat, snuggled against her stomach. She pulled a blanket over them both, locked the car doors, and prayed that ghosts and goblins, ghouls and forest witches weren't able to enter vehicles.

Virgie had been sleeping by the time Cleo returned after talking to Deacon on the phone. The thawed pizzas were sloppy plus she'd lost her appetite. Tossing them in a trash can outside, Cleo had escaped the castle and climbed into her Suburban. It was a large vehicle for just her and Murphy, but it felt safer than the castle. If she had to get away at a moment's notice, she could simply start the engine and hit the gas.

Cleo hated nights like these. When she lay wide awake, when worry melded with memories. She reached for the pink hat with its sparkly unicorn and ran her fingers over the cheap plastic sequins.

God knew. He knew why she was here and not *there*. Every night, Cleo asked His forgiveness. Every night, God remained silent. His critical judgment was deserved; she could hardly be angry with Him. Cleo tossed the hat into the far back seat of the Suburban, hearing it land on the paper bag that held the unopened bottle of whiskey.

She'd bought the liquor on a whim. It called to her like an old friend. And she needed a friend right now. Whiskey had been around her since her childhood. Its smooth taste, its scent, were familiar. A warm embrace. She remembered *him*. He would laugh, his cigar perched in the corner of his mouth. His words would slur. When she was in middle school, she'd sneak sips, cough, make faces, and cough again. He'd scold her for being too young for whiskey, but he never did anything but drink more. Still, he was her grandpa. She was his buddy. And by middle school, he and Grandma were home. The only safe people in her life, and a huge step up from a dad who'd left shortly after Riley was born, and from a mom who preferred methamphetamines over her girls.

It was natural, then, to view an inebriated man like Grandpa as safe. The smell of whiskey was always on his breath, saturating the cotton of his western snapped shirts, and along with the cigar smell, it was warmth to her.

Without further thought, Cleo launched herself into a sitting position and crawled over the seats. Murphy, yowling at being disturbed, followed her, sniffing the skin of her bare arm, his whiskers tickling her.

Cleo recalled her grandpa's oft-repeated words, *"What whiskey will not cure, there is no cure,"* as she pulled the squat bottle from the paper bag and opened it. As she drew a deep, reminiscent breath, the liquor's aroma wafted through her nostrils.

"Grandpa . . ." she whispered.

But he was dead now. And Grandma was . . .

Cleo closed her eyes against any further memories and kissed the opening of the bottle, tipping her head back. The golden liquid scorched a path down her throat, filling her sinuses. Her ears even seemed to ring with familiarity.

If whiskey had taught her anything, it was that it offered an embrace in exchange for dead dreams.

The scream wrenched from her throat, leaving it scraped as though someone had dragged a knife through it. Cleo fell onto the floor of the Suburban, Murphy hissing and screeching as he flew toward the front seat.

A fist pounded on the window again. Cleo squinted, her vision blurry, her head ringing with the pounding of a hundred jackhammers.

She scrambled from the floor, struggling to her knees, as the vehicle's seats restricted easy movement.

"Open up!" the man demanded, then emphasized it with another firm thud against the window.

Cleo fumbled with her shirt, pulling it down over her bare belly. Somehow it had wrestled its way up to the bottom of her bra. Her jeans were still on, but the button was undone—probably to give herself room to breathe? She eyed the whiskey bottle on the bench seat, propped up and capped. The amount had decreased significantly.

Nausea roiled in Cleo's stomach. Feeling sick from being hungover wasn't as awful as feeling sick from the knowledge that she was hungover. It'd been three months. Three.

She swore under her breath as she reached for the door, popped the lock—before thinking through the ramifications of an angry man standing outside—and swung it open.

"For real?" The man's voice was deep and exasperated.

Cleo squinted as the morning sun shone behind him. The sight of him caused her drink to begin an unwelcome journey up her throat.

He was a dark, handsome man. The kind who just needed a shave and he'd be perfect. His chiseled jawline was covered in stubble that was almost a full beard, his eyes were gold with a dark-brown perimeter, and he had curly raven-black hair combed back from his forehead. Overall, he had a definite Mediterranean look to him.

It was Deacon Tremblay.

She didn't need the internet to verify his identity. His picture, his profile, his *every feature* were embedded in the minds of all American women. Probably in the minds of international women too.

Cleo puked, the splatter landing on the grass by his Italian leather shoes.

"Good grief!" Deacon leaped backward.

Cleo retched again, hating herself. Hating this moment. Mortified and horrified and everything-a-fied. Moaning, she wiped her mouth with her forearm.

"Nasty." Deacon wrestled out of his outer shirt that hung open over a T-shirt. "Use this." He tossed it in her face.

The fragrance of Deacon's expensive, musky cologne mingled with the smell of whiskey in her sinus cavities. She moaned once more, sinking onto the car seat, burying her face in a shirt that probably cost over two hundred dollars on sale.

There were no words.

None.

Mortification always came at a cost, and this? This was probably the highest one yet.

Deacon reached up and braced himself against the Suburban's doorframe with his palms. The corded muscles in his olive-skinned arms did nothing to still Cleo's stomach. Instead it churned at the sight. The idea.

Deacon Tremblay.

Multimillionaire.

A French American from the south of France, whose family proudly boasted as much at every turn, leaving a lingering European air about their very, very American ties.

He was here.

In person.

Sidestepping her vomit.

"You done?" he asked.

Cleo couldn't look at him. His shirt smelled really nice, and it provided an element of hiding from her shame and humiliation.

Deacon yanked the shirt from her grasp.

Cleo yelped, immediately regretted it, then shrank back into the seat. If golden eyes could ignite into a fire, his certainly would. It was a righteous fire too, which probably had been fueling itself since the phone call when he interpreted her words as a threat. And it had turned into an all-out blaze when he arrived to find her a withering, pathetic mess.

"Well?" he pressed sternly.

Cleo nodded. "I'm done." She was. At least with throwing up. For now.

Murphy meowed from the front seat. Deacon's eyes roved to meet the cat's.

"She always like this?" he asked the cat.

Murphy's meowed response was uninterpretable.

"I'm sorry," Cleo managed. She reached up to smooth back her hair. She could feel the runaway waves beneath her fingers, tangled and snarled. No doubt she looked like a drunk Medusa.

"Listen." Deacon returned his amber gaze to her. "Get yourself cleaned up. We need to talk."

Cleo gave him a wordless nod.

Deacon pushed himself off the vehicle and strode toward the castle. His blue jeans were trim, his riveting forest-green T-shirt likely tailored. His neck was strong, like a Roman column. He was . . . perfection.

Cleo slid down the seat until her knees hit the back of the driver's seat. She sat up slowly and leaned her forehead against it.

God must be laughing at her right now.

Grandpa too.

Both for entirely different reasons, and neither for reasons Cleo could find any irony or humor in at all.

There was no saving herself from this wretched experience. Apparently, after their conversation yesterday afternoon, Deacon had hopped what had to be his own private jet and flown to the La Crosse Airport. Cleo scanned the expansive drive as Deacon headed toward the castle. She saw a black sports car parked in plain sight. For someone who wanted to fly under the radar, Deacon was making a poor start of it.

Thankfully, no press seemed to have followed him here. The surrounding woods remained quiet, and there were no paparazzi pulling in the driveway, no helicopters overhead. Or was it only in the movies that helicopters pursued famous people?

Cleo moaned yet again and slid out of the Suburban. She buttoned her jeans and brushed them clean with her palms. Cheap jeans with factory-made holes in them so as to look worn. They hugged her hips, which were probably twice the width of Deacon's last girlfriend's hips. Wasn't she Asian? A lithe beauty, with stunning eyes and gorgeous skin and a smile that made the sun shine brighter. They had broken up last year, citing competing schedules as the reason. It wasn't that he didn't like his ex. It was that the calendar turned out not to be their friend.

Why did she even care? Cleo mentally berated herself. On a good day, she'd garner no more than a sideways glance from the man. Today? Oh, it was a full-on scowl. And Deacon Tremblay was a flirt! Known for his charm, his ease, his—

"I brought you coffee." He appeared before her once again.

—his outright heroism.

Cleo reached for the travel mug Deacon held out for her, still avoiding his eyes. She hadn't seen him go to his car, but he must have.

"Thank you." Cleo's voice trembled.

Deacon tilted his head, attempting to coerce her to look at him. His brow was furrowed. A slight smile touched his mouth, which made his beard remarkably manly and maybe not a faux pas after all.

"It should help some. Not why I brought it—in fact, I've been trying to cut back on my caffeine intake—but it'll help you."

Cleo realized the travel mug was half empty. She stilled her repeated lifting of it to her mouth and stared at him over the top of the mug. "It was *yours*?" she whimpered.

He shrugged. "Sorry for the secondhand germs."

Her lips had touched the same plastic lid, in the same spot that Deacon Tremblay's lips had touched.

Cleo's insides warmed with pleasure, and she closed her eyes in a tight squeeze.

"Sink me to China, Lord, please." She muttered the prayer she'd prayed many times as a little girl. Grandpa had told her that if a person dug deep enough into the earth, they could dig all the way to China. So whenever she'd wanted to escape, she prayed God would help her sink deep into the ground.

"Not advisable," Deacon said, causing Cleo's eyes to fly up to meet his.

She'd said the prayer aloud?

Fabulous.

"I prefer flying to China," Deacon finished.

"Mr. Tremblay—" Cleo started in a flurry.

"Deacon," he interrupted.

"Deacon," she managed. "I am so, *so* sorry."

"Not gonna lie. You took me off guard." Deacon didn't fully smile, but he didn't fully scowl either. She couldn't tell if he was still annoyed or now amused by her. "I didn't expect my grandmother to drive you to drink so quickly."

Cleo gave a polite little laugh. "I didn't know you'd planned on coming here." Her response sounded weak even to her own ears. Or as if she wanted him to leave. Which she did. And she didn't. And she—

"I didn't know either." Deacon's smooth-as-honey voice left her mesmerized. Unfortunately, though, none of the earlier mortification was wearing off.

He waved his hand in front of Cleo's face, breaking into her wandering and fuzzy thoughts. "Yeah. You're going to need more than just the coffee. C'mon." Deacon steered her toward the castle with a light touch to her arm. "I'm a pro at the morning after. I've got you covered."

Cleo followed. More because she was at a complete loss of what else to do. Or say. Or think.

No wonder Castle Moreau sucked women in and never spit them back out. If all the past decades had a Tremblay or a Moreau man within the castle's vicinity, there wouldn't be one woman in her right mind who would ever go back home.

ten

Daisy

1871

A cobweb stretched across the archway of the door into the servants' hall of Castle Moreau. Though Daisy despised spiders, she ignored the cobweb and instead focused on hoisting Elsie against her side.

"Just a wee bit to go and I'll have you settled." The image of the servants' quarters she'd discovered prior seemed like the best place to sequester the injured girl. Daisy suspected it wouldn't be well received that she'd offered refuge to her. Especially without seeking permission, and with no authority of her own to stand on.

"Here we go." She assisted Elsie to a cot that was adjacent to the single window. Its bare mattress was unappealing, but it was better than lying in the woods with your leg in a trap.

Elsie whimpered as she lowered herself onto the mattress, then expelled a sigh of relief as she was finally able to relax.

"I'll need to tend the wound now." Daisy pointed to the bloodied, makeshift bandage around Elsie's leg.

Elsie nodded, a bit more color in her face.

"I could fetch a doctor," Daisy offered again, hesitating as she realized what a ruckus that might bring. There would be no sneaking a doctor into Castle Moreau. She'd have to explain herself to Festus, or worse, Madame Tremblay.

"No. No doctor." Elsie's resistance relieved Daisy instantly.

Daisy offered an empathetic smile and didn't press Elsie further, ignoring the pang of guilt that insisted medical care would be the wise choice regardless of Elsie's opinion.

After Daisy assured the girl that she'd return soon, she hurried down the halls and stairways to where the kitchen was located. Seeing that the stove was stone-cold, she decided it would take too long to stoke a fire and then boil water, so she opted for pumping ice-cold water into a basin in the sink. She found a cupboard stocked with linen towels and sequestered a few under her apron. Carrying the basin of water with careful attention not to spill, Daisy made her way back to Elsie.

The poor girl lay flat on her back, staring at the ceiling. Daisy set the basin on the nightstand.

"I don't have hot water to wash your wound with."

"Is that important?" Elsie asked, her eyes round.

"I'm not sure, to be honest." Daisy set the linens next to the basin. "I've never doctored a wound before."

Doubt washed over Elsie's features, and Daisy could hardly blame her. "Are you sure there's no one I can fetch for you?" Daisy felt she had to offer, even though she wasn't certain what she'd do if there were such a person.

Elsie shook her head and sat up straighter on the cot. "I've no one."

Daisy dipped a linen into the cold water, soaking it. "Then we'll do our best, yes?" Her tone was far more optimistic than she felt. Daisy knew there should be ointments, poultices, and medications to assist with the pain and fight against infection. But what those were, she wasn't sure.

As she cleaned Elsie's mangled leg, she tried to envision ways to ask Festus if he or his wife would know how to treat such an injury. But then that would prompt an admission of Elsie's presence in the servants' quarters, which would in turn threaten Daisy's position at Castle Moreau.

She had gotten herself into quite a fix. All for cotton for new pillowcases and a lump of cheese, both of which now lay discarded and forgotten in the woods. But one look at Elsie's pale face and Daisy didn't regret her decision to come to the girl's aid. She only prayed that the aid she offered would not only keep Elsie safe but also keep infection at bay.

It was past midnight and Elsie was finally asleep. Daisy had snuck her some food from the dinner left in the kitchen by Festus's wife, as well as blankets and a pillow she'd pilfered from a bedroom suite next to her own. Though it would be easier to care for Elsie if Daisy was also staying in the servants' quarters, since Festus had lodged her in the wing opposite the Tremblay family wing—for guests of the wealthier sort—she hadn't come up with a good enough reason to explain why she would have traded down in rooms. Festus would notice. He roamed the castle halls during the daytime more than Daisy had expected. He was strangely absent when it came to giving her any help or direction regarding her tasks, but then he would appear at odd moments when Daisy felt she didn't need his guidance.

Thankfully, she was able to avoid Madame Tremblay. There was something about her regal stance, her cold expression, her mind that ventured into places no woman's—or man's, for that matter—should properly go.

Daisy slipped up the main staircase, pausing long enough to cast a surreptitious glance at the doors that led to the study where Lincoln Tremblay was not to be bothered. Her stomach tickled a bit at the thought of him. That disturbed her more than the way he would simply stare at her were he to know what was going on inside the castle walls. Stare at her with those brooding eyes of his that made her wonder what was going through his mind. His heart. She shivered. He had a heart—and a soul. She'd seen it in his eyes that first meeting. That was what drew her to his door as much as what warned her away. It was the look of a prisoner. A prisoner with much strength and confidence, with hurt and wounds, and with bitterness and mistrust.

Daisy shook off the curiosity that made her want to wrench open the doors and come face-to-face with Lincoln Tremblay. She had suffered enough to see the pain in another's expression. She'd just never seen it in a man's before, and it had both terrified and captivated her.

She chose instead to wisely hurry to her room—after getting lost twice—and close the door that rose in height over her head by a good five feet. It shut with a resounding clank as the latch clicked into place.

Daisy turned and eyed the bedroom, its canopied bed and shuttered windows, the pale-blue wallpaper with translucent flowers dancing in a lacy pattern along the edges. There was an ethereal quality to the room, brought on by the moonlight that seeped through the cracks in the shutters, and a stillness that belied the sound of her own breathing.

Padding across the floor, Daisy unlatched the shutters and pushed them open. The moon was full, its bluish light turning the grass, the trees, and the drive various shades of navy blue. The yard was still, everything in its rightful place, and yet Daisy couldn't shake the feeling that there was movement outside her window. No, a *presence*. A presence of someone lilting in the night air, drifting behind trees, staying just out of sight.

She'd read too many stories. Her imagination had her sensing things that didn't exist. But this place. This castle. The stories from the mercantile. The missing women. And now Elsie, tucked away in the servants' quarters by her lonesome, in hiding because Daisy was terrified her employer would banish them both from the walls of Castle Moreau and send them into the night.

According to the gossips in the mercantile, that would be preferable. Moreau was not a haven, not a place where one went for safety. Rather, it was a place of question, of suspicion, and of unanswered speculation.

And she lived inside its walls.

A rattling startled Daisy, causing her to whirl from her place in front of the window. Her muscles tensed as she scanned the bedroom. All was still. Not even the draperies on the bed shifted.

She held her breath.

She was not alone.

Her skin prickled, and her nerves grew chilled. Daisy held her breath as she stood frozen by the window because she was certain if she released it, something frightening would awaken.

Finally, Daisy took a tentative step toward the bed. Someone could be hiding under the bed frame, then in the middle of the night scurry from beneath it to clutch at her ankles, or drive a knife into her chest, or smother her face with a pillow.

Eyes wide in nervous anticipation, Daisy crouched a safe distance away but with every intention of releasing a blood-curdling scream should she see another pair of eyes with malicious intent staring back at her.

But there was no one there.

Nothing alive anyway.

Daisy sat back on her heels, her palms pressed against the floor from when she'd crouched to look under the bed. A castle cursed with the vanished might be saturated with the remnants of murdered souls, wailing in a language foreign to the living's ears but familiar to the dead.

Daisy's gaze swept the corners of the ceiling. She wasn't sure if she believed in spirits, but she wouldn't be surprised if they did exist. Angels existed, she believed that, though she'd never actually seen one. God said they existed, and who was she to question God? Yet had He weighed in on the existence of the dead wavering in the afterlife? Daisy wasn't certain. It seemed logical that spirits who felt incomplete would wander. It also didn't stand to reason that God would leave any spirit incomplete. So Daisy chose to leave the conundrum alone.

The rattle echoed through the massive bedroom again. She jerked upright from her position on the floor and stared at the bedroom door. The doorknob turned left. Then right.

It rattled as someone shook it.

Daisy had locked it, just as she always did with every door that she slept behind. Her time with the Greenbergs had taught her that.

The knob twisted again. Left. Right. Left.

Slowly, Daisy rose to her feet and tiptoed across the floor, her eyes fixed on the crystal doorknob.

It stilled.

Daisy stilled.

Doors didn't keep spirits out. The spirits floated through them uninhibited. Didn't they?

She held her breath.

Waiting. Waiting for the moment a translucent wraith passed through, extending a bony hand, releasing a wail from deep in its soul, beseeching Daisy for help while strangling her to punish her for the sins of others.

Any announcement from the other side of the door that would indicate the presence was human would be welcomed by her. But there was none.

No voice to declare its humanity.

No further sound to identify its source.

Simply stillness.

Silence.

And it was the silence that was the most frightening of all.

eleven

He raised his voice enough to be heard from behind his closed door. Daisy skidded to a halt. A glance over the balcony told her the main entrance and adjacent rooms were unoccupied. Her eyes drifted to the study to the left of the stairs.

Lincoln Tremblay.

A shudder traveled from her head to her toes. Daisy sucked in a breath. He knew . . .

Somehow he knew about Elsie's presence in the servants' quarters.

He would oust her now. Or maybe murder her. Yes. That would be the end for her, she was sure of it. Daisy froze as her imagination conjured up every scene in every novel she had ever read.

Death by stabbing? Smothering? Strangulation? Drowning might be preferable because she could suck in the water and allow it to flood her lungs, hastening death. But how did a man drown a woman when he sequestered in his dark and imposing study with no water source? No. It would be strangulation. Stabbing was far too bloody. Smothering too . . . necessary to have a pillow.

"Miss François!" Lincoln Tremblay's voice bellowed this time, and Daisy jerked from her wicked thoughts. Between last night's frightening door rattles and terrible aloneness to today's unorthodox summoning from the man behind the door, Daisy wasn't sure she had many more minutes left to her life. If nothing else, fright alone was going to do her in.

Death by fright, that made the most sense.

She twisted the knob to open the door. Her eyes adjusted slowly to the darkness of the room. The drawn draperies and the sweeping spiderwebs in the corners of the ceiling only added to the bleary dullness.

Lincoln Tremblay's habit of staring had not changed since their first meeting. Nor had his position behind his remarkably large desk, with four piles of books at one end and another pile at the other. A large tome lay open before him.

"Do you talk?" His question startled Daisy. He didn't bark, or glower, he just . . . peered into her very soul, matched her unspoken pain with his eyes, and challenged her to speak in spite of it.

"Yes. Yes, I talk." She couldn't help the bit of offense that made its way into her voice.

Lincoln Tremblay grumbled something, but he didn't blink, and he didn't look away from her.

Daisy, attempting to squelch her nervousness, sucked in a loud, rasping gasp.

Lincoln's dark brows knitted together. "You are well?"

"I can't breathe." Daisy coughed, clearing her throat. She felt as if a four-hundred-pound weight had been lowered on her chest.

"Are you ill?" he asked with no shift in his tone and no apparent concern other than mere curiosity.

Daisy stared back at him. They locked eyes, neither of them blinking. At last she waved her hand and said, "Please look away!"

"Pardon?" He drew back.

"You're staring." Daisy coughed again. "It's savage!"

This time his brows rose to his hairline and hid beneath the strands of black hair dangling over his forehead. He blinked, averted his eyes downward, and tapped the open book with his index finger. "I had no idea I held such power over someone as to be equated with savagery."

Daisy swallowed, air filling her lungs once again. Lincoln Tremblay was intimidating. Powerful. He held sway over her very breath, and that was dangerous, though Daisy wasn't sure why other than that if it really were true, it threatened her life. Yet it didn't seem possible. He wasn't a wizard. Therefore, his staring stole her breath for an entirely different reason.

It also piqued her curiosity. There was something compelling about Lincoln Tremblay. Something that told her they were more kindred in spirit than she would expect. But then he was a man, and men weren't to be trusted. Life had taught her that many years ago. Mr. Greenberg was a glaring example of that fact. There was no way Daisy could find commonality between her and a man. Even to flirt with the idea was dangerous in and of itself.

Lincoln tapped the book again with his finger. "May I lift my eyes now, or do you believe I will end you with a glance?"

"If it were a glance, it wouldn't be near so bad," Daisy admitted without thinking. She caught herself from saying more and instead added, "Sir."

Dark eyes settled once again in her direction. Not even the lines at the corners of his eyes deepened.

"My grandmother is ailing," he said. "She'll never tell you

this, but it is true nevertheless. While she believes we brought you here to housekeep and to relieve Festus, in reality you are here to keep watch over her."

"I am?" Daisy's voice squeaked. Mr. Tremblay had kept his silence for several days. Festus had said nothing. On one hand, it made more sense than her being put in charge of housekeeping for an entire castle. On the other hand, she was taken aback at the idea—it was terrifying and wholly unwise. Lincoln Tremblay should know how monumental this sort of duty was.

He folded his hands and rested them on the book in front of him. Once again he stared darkly at her with a blank expression. "She will make your days miserable if you hound her. So leave her alone."

Confused, Daisy sniffed. "And how am I supposed to manage that?"

"Manage what?"

"Watch over her while not watching over her?"

"I never said that. I said to watch over her but not to hound her."

"And the difference is?" Daisy winced at her utter lack of deference to Mr. Tremblay.

"The difference is," he answered, lowering his voice—perhaps due to impatience—"that *hounding* means chattering and asking questions. It means being a pest. You can avoid that, yes? Being a pest?"

"I've never been called a pest in my life," Daisy stated emphatically.

"No?"

"No."

"Well, *watching* over my grandmother means bringing her tea in silence but observing her. Is she pale, is she chilled, are her hands shaking, has she eaten, is she writing? And so on."

"And if I notice something is wrong?" Daisy thought of Elsie in the servants' quarters. She would have two to watch over now. One a withering elderly woman with the mind of a Gothic killer, the other a girl just shy of sixteen with a serious leg wound.

She met the man's eyes again. That infernal, expressionless look.

He gave her a slight nod. "If something is wrong, you will alert me."

"Very well." It wasn't very well at all, but what was she supposed to do? Refuse the instruction and be dismissed? Still, it left her in a conundrum. "Do you still wish for me to clean?"

"Clean?" Mr. Tremblay raised a brow.

"I thought I was here to housekeep. Am I to clean or not?" Daisy knew she needed to work on her tone. She sounded sassy. "I don't know what the expectations are."

"This house has gone many years without polish and shine. I've little expectation of you in that regard."

"But if your grandmother believes I am here to housekeep?" Daisy connected the points for Mr. Tremblay.

He waved a hand. "Fine. Then clean. Sweep away the spiders and polish the balustrades if you must to keep up pretense."

"Do you never smile?" Daisy asked suddenly, then wished she hadn't. She knew better than to question him, to step out of line. Best to stay quiet, stay out of sight. Don't draw attention or engage. Safety required that she shrink down until she was barely a shadow of herself. Coming to Castle Moreau—no, *escaping* to Castle Moreau—had been the new beginning she'd longed for since she could remember. No man, ever, would make her feel small and helpless ever again. Yet here she was, unable to bite her tongue in spite of herself.

Mr. Tremblay sniffed, but his mouth remained in a straight line. "There must be a reason to smile, Miss François. Will you supply one?"

It was Daisy's turn to stare.

For a long moment they held each other's gaze. His dark, hers a bright green that probably made him unhappy that her eyes naturally smiled. But then, to Daisy's surprise, the corner of his mouth quirked. Just a bit.

"Perhaps having you here will provide a reason to smile. There is so little in Castle Moreau that inspires joy."

Daisy nodded, this time refusing to put her thoughts into words.

Lincoln Tremblay drummed his fingers on the book while searching her face. "You are not what I expected."

Daisy bit the inside of her upper lip.

He smiled then. It was small, but it reached his eyes and tilted the sadness that lingered there into a hint of admiration. "Green eyes are compelling," he admitted, and it struck Daisy with surprising force. "As are others who care for those in need. You may go now. Care for the stray you're hiding downstairs. But be quiet about it. If my grandmother discovers her . . . well, we won't consider that, now, will we?"

Green eyes? He'd noticed her eyes just as she'd feared, only he complimented them. And her stray? He could only mean Elsie.

Daisy was afraid to say anything in response. For fear of him, for fear on behalf of Elsie, and truthfully, for fear for herself. For her safety. For her heart. For all her hidden romantic notions that were going to be crafting Lincoln Tremblay into a storybook character that would never—*could* never—exist in real life. There was no possible way a man could brood, could stare, could lord over others and still show kindness. No way at all.

Daisy scurried down the corridor, ignoring the long line of Moreau family ancestors who stared at her from portraits that went back to the eighteenth century.

Lincoln Tremblay had not communicated displeasure at Elsie's presence, but neither had he indicated that she was welcome at Castle Moreau.

Daisy had promised to keep Elsie safe, but how could she be safe if Mr. Tremblay knew she existed? He could insist that Elsie be taken back to town, dropped at the doctor's doorstep, and left to incur her own debts for her care.

Daisy had no intention of breaking her promise to Elsie. If she must, she would go with the younger woman. She would find lodging for them both. She would *not* leave Elsie alone. Not like she had the other girls she'd left behind at the Greenbergs'. Left behind to live out their own nightmares and become souls begging for escape and finding none.

When Daisy entered Elsie's room, the girl was sitting up on the cot, her blue eyes fastened on whatever she saw out the window. She quickly turned toward Daisy, her eyes narrowing in question and concern.

"I'm so sorry," Daisy said breathlessly. "I meant to be here sooner but was delayed by . . ." She thought better than to mention Lincoln Tremblay. "I was delayed," she finished lamely. "How is your leg?"

Elsie glanced at her bandaged leg that was propped on a pillow. Her foot was bare and appeared swollen and a bit black-and-blue, including the toes. The bandage looked clean, though, without further seepage.

"I think it is all right," Elsie said. Her voice sounded tiny in the large room, with the stone walls swallowing up her words.

Daisy hesitated. She wasn't adept at nursing an injured person. And she didn't know what she would do for food, as she had yet to fetch whatever Festus's wife had supplied for breakfast. "Are you hungry?"

Elsie shook her head. "No."

That solved that problem, for now anyway. Daisy moved to Elsie's cot and gave her a smile meant to reassure her. "I suppose I'd best check your leg."

"If you must." Elsie sounded rather bored, almost disinterested. It gave Daisy pause. After having metal teeth biting into her flesh, she doubted that Elsie lacked concern for the wound. Daisy knew that if it were her leg, she would be fretting over possible infection, gangrene, or amputation. The horrific results were daunting.

Daisy unwrapped the bandage, then grimaced at the sight. The area where the trap's teeth had dug into Elsie's flesh was bruised deeply, the skin red and aggravated. But there were no signs of infection, no horrid smell.

Elsie watched Daisy as she wrapped the wound with a fresh dressing. "Thank you," Elsie said softly.

Daisy met her eyes. "You're welcome."

Elsie shook her head. "You've been so kind to me." Her eyes shifted from wall to wall, her hands gripping the covers with nervous energy. "But I-I believe I am well enough now."

"Well enough?" Daisy drew back.

Elsie nodded. "To leave Castle Moreau." Her voice wobbled.

Daisy eased herself onto the edge of the bed, her hand resting lightly on Elsie's leg. She wanted Elsie to know that she cared, that she wouldn't abandon her. "I realize it can be frightening here, what with all the stories about the castle. But I'll keep you safe, I promise."

Elsie shook her head again. "You can't promise that." She

averted her eyes and sat up straight on the bed. "I don't want to be here."

"I know." Daisy focused on Elsie's wounded leg. There was no way the girl could travel on her own. "But you cannot travel. Not yet."

Elsie sagged back onto the bed, but fear danced in her eyes. "This place—it will eat us alive."

"No. I won't let it." Perhaps it was an empty promise, yet experience had shown Daisy far worse than imagined legends about a castle and vanishing women. Images of the two girls she'd abandoned at the Greenbergs' annihilated her sense of peace with gut-splitting guilt. Of course, Elsie's circumstances weren't the same, and perhaps they weren't as threatening as Mr. Greenberg, lurking in the shadows at night, or Mrs. Greenberg's jealous temper, but the injured girl still needed to be with someone. Someone she could trust.

"First, we will get you well." Daisy's assurance came with a flash of Lincoln Tremblay's dark expression. She chose not to mention to Elsie that the master of the house—the *castle*—had somehow learned that Elsie was here.

Daisy was moving to rise when Elsie's hand shot out and grabbed her arm. Her fingers felt cold against Daisy's skin, and her grasp pinched. Startled, Daisy looked up at Elsie.

"Then you must at least look for her. While you keep me here. Look for her, please!" Elsie leaned forward, rising from the pillow propped behind her.

"Who?" Daisy eyed Elsie's nails digging into her flesh. She wondered if Elsie realized the intensity of her grip.

Elsie gave Daisy's arm a little shake as she looked toward the doorway, toward the hall that split the servants' quarters, and toward the cavernous castle itself.

"Hester May," she hissed.

"But . . ." Daisy tried to pull her arm away, but Elsie only squeezed tighter.

"She's been missing for *seven* months!" Elsie shot another glance toward the door, as if someone were lurking just outside, listening. Elsie lowered her voice. "If you think you can guard us from this place—protect me—then you need to consider the truth of it all." It was obvious that her attempts to comfort Elsie had fallen short. "Addie, my best friend, last saw her sister Hester May when she left their house for a walk in the forest to enjoy the autumn colors."

"B-but I wouldn't know where to look." Daisy knew what Elsie was assuming, placing the blame for Hester May's disappearance on Castle Moreau, just like everyone else in Needle Creek seemed to have done.

Elsie drew her blond brows together in earnest petition. "Everywhere. *Anywhere.* No one ever gets to go inside Castle Moreau, but *we* are *here.* And if I must stay, then we must find Hester May."

Daisy had no investment in Hester May. She knew nothing about the girl except that she'd disappeared, along with what was supposed to be a long history of such here at the castle.

A tremor raced up her spine.

Lincoln Tremblay. His brooding visage. Madame Tremblay and her Gothic tales. It all fit, didn't it? It's what castles were—mysterious and filled with secrets.

But vanishing women?

Where did one begin to look?

"You have to look for Hester May." Elsie's plea was accompanied by the release of Daisy's arm, but her words hovered in the room like an omen.

You have to . . .

What had seemed like an escape merely days ago was

117

already becoming a prison of sorts. One of obligations, all of them beyond Daisy's know-how and understanding.

Between Elsie, Madame Tremblay, and now Hester May, it seemed Castle Moreau was subtly shifting to encompass Daisy. To envelop her in its maze of unfamiliar rooms and people.

Yes. Castle Moreau was alive.

She could feel it.

She could feel it breathing into her soul. Wrapping itself around her like roots that grew into her body, curled around her bones, establishing its mark upon her.

Whatever lived here was coming for her. For *them*. It wouldn't stop until she discovered what had happened to Hester May, and it wouldn't return her once she did.

twelve

Cleo

Watching Deacon Tremblay in the cluttered kitchen of the castle was like watching a cinematic masterpiece. He'd enveloped his grandmother in a warm embrace, and she'd blustered around him with an adoring smile. She moved newspapers and magazines onto the floor to make room on the counter. The kitchen had been updated at some point in the castle's history to accommodate modern appliances. A long butcher-block table was positioned in the center, but it was mostly unusable, as Virgie had covered it with plates from different china sets, glassware, and more books. There was also a box of porcelain knickknacks, which appeared to be a collection of owls.

Somehow, Deacon navigated the clutter with ease and didn't seem to be astonished or appalled by the chaos. Instead, he opened the door of an antique Hoosier cabinet that was packed so full of glasses and mugs that it made Cleo's stomach clench at the mere idea she was supposed to organize the mess. Reaching for a simple clear glass, Deacon returned to the sink and ran it under hot water.

"Do you have dish soap?" he asked his grandmother.

Virgie shook her head. "I use that." She pointed to a bar of soap that looked like it'd sat there on the sink's edge for months without meeting water. It was cracked and gray.

Deacon ignored the old soap and instead switched the water to cold and let it run awhile before filling the glass. He brought it to Cleo, who sat at the table in the only chair free of clutter.

She took it from him, avoiding his eyes—well, avoiding looking at all of him really, except for maybe his feet.

Deacon held out his other hand. "Three ibuprofens. You don't want acetaminophen 'cause that will make you throw up again."

Cleo took the pink pills wordlessly and popped them in her mouth, downing them with a gulp of water, all while praying the glass was sanitary enough.

"Drink more," Deacon instructed. "Your body gets dehydrated from the alcohol, so you need lots of water to counter it. The headache will go away, eventually. I'll get you some bread."

"I don't have any," Virgie piped in. Cleo could feel the woman's eyes on her, but the floor remained the preferable place to aim her gaze.

"Rice?"

"If I don't have bread, I don't have rice either," Virgie added.

"Looks like we need groceries."

Virgie nodded. "You can drive me."

"No." Deacon's word was firm but gentle. "I can order the groceries online and have them delivered. I've no intention of showing my face in Needle Creek."

Virgie clucked her tongue. "Still afraid of people, are you?"

"Never afraid, Grand-mère, only distrusting. Have you ever had your face on the internet with the headline 'American Royalty Does the Director's Daughter' touting your previous night's adventure?"

Cleo was glad neither of the Tremblays was looking at her. A hot blush covered her face at how cavalier Deacon was about his past escapades, not to mention his choice of words.

Virgie gave a little snort. "No, because I never fooled around. In my day, we remained faithful for the sake of appearances, if not morality."

"Mmm, good advice, but a tad too late for me, Grand-mère," Deacon said.

Cleo's cheeks were blazing hot now. She studied the water in her glass as if it were a fascinating exhibit at an art museum.

"Well, you're all I have left, so I suppose I'll overlook it." Virgie sidled past him and tapped Cleo's shoulder.

Cleo forced herself to look up and meet the woman's frank gaze.

"If you have designs on my grandson, it's a lost cause. He's sworn himself to a life of celibacy now that he's *found Jesus*, but minus the priesthood. He's not here for you."

Cleo choked on her water. "I—" she coughed—"I didn't think he was here for me."

"Good." Virgie held Cleo's gaze for a moment before turning back to Deacon. "I know you think I'm out of my wits. Talk behind my back all you two want and make your plans to have some massive garage sale to get rid of my junk. But remember, Deacon, this is *my* property. You've not inherited it yet. If I say you're not touching something, you're not touching it."

"Grand-mère—" Deacon began.

She held up a crooked, arthritic finger. "Tut, tut, tut! Not another word. I am still the matriarch of this pathetic excuse of a leftover family. You will listen to me." With that, she waddled from the room on her orthopedic shoes without a backward glance.

Silence reigned for a long moment, and then Deacon pushed himself off the counter he was leaning on and moved to crouch in front of Cleo in order to command her attention.

She gave it to him, albeit reluctantly. It was difficult to look anyone in the eyes, especially when she was hiding everything about herself. But vomiting one's bad habit all over a celebrity's shoes made it so, so much worse.

Amazingly, Deacon seemed to have moved past it. "We're going to need to strategize how best to handle my grandmother and the mess here. I have a few days I can give up, but after that, I have some events I need to attend. I'd hoped to avoid coming here at all, but I can see my grandmother is going to be a handful."

Cleo didn't remark on the fact that Virgie was "a handful" when she was lucid, but what about when she fell into that creepy stupor and started uttering nonsense? Deacon had yet to see that.

"So," Deacon continued, "you need to forget about last night and move into Castle Moreau. Move your cat inside too. It's not cool to leave it in the car, especially with a litter box in the far back. That's not sanitary for either of you."

Crud. He'd noticed. Cleo shrank into her chair. That she was a younger version of Virgie minus the clutter was becoming clearer to her. They were both alone, wayward, and sorely lacking when it came to life skills.

"Also," he said, his knees cracking as he crouched, "you're going to need to shape up."

Cleo lifted her eyes then. His charm was still oozing from

his eyes, but his expression was firm, like when he'd palmed the doorframe of her Suburban after she'd puked.

"No more drinking. No more acting like a victim. No more looking at the ground when we're with each other. I don't bite. Whatever you've read or heard about me is ninety percent false. My grandmother has her own opinions about me—well, about the entire family history. But she's right. It's just her and I now, and I *will* protect that. That means you need to be on our side, and you need to be of the right mind so you don't screw it up."

"Screw what up?" Cleo half whispered, feeling intimidated, offended, and ashamed all at the same time.

Deacon's eyes blazed into hers. "Screw up the Moreau-Tremblay name. Meaning don't talk about anything that goes on here. Stick to the agreement and stay anonymous. I'll pay you in cash and we're good, right?" He studied her, doubt reflecting on his face that she was even capable of what she'd claimed. That she could organize the catastrophic collections Virgie had accumulated over the decades, and that she could help Virgie attain new, healthier living habits.

The task was insurmountable.

But Cleo would not tell Deacon Tremblay that was what she thought.

She nodded.

"Good." Deacon moved to stand, then thought better of it and gave her one last golden stare mixed with a side of luscious smile. "And don't worry. I don't have any intention of acting like a playboy. You don't need to worry about me."

He was conceited to think she would be worried about his intentions. But then Cleo admitted to a slight pang of disappointment too. Every girl dreamed of a handsome, wealthy celebrity to sweep her off her feet.

Deacon Tremblay would not be that celebrity.

That she would be staying in the castle going forward had been decided for her when Deacon marched through the halls with Murphy tucked under his arm. He deposited her cat in a bedroom on the second floor of the east wing. The room was covered in dust with stacks of old photograph albums scattered about.

Cleo chased after Deacon for no other reason than to preserve him from Murphy's tendency to go tiger on anyone who wasn't her. But by the time they'd reached the bedroom, Murphy was purring—*purring!*—and had already fallen under the charms of the man who held him.

"I'll order a new litter box with fresh litter when I place the grocery order." Deacon allowed Murphy to jump to the floor. The cat's feet landed with a thud on a faded Oriental rug that spanned the expanse of the floor but was hidden under boxes and paraphernalia.

"Gosh, my grandmother hasn't spared a single room in this place." Deacon heaved a sigh. "This is going to be more work than even I thought."

Thank the Lord he could see that.

"It may take you months," Deacon added.

Cleo raised her brows. *Months?* He would pay her for months to stay in a castle? With an old lady? And with rumors of the castle eating women for breakfast and never spitting them out?

"Have you heard of an Anne Joplin?" Cleo asked before considering her words.

Deacon was eyeing the bedroom's recessed ceiling and the dust that had collected over the years and settled on the molding.

"Yep." His head was tilted back as he walked across the

room, focusing on the west side of the ceiling. "Is that a water stain?" he mumbled to himself.

"She disappeared. In the eighties," Cleo supplied, as if he hadn't just admitted to knowing who Anne Joplin was.

"Every missing woman in the state of Wisconsin has somehow been associated with our castle. It adds to the mystique of the place." He tossed her a lazy grin, then reached for a ladder-back chair that had been shoved into a corner. He slid the chair over and hopped onto it, his height helping him get closer to the stain on the ceiling.

Cleo let the matter drop. He didn't seem bothered by it, so what good would it do to mention the cassette tape so coincidentally placed on the hood of her Suburban, or to mention Dave's cousin Anne, or that Stasia had parroted the castle's morbid rumored history as if enamored with death itself?

"Why do you ask?" Deacon ran his hand down the molding in the corner and along the wall to where it abutted a window seat. The seat had once been a blue brocade cushion, but now it was faded gray and filthy.

Cleo hesitated.

"Well?" He'd stopped his inspection and was looking down at her from his perch on the chair.

She could see the outline of his pecs through his T-shirt. God help her.

Cleo cleared her throat—and her mind. "I was just wondering," she finished lamely.

Deacon hopped off the chair and faced her, his alluring eyes making her squirm under his assessment. "Look, I get that this whole"—he waved his hand around—"setup we have going on here is unorthodox, but I need to know the job will get done and you won't join the gang of conspiracy theorists out there who claim Moreau is haunted or that it's some Bermuda Triangle for women. It's an old castle. On the Mississippi River. That's all."

"Okay." Cleo accepted his admonition. What else could she do?

He frowned. "You agree to things easily, don't you?"

"What?" She was surprised by his observation.

"I guess I'm more accustomed to super-feminist women. Strong ones. Heck, look at Grand-mère! But you're just very, well, agreeable."

"That's bad?" Cleo was wishing for China again.

"Not bad, no. It's just . . . I've a feeling there's more to you under the surface."

And he would try to find out? No, thank you. Cleo shook her head. "I'm just me."

"Who doesn't care to find regular employment and fill out the required tax documents." His lopsided grin matched his haphazard dark curls. "It's okay!" Seeing her anxiety spiking, he held up a hand. "I'm not going to dissect you." Deacon moved the chair back to the corner where he'd found it, muttering under his breath, "I know what being under a microscope feels like."

Cleo waited. Murphy rubbed against her legs, and she bent to pick up the long-haired cat. His purr was comforting, vibrating against her chest, reminding her that at least one thing in her life stayed consistent.

"Now that you got me here with your concerns about Grand-mère's mental state, I'm going to go check on her."

"I didn't mean to worry you and make you feel obligated to come," Cleo inserted, immediately feeling guilty.

Deacon shrugged. "She's all I have left." He gestured to the overpacked bedroom. "Take today to get your sleeping quarters here cleaned up. There's a laundry room in the basement. Assuming Grand-mère has kept up with the maintenance appointments we have scheduled, all appliances should be working. You can wash sheets, blankets, whatever you need."

"Okay," Cleo said. "Thanks."

Deacon was assessing her again. He gave a small, dismissive shake of his head. "Yeah. You bet." He eased by her and reached the bedroom doorway, then turned. "Tomorrow, since I'm here, you may as well take me through your plan to go through Grand-mère's collections."

A smile and he was gone.

Her plan? She had no plan.

Cleo stared at the bed in the middle of the room, piled high with clothes. That should be *job one* of her plan—clear the bed—or else she'd be sleeping in the Suburban again, and the rest of the whiskey would call her name with more assertiveness than she'd be able to resist. Regardless of the consequences.

thirteen

Light flickered under the door. It wavered, as if someone were standing just outside holding a candle, debating on whether to twist the knob and enter unannounced. Cleo hadn't fallen asleep yet. The creaks in the castle made her half convinced that every missing woman ever attributed to the place was still roaming the halls in the form of an apparition. Murphy was edgy too. He jumped from the now-clean bed to the window seat, then to the dresser, where he knocked over a cardboard box filled with notecards.

Cleo watched the light dissipate.

She sat cross-legged on the bed. It was nights like these she wished she had a phone with data, social-media accounts, anything to connect her to the outside world. She didn't want to be alone with her thoughts. Didn't want to conjure up things that weren't there. Worse, she didn't want to remember what *was* there, in the back of her mind, never far away. Enough to eat at her stomach and make her feel nauseous.

She'd failed. Truly. Living and surviving hadn't equated to any form of success. Instead, it merely reminded her daily of the struggle to keep going and the pitiful deficits she tried to ignore existed.

A bang outside the bedroom jerked Cleo from her dismal thoughts. She moved from the bed, noticing that Murphy had arched his back and was staring with wide yellow eyes at the door.

"What is it, Murph?" Curse all the tales from that girl Stasia. Cleo was half frightened to open the door for fear they'd all come true and she'd be assaulted by a barrage of vintage murdered souls, all clawing at her for revenge.

Cleo shook her head, ridding her mind of such a scenario, and forced herself to open the door. The dark, mahogany-paneled hallway was dimly lit by small wall sconces, probably from the 1930s. They were yellowed with age and cast a golden hue. The hall was empty. Nothing moved, nothing accounted for the bang she'd heard.

She knew that somewhere in the castle, Virgie was ensconced in her own bedroom, and Deacon must have found some other room in which to spend the night. The place seemed more abandoned than inhabited, and even though it was nighttime, Cleo tried to calm herself with the knowledge that she wasn't the only one in Castle Moreau. She reassured herself that Deacon Tremblay wasn't about to let anything happen here that would sully the Moreau-Tremblay family legacy.

Another bang echoed through the air, and Cleo gripped the doorjamb. She glanced at her watch. Just past two o'clock in the morning. There shouldn't be anyone moving about. But then she was awake, wasn't she?

A glass of milk might help in calming her nerves. As a child, milk had been her go-to—before she was taught other ways to dull her senses. It was Grandma's plan to counteract Grandpa's influence. Milk. Whiskey. Friend. Foe. But she'd never been close to Grandma. It was always Grandpa. Cleo reached for her necklace and rubbed his thumbprint, then stuffed the chain under her T-shirt.

She reminded herself that haunted castles were objects of speculation that couldn't be proven. Milk had been proven. It was tangible, and it was in the kitchen. She was still wearing joggers and a T-shirt, and she was used to going barefoot. She shot a look toward Murphy. The cat had relaxed and was nosing around the bottom of the bed.

"I'll be right back," she told Murphy, as if he were keeping tabs on her whereabouts.

Cleo wove her way through the east wing until she reached the balcony overlooking the main entrance. Its cathedral ceiling cast eerie nighttime shadows. She could hear the ticking of the grandfather clock.

Tick. Tock.

Tick. Tock.

Padding her way across the balcony toward the staircase, Cleo paused, eyeing the half-open door to the left of the stairs. A former study, she'd been told earlier by Virgie, who had reluctantly given her a tour of the castle.

"I put all my father's things in there, so don't mess with that room. It doesn't need any organizing," Virgie had warned. She hadn't invited Cleo even to peek into the room.

Now Cleo was pulled toward it out of pure curiosity. She stretched out her hand, pushing the door all the way open.

The study was unlit, but the three floor-to-ceiling windows across the room were void of draperies. Cleo could see out into the expanse of woods—a deep green turning almost to black—just beyond the lawn. The moonlight was dull, as it wasn't full, and yet it gave enough light for Cleo to locate a light switch to the left of the door. She flicked it.

Nothing.

She tried the switch again: down and up. Still nothing.

Then a low moan from the far corner of the room stole Cleo's breath from her, chilling her into a frozen stare.

The form of a woman stood there. Cloaked, shrouded, her features uninterpretable. Cleo could tell the woman was looking at her and yet she couldn't see her eyes.

"Hello?" Cleo didn't move. She wanted to move *backward*, out of the room, but she couldn't get her legs to cooperate. There was something inhuman about the woman. Something otherworldly. "Can I help you?" Her voice trembled.

The woman remained still, unmoving. Cleo squeezed her eyes shut. Was it an apparition or were her eyes playing tricks on her? There couldn't be a woman standing there— not garbed as if she were from the turn of the century!

Cleo released her breath when her eyes opened and focused again. The woman was gone. The form, the apparition, or whatever she was, was no more. Had she ever been there?

Giving life back into her blood, Cleo hurried from the study, not bothering to shut the door behind her. She dispensed with the idea of a glass of milk. Instead, she longed for the whiskey in her vehicle, but wild horses couldn't drag her outside in the dead of night to retrieve it. No. She would retreat to her bedroom with Murphy and the collections of photo albums and books and notecards and dusty old magazines. She would bury her face in her pillow like a child and whisper bedtime prayers until all the ghosts of Castle Moreau fell asleep too. Fell asleep and left her alone.

The Girl

AUGUST 1801

Papa told me that *Maman* was not long for this world. I stood by her bedside and stared into the face of the woman who had nurtured me to the age of six. I was young, but even I could recognize death. It hovered over her body like a vulture over a carcass in the field. It sucked life from *Maman*, leaving her face gray, her eyes sunken into her head, and her mouth hanging open in a silent scream. Only instead of a scream, it was a gurgle. A rattling that formed deep in her chest and made its way up her throat, a gasping breath for life.

"Bid your *maman* farewell, *mon chéri.*" Papa nudged me closer with his hand.

I did not want to go closer to *Maman*. This woman holding hands with death was not the woman I knew as *Maman*. She was a shriveled-up shell with bloodstains in the corners of her mouth where she'd coughed it up.

"*Chéri* . . ." Papa nudged me again, and this time I resisted. It was the first time I recall ever being disobedient to my father. It would not be the last, for I was soon to discover that in my father's world, disobedience was rewarded with acquiescence.

I backed away from *Maman's* bedside. I remember my eyes were wide and burning because I forgot to blink away the sight of her.

"It is not *Maman*," I whispered.

"Kiss her farewell," Papa urged. This time there was a crack in his voice. Yet his emotion did not sway me. Not the mind or heart of a child held only by the grips of terror. Death was a frightening thing to look upon, and bestowing affection by way of a kiss was abhorrent.

I turned and fled the room. My father's shout followed me as I raced down the hallway, my thin shoulder bouncing off the mahogany-paneled walls. Out of the west wing my feet took me. Across the balcony and into my father's study.

I found a reprieve from the horror underneath his desk, curled into the darkness there, huddled in its shelter. I could not weep, for I had no tears. Tears were becoming rarer as I aged. Things like disappointment and sadness sometimes intrigued me more than they toyed with me. But now, at this moment, I stared out from my hiding place.

The smell of Papa's tobacco lingered in the air.

I could hear the ticking of the tiny brass clock that sat above me on his desk.

My hands pressed against the floor, the wool of the carpet prickly and itchy against my palms.

Then, in the stillness, I heard her.

The rustle of her skirts.

I saw the outline of her feet as they stood in front of my father's chair.

She never made a sound. The woman with the crooked hand. But, unlike everyone else in the castle, she would not leave me alone either. It was both exhilarating and terrifying. I could not see her face, only her feet.

I closed my eyes against her presence, and when I opened them moments later, she had vanished.

Such was the way of the woman with the crooked hand.

fourteen

Daisy

1871

Very conscious of Lincoln Tremblay's instructions, Daisy assumed she should begin her day with a peek into the world of Madame Tremblay. She could not get Elsie off her mind, and her instinct was to check on the young woman first. Her leg, if it became infected, would create a whole new set of difficulties. What would she do? Ask Mr. Tremblay for help, since he knew of Elsie's existence and yet had made no attempt to throw them out?

It wouldn't be good to get on his bad side, and Daisy figured the fastest way to do that would be to shirk the duty he'd given her to observe his grandmother.

She hesitated outside the room where Madame whiled away the hours, pen to paper. How many more years could the aged woman write such Gothic horrors? A rap on the door garnered no bid to enter. Daisy hesitated, then twisted the knob and peeked inside. Madame was bent over a small writing desk by the window that overlooked the drive and the front lawn. Her spine looked gnarled and crooked, but she wore an elegant violet dress like a queen, her hair swept into an updo that was impressive considering she had no ladies' maid to assist her. She wore spectacles, Daisy could tell, because a delicate chain looped against the side of her face, attached to the brass arm that rested behind her left ear.

"It's rude to stare at a person's back," Madame announced without lifting her head, turning, or ceasing the scratch of her pen against paper.

"I'm sorry, Madame," Daisy answered quickly. How was she to explain her presence here? "Would you—like some tea?"

The pen stilled. A small sigh. And then, "I told you not to pester me with things like tea. Do I look English? No. I am French."

And French people didn't drink tea? Daisy did not know so she sealed her lips. She thought she'd read of Frenchwomen having afternoon tea in a novel. Surely, the English weren't the only ones to enjoy such a tradition.

"And in America, unless you're *trying* to be aristocracy, you do whatever you please," Madame said, her pen picking up its scratching again.

"Yes, Madame." Daisy nodded, even though the old woman wasn't looking at her.

"You are quite the mouse, aren't you?" Humor laced Madame's voice now. "Perhaps I should make you a character in my story. You could be the young woman plagued with the pox, who is gnawed upon by rats in the dark hours of night but is too polite to shoo them away."

Daisy blanched. Madame was no Jane Austen, that was certain.

"Go to my desk, child," Madame instructed, her head still bent over the paper.

Daisy turned toward the large desk that sat at the opposite end of the room. It was far more masculine and imposing, similar to Mr. Tremblay's desk. She hurried to the desk, her eyes scanning the walls. She was being watched. Watched by the portrait of a gray-haired, thin-nosed man with a blue cravat, pale-blue eyes, and skin so pasty he looked half dead.

"There's a box by the lamp," said Madame. "Bring it to me."

Daisy tried to ignore the portrait and the way the man's eyes seemed to follow her. Instead, she swept her gaze over the desktop, settling on the wooden box intricately carved with forget-me-nots. She lifted it and was surprised by how light it felt in her hands.

Daisy brought the box to Madame at her writing desk, and the old woman set down her pen and twisted in her seat to reach for it. As Daisy placed the box in Madame's hands, she saw that the woman's fingers, though stained with ink, were straight and young-looking. Her skin was weathered, yes, but her knuckles weren't arthritic, and her nails were well-trimmed and fine.

She caressed the box before setting it beside her papers. "I suppose you wish to know what it contains, don't you?"

Daisy did but wasn't sure she should admit it.

Madame lifted her chin, a smirk settling on her lips. "I married Raphaël Tremblay when I was but sixteen. He was the son of a French trapper, who had married—marriage by common law, not a legal marriage—a woman of ill repute. Raphaël was their third born. He was handsome, and my father did not approve of him. But I did as I wished, and we were married."

Daisy wasn't sure why Madame was telling her this.

She tapped the lid of the box. "When my husband died—

twenty years after our marriage—I asked for his heart as a keepsake."

Daisy blanched. Her breath caught midway in her chest, and she stared at the box. It couldn't be true!

Madame's smile stretched across her wrinkled face. Her white hair accentuated her dark eyebrows, which winged upward. "They would not give me Raphaël's heart. They found my request barbaric. One person even condemned it as 'pagan.'"

Daisy swallowed with difficulty.

Madame continued. "I argued that we keep locks of hair from a loved one's corpse. Why can we not keep a heart—especially if it is calcified?"

Daisy didn't know what that meant.

Madame chuckled and turned, resting her hands on her lap and looking up at Daisy with a bold stare, not unlike her grandson's. "So, do you know what I did?"

Daisy shook her head wordlessly.

"I paid them to remove my husband's heart and to bring it to me." This time her laugh was a trill and filled the room. "Money causes so many miraculous changes of the heart!"

Madame's eyes narrowed as she studied Daisy's face. Daisy attempted to maintain an impassive expression but knew the shock and horror of the story was etched into her every feature.

"Humanity takes itself too seriously." She waved off Daisy's silence, drumming her fingernails on the box that held Raphaël's heart. "It is in the dark corners, in the places we avert our eyes from, where truth lingers. Truth is not palatable. In fact, most cannot manage the truth."

Festus dropped a basket of bread and cheese on the table in the kitchen. He had already brought in a steaming pot of stew that made Daisy's mouth water.

"Give your wife our thanks," Daisy offered.

Festus shot her a quick look from under bushy eyebrows. "Sure. She don't need no thanks, though."

"I would like to meet her sometime," Daisy tried again.

Festus groused as he fumbled around the cold kitchen, collecting the remnant containers from the noon meal at the castle. He haphazardly tossed a cloth napkin into a basket. "My wife don't like to meet no one."

His declaration disappointed Daisy. She'd hoped that perhaps she could befriend Festus's wife, who had to be an older woman. Perhaps find a kindred soul in a castle filled with dark, brooding characters—one of whom had paid others to remove her late husband's heart, and another who had hired a woman under the guise of a maid to spy on his own grandmother.

Festus himself was no parcel of joy, and even now the storm clouds on his face made Daisy bite her tongue. "Make sure you get some soup into Elsie," he admonished.

Daisy startled, locking eyes with Festus. Not only had he also become aware of Elsie's presence in the servants' quarters but he knew her name!

His chuckle was congested with age. "You think you're a mite sneaky, eh? This place has eyes, girl, and don't you forget it."

Daisy frantically searched for something to say, something to convince Festus that Elsie wouldn't get in their way.

"She is injured," Daisy began.

"I know." Festus gave a nod. "There's a poultice in the basket there my wife made up. Bind it around her wound. It will help keep out the pus."

"Th-thank you," Daisy said helplessly.

Festus waved a knobby hand toward the stairs that led to the lower servants' quarters off the kitchen. "She don't belong here. Once she can walk, she goes home. I know her brother ain't here, but she goes home all the same."

Daisy opened her mouth to reply, then snapped it shut.

"Speak your mind," Festus barked.

Daisy considered whether to question him. She'd promised Elsie after all. Or perhaps not promised, but she'd heard the plea and was hard-pressed to ignore it despite her own misgivings. "Did you know Elsie's friend, Hester May?"

Festus's head shot up so fast, his newsboy cap fell off and landed with a plop on the stone floor. His hazy eyes drilled into hers with a ferocity she'd not anticipated. Apathy or disinterest toward Hester May's disappearance, Daisy would not have been shocked at that. But Festus's expression was severe.

"Whaddya want to know of Hester May?"

"I-I . . ." Daisy fumbled. "Elsie told me she—"

"That this place ate her up, eh? Made the girl disappear? Along with the others?"

Daisy nodded.

He shook a finger at her. "Says everyone, that. No-good Needle Creek gossips. On second thought, you can send Elsie packin' for all I care. No one needs bother about Hester May. The Tremblays had nothin' to do with her going missing."

"I never said—"

"Didn't have to." Festus bent slowly to retrieve his fallen cap. He smashed it on his head of thick graying hair. "Don't say that name here. Ever again. Ya hear?"

Daisy nodded fervently.

Festus grumbled under his breath, snatched his wife's basket and empty containers, and charged from the kitchen, leaving through the door that faced the stables.

"Please!" Elsie was sitting straight on the bed, her wounded leg propped on a pillow, her face white with terror. Wide-eyed, she reached for Daisy as she entered with a tray of stew and bread. "Please don't leave me here alone anymore!"

Concerned, Daisy set the tray on the dresser and glanced toward the window. It was midafternoon. "What is it?" She noticed Elsie's trembling hands.

"You don't hear it?" Elsie lowered her voice as if someone were in the hallway eavesdropping.

"Hear what?"

Elsie shivered involuntarily. "The knocking on the wall!" she replied in a loud whisper.

Daisy listened. She shook her head. "I don't hear it."

"Not *now*," Elsie hissed. "Every so often, though, I hear it. *Tap, tap*. Like someone is knocking on the door—only they're not."

It might have been Festus, who for some reason had come upon Elsie in the servants' quarters. "The handyman, Festus—" Daisy began, but Elsie interrupted.

"It wasn't the old man!" Elsie's voice turned watery, panic-stricken. "I saw him outside the window. He saw me. No. This is *inside*. Inside the room. As if I were to lift my eyes and look into that corner"—she pointed to the far wall—"I would see someone standing there, rapping their knuckles on the wall."

Daisy wasn't sure what to say. She struggled to come up with an explanation, something to bring comfort to the young woman, to ease her mind and help her rest.

Elsie shifted on the mattress, wincing as she dragged her injured leg in an attempt to swing herself off the bed and onto the floor. "I will not stay here another night. Not alone."

Daisy reached for Elsie, but Elsie batted her hand away,

leveling a determined look on Daisy. "They're coming for me. I need to get out."

"Who is coming?" Daisy felt her fear lodge in her throat.

Elsie shook her head, her hair falling about her face. "I don't know! Whoever took Hester May. The woman, Elizabeth, before her. And the women of low morals. All of them! Disappeared. I don't want to be one of them. I *won't* be one of them." Elsie was frantic now, pawing at the bed, attempting to stand on her good leg.

Flustered, Daisy reached for her, and Elsie instantly took reprieve by leaning against Daisy. There was a slight unbathed scent hovering over the girl . . . and something else. Something putrid that made Daisy catch her breath. She eyed Elsie's leg and the bandage wrapped around it.

"Elsie, your leg—it's infected."

"I don't care." Elsie hopped toward the dresser and the food. "I'll take this bread with me. I'll find my way back to Needle Creek."

"And stay where?" Daisy asked, growing more worried by the second. "You already said you've no place to go."

Elsie swiped the bread from the tray. "It doesn't matter. At least I'll be alive."

Daisy reached for Elsie's wrist, and her touch stilled the young woman. Harried and glazed eyes met Daisy's. She could see Elsie's cheeks were flushed, and her shivering body bespoke a fever.

"Elsie, you must lie down. You must stay." Perhaps what Daisy believed to be infection setting in was causing Elsie to hear things. Imagine things. That she was afraid of Castle Moreau and its secrets was already a given, so it made sense Elsie would fixate on such in a delusional fit of illness. "Come with me. I will take you to my room. You will not be alone—at night at least."

Elsie hesitated. "But Madame Tremblay—"

"Will not know you are even here," Daisy interrupted. "She rarely leaves her front room where she writes." She didn't feel it wise to mention Lincoln Tremblay, though he hardly ever left his study. And Festus posed no real threat—she hoped. Still, Daisy felt more confident receiving Elsie into her own room now that Lincoln and Festus knew of the girl's presence and didn't seem to mind all that much. "Please," Daisy said.

Elsie considered for a long moment, then slowly set the bread back on the tray. She nodded, her face growing paler under the strain of standing heavily on one foot.

"Come," Daisy instructed. She would settle Elsie back in her bed, apply the poultice from Festus's wife, and then she would try to muster the courage to ask Mr. Tremblay if she could seek out a doctor. He wouldn't deny care to a woman in need, would he? Daisy was determined to ask, and she was determined to say nothing to Elsie. She would see Lincoln as not only a surprise but also a threat.

As she gathered what little Elsie had in preparation before helping the girl up the flights of back stairways to the north wing, Daisy's eyes swept the far corner of the room. No one was there. No one knocking or making a sound. And yet, in the labored silence, Daisy felt as if she and Elsie were not alone. And if they weren't, then it was a summoning of an old story of ghosts and spirits, of walls that came to life, and of a castle that breathed, filling its lungs with malice and evil intent.

fifteen

Cleo

hat I want to keep." Virgie hiked up her green polyester pants and pushed past Cleo. She snatched the spoon from Cleo's hand. "I went to Nashville when I was in my fifties. A fine city. This spoon is part of a collection." She waved it in the air.

"Where are the rest of them?" Deacon asked, a slight challenge in his tone.

Virgie eyed him. So did Cleo, but for altogether other reasons. It was impossible to concentrate on any type of plan with Deacon Tremblay standing there with his muscly physique, his half-buttoned blue oxford shirt and designer jeans.

"Don't get sassy with me." Virgie raised a white eyebrow at Deacon. "They're here. Somewhere." She shook the spoon over the mounds of clothes and boxes filled with trinkets and paraphernalia.

"Grand-mère . . ." Deacon started to intercede.

Had he really never watched an episode of the TV show where they did interventions for hoarders? Maybe Virgie hadn't trashed the castle, but she had turned many of its rooms into a warehouse of random inventory that was, for all sakes and purposes, worthless junk. Getting Virgie to agree to cleaning house would probably take professional help. A therapist who'd been trained to walk her through the mental and emotional implications of releasing her hoard.

"Give me back my spoon!" Virgie shrieked at Deacon, who had swiped it from her hand.

He studied the spoon, an expression of mixed humor and exasperation on his face. "Grand-mère . . ." Deacon lifted his eyes from looking at it. "This is a spoon from Nashville dated 2010. You weren't fifty ten-plus years ago."

"And your point?" Virgie snapped.

"My point is this isn't a souvenir from your trip to Nashville."

Virgie snatched the spoon back and held it to her chest, glaring at Deacon. "But it's from Nashville."

"Why is Nashville so important? What happened on the trip to make it sentimental to you?"

Cleo looked between grandmother and grandson. One would never pair them up as family. Not with Virgie looking dressed from the garage-sale pile of a nursing home while Deacon stood there giving every single Avengers actor a lesson on how to be hot.

"It's the city of music." Virgie pressed her lips together and looked down her nose at Deacon. "Leave me alone." She started for the broad doorway of the room, Deacon trailing behind her with an expression that made Cleo hide a sudden smile. He hadn't expected *this* much trouble from his grandmother!

Taking advantage of the time alone, Cleo rested her hands on her hips and the waistband of her cheap jeans. She looked around the front room that must have, at one time, served as a sitting room. There was a lovely large window overlooking the drive and front lawn. The opposite end of the room had a set of floor-to-ceiling bookshelves, a fireplace lodged in the middle of them. The shelves were stacked with books—old ones, by the looks of it—but Cleo wouldn't be able to get near them until she dealt with the boxes and junk that blocked the way. The walls were a pale yellow, pleasant if they weren't so stained with age, making it look as though someone had smoked one too many cigarettes in this room. Yet the only smells came from the must and mold of all the old junk.

A plan. She needed a plan. Cleo hefted a breath to steady her nerves. A plan was needed because Deacon expected one. Assuming she found a way to execute her plan without having to deflect Virgie's acts of sabotage, it should be a simple matter of organizing the items into three categories: keep, throw, and donate. Ideally, Cleo would ask Virgie to give input, but she already knew Virgie would come back with "Keep, keep, and keep." Dare she just toss out the things that were obviously trash? She glanced out the window. It'd be great to have a dumpster—or three—brought in. Would Deacon be opposed to having someone deliver them? He could hide and pretend he wasn't here, maintaining his anonymity.

Cleo opened a few cardboard boxes to get an idea if there was any rhyme or reason to what Virgie had spent years tucking away in this room. The first box contained magazines: *Country Life, French Cuisine, IT Magazine,* and several others. Cleo thumbed through an *IT Magazine.* It'd be ironic if there was a picture inside of Deacon at some Hollywood event. But a glance at the date told her he was just a child when this particular issue had been printed. In her opinion, the entire box could go in the trash pile. What was the point of keeping a box of magazines from the 1980s?

"Don't throw those!" Virgie's strident voice was laced

with urgency. She hurried into the crowded room as fast as she could given her age and the amount of stuff lying all over.

"I wasn't going to," Cleo assured her. But she might—later.

Virgie reached into the box and took out one of the French cooking magazines. "I was going to use the recipes in this one."

"You cook?" Cleo asked the question before thinking about how insulting it probably sounded. She was coming more from the angle that there was barely a scrap of edible food in the kitchen before Deacon had ordered groceries. It looked as though Virgie lived primarily off ramen noodles and a high quantity of boxed fruit snacks.

"I intend to," Virgie answered, clutching the magazine to her chest. "Please." Her voice lowered, and her eyes lost their stubborn obstinacy and filled with tears. "You can't take them. You can't."

"Okay," Cleo said, her empathy trumping common sense. She gave Virgie a reassuring rub on her shoulder.

Virgie sniffled, her fingers curling against the magazine and crinkling its glossy pages. "We need them here. They're important."

"I understand," Cleo reassured again. She looked up, hoping Deacon was there to witness this shift in Virgie's personality. He wasn't. They were alone. "We can work together, all right? To clean things up?"

A tear trailed down the finely wrinkled face. Virgie sniffed. "I didn't ask him to do this. I don't understand why we must go through my things."

Cleo bent to look into Virgie's face and attempted to capture her gaze. The older woman was staring past her, toward the fireplace and the bookshelves. Cleo gave Virgie's upper arm a gentle squeeze. "It will be healthier for you to clean things out. It's not even safe with these towers of boxes in here. If they fall—"

"I need the towers!" Virgie's voice trembled. "I need them."

"They're cardboard boxes of things, that's all. How about we go through them, and if something is critically important, we can—"

"He told me *never*. Never to clean." Virgie sucked in a weak sob. She lifted a hand to her lips to stifle the sob. "I can't begin now."

"Who told you that?" Cleo pressed.

Virgie's eyes locked with hers. "*He* told me. And I always listen." With shaking hands, Virgie set the magazine back in its box. She looked so frail at that moment. So lost.

Cleo almost hated the idea of touching any more of Virgie's possessions. But whoever *he* was, he had done a number on Virgie's psyche. The command had been etched into her mind many years ago, and now for her to do anything but leave her things alone would be tantamount to betraying him.

Virgie gave Cleo a small smile, her eyes still watery. "We'll do what we must. He'll have to understand."

"Deacon will understand," Cleo baited to see if Virgie was transferring some old memory on to Deacon.

Virgie shook her head. "Not Deacon." She patted Cleo's hand. "Never mind, dear. It's not worth going on about anyway."

The knock on the front door of Castle Moreau caused Deacon and Cleo to freeze, both exchanging a look of surprise. The knock sounded again, louder this time, echoing throughout the castle. Whoever was there had banged the massive brass door knocker with emphasis.

"Did you call someone?" Deacon whispered.

"No," Cleo answered, holding an LP record of John Denver in her hands. Deacon leaped over a crate filled with cassette tapes. He'd approved of her plan—the whole keep-throw-donate idea. Virgie was pouting in her room. At least that was what Deacon had told Cleo. Meanwhile, she felt a growing ache inside, one that stung. Virgie was holding on to all of this—for whatever reason—and they were here, at Deacon's insistence, rummaging through her lifetime of collections and memories. Her security. They were pilferers, grave robbers, no better than thieves . . . Cleo knew how she'd feel if someone were digging up her past and rifling through it. Granted, these were *things*, not memories, but still—

"Can you answer it?" Deacon interrupted her thoughts.

Cleo drew back. "Me? Why me?"

He raised his brows as if she should know. "Do you really want the paparazzi hanging out in trees outside the windows?"

Cleo blew out a breath of nervous energy, and Deacon's grin almost irritated her. It would have if it wasn't so darned intoxicating. Instead, her retort stuck in her throat as that infernal shyness took over. She nodded, zigzagging between the piles.

Reaching the grand entrance, Cleo tugged on the door handle, pulling open one of the heavy wooden doors. It felt as though she were opening the castle gates to the enemy.

"We need to talk." It was Dave, cassette-tape-player man. Cousin of Anne Joplin. Behind him stood Stasia, her green eyes wide, her nose ring smaller than last time, with emerald-green eyeliner that winged upward toward her bedazzled brows. So, Dave and Stasia knew each other?

Just her luck. Accusatory and morbidity in stereo.

"Can I help you?" Cleo really didn't want to be reminded

of the cassette tape. Of Anne Joplin. The last twenty-four hours had gone without too much of a hitch, outside of dealing with Virgie's unpredictable reactions. It was easier to forget the lore around Castle Moreau if people would just let sleeping dogs lie.

Dave had his hands stuffed in the pockets of his athletic joggers. His eyebrows had launched halfway up his forehead, his eyes taking on an expectant look. The morning sun gleamed off his bald head, and there were red tints in his mustache that would make an old Tom Selleck jealous. He was a nice-looking guy, though a bit intimidating just now.

"I'd like to listen to that tape again," he stated, rocking forward on his toes.

Stasia peeked around him, her expression alive with anticipation. Her Nirvana T-shirt hugged her form, yet she wore an oversized zip-up hoodie, black, that hung loosely over her jeans. "Seriously, Cleo, do you have any idea what you landed on?"

Cleo shot a furtive glance over her shoulder. Protect Deacon's anonymity? Check. Talk about the mysterious tape of Anne Joplin's friend who escaped her own disappearance? Preferably not. Especially with Deacon in the other room and within earshot. She had a distinct feeling he would not appreciate a new group of conspiracy theorists snooping around Castle Moreau. "I really don't—" she began.

Dave stepped forward, which made Cleo stop talking. "Please. My cousin—my family—all these years of unanswered questions. Where did she disappear to? That girl on the tape. It was Anne's best friend, Meredith. We haven't spoken to Meredith in years. She moved away and we lost all contact with her. Until now, we've had nothing to go on that might answer the question of why Anne disappeared."

Helplessness washed over Cleo. "I can give you the tape—I don't know why it was left on my car anyway."

"What tape?" Deacon's voice from over her shoulder gave Cleo a start.

Dave drew back a bit, his brows rising even higher, while Stasia's eyes rounded to the size of ping-pong balls.

"Umm . . ." Cleo searched frantically for words. It was Deacon's choice to out himself to these two, not her fault. Still, guilt surged through her—just like it always did, as most things were usually her fault.

"Hey, Deacon." Dave lifted his hand in a slight wave.

"Dave." Deacon dipped his head.

"You know each other?" Cleo squeaked.

Deacon kept his focus on Dave. "Yeah. I do know people in Needle Creek, Cleo. My family is from here." There was a cynical element to his response, and Cleo reddened even though she had a feeling it was aimed at Dave.

"Listen, Deacon—" Dave started to say.

"No, *you* listen." Deacon stepped just ahead of Cleo, his hand settling on her waist and pushing her gently back into the castle. It was an oddly protective gesture, and Cleo felt a flush creep up her neck as Stasia met her eyes with celebrity-glazed awe. Deacon didn't notice Stasia, his amber glare instead focused on Dave. "You and your family have spread lies about mine since the day Anne disappeared. Frankly I'm sick of the stories about this place. It's a castle. Get over it. Doesn't mean it's haunted, or that victims are hidden away in the dungeon, or there's some sadistic history here that sucks in helpless females. Look at Cleo. She's here. She's okay. You haven't vanished yet, have you?" Deacon turned to Cleo.

She shook her head obediently. "No."

"Have you heard anything strange going bump in the night?" Deacon challenged with the intent of proving his point to Dave.

Cleo bit her tongue. The apparition in the study . . . had it been real or just her imagination working overtime. Her hesitation left an opening for Dave to press his argument.

"See?" Dave nodded at Cleo. "She's not convinced."

Deacon hefted a very audible sigh. "Go away, Dave."

"Not without the tape," Dave said.

"That's right," Stasia interjected. "We want the tape."

"What tape?" Deacon insisted.

Dave looked around Deacon at Cleo. "You didn't tell him?"

Deacon twisted to direct his stare at Cleo, and now all three of them were looking at her. Waiting.

She swallowed hard, like her throat was sore, only it wasn't. "Umm . . . when I got into town the first day here, someone left an old cassette tape on the hood of my Suburban. I stopped at Dave's store—not knowing the connection—to find a tape player." She paused.

"And?" Deacon prompted.

"And on the tape was a woman being interviewed about Anne going missing."

"It was Meredith Bell," Dave supplied.

"Meredith?" Deacon's voice was sharp. "She left Needle Creek years ago."

"I know," Dave agreed, "which is why I'd like to have the tape."

"So you can use it to smear the Moreau-Tremblay legacy even more?" Deacon lost his charming side when confronted with Dave.

Dave held up his palms. "Hey, I'd like to be civil about all this. I'm not out to cause more trouble. I've matured, and I regret being so vocal years ago."

"Blaming my grandmother for hiding information that would help find Anne? Yeah. You were *quite* vocal. I've had to ward off the press for the last decade over a missing-persons case that's forty years old."

"I know, and I'm sorry." Dave's apology seemed sincere to Cleo. She looked up at Deacon, who eyed Dave with continued suspicion. Dave didn't let that intimidate him. "I was just a kid when Anne disappeared, but I remember how it tore up my grandmother, my aunt, my entire family. When I had the chance to start investigating it myself, I got carried away with the intensity of it."

"An understatement, I'd say," Deacon muttered.

Stasia fingered a strand of black hair that had slipped from her headband. "There are a lot of stories about this place," she stated needlessly.

Deacon shifted his gaze to her and looked unimpressed by her observation. "Sure, and there are a lot of stories about haunted houses, but most of them don't have family still alive. Prominent family. Whether you like us or not, we have a name to uphold, and your spreading slanderous conspiracies will get you sued."

Cleo's eyes widened. Wow. Deacon was serious about this. She glanced at Dave, who seemed to take it in stride.

"Got it, Deacon. I won't make an issue of it. But, please, don't stand in the way if I can find some answers here."

Deacon considered for a moment, then said to Cleo, "Go get the tape for him. But I want to listen to it before they leave."

Fabulous. So much for avoiding the dark and dismal. The abyss of Castle Moreau. Cleo could see the sparkle of excitement in Stasia's eyes, but she didn't feel the same. Not the same at all! She knew what it was like to have a history without answers, with stains that never washed out, and with demons that hounded you for years and refused to give up. She was still running from them.

In a weird way, she and Castle Moreau weren't all that different from each other. Not really. And *that* was what bothered Cleo the most.

sixteen

Deacon didn't invite Dave and Stasia into the castle. Instead, he hauled out some camp chairs he'd found in one of the many rooms and arranged them in a circle on the front lawn. The hospitality wasn't the greatest, but Virgie wouldn't do well with strangers entering the castle and violating her privacy.

Dave had brought a tape player with him, and after Cleo retrieved the tape, they took their seats and listened to the scratchy recording of Meredith being interviewed. When it was finished, Dave clicked it off.

Deacon nodded in understanding. "Okay, I get how that brings it all back for you."

Dave pressed the rewind button. "I have a few questions, if you don't mind?"

"Shoot," Deacon replied. "But I may not answer them all."

"Actually, they're for Cleo."

"Me?" Cleo shifted uncomfortably in her chair. "I don't know anything."

Dave's eyes were kind, which she appreciated. It was easier

to talk to him when he wasn't acting so intense. He leaned forward, elbows on his knees, hands folded in front of him.

"Do you have any idea why someone would leave this tape on *your* car?"

She'd wondered that herself. Cleo shook her head. "No. I don't know. I assumed it was coincidental." She palmed her fist nervously, debating on cracking her knuckles as a diversion from the anxiety welling within her. She shouldn't be anxious. She had nothing on the line personally as far as Anne Joplin's disappearance was concerned.

"Nothing about Castle Moreau is coincidental," Stasia stated, then was wise enough to bite her tongue when she received Deacon's dark look.

"You've never heard of Anne's case before? Talked with someone from your home about her?" Dave asked.

Cleo cracked the knuckle of her left index finger. An X-ray into Cleo's life was not where this conversation was supposed to go. She hadn't agreed to that. "No," she answered quickly. She noticed Deacon's quick glance. He knew she was secretive and he'd been kind enough—or maybe foolish enough?—to not press for answers.

"Have you ever heard of Anne Joplin?" Stasia asked on Dave's behalf.

Hadn't Dave just asked that? Cleo hoped she could maintain a polite tone and disguise the tremor she felt go through her body. She cracked her middle finger knuckle. "No. Never. I'd never heard about Castle Moreau, or the stories, or the whole history of vanishing women. It's creepy." Not to mention when she saw spooky ghosts lurking in the castle at night. Now *that* shed an entirely different perspective on Stasia's theories. Cleo kept that information to herself.

"You're sure?" Stasia scooted to the edge of her chair.

Cleo cracked another knuckle, then froze when Deacon's

palm lowered to rest over her clenched hand. She shot him a glance. He wasn't looking at her, but his thumb gave the back of her hand a reassuring stroke. A simple gesture. One she felt to her toes.

"She's sure," Deacon answered for her. He turned his attention to Dave. "How old was Anne when she went missing?"

"Nineteen," Dave said. "The story goes—at least from what we know of Meredith's side until this tape surfaced—Anne and Meredith had gone to a late-night party. You know the kind. High schoolers in the woods, campfire, beer, and the like. Meredith said it wasn't far from the castle here, and it was on Moreau property."

Deacon nodded. Apparently, he was familiar with the story but didn't mind being refreshed. He also hadn't moved his hand. His touch seared her skin. Stasia had noticed too, and she gave Cleo a smirk.

Dave continued, "The party broke up about two in the morning. When Meredith and some others were splitting up in different rides to head out, no one could find Anne. She just disappeared."

"And that's it," Stasia interjected.

"Yeah. That's it." Dave heaved a sigh. "Now this tape shows up, what, forty years later? Why? And *who* had it all this time?"

"The recording doesn't say a lot more than what you already told us," Deacon said.

"No," Dave agreed, "but Meredith's testimony is . . . more personal."

Stasia nodded, keeping a calm demeanor, but in her matter-of-fact way making it clear there was more to the tape than either Deacon or Cleo were understanding. "Think about it," she said. "Meredith says she was barefoot. She indicates she was running. She didn't stop. That doesn't align with the overall story from everyone at the party, who said they were splitting up into different cars to leave and then noticed Anne was missing. On the tape, Meredith makes it sound like she and Anne were being chased. Hunted."

Cleo shivered, though no one else seemed to find the idea unusual. This story was on the creepier *Investigation Discovery* side of things. Also, she should move her hand from beneath Deacon's. Really. She should.

"And the words 'isn't anymore'?" Dave said, picking up where Stasia left off. "I mean, what is that? No one says such things about missing people. It's as though . . ." He broke off.

"As though Meredith knows Anne is dead," Stasia finished, then bit her lip. "I'm sorry," she added quickly with a wince toward Dave.

"Don't be," Dave responded bluntly. "I feel the same way. I don't like it, but that's how Meredith sounds. Like Anne is dead, and Meredith knows it."

"You think Meredith is to blame?" Deacon offered. He leaned back casually in the camp chair, withdrawing his hand from Cleo's in an absent gesture. He probably didn't even realize he'd touched her. He propped a leg over his knee, looking as if he were interviewing with some Hollywood reporter instead of dissecting a missing-persons cold case.

"Maybe?" Dave shrugged. "But where is she now?"

Stasia held up her index finger to make her point, and Cleo noticed she had long fingernails with skulls painted on them. "Meredith left Needle Creek in 1990, nine years after it all happened."

"Does she have family here?" Cleo tried to help.

Dave shook his head. "That's the thing. Meredith was a foster kid—she had a rough life. By the time she up and left, she had no ties to anyone. Not even a boyfriend."

"But Anne had lots of ties," Stasia said, "and nobody has forgotten. Meredith had to know we never would."

"What's *your* interest in all of this?" Deacon shot the question to Stasia, who offered him a lopsided grin.

"I'm a crime junkie."

"That's cold," Deacon quipped.

Stasia pursed her lips. "Someone's gotta remember the cold cases. The cops sure don't."

"They can't," Dave said. "The number of unsolved cases is more than they can handle, what with their limited resources. It's not uncommon for family or well-meaning citizens to pick up the case and keep searching after the investigation gets shelved by the authorities. Stasia helps me with our personal investigation. She's got a sharp mind for this sort of thing."

"So, if Meredith is gone now, who was the cop in the recording?" Cleo felt like she'd earned back control of her emotions.

"That's what I want to know," Stasia said. "He could still be around, still have some answers. Maybe Meredith said something to him after they stopped the recording."

"Well . . ." Deacon slapped his knees to end the conversation and show he needed to get back inside. "You all have fun figuring it out. I'm sorry I can't be of more help."

"You can," Dave quickly stated.

Deacon paused.

Dave didn't miss a beat. "The fact is, Castle Moreau *is* intertwined in this because it was on Moreau property that Anne disappeared. You have a vested interest in helping us solve the case."

"No, I don't." Deacon furrowed his brow. "I have *zero* vested interest in this. Are you threatening me with more publicity stunts?"

Dave shook his head. "Not threatening, just being honest. Think about it. If we find out something *did* happen here at Castle Moreau, that somehow this place *is* involved, it'll leak to the public eventually whether we want it to or not."

"No one's found anything to substantiate that accusation in forty years," Deacon argued.

"Sure, but they didn't have a lead like this one with the tape. It's a whole new angle. Meredith and Anne being chased? Not the party scene like everyone believed it to be? Anne being presumed dead by her own friend? A potential cop we can talk to? This could bust the case wide open."

Deacon's mouth settled in a grim line. Cleo was surprised when he met her gaze and seemed to search her face for some answer or help with the situation. She offered him a small smile. She could be a friend if he needed one, and any person who tried to live under the radar and avoid attracting attention to himself needed a friend. It was just who could and couldn't be trusted that was the problem.

She entered the kitchen looking for something warm to drink, coffee or tea. It was past nine at night. She gripped a flashlight, not trusting the castle's vintage electrical system to not flicker out and leave her stranded in the dark. Cleo had no issue with admitting she was a fraidy-cat, and then add her debacle the other night with the unidentified apparition, and yeah, she felt safer with a flashlight in her hand.

"Scared of the dark?"

"Gosh dang it!" Cleo yelped and swung her flashlight beam directly into Deacon's face.

He held up a hand to block it, and she flicked off the flashlight.

"Wow, a little dramatic?" Deacon grinned, and if the light over the kitchen stove wasn't already on, Cleo figured there was enough electricity in that smile to light up the entire room.

"You scared me!"

Deacon propped his feet up on a spare chair and leaned back in the one he was sitting in. In front of him on the butcher-block table was a mug of something piping hot.

Good grief. The man was wearing flannel pajama pants. Flannel! She figured a man who was wealthy and chic would have luxury silk pajamas, but flannel? It was so Midwest and so . . . sexy.

"There's more coffee in the pot," Deacon offered.

"Thanks," Cleo mumbled. Her thoughts were a dramatic mixture between a middle school girl at a slumber party and a grown woman struggling to understand a tumultuous attraction.

She padded over to the coffeepot, thankful she still had her bra on under her T-shirt and was wearing knit shorts that covered well past her thighs. She had no desire to be lumped into the typical Deacon Tremblay grouping of women seeking his attention. She'd *take* his attention, but she wasn't going to grasp for it desperately. No. Cleo corrected her thoughts. She wouldn't take his attention either. The dream of a drop-dead gorgeous celebrity falling for her was a trope any female would fall for, but then there'd be press and publicity, and her ability to stay hidden would fly out the window like an uncaged bird.

"Coffee doesn't pour itself." Deacon observed her standing by the pot, not moving.

"Oh," Cleo responded. "Yeah."

"I have to say, you're probably the least talkative woman I have been around in a long time."

"Sorry," Cleo said.

"Don't be." Deacon used his foot to push the spare chair out toward Cleo. "It's refreshing. Not that you're practically trembling like a scared kitten, but at least you don't talk my ear off or try to impress me."

"I don't have anything to impress you with," Cleo admitted against her better judgment.

"Hmm" was all Deacon said. He then sipped his coffee and stared at her over the rim of the mug.

"I'm not a scared kitten," Cleo protested, though she wasn't so sure she believed it.

"No?" Deacon tilted his head to study her. "A bunny then?"

"I'm not a rabbit."

"Fish?"

"I don't swim."

"Ah!" He snapped his fingers. "You're a leopard gecko!"

"A what?" Cleo frowned. She'd not expected that at all.

"You know, one of those lizards people have as pets. They prefer to stay hidden but can be very loyal and friendly companions once you earn their trust."

It was too apt to argue with. Still, she didn't care for the comparison. She chose not to comment.

Deacon leaned forward with his elbows on the table, his thumb tapping the mug. "You know, Dave's wanting to find out what happened to his cousin is noble."

Cleo nodded in silent agreement.

"But it could cause one heck of an issue." Deacon seemed to want to confide in her, which was something Cleo had a hard time relating to. She was used to internalizing her thoughts, chewing on them, arriving at conclusions—right or wrong—within herself. But Deacon didn't appear to be the same. "You're familiar with all the lore around this place?"

"Yes," Cleo said.

Deacon scrunched his face, and it only made him cuter. "So, my great-great-grandfather—however many grandfathers back in time—built this castle in the early 1800s. His daughter was Ora Moreau Tremblay, the great American Gothic novelist—in the style of Mary Shelley."

"Mary Shelley who wrote *Frankenstein*?" Cleo was vaguely familiar with the author and her association with the legendary monster.

"Yeah. Only Ora Moreau Tremblay was more real-life. No monsters unless they were human Jack the Ripper types."

"And that's how the Moreau-Tremblay name became all-American?" Cleo ventured. She sipped her coffee as a way of coping with her nerves.

Deacon nodded, a dark curl flopping over his forehead. "I guess Ora's father was a wealthy Frenchman. Yet it wasn't until Ora that the name became synonymous with American literature. From there we became American royalty—sort of." He gave her an apologetic wince. "I'm not trying to sound arrogant."

"You can't help what you were born into," Cleo offered. She knew that better than anyone.

"So true." Deacon nodded slowly. "Anyway, it's been generation after generation since Ora."

So, Ora Moreau Tremblay the woman had been strong, of her own mind, and willing to take risks. The nineteenth century could not have been friendly to a woman who wrote Gothic novels surrounding murder.

"You want to protect your family." Cleo voiced her thoughts quietly. It was an observation, yes, but one she related to more than she would ever let on.

A look of gratitude crossed Deacon's face. He nodded again. "Yeah. See? You get it. It's not that I don't want to help someone find closure like with Anne Joplin's case. I just . . . Grand-mère doesn't need the press in her life." He had the grace to look guilty when he added, "I gave her enough of that when I was younger and clueless."

Cleo remembered the tabloids. The photos of parties, of the wild boy Deacon Tremblay.

"What changed you?" she asked, then regretted it. Too deep, too intimate, too uninvited. Cleo hurried to say, "You don't have to answer that."

"It's a good question." Deacon took another sip of coffee. "Hard lessons, that was what changed me. I'm sure you're familiar with the media's version of most of them. The fact is, though they're an exaggeration, there's still some truth in all of it. I wasn't . . ." He paused and scrunched his face again. He needed to stop doing that. It was too adorably attractive. "I wasn't taught much by my parents. Morals, I mean. Ethics, sure, but morals? Meh. They were gone most of the time. I spent most of my summers here with Grand-mère. Some school years overseas. It's hard to stay grounded, you know?"

Cleo nodded. She knew, but for entirely different reasons.

Deacon continued. "I had a buddy who talked about faith a lot. Not the in-your-face, Bible-beating type. Just—well, he lived it. What he believed."

"You're a Christian?" Cleo found it hard to believe that Deacon Tremblay would have had a conversion experience.

He smiled a little. "Not one on fire exactly—I still get un-comfortable in church. I don't get the whole raise-your-hands thing during worship. I mean, I *get* it, I just don't feel cool with it. But the idea of God. Of faith? Of grace? Yeah. I can get behind that."

Cleo didn't reply but instead focused on her coffee cup, hoping Deacon took her lack of response as closure to the topic. She shouldn't have ever brought it up.

Deacon didn't get the hint. He leaned back in his chair, taking his mug with him. "What about you, Cleo, whom I pay in cash and know nothing about? I've entrusted a perfect stranger with my most valued relative and our family name. Kinda laughable, yes?"

Cleo gave a small laugh to prove him right. For someone so concerned with preserving his reputation and privacy, welcoming a stranger into his home was a risk in and of itself.

"Seriously, where are you from? Or is that a secret too?"

It was hard not to squirm under Deacon's gaze, for a variety of reasons. Cleo smiled sheepishly. "I-I don't usually talk about where I'm from." She hoped the smile diverted him from seeing past it to the fear and panic that instantly gnawed at her stomach. He couldn't find out. It would endanger . . .

Cleo pictured the pink hat in her car with the sequined unicorn. *Protect. Save. Run.* Her mantra in life.

"It's okay," Deacon said at last. "You don't have to tell me anything you don't want to."

She felt like she should offer him something. "I believe in God."

"Yeah?"

Cleo nodded. "Although sometimes He seems not so interested."

"Not personal?" Deacon's voice was gentle. "I get that."

Cleo met his gaze. "I wish He was. I wish I could know He really does care. Just believe it. But I can't."

"It's that whole 'if God is good, why does He allow evil' thing, isn't it?"

Cleo nodded. "It is." She waited for something profound. Some answer that Deacon Tremblay might give that would bring comfort.

Instead, he studied her, his amber eyes warm and intoxicating. Finally, he said, "I'm sorry, Cleo."

She frowned, drawing her brows together.

Deacon finished, "For whatever happened to you to steal the life from your eyes. To make you so afraid."

Cleo hated that her eyes filled with tears. She looked away. From Deacon. From his ability to see into her heart. From the way his soul knew without her saying a word that fear was, and would always be, her closest companion.

seventeen

Daisy

1871

Daisy stood in front of Lincoln Tremblay's study. It took courage to knock and request entrance. She wasn't sure she had the courage, except the image of Elsie writhing on her bed with fever this morning urged her on. The girl needed a doctor more than anything. Elsie's condition—her leg injury—was far beyond anything Daisy could help with.

She'd debated about the worst of three possibilities of which to inquire for help. Madame Tremblay was utterly terrifying. With her willingness to have her husband's heart carved from his corpse to be preserved, Daisy wasn't entirely sure Madame Tremblay wouldn't use Elsie for some object of study in order to write her into a novel.

With Madame Tremblay a firm *no*, Daisy considered Festus. His wife had offered a poultice. That was kind. Perhaps he could bring her here or take Elsie home to her? But Festus had been nowhere to be seen this morning. Daisy had looked everywhere, and that alone had taken some time considering she had to search the grounds, the stables, then inside the castle with all its wings and staircases. Festus might be somewhere inside, but their paths simply didn't cross!

So it was Lincoln Tremblay's door Daisy now stood before. She ran her hands down her dress front. It was gray cotton. Mrs. Greenberg had insisted it be plain. But it was clean, and Daisy liked the navy-blue buttons sewn on its front. A bit of color—of the night sky—captured in a button.

She touched her hair. The red ringlets were springing in different directions. Daisy had pinned it as best as she could, but it was of no use. Flustering about outside Mr. Tremblay's door would do Elsie no good. Daisy mustered her bravery.

"Knock," she whispered to herself. So she did. A light rap. One that would probably take a miracle or remarkably good hearing to notice.

"Come in." Mr. Tremblay's deep voice answered, and even though it was the hoped-for response, Daisy still jumped a little at the sound.

She turned the knob and pushed the heavy door inward. The study was still shrouded in shadows, the draperies all drawn. No fire crackled in the fireplace. She looked around and wasn't surprised to find Mr. Tremblay sitting at his desk as though he'd never left it since the last time she'd seen him there.

And he was staring again. That dark, studious stare that made Daisy wonder if he saw right through her body to something beyond her. Or if he was trying to see inside of her. Into her soul.

"Pardon my interruption, sir," Daisy began, attempting to copy the polite expressions she'd heard Mrs. Greenberg utter in the past. "I-I have an issue I need help with."

The staring continued.

Daisy tried again. "I realize I didn't ask permission, but a few days ago, as y-you know, I came across a young woman, Elsie, who had her leg caught in a trap."

Mr. Tremblay's expression didn't change.

Daisy coughed. "She is in my room now, but she's awful sick, sir. Feverish." Daisy didn't expound on the way Elsie's wound was turning a putrid color or that the smell of infection was becoming overwhelming.

Mr. Tremblay finally spoke. "And you wish for me to heal the woman?"

"No!" Daisy was quick to respond. "No. I merely hoped that we could call for a doctor."

Silence.

She swallowed. Waiting.

Mr. Tremblay picked up a pencil and toyed with it for a moment, breaking his stare long enough to look at the tip of the writing instrument and poke his thumb against it. "My grandmother may be of assistance."

Daisy blanched. She could *feel* the color leave her face. "I—"

"She would find it morbidly fascinating as well," Mr. Tremblay said, lifting his eyes again.

"Mr. Tremblay—"

"Lincoln. I really dislike superfluous titles."

Daisy choked and then coughed. It would take the threat of being returned to the Greenbergs for her to call Mr. Tremblay by his first name.

"Mr. Tremblay," she tried again.

His expression darkened. "You don't listen well, do you? I will not help at all if you insist on *mistering* me."

"I'm sorry, sir."

"Lincoln," he retorted.

"L-Lincoln." Greenbergs or not, he was intimidating enough as he drilled her with his brooding demeanor, his rakish black hair sorely in need of a trim, and his hands that were quite handsome in and of themselves. Strong. Olive-skinned.

He didn't smile as he dipped his head in acknowledgment that he'd won that little battle. "I'm not keen on inviting the doctor of Needle Creek. He is a joke at best, and at worst, it means inevitable death for his patient."

Daisy was tongue-tied as all hope for Elsie flew out the window. "What do you suggest I do, sir?" Perhaps her question was bold, but desperation sometimes superseded one's need to be timid.

Lincoln tapped the pencil on his desk. "I will summon Grand-mère. She can assist you."

This was not what Daisy had hoped for. The absolute opposite, in fact. Her hesitation must have snagged Lincoln's attention. A midnight-black eyebrow winged upward.

"You disapprove?" he said.

"I'm . . . no, thank you. I—"

Lincoln set his pencil down and leaned forward over the desktop, folding his hands. "You realize that if you aren't an ambassador for your own feelings and thoughts, then no one else shall be either?"

Daisy wasn't sure what he meant, but there was a warmth to his tone, a tiny quirk to his lips that made her believe—or want to believe—that he wished her to be honest with him. Openness and honesty had never been encouraged before. Rather, submission and acquiescence were the expected responses, not only of women but especially of orphans such as Daisy. An orphan like her simply had no occasion for speaking her mind. That privilege had been stolen in childhood and wasn't to be returned.

"Well?" Lincoln pressed, his gaze never wavering from her face.

Daisy summoned a small bit of courage from deep inside herself. She cleared her throat with a tiny cough. "Your grandmother is . . . quite intimidating, sir," she said.

Lincoln's jaw worked back and forth, but other than that, there was no alteration in his expression. No sign as to whether he was offended, angered, amused, or impartial. Then he said, "Be that as it may, I will summon my grandmother."

"Yes, sir." Daisy dipped her head. It had been silly of her to fall for his goading. Lincoln Tremblay had no intention of taking her arguments into consideration. He was a Tremblay, after all, and Tremblays did as they pleased.

Daisy tried not to hover as Madame Tremblay's regal stature swept down the hallway toward the bedroom Festus had assigned Daisy. There was a chill in the air. The kind that followed one person—namely, Madame—and made anything in her way cower and step aside. Granted, Daisy recognized nothing really stood in her way, but she was certain, if they could, those whose portraits hung in the hall would have fled from their frames and gone into hiding.

Madame Tremblay paused before Daisy's room and eyed her over her shoulder. "This is the room you've chosen to be yours?"

Hearing censure in the woman's voice, Daisy offered a weak nod. She wanted to pass the blame on to Festus but felt it would be unfair to do so, so she opted for silence instead.

"Hmm" was all that Madame said. She pushed the door open and scanned the room, her stiff shoulders drooping a bit. Daisy watched her curiously, noting that the woman's face softened a bit before she seemed to heighten her resolve and summon her previous demeanor of control.

Elsie lay on Daisy's bed, her wounded leg supported by pillows, her face pale and sweaty. Hair stuck to her damp cheeks, and her neck was exposed as she had clawed at her nightgown as if it were shackles that held her to the bed and not sickness. She mumbled something in her feverish state, and Madame Tremblay moved to the bedside.

"She's very ill," Madame observed.

"Yes," Daisy acknowledged. She ventured to explain further in case Lincoln had not relayed to his grandmother the full story. "I found Elsie in the woods. Her leg was caught in a trap."

"Fiendish devices. Devices of torture scenes in my novels." Madame pinched her lips together in distaste, and for a moment Daisy wondered if the woman hid compassion deep in her soul and her stories of Gothic morbidity were merely a façade.

The aged woman reached for the haphazard bandage Daisy had applied to the wound. It was yellowed and stained, a stench rising from it that was a mixture of infection and the poultice Festus's wife had sent.

"Putrid." Madame ran her finger beneath her nose. "We'll be lucky if her entire leg doesn't fall off from infection—or be cut off by the doctor."

Elsie whimpered, clutching at the sheets.

"Shush, child," Madame instructed.

Daisy winced. The idea of amputation was much further than her own worry had taken her.

Madame turned her attention to Daisy. "What has the doctor said about her condition?"

"The doctor has not been called yet," Daisy answered.

"For pity's sake!" Madame's eyes widened, deepening the

creases at the corners. "Not been called? Are we pinching pennies? Send Festus for him immediately."

"May I?" Daisy couldn't disguise the eagerness that filtered into her voice.

Madame Tremblay's sharp look made Daisy reconsider. "May you? Of course you may! The doctor must be called immediately. Meanwhile, we'll ready the young woman to be transported off the premises. She will receive better care under his watchful eye."

"Off the premises?" Daisy squeaked. "Elsie cannot be moved! She has no family—"

"Who says she can't be moved?" Madame's countenance darkened. "No family? What are we to do with her here?"

Daisy felt a lump of fear swell in her throat. Fear of being intimidated by this woman, coupled with the fear of doing nothing on behalf of Elsie. Even so, she summoned the quiet courage of Jane Eyre, Charlotte Brontë's heroine whom Daisy so loved to read about.

"Tend to her here," Daisy retorted plainly. "Give her the care she needs right here—under direction of the doctor."

"And if it requires sawing off her leg? Then what?" There was challenge in the old woman's eyes.

Daisy fumbled for a reply. "Well, then we . . . we saw it off."

"*We* saw it off?" A crooked smile touched Madame's lips, and a twinkle of amusement entered her eyes. "My dear, you're as gory as they say I am. Shall we look at her wound now?"

Somehow, Daisy felt as though Madame had never intended on allowing her to call the doctor but instead had been toying with Daisy's sensibilities. Daisy sidled up next to the bed as Madame unbuttoned the cuffs of her sleeves.

She'd not meant to turn Elsie into a science experiment or to arouse the unearthly curiosity of Madame Tremblay.

The older woman began to unwrap the bandage, not offering so much as a cursory look of concern at Elsie. Daisy did that for both of them and sucked in a sigh of relief that Elsie now appeared quite unconscious.

As the bandage was unwrapped, the interest on Madame's face grew. Despite her white hair, her papery white skin, and her elegant dress, she was anything but a lady of an American castle. Instead, she was the epitome of a writer who sequestered herself in her study to write horrific tales of death and mayhem. That she drew inspiration for her stories in real life was clear by the way she examined the now-exposed wound on Elsie's leg.

"Fascinating," she muttered.

Daisy had to look away. She did not share Madame Tremblay's fascination. The wound was seeping, fiery-red at its edges, the teeth of the trap having done a wicked deed to Elsie's flesh.

Madame leaned forward, probing the skin outside the wound with her fingers. Elsie whimpered beneath the touch.

Madame ignored her. "Her leg is very warm near the punctures. The skin hasn't begun to discolor—that alone is a sign we needn't fetch a saw just yet." Humor laced the woman's tone, and Daisy didn't know whether she should breathe a sigh of relief or be repulsed by Madame's making light of a dire situation.

"Shall I have Festus get the doctor from town?" Daisy asked.

Madame settled a blue-eyed stare on Daisy. "No." She offered no explanation as to why she'd suddenly changed her mind on seeking medical help. She straightened, and Daisy stepped back.

Madame rolled her sleeves down, slipping the pearl buttons of her blouse's cuffs into their buttonholes at her wrists. "She will need to be moved. Ask Festus to help you. She should not be in this room."

"I don't mind sharing with her—" Daisy tried to reassure Madame but was interrupted as the woman's hand went up to stop her.

"Have Festus move her to the east wing. There's a bedroom there that . . . is closer to my suite. I will tend to her there."

"You?" Daisy couldn't help the surprise that leaked into her voice.

"Young woman"—Madame half sneered and half smiled simultaneously—"I have many years' experience caring for others, which far outweighs your own paltry knowledge as evidenced by this pathetic bandage you've applied. Thank the saints that Festus's wife saw fit to provide a poultice. It is helping, but it also isn't enough. Now do as I say. Fetch Festus and help him move this female to the other room in the east wing."

Daisy didn't miss the very scientific way Madame Tremblay referred to Elsie.

The woman continued. "Once she's moved, boil water and bring it to the room, along with clean linens. Tell Festus we need more of his wife's poultices. I will fetch my oils. We will also need camphor to help reduce the infection. I have morphine in my study, and I shall retrieve that myself. This young lady needs some relief."

On that, Daisy could agree.

Madame Tremblay blinked at her, her icy stare not unlike her grandson's dark one. She tilted her head. "Well?"

"Oh!" Daisy startled, realizing that Madame was waiting for her to act. "Yes. I'll go right now." She spun on her heel and hurried for the bedroom door, for Festus, and for the slim hope that the Gothic-horror authoress could somehow bring healing to Elsie. If she was being honest—and Daisy preferred not to dwell on the truth of her thoughts—she hadn't much hope.

eighteen

Cleo

PRESENT DAY

Virgie hovered as Cleo sorted through a box of knick-knacks. Everything from toothpick holders to miniature figurines were packed in the box, each item wrapped in newspaper. If God kept an inventory of all the unnecessary items in the world, there was a good chance Castle Moreau would cause His inventory software to crash. Cleo wiped her hand over her brow, feeling uneasy due to Virgie's nearness, and nervous because Deacon had gotten under her skin last night. He hadn't been nosy. He'd been . . . caring. She wasn't used to that. Not since her grandfather had passed away years ago. Caring was a foreign sensation. Not that she didn't care, but that she hadn't been cared *for*.

"Not that one!" Virgie's half shriek of panic startled Cleo, and she tightened her grip on a porcelain cat with a chipped ear. Virgie wagged her finger at the cat. "I had a cat that looked just like that when I was a little girl." She nudged her way closer, her knee bumping an empty box and sending it and plumes of dust falling to the floor. Virgie reached for the cat, and Cleo relinquished it, not trying to hide the perplexed rising of her brows at the rather emotional outburst over a figurine that had been buried in a box for heaven knew how many years—or decades.

Virgie clutched the cat to her chest, her wrinkled hands looking even more aged today as the blue vessels that ran through them stuck out like a web of mazes. "This is my cat."

Cleo nodded, praying for patience and a brief bout of wisdom from above. God could grant her that at least, couldn't He? "All right. So you can keep the cat, but then we need to dispose of three items."

"Dispose!" Virgie gasped. "I thought I had the option to donate!"

Cleo rolled her eyes at herself and tipped her head up and down. "Okay, yes, I just meant—"

"You want me to throw it all away. He told me—"

"Not to get rid of anything," Cleo interrupted. "I know." She gentled her tone at the sight of hurt streaking across the older woman's face.

Ease up, Cleo. She was cranky. On edge. The whole Anne Joplin fiasco had not dissipated, and she'd heard Deacon talking to Dave on the phone this morning. That and Deacon . . . well, c'mon *Deacon Tremblay* was enough to set a girl's nerves on edge—and on fire.

Cleo reached out to give Virgie a reassuring touch, but the elderly woman shrank back, her eyes wide. "My family has owned this property for two centuries. You've not a bit of say what I do with it or its belongings."

The bark was worse than the bite, and Cleo allowed understanding for Virgie. How awful it was to be uprooted by one's grandson. Simply *told* that the boxes of collections, the hoard of random items, all of which formed some strange and unrelatable form of security blanket around her, must go. Be organized. And for what reason? Cleo knew if she were in Virgie Tremblay's shoes, she would want to know why. Why now? Why had Deacon determined this year to be the year to return Castle Moreau—with its old fixtures, worn-out carpets and scuffed wood floors, its cluttered rooms full of dust and spiderwebs—to its previous glory? What purpose did it serve but to unsettle an old lady, who had built a nest of contentment within these walls?

It wasn't healthy, Cleo knew, would be the answer. Not mentally or emotionally, and while Virgie wasn't a hoarder who surrounded herself in filth, the piles of crates and boxes and clothes and trunks would be overwhelming for anyone, let alone a woman in her eighties.

Cleo sat back on her heels, ignoring the random junk splayed about her on the floor. She met Virgie's eyes and compassion flooded her. Had this been her own grandparent, she would have pleaded for the person coming in to be understanding, loving even. To take feelings into consideration and not just be clinical in one's approach to organization.

"Tell me about your cat, Mrs. Tremblay," Cleo offered.

Virgie's eyes relayed suspicion, but she answered anyway, thumbing the rough part of the cat's broken ear. "Her name was Curly. She was white, like this, with an orange back and orange-tipped ears. I found her as a kitten. She was outside in the rain, huddling under the eaves of the stable."

The stable. Cleo realized she'd not yet explored the outbuildings of the nineteenth-century castle. But considering it had been constructed within fifty years of the American War of Independence, it had to boast outbuildings that had once serviced horses and carriages and other necessities.

"Curly lived to be nineteen," Virgie went on. "She died

at the end of my bed. I woke one morning—I was newly married—to find her having simply fallen asleep."

Cleo offered Virgie an empathetic frown.

Virgie's features had softened with the memories, and her panic at losing the figurine seemed assuaged for the moment. She shifted her feet in her orthopedic shoes. "My husband helped me bury Curly under the old maple tree behind the stables where I first found her." Virgie stroked the glass back of the cat. "I miss her." All spunk had left the woman's voice, and a distant look came over her face. "I miss him."

Him. Her husband? Was that the "him" Virgie referred to? "What was his name?" she asked.

Virgie shuffled to a nearby crate and lowered herself gently onto it, her knees cracking from the exertion. "Charles Thorndike. I met him in the late fifties. He was a pharmacist."

Interesting. Cleo had expected him to be a Wall Street broker, or a famous actor, or something altogether far more impressive.

Virgie stared at a box filled with towels. "Charles was wonderful. A caring man. Not as bossy as my grandson. No." Virgie lifted her eyes toward the ceiling in exasperation. "I trusted Charles. He proved his faith in me from the first day we met. He allowed me the privilege of keeping the Tremblay name alive—I was the only remaining heiress—and so the name has continued, while his name of Thorndike died with him. Our son, Deacon's father, took after my Charles."

"And your son has passed away?" Cleo recalled reading a news article from a few years ago that something had happened to Deacon's parents.

Virgie swallowed hard and avoided answering Cleo's question directly. "You will know pain, dear, when you bury your spouse and your child before you ever have a chance to even flirt with the grave."

"I'm sorry," Cleo responded. And she was. She was sorry for the pain that death brought with it. The unanswered questions that always linked arms with death. Whether it was Anne Joplin's disappearance and unanswered end to her life, or her own story she'd rather not revisit.

Virgie's chest rose in a deep sigh. She pocketed the figurine. "I never wanted to be friends with death. Unfortunately"— she glanced about the room—"it is the essence of this place. This awful, godforsaken castle and all its secrets."

Cleo wanted to ask what she meant, but the expression on Virgie's face stopped her. Or perhaps it was the lack of expression. Her eyes and her face had gone vacant, as if she had drifted away somewhere and held no further thought or opinion on the matter.

She had spent most of the day with Virgie overriding her recommendations to toss or donate. The "keep" pile had filled three boxes of mostly figurines and assorted pieces of glassware. Her stomach was feeling dodgy with the lack of protein and proper hydration, but now she sat cross-legged facing a bare section of wall in the downstairs study just off the foyer. A bare wall meant she had made a dent in this room's collections. She would take any small victory, even though it meant in reality she'd made but a small dent in the room. And this was just one room. She hoped Deacon was prepared for her to live here through the winter months because there was no way this was a mere summer job!

Cleo stared at the wood paneling that ran halfway up the wall where it met with faded wallpaper. The vintage wood was beautiful. She moved to her knees and leaned toward it, running her hand along the scrolled woodwork. She tried to imagine what this wall had seen, the stories it could tell.

What had life been like here the week the Moreau family moved into the Midwestern castle? Hadn't Moreau started his life in the United States as a fur trapper? Whatever the original history, this wall had seen decades pass by. The Civil War had played out in the South, then World War I, and Virgie Tremblay had grown up in these halls under the umbrella of the Moreau family name. All of it was rich in history. No wonder the Moreau fortune and legacy had woven the Moreau-Tremblay family into the very fabric of Midwest America and then stretched to the very public media outlets that had made Deacon into a wealthy playboy.

Cleo's thoughts ground to a halt as her fingernail hooked on a splinter in the wall paneling. She slid forward until her eyes were level with the wood. She studied the splinter, squinting to see it better, then sucked on her fingertip where the nail had bent just enough to draw blood. Cleo reached out and toyed with the end of the splinter. It . . . wasn't a splinter. It was—

"A loose piece," she mumbled to herself. Cleo ran her fingers along the rounded molding that butted up to the wallpaper. It was smooth and well attached until her fingers met with the piece of loose wood again, small and thin. Like a narrow piece cut to fill an accidental gap between the molding and the wall. Cleo fumbled with it more until the piece gave way.

She rose to her feet and leaned closer until her forehead was pressed against the wall.

"What on earth?" Cleo could see a tiny piece of metal, like a hook attached to a hinge where the wood shrapnel had been. She was able to fit the tip of her finger into the gap and press on the metal. A clicking sound met her ears, and Cleo sucked in an astonished breath as the wood paneling split down the middle to reveal not a seam between pieces of panel but an actual door.

Cleo tugged at it. The door in the wall only went as high as the wood, so she crouched to see behind it.

Abolition era? A place to hide liquor? Those were her first thoughts, but they were quickly dismissed by the knowledge that the castle had been built just after the turn of the nineteenth century, way before whiskey and gin were hidden behind walls and in cellars.

A strong musty smell came from behind the door. She peered inside. It was black, unlit, and going by the stale air that escaped, hadn't been opened in decades.

Cleo glanced over her shoulder. Should she go get Deacon or Virgie? This was their property, their secret to uncover. But the void behind the wall was appealing to her. *She* had discovered it. Cleo's instinct was to investigate this for herself, to see if anything was even there. So she reached into her jeans' pocket and tugged out the phone Deacon had given her. Flicking the screen on, Cleo opened the flashlight app, allowing its beam of light to reveal what the wall had been hiding from the world.

A trunk, its lid half rotted through, greeted her. Cleo could see inside through the slats of old broken wood to cloth, which was moth-eaten—or mouse-eaten. She edged in farther, ducking so she could fit her head and shoulders into the small alcove behind the wall.

When she set her phone on the floor, the light bounced off the ceiling of the tiny space. Cleo reached out hesitantly, her fingers connecting with a velvety fabric that felt fragile. A tassel, frayed and chewed, was piled on top where the material was closed tight. A velvet bag in an old trunk.

Cleo's mind instantly filled with the image of jewels. Of

gold or hidden treasure. Perhaps this was a Moreau family hoard of some kind.

Without thinking, Cleo slipped her finger into the velvet bag's drawn opening and worked on widening it. After a moment of struggling with the bag, she was able to slide her hand inside it, grazing something cold to the touch. Smooth. Polished.

Gold.

It had to be gold.

Holding her breath, Cleo snatched up her phone from the floor of the alcove. Holding its light over the open and aged bag, she peered inside.

It wasn't gold that greeted her.

The cavernous eyes of a skull stared back at her. Bones were arranged neatly beneath it, with the skull positioned in a way that seemed to guard the bones.

There was only one thing left to do.

Cleo's scream filled the castle and echoed off the walls. A haunting scream that brought with it the reality that she had unearthed the truth behind a dark and rumored secret of the Castle Moreau.

nineteen

"You *have* to report it." Cleo was shaking, her hands trembling so much that she couldn't even tuck her hair behind her ears to keep the waves out of her face.

Deacon was wordless as he stared into the abyss behind the wall. A small closet really. Not even. It was a cozy nook just large enough to house a "freaking human skeleton!" as Deacon had not so subtly exclaimed moments after hurtling into the room, following Cleo's scream.

Cleo tried again, tugging on Deacon's shirtsleeve and not even bothering to notice how warm his skin felt through the cotton. "Deacon. It's human remains. We have to report it."

He wasn't blinking. He seemed shell-shocked. His mouth was a grim line, his eyes round in disbelief.

"Deacon?"

"What?" He shook himself out of his stupor of surprise.

"We need to call the police," Cleo announced, then instantly bit down on her tongue. No. That wouldn't be good. She couldn't be a part of an investigation!

Seeing Deacon shake his head brought her a bit of relief from her instantaneous panic. "I can't. No—no cops."

"Okay," Cleo breathed, choosing not to argue now that she was thinking clearer. Cops would mean questions. Checking IDs. Heck, human remains in Castle Moreau meant a lot more than police. It meant media. Conspiracy theorists. Complete and utter chaos.

"This stays quiet." Deacon's voice was low, almost regretful. "We can't afford to have . . . no. Not this."

"What if it's recent? What if it's—?" Cleo swallowed her nausea at the idea. "What if it's Anne Joplin?"

Deacon's golden eyes denied her statement. "Look at it." He waved his hand toward the rotting trunk, the worn velvet bag. The skull was dull—Cleo could see its dome, while the bag hid the rest of the gruesome remains. "It's old, Cleo. Like *ancient* old."

"You don't know that."

"The trunk is at least a hundred years old."

"Are you sure it's that old? Not . . ." She couldn't say Anne's name again.

Deacon gave a small laugh. "I'm not sure about anything *except* it's old. And we're not calling the authorities."

Cleo crossed her arms over her chest, protecting herself against . . . what? Ghosts? Invisible law-enforcement officers who could bring charges against them for not immediately reporting what they'd uncovered? She didn't want to go to prison for hiding human remains! Could she be facing criminal charges if they didn't call it in? She didn't want to be discovered. She *couldn't* be. There was enough danger there to make her skin crawl and cause her to look over her shoulder and—

"Close it back up."

"What?" Staring at Deacon, she snapped back to attention.

"The door, the wall panel—close it up. Leave it the way it was. Just let it be."

186

"But . . ." Her conscience warred with her desire to follow Deacon's instruction.

He leveled a dark look on her. "Listen. You call the cops and then what? If it's not recent—which it doesn't appear to be—then they call in government archaeologists. Castle Moreau not only *shuts* down, we'll be on the ten o'clock news by tonight. I'd need to call in security because reporters and paparazzi will soon be *crawling* all over the castle grounds. I know *you* don't want that either."

Cleo shuddered, shook her head. "What about the family?"

"I'm trying to protect the family, Cleo," Deacon answered.

"No, I meant the *victim's* family." She pointed at the trunk. "Someone is missing . . . *them.*"

"If it's as old as I think it is, those missing them are probably dead too by now."

Cleo didn't think Deacon meant to sound callous or insensitive. They were both reeling from their discovery and the implications of what could follow were they to report it.

Silence bridged an invisible bond between them as they both stared at the trunk. Though Deacon had stated very clearly his intention to put the remains back the way they were, hidden, neither of them moved. Cleo could feel him beside her, the strength of his body, his breathing slowly in and then out. In that moment, she realized how *human* he was. Not just a face or a symbol of something women regarded as eye candy. He wasn't just wealthy or the last in a long line of prominent members of an American dynasty. He was . . . a man. In his own way, he was frightened. Frightened by the backlash of the news that actual human remains had been found in Castle Moreau.

The stories—ones like Stasia had repeated—would become true stories to most. Sensationalized even more. The

Moreau-Tremblay family name would be obsessed over and garner even more spotlight attention—both positive and negative—and perhaps they would be viewed as criminals in the eyes of some who felt they were voices for the voiceless dead, those who'd vanished in the shadows of Castle Moreau.

"I need to call my lawyers." Deacon raked his hand through his curls, giving off a whiff of spicy deodorant.

Cleo looked at him, this time with more empathy. "Deacon?"

He returned her gaze.

"I understand that neither of us wants this for our own personal reasons. But this was a *human being*. Even if the remains are old, they belonged to someone."

"I know." Deacon's tone was grave. Resigned. He squeezed the bridge of his nose. "That's why I need to call my lawyers first. Before I do anything else. I need counsel to make sure this is handled legally, but also in a way that protects my family." He shot her a sideways glance. "And you."

She knew he didn't know why she needed protection, but the relief his words brought her was significant.

"Thank you," Cleo breathed.

Their eyes met in mutual understanding. Someone had died here. At Castle Moreau. Now both of their lives were inexplicably woven together with that of the bones hidden in the wall. The worst part was the realization that Castle Moreau really *was* what the stories had claimed. It was a coffin, and it buried secrets that had now come back to haunt them all.

The Girl

She came to me mostly at night. The weeks following *Maman's* death were horrifying. Papa became reclusive, never leaving his study. It was as if I did not exist any longer either and I missed him. I missed his laughter, his perfect words that always brought me comfort.

Now I was left with a woman he believed did not exist. An apparition that came into my bedroom, hovered over me, and watched me as I slept. This was not comfort. This was not the solace I needed as a grieving child, lost without her mother and now without her father.

"*Laisse-moi tranquille,*" I would whisper into the darkness. "Leave me alone." And the caped vision would drift away from my bedside, but never fully go away. I would see her form in the moonlight, the crooked deformity that was her hand highlighted.

The ghost never spoke.

I wished she would. I wished the hood would fall from her face, and I could see it fully. That the hollows of her eyes would suck me toward her, that her gaping black mouth would open, and that she would swallow me whole. While

189

it was a terrifying prospect, it comforted me in that it would be the end. The end of the hauntings. The end of the inexplicable sorrow that knifed my soul and left me, a small girl, bereft of comfort.

But I remained there to survive. Alone. With a phantom for a wicked companion that ate at my soul while I slept and left me aching when I awoke.

"*La femme fantôme,*" I began to call her. *The phantom woman.* No one believed the mutterings of a little girl. No one listened when I begged to have a nursemaid sleep with me at night.

"You are too old," I was told.

At six years of age, I didn't feel too old. I was still a child, *n'est-ce pas?* Perhaps it was because my papa was not capable of making decisions to hire a nurse or a governess. Perhaps it was because there was simply no one to employ. The housekeeper was unfamiliar with children and had little patience for me. The servants were schooled to give me berth when I passed and to treat me with an aristocratic respect I hardly deserved as the daughter of a French trapper who had made his fortune through various means and methods no one understood.

And so I curled under my blankets at night, afraid to grieve for *Maman* for fear of making Papa angry, and afraid to peek from beneath the covers in case I saw the phantom woman staring down at me with her featureless face and deformity.

That was the moment I became inebriated with fear. And then, in the solitary prison of nighttime, a mere four weeks after *Maman* winged her way to eternity, the phantom woman appeared again.

This time she did not back away when I demanded she leave.

This time she did not obey me as a servant should.

This time she seemed to grow both in size and monstrosity in the blackness of my room.

And this time the woman with the crooked hand finally spoke.

twenty

Daisy

1871

They had moved Elsie to the room Madame Tremblay requested. Though Daisy had no real attachment to the young woman, she still felt protective of Elsie. This made the distance from the wing in which Daisy slept to the wing where Elsie was being tended seem very far.

Daisy hurried from the kitchen that was now overly warm from the stove being stoked into a roaring fire to boil water. Festus had taken care of that deed, and perhaps his old bones made the heat feel good to him. As for Daisy, her dress was damp at the small of her back and underarms.

Festus met her coming down the stone steps of the servants' hall while she carefully made her way up, carrying a kettle of boiling water to replace what she'd taken to Madame earlier. The mistress of the castle had taken up residence at Elsie's bedside. One might argue it was endearing of the woman to give the patient such focused attention, but a gnawing in the pit of Daisy's stomach made her anxious. Madame was far too intrigued by Elsie's wound.

"Where're you goin' with that?" Festus growled.

"Madame needed more hot water."

Festus frowned. "When you've delivered the water, the master needs you in his study."

Daisy drew back, her shoulder bumping into the wall of the narrow stairway. She'd never been asked to Lincoln's study. More anxiety welled inside her. Not that Lincoln had proven to be anything but kind, though brooding, but because being summoned anywhere was . . . well, it never ended well in her experience.

"Is there a problem?" Festus asked.

"No. I just—"

"You don't need to know why, girl. Just do as you're told." The aging man pushed by her, causing Daisy to have to flatten herself against the wall so he could pass. She wasn't accustomed to many conversations with Festus, but those she'd had were congenial. He seemed different today. Preoccupied and annoyed. Perhaps Elsie's appearance and upsetting of their daily routine had him on edge.

Festus disappeared into the kitchen as Daisy continued her climb until she reached a hallway, which led to another set of stairs, then through several doors until she reached the wing where Madame had them place Elsie. Daisy noticed the suite of rooms that Madame occupied had an open door, and she dared to peek in as she passed, noting the rose-colored walls, the luxurious carpet and clean hardwood floors. She'd never cleaned the room herself. She'd never been instructed to or even expected to. As Daisy proceeded to Elsie's room, she wondered how Madame's suite could appear so clean and polished at first glance.

Daisy nudged Elsie's door open with her toe. On second

thought, Elsie's room was much the same. It didn't dawn on Daisy until now that when she and Festus had moved Elsie here, the bed was made, the drapes pulled back to reveal sunlight and clean windows. The floor and furniture had no dust on them. The wallpaper featured little bouquets of bluebells and was free of spiderwebs and the evidence of time.

Madame, who was hunched over Elsie, looked up at Daisy's approach. "You can place the kettle there." She motioned with her hand toward the stand that held a basin of water with clean folded linens beside it. "Then you may go."

Daisy tried to hide her frown as she did Madame's bidding. Elsie was still asleep—or maybe unconscious, Daisy wasn't certain—but the feverish flush had lessened on her cheeks. After Daisy put down the kettle, she turned and clapped her hand over her mouth to keep from squealing in surprise.

Madame Tremblay had opened Elsie's bandage and was poised with a sharp blade over the wound. With a calculated motion, she sliced a piece of flesh near the largest puncture wound from the trap.

Daisy gagged, raising her other hand to cover her mouth.

Madame seemed oblivious to Daisy's retching as she dropped the piece of flesh into a glass vial and corked it. "Wet a clean cloth for me," she ordered Daisy without looking at her.

Swallowing back bile, Daisy did as the woman asked, squeezing hot water through the cloth, then handing it to Madame.

Madame took it and started to clean the wound. She offered no explanation as she once again lifted the blade and removed another small piece of skin.

Elsie moaned, shifting in her position on the bed.

"Keep her still," Madame directed.

Aside from forcefully pressing Elsie's shoulders into the mattress, Daisy wasn't sure how to accomplish that.

Madame mumbled something about "infected skin." When Daisy didn't respond or move, Madame groused louder, "Take your leave if you're to be worthless."

Daisy hesitated until Madame lifted her head and glared at Daisy. "Leave."

Daisy hurried from the bedroom, pulling the door shut softly behind her. Cutting flesh from the wound was something that could be explained if it was gangrenous, but saving the flesh in a vial? Was the woman mad or simply deviant enough that she was keeping it as a souvenir of sorts?

She knew what she needed to do. Daisy rushed through the maze of hallways, winding her way toward the balcony that overlooked the front hall. A glance at Lincoln's study reminded her that he was waiting for her to answer his summons. And she should. But something else urged her forward and down the stairs, steering herself away from Lincoln and toward Madame Tremblay's work area.

Slipping into the room, Daisy shut the thick door behind her. The window allowed the daylight to spread beautifully through the room. The writing desk was unattended, of course, with Madame upstairs. For a moment, Daisy stood there catching her breath. She surveyed the shelves along the far wall until her eyes settled on the gold-embossed title on the spine of a green hardback book: *The Phantom Woman.*

Daisy knew it was one of Madame Tremblay's most popular novels, one that had catapulted her into the ranks of the Brontë sisters, Mary Shelley, George Eliot, and other female authors of the last century. Still, for all the stories Daisy had read, she had not read anything by Madame Ora Moreau.

She went over and pulled the book from the shelf, then started thumbing through it. What was it about Madame

Tremblay—or rather, Ora Moreau—that was so intoxicated with the gruesome that she would abandon her writing room to cut flesh from a wounded woman?

Everything Daisy had heard about Castle Moreau seemed truer as she perused the pages of the work of fiction. It was enough to show Daisy that Madame had a very dark, very fearsome side to her.

When Daisy turned a page and an ink sketch of a phantom woman appeared on a portrait plate, she nearly dropped the volume. As it was, Daisy plopped onto a nearby chair and stared at it. The image was dark, short lines of black ink sketched delicately but strategically to depict a cloaked and hooded figure of a woman, poised over the bed of a child, her hand—or what should have been a hand but instead was gnarled with its deformity—raised as if she planned to bring it down upon the sleeping child in an act of violence.

Daisy slammed the book shut. No. The Brontë sisters had never entered the depths of evil like Madame had. Mary Shelley and the others? Daisy couldn't recall anything so dark as a spirit haunting a child with intent to kill.

"The master is waiting." Festus stood in the doorway, displeasure etched into every crevice of his face.

Daisy yelped, dropping the book onto a table next to her.

"Snoopin' in Madame's things will come to no good for ya." Festus pushed the door wider and stepped aside in a gesture that said Daisy was to exit the room immediately.

When she did, Festus reached out and the grip on her elbow was tight. Not painful, but for sure it communicated a sternness that was not to be ignored.

"Never come into this room again if Madame isn't here, ya understand?"

Daisy nodded.

"Now git." Festus gave her a slight shove, and Daisy hurried away from him. She wasn't afraid of Festus. She was afraid of what she left behind in Madame Tremblay's writing room—the story of the phantom woman and the child being haunted by a spirit that obviously meant her harm. And worse, it had been penned by the very woman who now hovered over Elsie's bed like a vulturous soul exacting her curiosities onto the unsuspecting Elsie.

Daisy shuddered as she hurried back up the flight of stairs to the balcony and toward Lincoln's study. If Madame Tremblay was dark enough to have her dead husband's heart removed and to save flesh from Elsie's wound, what did that say about the state of any of the Tremblays? Of Lincoln?

His kindness seemed dwarfed in the shadows of Castle Moreau, and his dark eyes turned from studious stares in Daisy's mind to the hungry look of a man who preferred to toy with his prey.

She wished she were braver. She wished she had the heart of a warrior, bold and willing to walk into danger. With her red hair, Daisy figured she should have a smart wit about her and the determination to accompany it. Maybe life had merely stripped her of that. What with living with the Greenbergs, succumbing to the abuses of Mr. Greenberg and the ill temper of his wife. Perhaps there was such a thing as beating the spirit out of a child? If so, it had certainly happened to her, and now Daisy entered Lincoln Tremblay's cave-like study realizing even her legs were trembling. Brave was not a quality she was well accustomed to.

He watched her enter, and this time Daisy saw in his stare a monster waiting to pounce. The atmosphere at Castle Moreau had plummeted even darker to Daisy, and she wondered if staying with the Greenbergs would have been better in the end. At least she would have known what to expect.

"I told Festus I wished for your company. I've waited quite a long time." Lincoln's voice filled the room. He was in his customary position behind his desk, hands folded, leaning forward.

Daisy cleared her throat. "I'm sorry. I—"

"My grand-mère is demanding, I know." Lincoln gave a slight smile. "Tell me, how do you believe she fares? What are your observations?"

Yes. He had asked her to watch Madame. That was her primary purpose in being here. She had plenty to offer him by way of opinion, but none of it felt appropriate to share with honesty. Instead, Daisy clasped her hands in front of her, tilting her chin down just enough to communicate humility before the man of the house, or in this case, the castle. "She fares well," Daisy responded.

A short bark of laughter erupted from Lincoln, and it made his face momentarily appear friendlier. Handsome even. "Grand-mère fares well," he repeated as if his tongue caressed her words. "Now tell me your true thoughts of my grand-mère, Daisy François."

The use of her full name astonished her. Not that it was of any import other than that Lincoln Tremblay had bothered to educate himself about her surname. If so, what else had he schooled himself on?

"I'm waiting," he prompted.

Daisy shifted in front of his desk, putting her weight from her left foot to her right and then back again. "Your grandmother is . . . determined."

Lincoln dipped his head in acknowledgment. "I know that." He narrowed his eyes. "She is watching over the young woman, yes? The one you rescued in the woods?"

"Yes," Daisy answered, not expounding.

"And the woman is recovering?"

Daisy nodded. "I think she may be a little better."

"A little? Is my grand-mère giving adequate care? She should, as she's quite capable."

"Yes," Daisy replied.

Lincoln's palm came down on his desk with a heavy slap, startling Daisy and causing her body to jerk in reaction. He glared at her. "Talk to me!" he demanded. "Your paltry sentences make my brain hurt."

Daisy swallowed hard. He had frightened all the words right out of her.

Lincoln's eyes raked her face. "You have thoughts, yes? Ideas and opinions. You've locked yourself away in your mind. This may be a castle, Daisy, but we don't practice the medieval approaches to gathering information. I've no dungeon, no torture devices, no rack to stretch your arms and legs from your torso."

Daisy felt herself blanch.

Lincoln continued. "I abhor beheadings, though I've never in my life seen one, and I've zero intention of shackling you to a wall and letting the rats gouge out your eyes."

Daisy couldn't help but widen hers at his outburst.

"So then"—Lincoln slapped his desktop again—"speak your mind. What's the worst that can happen to you?"

She really shouldn't answer him honestly, but then something inside of Daisy broke in that moment. Perhaps he had drilled a tiny hole of trust into the dam that hid her most private fears, or perhaps fear itself had made her irritated enough. Daisy acquiesced and answered him literally.

"You could fire me and send me away. Then where would I be? You know what happens to girls like me, who have no home to speak of? We end up riding the trains westward, picking up work at brothels, being worthless women in the eyes of society. Castle Moreau is a terrifying place, Mr. Tremblay. Your grandmother is horrific, and you, sir, are nothing short of a beast behind a desk ready to spring on me. So no, I do not speak my mind. I bite my tongue to stay alive, stay employed, and stay free of the defiling way of life many women in my shoes find themselves."

She bit her tongue, contrary to what she'd just said, and everything inside of Daisy quivered at the realization. Perhaps her red hair *did* hide a smart wit after all, but a smart wit didn't imply a smart mouth, and she'd shown little wisdom in allowing Lincoln Tremblay to goad her into an honest outburst.

Lincoln stared at her darkly, this time rolling a coin up and down his fingers without even looking at them. "So you *are* afraid of me?"

"Of you?" Daisy shook her head. "Of Castle Moreau perhaps. Maybe all of you. Or maybe none of you. I've no idea what to think." She thought better of her words and added, "Sir."

"Don't think." Lincoln leaned back in his chair. "That is what seals your lips together." He stopped and studied her mouth.

Daisy felt a flush creep up her neck.

He continued, "This castle is a prison of sorts, that I understand. So here is my plan. I want you to visit me here every day."

"Every day?" Daisy squeaked.

"Yes. Tell me your *honest* impressions of my grand-mère's health. Not just her body, but her mind. She has been troubled since I was a child—as evidenced by the stories she writes. But then I would also like to just talk."

"Just talk?" Daisy echoed.

Lincoln's black eyebrow winged up over his left eye. "You read books, yes? Let's discuss them. The weather. A boring subject, but a topic nonetheless. News of Needle Creek—you escape the castle at times to go to town, don't you? What do they say about us Moreau-Tremblays? I would find their suppositions humorous."

"You wish for me to spy on your grandmother and also the people of Needle Creek?" Daisy couldn't help but interpret his words as such.

"Spy? No. I'm not at war with anyone, least of which my own grand-mère. I just want . . ." His voice waned and he ducked his head, and then when he lifted his eyes, an element of confidence had fled and for a moment Daisy thought he looked almost vulnerable. "I would just like your company. We can discuss the grass outside if that makes you feel better."

"I don't like grass very much. It makes my eyes itch."

A smile split his face. Long creases in his cheeks deepened. His eyes took on an altogether friendly appearance, and Daisy was moved by it for reasons she wasn't entirely sure of.

"I'm not fond of grass myself. How about clouds? I'm assuming that would be a safe subject."

"I do like books." Daisy reverted to one of Lincoln's original suggestions.

"Which is your favorite? And if you say one of Grand-mère's, I may change my mind about the beheading."

Daisy felt her own smile play at her lips. "No. I've not read hers." She didn't dare mention her earlier visit to Madame's writing room. "I quite like *Northanger Abbey*."

"Hmm, I've not read that one."

"It's by Jane Austen."

"English?"

"I assume so."

"Have you read Edgar Allan Poe?" Lincoln asked.

Daisy shook her head. "He's quite dark."

"True. But his poem 'Annabel Lee' is hauntingly beautiful."

"I've not read that one either."

"You should." Lincoln's voice had lowered, which sent shivers through Daisy, even though her fears seemed to have lessened.

"Who's Annabel Lee?" Daisy ventured.

"I think she was a woman Poe loved," Lincoln replied, "and the poem tells her story."

His gaze drilled into hers, and Daisy was quite unable to look away. The intensity of Lincoln Tremblay's presence drew her to him as if she were a ship looking for port. But ports could be dangerous too, and one shouldn't trust too readily when anchoring in an unknown place. Lincoln was still speaking, and Daisy fought to focus on his words. Instead, she watched his carved lips move as he spoke, almost hypnotizing her with the way his jaw worked with strength and confidence.

"A woman is a powerful creature, Daisy François. Do not underestimate the power you wield."

twenty-one

Everything magnificently terrifying happened at night. This was a promise, tried and true, made by every frightening novel, every personal experience, and every ghost story ever told.

Daisy cursed this fact as she stood stock-still in the middle of her bedroom. The moon had hidden itself behind clouds tonight, and though her eyes were adjusted to the depths, Daisy still had a difficult time making out the objects in her room. The wardrobe, the bed, the desk were all bulky shapes. The door was closed, locked, yet even now the knob twisted one way and then the other.

Daisy held her arms around herself, fixated on the door. She was alone in this wing of the castle. Desolately alone . . .

There it was again—the rattle of the doorknob. She didn't ask who was there. Daisy knew there would be no answer. She was alone. Alone with night phantoms.

The phantom woman.

It was a horrible time to recollect the title of Madame Tremblay's novel. A horrible time to recall the ink drawing of the phantom poised over a sleeping child.

Mrs. Greenberg had told her once that spirits of the dead were not kept away by locked doors, or walls, or even by the prayers of a righteous man or woman. No. They were unstoppable demons of the night, wandering souls, aimless and determined to take the living into their merciless dangling between heaven and hell.

Daisy took small comfort that the door into this particular bedroom seemed to refute Mrs. Greenberg's superstitions. And regardless of the inadequacies her previous guardian had applied to prayer, Daisy felt her lips move in an urgent plea that God and all His angels would descend on the creature outside her room rattling the doorknob.

The knob stopped moving.

Daisy sucked in a breath and held it.

Silence drifted through every crevice and every crack in the room.

She slowly released her breath, but as she did so, a scraping sound dragged along the floor just outside her bedroom. It sounded like nails against the floor. In her mind's eye, Daisy could see the image of a ghostly woman being dragged from her bedroom door by an unseen figure, her dead fingernails scraping the wood, her face twisted in agony as the demon pulled her into a hellish unknown.

The scraping ceased.

Daisy held her body stiff. Motionless. As if they would sense the slightest movement.

She hated this place.

Her earlier interaction with Lincoln Tremblay had been a surprise, enjoyable, but this snuffed it out completely. The Tremblays might not have medieval dungeons in their Midwestern castle along the Mississippi, but it had something far worse. It had the ghosts of women who had disappeared.

Like Hester May.

In all that had happened with Elsie, Daisy had almost forgotten the missing Hester May, not to mention the other women from Needle Creek who were yet unaccounted for. All of them had last been seen near Castle Moreau.

It was their spirits that haunted these halls.

If Madame kept her husband's heart in a treasure box, and pieces of Elsie's skin in vials, what else was being hidden in the castle? What atrocities were concealed behind its stone walls, wood panels, and rich tapestries? And what of this place's mysterious occupants? A grandmother and her grandson . . . with the rest of the Moreau-Tremblay line stolen by death? Was it not odd that Lincoln was still unmarried, or that no household staff busied themselves in keeping up the castle's appearance?

This place was not right. It was unseemly. It was dangerous, and it was now her home.

Daisy jumped as a wail echoed through the hallway outside her bedroom door. A lonesome cry from far off in some other part of the castle, yet still close enough for it to reach Daisy's ears.

She forced herself to approach the door. Without hesitating, she unlocked it and twisted the knob, creating an opening for the evil outside her room. If the crying was coming from Elsie, Daisy could not, *would* not, abandon her.

The hallway stretched before Daisy, empty and black. She couldn't help but glance at the floor and look for scratches from the ghost woman. There were none. It was a deathly still place now.

She stepped cautiously into the hall. Everything in her demanded that she flee back to her bed, but a strong sense of obligation to Elsie compelled her forward. She should have grabbed a lantern, a candle, something to light her path.

Daisy dragged her hand lightly along the wall as she tiptoed down the hallway, her bare feet cold against the floor. To get to the north wing, she must head down the back hall to the servants' staircase, climb the narrow stone steps to the third floor before turning left and arriving at the row of suites that included Madame Tremblay's. Or she could avoid the more frightening servants' route and instead weave her way to the balcony near Lincoln's study, then take the hallways to a flight of stairs meant for the family of the castle to the third floor, then across the main hall and past more rooms until she reached the north wing.

Daisy decided to avoid the servants' route. Something about it made her feel lonesome, less safe. Perhaps it was why Elsie demanded to leave the servants' quarters that Daisy had originally put her in. Castle Moreau was not a warm place; the servants' quarters were even colder.

She caught sight of the vast balcony at the end of the hallway. While there was no man-made light to guide her, enough light from outside added shades of blues and grays to make the balcony appear to be some sort of respite or haven. If she could make it there, she would be halfway to Elsie's room.

Another wail echoed, causing Daisy to stumble. She regained her footing and increased her pace. The wail sounded almost unnatural, a mixture of pain and confusion. It was distant and yet it ricocheted off the castle walls and the floors, making it impossible to tell where it had originated.

Daisy regulated her breathing and focused on coming to Elsie's aid should it be her who was crying. It *had* to be Elsie. Daisy refused to allow her imagination to run wild with the idea of a phantom woman roaming the halls.

The brush of cold fingers across the back of Daisy's neck sent terror through her. The icy touch toyed with the baby curls that had slipped from her bun, trailing across her neck . . .

A primal scream ripped Daisy from her restraint. Her body launched forward and away from the ghostly fingers, even as she spun to peer into the void of the hallway behind her. No one was there. Stumbling forward, Daisy sprinted toward the balcony, not caring if something was in her way or if she made any noise. She could sense the eyes, the presence, the hands of someone behind her, and yet there was no one. Only an invisible, vaporous force that was chasing her through the castle.

Daisy shot a panicked glance over the balcony, catching sight of the massive chandelier with its cobwebs and dust. Her bare feet slapped against the wood floor, and as she ran, all coherent thought fled from her.

She finally reached the study door and flung it open, rushing inside.

He was there, this time not behind the desk. The window silhouetted Lincoln Tremblay's profile. For some reason, this was the only room in Castle Moreau that Daisy could think of that felt safe. The strength of a man whose own darkness could battle someone else's and perhaps come out stronger. A champion. A hero.

Daisy barely registered her actions before she threw herself into his arms. Nor did she contemplate what possible good a man could do against a force of evil when he was sitting in a wheelchair, unable to rise to do battle.

twenty-two

Cleo

Deacon was not returning to New York as he'd planned. This much was obvious now as he had remained at Castle Moreau for four days instead of the original two he'd indicated. It was no longer the mission of determining if his grandmother, Virgie, was in need of physical and mental assistance, as Cleo had given him the impression, but it was to handle the new debacle of a literal skeleton in the closet.

Cleo watched Deacon as he paced the castle lawn, speaking into his phone. She stood at the front window by an antique writing desk supposedly belonging to the revered Madame Ora Tremblay, author of *The Phantom Woman* and other Victorian horror novels. She ignored the furniture in exchange for watching Deacon's long legs eat up the yard's patchy grass. He paused by a stone gargoyle statue that stood sentinel beside an iron bench, rusted from age and weather. His right arm was flailing about as he talked, expressive and agitated.

"What's he going on about now?" Virgie's presence behind

Cleo didn't frighten her. She was growing accustomed to Virgie's hovering, if not her mood changes.

Cleo offered the elderly woman a smile, attempting to hide any outward sign that she and Deacon had a secret of their own now. Bones. Human remains, tucked away neatly in a vintage and moth-eaten velvet bag, with a wooden chest acting as its coffin.

Her *life* was becoming a Gothic novel that rivaled an Ora Moreau classic, and Cleo wasn't exactly cool with that. She had enough proverbial ghosts haunting her. The *truth* haunted her. She had not signed up for this. She had signed up to sort through an old woman's junk pile—and for the record, Cleo reminded herself, she was making pathetically poor progress.

"Nothing to say?" Virgie quipped when Cleo failed to answer her inquiry. She stood next to Cleo, her curly white head barely reaching Cleo's shoulder, and followed Cleo's gaze on her grandson. "If I hadn't seen the news, I'd say he was arguing with his ex-girlfriend. But apparently she's dating some foxy son of a gun from Paris now." There was humor plus a little bite in Virgie's tone.

Cleo chose not to comment on that either. Discussing Deacon's love life was remarkably uncomfortable, especially with his well-toned body creating ruts in the lawn as he hiked back and forth between the gargoyle and a maple tree.

"So, do you have designs on him?" Virgie would not stop talking. This Cleo knew, because the woman had discovered Cleo couldn't do two things at once. If she was engaged in conversation, then she'd leave Virgie's things alone so she could concentrate on Virgie's conversation. Which was usually pointless, or nosy, or sassy, or all of the above lumped together. "Well? Do you?" Virgie pressed, her eyes innocently wide behind her black, round glasses.

Cleo glanced at her. "Umm, no?"

Virgie's pink lips smiled a little. A nice smile touched with disbelief. "Impossible. Any female in her right mind would have designs on Deacon Tremblay. If not for his name and money, then for his handsome face. Have you seen my grandson?"

Cleo choked.

Virgie patted Cleo's arm. "There, there. I know it seems odd for a grandmother to remark on her grandson's looks, but he's so much like my Charles was, and a bit like my grandmother Ora Moreau's husband. Did you see his portrait in the east wing? He too was handsome as all get-out. Throw all those genetics in along with my Charles's one-hundred-percent French and we have a smashing bloodline of fabulous men."

Cleo couldn't argue. She *had* seen the portrait of Ora Moreau's husband. She had also seen a portrait of Charles. And, yes, Deacon was . . . remarkable.

"I knew it." Virgie was studying her and must have seen something in Cleo's expression. "You like Deacon."

Apparently they were middle school girls now. Cleo tried not to let her mouth quirk into a smile of embarrassment and in doing so give Virgie more ammunition for her goading. "Yes, your family has very handsome men in it," she conceded.

Satisfied, Virgie looked back out the window toward Deacon. "I'm proud of him. He has been a rascal in the past, but he's maturing now. It's a shame my son and daughter-in-law aren't with us any longer. Dratted plane crash. They had to follow in John Kennedy Jr.'s footsteps."

Cleo vaguely remembered hearing about the airplane crash that took the life of JFK's son, as well as the lives of his wife and sister-in-law. Deacon's parents had suffered a similar fate. Until now, she hadn't known. Hadn't thought to question why it was that only Virgie and Deacon were left in the Tremblay line. But then avoiding the idea of parents altogether was her preference. With a father who'd never been named, and her mother . . . Cleo bit back a sudden onslaught of tears. The thought of parents was a trigger for her. She grappled for her grandfather's thumbprint and rubbed it absently, drawing comfort from his dysfunctional legacy of strength.

Virgie hefted a quiet sigh. "I miss them."

Cleo could relate. She missed her mother too. The mother she'd found lying in the fetal position after overdosing. The mother who had left Riley in a Graco Pack 'n Play in dirty diapers. The mother she shouldn't miss but did anyway. Just like Grandpa. She shouldn't miss either of them. That was why Grandma couldn't handle her. Cleo had been loyal to the wrong people—the people who'd hurt her and Riley, who didn't deserve her love.

"Anyway, you have mail." Virgie held out an envelope.

A pit settled in Cleo's stomach. A letter? Here? No one knew she was here. There was no reason she should be receiving mail. No reason at all.

"Are you going to take it or shall I add it to the pile of magazines you wanted to go through next?"

Ignoring Virgie's sarcasm, Cleo took the envelope gingerly.

"It's not going to bite you."

Cleo met Virgie's eyes and noted a wariness in the woman's study of her. Virgie was trying to read her, to understand her, and that she was curious about the origin of the letter was obvious.

"Thank you, Virgie." Cleo smiled thinly and moved away from the window. In fact, moving away from this room and taking refuge in her bedroom upstairs seemed preferable right now. With a glance toward the now-closed panel wall, she hurried from the study. Leaving Virgie behind in the same room as the hidden skeleton didn't worry her too much. The woman had lived in the castle for many years—as had generations before her—without the skeleton being exposed.

Cleo padded up the flight of stairs to the balcony, glancing at the chandelier and wondering when so many of its crystals had fallen off and if they'd ever hit anyone on their way down. Maneuvering through corridors, she made her way to her bedroom, shutting the door and leaning back against it.

Murphy was curled at the end of her bed, and he opened one eye.

She shook the envelope at him. "Who did you blab to that I was here?"

Unmoved, the cat closed his eye and resumed his nap.

Cleo sank to the floor, her back against the door, and lifted the envelope to read the return address. Her fingers shook, and images she didn't want to recall flooded her mind. They'd found her. It was obvious. Cleo wasn't sure how to process the panic and nauseating anxiety that surged through her.

She could run. Again.

Was it the phone Deacon had provided her with? Had they somehow traced it back to her, and if so, how? How was it even possible?

The handwriting on the envelope was so familiar and it tore at Cleo from the inside out. She bit her bottom lip until she tasted blood.

Open it.

Easier said than done. Her index finger slipped as she pushed it under the envelope's flap. The ensuing paper cut caused Cleo to yank her finger back and suck on it for a second. She could feel her hand trembling as she pulled it from her mouth.

"Get it together," she coached herself. Attempting again, this time she opened the envelope. The paper inside was yellow lined paper, the ink from a ballpoint pen. The handwriting . . . Cleo dropped the letter as if it had burned her. She scooted away on her backside, staring at it numbly.

Murphy jumped from the bed, a hiss escaping him at Cleo's sudden movement. She rubbed her hand across her eyes. Maybe if she opened them, it would be something different. *Someone* different. But when she did so, the letter lay discarded a few feet away, the writing a shaky, thick blue ink with looping letters, the words impressed on the paper where the writer had pushed the pen hard against it.

"It can't be," Cleo whispered. "Oh, God . . ." she breathed. A prayer of sorts? Maybe. A request to understand the impossible? Most definitely.

Carefully, Cleo drew the letter toward her.

"Dear Cleo" was written in bold letters, practically screaming at her from the top of the page, followed by *"Come home."*

That was all it said.

"Dear Cleo, come home."

But the writer of the words . . . Cleo drew in a deep, stabilizing breath. He couldn't have written this. He *couldn't* have! Grandpa was dead. He'd died three years ago. How he had sent her a note—and to her hiding place at Castle Moreau—was as unearthly and as terrifying as it could get. Hearing word from beyond the grave was never meant to be so tangible. But there it was, in blue ink and with shaky handwriting:

> *Dear Cleo,*
> *Come home.*
> *—Grandpa*

Virgie's screams catapulted Cleo to her feet, and her sudden surge upward caused her to fall against the door, lightheadedness almost taking her out completely. The letter from her grandfather stared up at her from where she'd dropped it, but Virgie's distress shoved Cleo into action. Her adrenaline was already soaring, and when she opened the door, Murphy darted out between her legs, his angry yowl telling her he wasn't happy that his peaceful afternoon had been disturbed.

Cleo raced back toward the room in which she'd left the older woman.

"No! No!" Virgie cried. "Leave it be! No!"

Cleo stomped down the stairs, dodged boxes and piles of stuff in the large entryway, and charged into the study.

Virgie was grabbing at Deacon's arm, clawing at him, her face wild with panic. Her white hair was in disarray for how perfectly styled it'd been only minutes before when she was bantering with Cleo. She was pulling backward on Deacon, even as he was pushing forward—in the direction of the paneled wall and the secret alcove.

"I said *leave it alone!*" Virgie shouted, her voice high-pitched and wobbly.

"Grand-mère!" Deacon tried to extricate himself from her grip as gently as possible. He cast Cleo a harried look.

Cleo entered the fray. "Virgie, let Deacon go."

Virgie's fingernails bit into the skin of his forearm where his shirtsleeve was rolled up. She turned her rage on to Cleo without letting go of Deacon. "You did this! You!"

"Did what?" Cleo asked, reaching out with both hands in a calming motion. "Virgie, what did I do?"

"Leave her alone!" Virgie twisted her petite frame and

moved her hands to Deacon's chest, pushing against him. Her fragile body was clad in polyester pants and a short-sleeve purple knit turtleneck that did nothing to hide the thinness of her bones or the saggy wrinkles of her arms.

"Grand-mère . . ." Deacon gently gripped her upper arms, bending to try to capture his grandmother's gaze. "Grand-mère, I need to open it."

"Leave. Her. Alone." Virgie seethed.

"We can't leave it there," Deacon stated firmly. "I talked to our lawyers and—"

"Lawyers?" Virgie shrieked. "What do lawyers have to do with her? She has been here at Castle Moreau for years! She's not harming anyone!"

"You knew about it?" Cleo broke in.

Virgie shot her an annoyed look. "I've lived here all my life. Of course I knew about her."

Deacon urged his grandmother toward a chair that was empty of random junk. She resisted. "It's illegal," he said. "We have to report it."

"You want to tell the police?" Virgie drew back, her voice increasing in volume again. "And then what? The world too? Everything everyone has ever lied about our family will come to life again! The lies. The slander."

"About women disappearing?" Cleo pressed her lips together when Deacon gave her a quick shake of his head.

"Yes! That! People believe this place is *evil*." Virgie's eyes widened with intensity. "She stays behind the wall. And we don't tell *anyone* about her."

"Who is she?" Deacon spoke in an even tone, trying to calm Virgie down.

A raucous laugh erupted from the old woman. "I'm not telling you! You'll only ruin it! You'll tell your *lawyers*," she spat, "and then people will be nosing around my castle and looking in places they're not supposed to look. Castle Moreau is *our* legacy, Deacon, no one else's. It's bad enough you brought *her* here."

"Who? Cleo?" Deacon sounded incredulous.

Virgie's face transformed then, taking on the look of someone who was gazing into the beyond, at something neither Deacon nor Cleo could see. "It's all right," she said calmly. Her voice was lower now as she soothed whoever it was she was looking at behind Deacon. Cleo glanced around to see if she could identify who or what Virgie saw. "It's all right," Virgie said again. "No one will ever know. I promise. Never."

Virgie smiled up at Deacon, her expression soft and caring. She stroked Deacon's arm where her fingernails had left scratches. "Honey, you need to be more careful." She rolled Deacon's shirtsleeve down and then patted his forearm. "There. Now, watch what you're doing. Let's go have some tea." She motioned for Deacon to follow her. He acquiesced, but his face displayed confusion as he passed Cleo.

"I'll be right back," he mouthed.

Cleo nodded, then wrapped her arms around herself in a protective manner as Deacon and Virgie exited the study. Something about this room—besides the human remains behind the wall—wasn't right. An aura embraced it, danced in the corners, and laughed when no one was looking. A sardonic laugh that said the rumored secrets were truer than some might believe, and declared those same secrets would stay hidden in the dark at all costs.

twenty-three

"*When it rains, it pours.*" That was what Grandpa always said. The thought of this old quote sent a chill through Cleo as she hurried toward the front entrance of the castle. The knock that had echoed through the hall caused Cleo to jump out of her skin. She'd been eyeing the wall that hid the skeleton while listening with one ear as Virgie chattered to Deacon, the two of them heading toward the kitchen for tea. Virgie was acting as if she hadn't had a near meltdown only minutes before.

Cleo pulled the heavy door open and tried not to roll her eyes when she saw Stasia standing there. Her black hair was pulled back into a headband, and she wore her customary facial jewelry. She had on a royal-blue T-shirt and black skinny jeans with blue Converse tennis shoes—the perfect meld of goth and pretty with a bit of Billie Eilish vibe.

"Hey," Stasia said. "I didn't know how else to get ahold of you except to show up here on your doorstep."

Cleo wasn't about to give Stasia her number. Not because she didn't trust her, but with her grandpa's letter still lying on her bedroom floor, she felt her anonymity slipping away at the speed of water through a funnel.

"Anyway, Dave and I figured out who the investigator on that tape was."

"Investigator?" Too much was coming at Cleo. Her brain was spinning.

Stasia frowned. "You know, the tape about Anne Joplin? Her friend Meredith?"

"Oh. Yeah." It wasn't as if she'd forgotten about Anne. Cleo shoved the mental image of the skull to the back of her mind. Deacon had been sure it was old, that it wasn't Anne. Although something about his chat with his lawyers had made Deacon change his mind about reporting what they'd uncovered in the hidden alcove to the authorities.

Stasia raised an eyebrow, assessing Cleo with a quizzical eye. "We want to go talk with him."

"With who?" Cleo frowned. She was losing her mind.

"With the investigator." Stasia's face scrunched, not hiding that she thought Cleo was acting weird. "Do you want to come along?"

"Me?" Cleo squeaked.

"Or Deacon."

"Um . . ." Cleo looked over her shoulder. Grandpa's letter. The skeleton. Virgie's flipping out. Now this? "No. No, I'm good," she sputtered.

"You don't want to talk to the investigator? I mean, someone left that tape on *your* car."

"Just a coincidence, Stasia," Cleo said, excusing it.

"Try again," Stasia retorted. "Besides, Deacon told Dave that we should keep him posted on anything and everything we found. Guess it's his right considering all the suspicion about this place over the years. And the fact that every woman in Needle Creek would be camping out on the lawn here if they knew Deacon Tremblay was around. Which means half the town's population would be at risk of disappearing—if women really *do* go missing at Castle Moreau. Congrats, by the way!" Stasia offered a crooked smile.

"For what?" Cleo was *not* keeping up with the girl's sharp mind and wit.

Stasia laughed. "For not vanishing like everyone else seems to do around here."

Cleo wished she could be as carefree as Stasia seemed. She wished her biggest task in life was to research conspiracy theories instead of being smack-dab in the middle of one. Or two, if she included her own life's story. Gosh, she could go for a stiff drink right now. She eyed her Suburban parked in the drive. The whiskey was still inside it . . . unless Deacon had taken it. Suddenly her mouth was dry.

"Okay then." Stasia held up her palms with a dismissive flick of her fingers. "It's obvious you're not interested, so I'll just, you know, wander back into town."

"Wait." Cleo made a motion to reach for Stasia, even though she didn't touch her.

Stasia looked at her expectantly.

"Um, Deacon will probably want to know what you're doing." Cleo realized her lack of functional brain cells at the moment wouldn't be a good excuse when Deacon found out he could have weighed in on the investigation into Anne's disappearance but hadn't been told about the latest developments. "I'll go get him."

Stasia frowned, this time with concern. She looked over Cleo's shoulder into the castle, then back at Cleo. "You *are* okay, aren't you?" She leaned in. "One woman to another, right? I'll kick some you-know-what if you're in danger."

Cleo gave a weak laugh. She believed Stasia would and

probably could too. "I'm fine. Really. Just—it's been a long week."

Stasia rolled her lips together and nodded. "I'll say. Dave is rampaging around town, looking at all the old archival news about his cousin Anne. Word is getting out he's looking into her disappearance again. I mean, this place will be lucky if it can avoid attention, at least from the folks in Needle Creek. Castle Moreau is a freaking legend—people both love it and hate it."

Cleo was on the side of hating it. "Okay, I'll get Deacon. Do you want to come inside?" Darn. Bad idea. What was she going to do, leave curious Stasia standing in the foyer outside the room that hid the skeletal remains of . . . well, whoever it was?

"Sure!" Stasia eagerly pushed past Cleo, who turned and sagged in relief as she saw Deacon coming toward them.

His eyes narrowed when he spotted Stasia. "What's up?" His casual greeting disguised a tense look given to Cleo.

Stasia explained her reason for being at the castle, and Deacon winced. That he was also feeling overwhelmed by the cacophony of events at Castle Moreau was apparent.

"All right. Umm . . ." He raked his fingers through his dark hair. Cleo noted how Stasia's eyes followed his hand. Yeah, she was right. Every woman in Needle Creek *would* risk life and limb to be near this man. Her own stomach swirled at the idea she'd just spent the last few days with him. In another life—in another world—she'd be living a dream. Here, she was just living a nightmare.

Deacon was looking at her, and Cleo snapped to attention. "So, we should go with Stasia."

"We should?" Cleo's voice squeaked.

Deacon looked as though he was trying to communicate something with his amazing eyes. "Yeah."

"Okay." Cleo nodded, still not understanding. But Deacon was her employer, after all, and they had a shared secret between them.

"Cool!" Stasia was looking weird at them. She was probably contemplating if they had both lost a bit of their minds. "I'll, uh . . . get in my car. Do you want to follow?"

"Right now?" Cleo shot a frantic look at Deacon. They couldn't leave Virgie alone, not after her near mental breakdown.

"Dave's already on his way to meet with the guy," Stasia said.

Way to give them a heads-up!

Deacon nodded. "We'll be right there."

Stasia looked between them, raised her brows, then turned toward the front door. "Ooookay. I'll just . . . you know, wait for you in the car."

Once Stasia stepped outside, Deacon was quick to close the door on her. He expelled a huge breath, enough to lift some of Cleo's hair off her shoulder. He noticed and reached out to straighten the wavy lock. Cleo didn't know that hair had nerves, but she was certain she felt his touch clear to her toes.

"My grandmother will be fine."

"How do you know?" Cleo whispered as if Stasia were eavesdropping through the door.

"We don't have much choice," Deacon answered. "I can't let Dave go digging into this Anne Joplin stuff without being there to monitor the situation. I don't trust he won't rush off to the local news station immediately after with some wacked-out theory."

"And your showing up at this investigator's place isn't going to jeopardize your own anonymity?" Cleo challenged.

"A chance I'm willing to take rather than let Dave run loose with this."

"He doesn't seem that bad of a guy," Cleo stated. "He just seems intense. Anne was his family, after all."

"Yeah, and my lawyers aren't convinced that the authorities won't believe what I already know to be true, which is that those bones in there"—Deacon waved wildly toward the study with an air of annoyance—"are older than my grandmother!"

"Oh." Realization dawned on Cleo. "Your lawyers are saying you need to report it."

He gave a sigh and nodded. "The legal risks far outweigh my concerns about privacy. They believe if the bones *are* by any slim chance Anne Joplin's, then not reporting it makes me complicit in covering up some familial crime."

"So the Moreau-Tremblay family is the French mafia of Needle Creek, Wisconsin?" Cleo couldn't help but crack a joke. It caught Deacon off guard, and his crooked grin was her reward.

"I guess so, yeah. There are a ton of legal implications. One of my lawyers is on a flight here. We'll report the remains and then my security team will cordon off the property as best as they can. Not to mention, I'm sure the authorities will want us out of the castle."

"Looks as though we have as long as it takes for your lawyer to get here to figure this out," Cleo said.

"Basically. And I don't even know what exactly we're trying to figure out. Old remains won't be easy for the authorities to identify, and it's not Anne."

"You don't know that for sure, though," Cleo said.

Deacon shrugged. "No," he admitted. "I guess I don't."

"We need to go with Stasia and see what this investigator has to say."

Deacon appeared completely unenthusiastic. "Yeah. I guess we should do it while we still can."

Cleo wasn't prepared for Deacon to touch her arm in a subconscious effort to move her forward as he opened the door. She especially wasn't prepared for his fingers to trail down her bare arm, leaving her skin hot and her mind more off-kilter than it had been even minutes before.

"Cleo." His voice mesmerized and terrified her simultaneously.

"Yes?" She tried to sound casual while drowning in the amber pools of his eyes.

His fingers caressed her arm in a light back-and-forth stroke. She wasn't even sure he realized he did it. "I know that you . . . want to stay in the background. We'll take care of you too. I won't let the media splay you out for the world to see."

Cleo couldn't deny the twisting anxiety in her gut when Deacon had explained his intentions.

"I've got you." He squeezed her arm gently, then dropped his hand.

For a long moment they stared at each other. Reading each other's eyes, the mutual need for anonymity colliding with the very different reasons why and the secrets she hadn't told that Deacon didn't seem to care about just now.

Cleo didn't know how to process it. Any of it. Not Deacon. Not the memories. Not her grandfather's letter. Not her own darkness.

All she knew was that there were human remains in the castle, Virgie had been hiding them, there was a slim possibility they belonged to Anne Joplin, and sooner rather than later, Castle Moreau would be crawling with people and Deacon's and Cleo's carefully ordered private worlds would then be robbed from them like thieves breaking into a grave.

twenty-four

Daisy

1871

It was strange how Lincoln Tremblay only increased in strength even as the reality of his limitations slowly revealed itself to her. It was Daisy whose weakness had sent her into his arms, so that now, balanced precariously on his lap and oh so indecently, she was very aware that he'd wrapped his strong arms around her waist. His lap was far less muscled, his legs lean and twisted in subtle but distinct ways. Still, he held on to her, probably in a gentleman's effort to keep her from collapsing onto the floor, if not from utter shock at what had just occurred.

"I'm so sorry!" Daisy dropped her arms from around his neck, pulling her face from where she'd buried it against his shoulder. He smelled of cedarwood and spice, and his face was close enough to hers that in the darkness she could see his black stare. So intense. So filled with questions that both challenged and reaffirmed an inner strength. Daisy could only pray that he was the trustworthy man she wished him to be. That he wasn't a legendary monster of Castle Moreau who ate women and spat them out into the hallways of memories of lost souls.

"Truly, I-I . . ." Flustered, Daisy attempted to squirm from his lap. She was aware now of the arm of the mahogany wheelchair that dug into her back. She was also aware of how silent the castle was. No screams. Nothing but the ticking of a clock somewhere in the study, the sound of a soft rain against the windowpanes, dancing in the night, and the steady breathing of the man beneath her.

Lincoln had yet to release her.

She tried again, twisting gently, afraid she might hurt him. She sensed a physical weakness in the lower half of his body that he'd hid behind his desk until now. He loosened his grip but didn't remove his arms.

"I'm not made of glass." His voice was a low rumble.

"Please . . ." She was embarrassed. No, she was mortified, as it suddenly dawned on her that she was clothed in a nightgown. Her feet were bare. Her curls were flying every which way in what had to be a wild red halo around her head. "I'm so sorry, I—"

"Don't apologize. Spare me your looks of pity and your sorrowful sighs."

"My sorrowful sigh is for myself, I'm afraid." Daisy had no qualms in admitting it, for there was no hiding the impropriety and impulsiveness of her position. "If I've offended you—"

"Offend me? Hardly. You're the first woman who has ever thrown herself at me, and I daresay you will be the last."

"I could hardly know why." Daisy's honesty silenced Lincoln for a moment. Then his chest rose in a deep breath that indicated he was composing himself. For what, she didn't know.

"My old friend here"—Lincoln released her waist with his left arm long enough to pat the arm of his wheelchair—"doesn't inspire womanly affection. Someone with my condition is hardly a hero, no?"

Daisy hesitated as his arm once again slipped around her waist, holding her against him in a way that she should never be held, let alone be comfortable with. Still, she could sense that the instant she resisted, the instant she fought his grip, Lincoln would release her. It was something Mr. Greenberg would never have done.

She shivered at the thought and said without censure, "We all have challenges in life, Lincoln. Things we must contend with, whether physical, mental, or otherwise."

"Lincoln," he repeated absently, as though he had never heard his name spoken from someone else's mouth before. The creak of his chair beneath their weight, the feel of the leather on the back of the chair by his shoulder, brought awareness back to Daisy. She could feel the warmth of his hands through her gown. Nothing about the man was weak, regardless of the self-deprecation he showered on himself. If in the light of day she were to recognize physical weakness, his inner strength far outweighed it.

"Now then," he started, "why not explain what sent you flying into my study in the dead of night like *La Velue* was chasing you."

"Who?" Daisy drew back a bit, attempting to see his eyes better, and curiously unwilling to change her position. Darkness shrouded his features.

"A French monster. Some call him the *Peluda*. He is a piecemeal creature, both snake and dragon, tortoise and porcupine. His quills are like arrows on fire." Lincoln seemed to enjoy regaling her with the legend and mystery of the tale. "Just one strike of his tail will send you into the eternal."

"He sounds dreadful," Daisy breathed, quite caught up in the description, though she hadn't forgotten where she sat. She moved again, but Lincoln's hands remained at her waist, not restraining, but not initiating her departure either.

"Dreadful? Mm, yes. He survived the Great Flood of the Scriptures by hiding in a cave and then rampaging the earth when it was over."

"But wouldn't his cave have flooded?" Daisy questioned, thoroughly curious now.

A low laugh, and then, "One would think."

"And Scriptures say there were two of every creature, so would he and his mate have fit on the boat?"

"The ark?" There was humor in Lincoln's clarification. "One would think not."

"So the legend cannot be true. At least not in its total," Daisy concluded.

Lincoln chuckled, and Daisy could feel the vibration through her palm braced against his chest. She moved then, enough to encourage Lincoln to release her. Very aware of herself, of her proximity to the man, she slipped from his lap. Hugging her body, Daisy allowed her hair to fall forward over her shoulders. It felt like a shield.

"What startled you, really?" Lincoln turned his head toward the window. The draperies were now pulled back to reveal the earth shrouded in night.

"I heard someone," Daisy admitted, following his gaze out the window.

"Did you?" he asked almost absently, as though his memories had somehow taken him out of the moment to a place far away.

"She was crying. It was why I came. And then . . ." Dare she admit the icy cold fingers in the corridor? The ones that had caressed her neck and made her lose her senses and flee?

227

Lincoln looked up at her, searching her eyes in the shadows. "You must have heard the woman with the crooked hand. The phantom woman."

Daisy's breath caught. She stared down at Lincoln. "But she is merely a story. A story of your grandmother's imagination."

"Is she?" Lincoln offered a tolerant smile. His dark hair fell over his forehead, hiding some of his features. His hands gripped the arms of his chair, the wheels large on either side, with a smaller third wheel in the back. He sat in it like a prince on his throne in a castle. A banished prince. One with secrets and wounds and scars. "Is she merely a story?" he whispered.

Was she real?

The question had kept Daisy awake long into the night. That, along with the fright of her doorknob twisting again, or moans echoing through the corridors. Not to mention her interlude—her highly *inappropriate* interlude—with Lincoln Tremblay, which had set her nerves on fire in a way they'd never been before. Together, they were all fearsome things. Processing the chaos of her emotions was like trying to come up for air in a swirling tide of water.

Now, with sunlight transforming the day into something beautiful, Daisy donned her gray dress, tied her curls into a neat bun, and gathered her wits—what little of them seemed to be left. She must check on Elsie this morning. Though the eerie cries had ceased after Daisy bolted into Lincoln's study, the fact remained: Elsie needed care, and Daisy could hardly assume that Madame Tremblay had devoted herself to bedside nursing throughout the night. The authoress's version of *nursing* left much to be desired.

And what of Lincoln? Now that the morning had dawned, so too had the stunning realization of his condition. It explained why he never seemed to leave his desk. Why his study was his haven. Had he always used a wheelchair? He must have been born with the malady. She felt no pity for him, only for those who refused to associate with Lincoln Tremblay. It was perhaps their own misfortune, not his. Was this why, in Festus's words, he did not "exist"? A family shame perhaps—also why Madame never mentioned her grandson, sequestered above her just off the balcony, as if tucked away, stored for safekeeping? Daisy's ire rose at the idea.

As she strode toward Elsie's room, she pushed Lincoln from her mind and prayed that Elsie had not been dissected during the night. Cut into tiny pieces and stored in vials and wooden keepsake boxes. Lorded over by a torturous old woman enamored with anatomy and gore.

It was decided. Daisy approached Elsie's bedroom door and made her determination with alacrity. She did not like Madame Tremblay. She did not wish to read the woman's stories. She did not take any comfort in Lincoln's grandmother being the only one tending Elsie. Today, regardless of the consequences, Daisy would fetch the doctor from Needle Creek. She would either send Festus or, if he refused to cooperate, she would go herself. She would see to it that Elsie received proper care and, God willing, was taken to a safer place in which to recover.

Daisy opened the bedroom door, immediately assailed by the smell of rubbing alcohol, poultice, sickness, and a sweet scent she could only compare to rosewater. The tall, arched window at the far side of the room allowed the sunlight to stream in across the floor. Before attending to Elsie, Daisy made quick work of opening the window to permit fresh air into the space. She then turned her attention to the bed while searching for any signs of Madame Tremblay's presence.

A stillness consumed Daisy with the awful realization that the room was empty of occupants—no young woman in bed, no Madame Tremblay. The bed had been cleared of sheets, the bedspread folded neatly at the foot. Dishware, washbasin, kettle, bandages—they were all gone. And the velvet wing-back chair, where Madame had sat by the bedside, was now repositioned in its original spot against the wall.

"Elsie?" Daisy's voice cracked the silence, the needless question coming from a growing panic inside her. She hurried to the bed as if, magically, Elsie would suddenly appear there. Instead, Daisy saw a perfectly puffed pillow, void of its case, as though Elsie's head had never lain there. "Elsie!" This time it was a cry.

Daisy flew to the door and looked into the hall, left and right. There was no one. Absolutely no one. Without thought to the consequences, she sprinted to Madame Tremblay's door that opened to her suite. She rapped her knuckles against it.

"Madame! Madame!"

There was movement inside, mumbling, and then the door opened to reveal a very stoic-faced Madame Tremblay, staring through cold, blue eyes, as if Daisy's interrupting her peace and solitude was akin to a repeat of the French Revolution.

"To what do I owe this appalling interruption?" Her lofty voice would have made the queen of France cower.

Daisy couldn't help but look beyond the woman in hopes of glimpsing Elsie in the room. But it appeared empty of anyone other than Madame Tremblay and her belongings.

"Elsie," Daisy breathed. "She is missing."

"Missing?" Madame drew back, a thin eyebrow winging upward.

"Yes!" Daisy's panic swelled again, especially with the look of utter calm on Madame's face. "Where is she? Do you know what happened to her?"

"Child, calm yourself." Madame Tremblay stepped from her room and closed the door behind her with a solid thud.

Daisy stepped back, allowing the woman room to go before her. Trailing behind, Daisy determined she would have answers. "Madame, tell me what has happened to her." Yes. It was a demand of her mistress. So be it. Daisy would accept the consequences.

A casual wave of Madame's hand over her shoulder at Daisy was all she received in return. Daisy hurried after the older woman. "I heard cries last night. Was that Elsie? Did something happen? Did she—?" No, she wouldn't accept death as a resolution to Elsie's disappearance.

"You do ask a lot of questions." Madame rounded a corner and glided onto the balcony, aiming for the flight of stairs that would lead them down to her writing room. "It is true, you heard . . . Elsie's cries."

Daisy didn't miss the hesitation in Madame's response. She seemed to be considering her words carefully.

"Elsie's fever broke during the night. The infection in her leg is clearing. The simple truth is that I had Festus move Elsie to his home. His wife will give her the care she needs, and better than I could. After all, I've a book to write. I don't have time to spare in urging the young woman back to health."

"She is all right, then?" Daisy expelled a breath of relief. "I can go see her?"

Madame's lips quirked in a small smile. "Festus's wife isn't keen on company. I would recommend you leave Elsie to her and consider your Christian duty appeased. We've done all we can. It's time now for you to return to your normal obligations. I've given you plenty of liberties regarding Elsie's care, and I would like to hear no more of it." Madame opened the double doors to her study.

Sunlight twinkled across the wood floor, illuminated Madame's writing desk, and gave the room a welcoming warmth. It seemed the authoress had no intention of continuing the conversation surrounding Elsie as she pulled her chair from the desk and gingerly lowered her aging body onto it. She reached for a pen, but rather than dip it into the inkwell, she trailed its nib along a page lying on the desktop. Scribbled handwriting was scattered across the page, with a sheaf of papers piled next to it.

"Would you like to know what my next novel is about?" Madame offered.

Daisy did not. She eyed the wretched box that held the heart of Madame's husband. Something about Elsie's removal from the castle did not calculate properly in Daisy's mind. Her fever had broken, but why move her in the middle of the night? Why not allow the poor woman to rest in a comfortable bed rather than be jostled about by an old man who most likely hadn't had the strength to carry her? Elsie would have had to walk, limping on her horribly painful leg while leaning on Festus.

"My story is about a young woman," Madame continued. "She discovers that her brother is a grave robber. She must hide among the corpses to determine what he does with them. Selling them to science is too easy of an explanation, so I am thinking up something far more . . . grotesque."

"What is Festus's wife's name?" Daisy interrupted the stream of the story being offered by Madame.

Madame tutted and straightened the sheaf of papers that

equated to her half-written novel. "Why don't you ask Festus? It is *his* wife, after all."

"And their house? Where do they live?" She hadn't noticed a building on the grounds that might be where the estate keeper and his wife lived. Perhaps it was located deeper in the woods or at the far end of the property. The meals delivered to the castle were well prepared, and yet it was always Festus who brought them, and Festus who returned the dirty dishes. And she hadn't seen him coming and going with a wagon or a cart to transport the meals.

"Child," Madame said, her lips pinched together, "I must write now, and your mistrusting questions are disconcerting. Please rest in the fact that your wounded Elsie is being cared for and leave me to my work."

Daisy could sense that pushing for more answers wouldn't be well received.

Madame's head was bent over her paper, her pen scratching against it, conjuring the words to compose the story forming in her head.

Daisy turned to exit the room. Elsie had been so frightened in the servants' quarters. She had insisted she heard scratching sounds and then *begged* Daisy to find Hester May. Daisy softly closed the doors to Madame's writing room, watching the woman's stiff back until the doors blocked her from view. Hester May had gone missing near Castle Moreau months ago, then the girl named Elizabeth, followed by the women of ill repute. Now Elsie . . .

Daisy leaned her forehead against the door. Was she succumbing to a horrid nightmare that riddled her senses? It seemed her staying at Castle Moreau was stealing her sense of reason. Elsie was with Festus and his wife. She was safe. There was no reason to doubt Madame Tremblay's word. None.

And yet Daisy did not believe that. She would need to see for herself that Elsie was all right. She would need to find out if Hester May and the other women had ever been inside Castle Moreau. She knew what it was like to live on one's own and without someone to fight for you, without a place of refuge in which to escape. To have the truth hidden from view, secreted away under a façade of something more impressive, more holy, or more right. Daisy carried the weight of abandoning Patty and Rose to the Greenbergs. She had left them behind to find her own escape. She could not do that again. That was her truth. The ugly past she'd fled from had made self-preservation her shame. She had abandoned the weak to save herself. She would not do that to Elsie. And not to the other nameless women who had vanished at Castle Moreau.

The Girl

Phantoms were not supposed to speak, and yet she did. The woman with the crooked hand told stories to me in the darkness. Frightening stories of sea monsters who feasted on children for dinner and ate their fathers for breakfast. She told of dwarves with eyes of red who danced around fires and summoned the gods to rain fire on those who acted unjustly. She told a tale of a maiden who was lost in the forest and came upon a river. While she was there, the river stopped flowing, its current stilled by the power of a mighty warrior who had been cast under a spell and lived beneath river stones.

On seeing her, he refused to let the waters pass until she drank of them, thus drinking of him. And when the maiden finally drank the cool waters, the warrior reached from his watery prison and claimed her as his own. Later, the maiden's body was found floating at the mouth of the river, her eyes missing. They said the warrior had taken her eyes so her remains could not share the vision of what she had seen.

The woman with the crooked hand sat at my bedside and lulled me to sleep. Nightmares and terrors became merely dreams as I grew accustomed to the tales she told. Some were tales of my French ancestors, but most were of her own making. I would close my eyes to listen, and her voice would soothe me. When I opened my eyes at the story's end, she had vanished. Taking with her the horrors of the night and leaving behind an empty void.

I was safe.

The woman with the crooked hand taught me to taste fear. To eat of it. To spit it out.

She was fear.

La femme fantôme.

twenty-five

Cleo

PRESENT DAY

Deacon's baseball cap was pulled low over his forehead. He wore sunglasses too. Apparently, the proverbial disguise of the Hollywood elite was his go-to when trying to remain out of the spotlight. Stasia's car whizzed by the grocery store, the hardware store, the library . . . Cleo stared out the window from the front passenger seat, trying to ignore that Deacon was sitting directly behind her, squashed in the back seat. He told her it was less conspicuous that way, but to Cleo he was remarkably conspicuous. She could feel his knees pressing against her seat.

"So that's the old mercantile of Needle Creek." Stasia pointed to an old brick building that was adjacent to a gas station. "It's one of the few historic buildings left in town." She sounded like a tour guide, but Cleo didn't mind. "It was said that in the mid-eighteen hundreds, two local girls went missing from Needle Creek a few months apart. The rumor mill was rampant about it at the mercantile. It's where people gathered to talk."

"People still talk," Deacon muttered from the back seat.

"Did they find the girls?" Cleo had to ask, already guessing the answer.

Stasia shook her head and adjusted her grip on the steering wheel. "Nope. I heard there were some local prostitutes who went missing too. My great-great-grandmother's sister was one of the girls who disappeared."

"You have a connection to the missing women of Castle Moreau too?" It was the first time Stasia had mentioned anything outside of her insatiable interest in solving cold cases.

Stasia cast her an apologetic look. "Well, yeah, but not like Dave's. I mean, his cousin's disappearance is more recent. A great-great aunt from the 1870s? Not so worried about her anymore."

"Your family would want closure, though, wouldn't they?" Cleo eyed a liquor store as the car zoomed past it. *She* wanted closure. To a lot of things. The letter from her grandfather was still in her room at Castle Moreau. It was like leaving a can of worms open. There was no recovering from that. No closure.

"I don't know." Stasia turned the car onto a side road. "With over a century between us, it's a curious bit of family lore."

"Too bad *family lore* never seems to go away when you're on the side of the villain." Deacon was staring out the windshield.

Stasia glanced at him in the rearview mirror. "I don't think anyone is blaming you."

"Not me. Just my family and our entire legacy," Deacon said, sarcasm in his voice.

Cleo could tell he was nervous. He was picking at his

fingernails. She couldn't blame him. Castle Moreau felt like a ticking time bomb that had been ticking for many decades and was now down to its last minutes.

Stasia parked the car in front of a green ranch-style house. "So, the investigator's name is Detective Germaine. He's retired now." She opened her door and looked at them. "You guys coming?"

"Yeah," Deacon said, sounding resolved. He got out at the same time as Cleo. She startled when his hand found the small of her back. His breath brushed her ear as he leaned in and whispered, "Nothing gets said about the castle. *Nothing.* My lawyers would kill me if they knew I was here without consulting them first."

She nodded. She had no intention of saying anything for fear of what might backfire. The last thing she needed was to be pulled deeper into the conspiracy theory that Castle Moreau was a vortex for missing women. Technically, *she* was a missing woman.

The irony of that made Cleo sick to her stomach. She felt a pang of guilt for leaving Riley behind to wonder and worry. And she feared they would find her, that it would all come to fruition and—

"Hey!" Stasia called to Dave, who was standing just inside the front door of the house.

Dave motioned for them to come inside. "I got here a little bit ago, but we've just been shooting the breeze. Come on in." He stepped aside for them to enter.

The square living room was tiny, dwarfed in comparison to Castle Moreau's gathering spaces. The house, probably built sometime in the seventies, looked shabby, the shag carpet original, and there was a strong odor of cigarette smoke. A dog lay on the floor by the couch, whining and thumping its tail. An elderly man's feet rested near the dog, his legs encased in wraps to help with swelling. The man wore a buttoned-up shirt with western-style pockets, which hung untucked over navy-blue sweatpants. He was balding, and a pair of bifocals balanced on his average-looking nose. His hazel eyes rested on Cleo. There was a sharpness in them she wasn't sure she was comfortable with.

"Detective Germaine," Dave introduced, "this is my friend Stasia, and this is Deacon Tremblay and his, um . . ." Dave frowned, searching for how to define Cleo's role in all this.

"She's my friend," Deacon finished for Dave, swiping his sunglasses from his face. He offered a charming smile, reached for the retired detective's hand, and gave it a firm shake. "Thank you for meeting with us."

"Never thought I'd have a Tremblay in my house." Detective Germaine's chuckle was raspy. He reached for a pack of cigarettes and knocked one out into his hand. "Mind if I smoke?"

Dave grinned. "It's your house."

Cleo minded, but she didn't say anything. Her allergies were sure to kick in, and her sneezing fit would soon indicate her aversion to cigarette smoke.

"Have a seat." Germaine waved them toward a couple of overstuffed chairs. "This is Fido." He nudged the mutt with his toe, and the dog turned and gave the man's age-spotted hand a thorough licking. "Couldn't think of anything else to name him."

"Hey, Fido." Stasia extended her fingers, and the dog sniffed her before accepting Stasia's scratch behind his ears.

"Dave here says you all got a copy of the tape of Meredith Newton's interview with me?" Germaine went in for the guts of the conversation.

Deacon nodded, perched on the edge of his chair. Cleo sat

in one beside him and tucked her hands under her legs. She was going to stay as mum as possible.

"We have some questions for you about it." Dave was standing, too excited and agitated to sit. "Now that we're all here, I'd like to—"

"Hold up." Germaine held his palm out. "First things first. How'd you get a copy of the tape?" The hazel eyes drilled into Cleo.

Gosh, she hated cops. She squirmed in her chair. A quick glance around the room told her Detective Germaine didn't have a laptop or tablet handy. Which meant he wasn't going to jump on the internet and do a background check on her, at least not right now. Of course, that didn't mean he couldn't or wouldn't do so later.

Cleo shifted nervously again.

Germaine's eyes narrowed.

"I found the tape on the hood of my Suburban. When I came out of the grocery store." A simple explanation should not have been that hard to spit out.

Germaine's gray brows drew together. "That's odd."

"It is," Dave inserted eagerly. "She came to my store shortly after to hear what was on it."

"Convenient she picked your place." Germaine, despite his smoking and run-down house, was remarkably on point. "Okay. Fire away—what do you want to know?"

Dave ran his palm over his bald head. "Meredith, she made it sound like my cousin Anne just disappeared. That doesn't fit with the original story."

"No. No, it doesn't," Germaine agreed.

"What sort of follow-up was there after she gave her account?" Dave asked.

Germaine took a puff of his cigarette. He widened his eyes in dismissal. "None."

"None?" Dave frowned.

Germaine shook his head. "Wasn't anything to follow up *on*. She said Anne disappeared, the rest of the group said they were all dispersing to their vehicles when they noticed Anne was gone."

"But Meredith states on the tape that she and Anne were running—like running away from someone," Stasia interjected.

"Yep. And we asked others, and they refuted her statement. Meredith liked to tell stories. Embellish things." The old detective took another pull on the cigarette.

Dave looked irritated. "You didn't believe her because she was in the system, is that it?"

Germaine quirked an eyebrow. "The system? You mean foster care?"

Dave nodded.

"Maybe. Not sure it had much to do with that, so much as she had a reputation at the high school for telling tall tales, getting other kids in trouble. When you have a single eyewitness testimony from a not-so-credible source, you tend not to take it seriously when the other unanimous testimony says the opposite."

"But they just said Anne wasn't there when they got into their cars. That doesn't mean she wasn't chased—that Meredith wasn't chased," Dave argued.

"Meredith *wasn't* chased." Germaine ground his cigarette in an ashtray sitting on the end table next to him. He leaned forward. "She hitched a ride home with her boyfriend that night. It was later when she said she and Anne were chased and ran through the woods. Her story didn't add up."

"Did you investigate *her*?" Deacon introduced a new theory, which didn't appear new to Germaine, going by the look he gave Deacon.

"Of course we did. Didn't find anything suspicious, other than her story. No evidence at all that Meredith Newton had any part in foul play."

"What do *you* think happened?" Stasia asked.

Germaine looked at her quizzically. "What do you mean?"

Stasia crossed her leg over her other knee, her eyes sharp with energy. "Detectives always have their own personal theories, right? Even if there's circumstantial evidence—or no evidence?"

"You watch too many crime shows." Germaine snorted. "Sure, I had a theory. Nothing to prove it, though."

"Well, what was it?" Dave leaned forward.

"Same as a lot of folks." Germaine leveled his stare back on Deacon. "Castle Moreau has always had weird things goin' on around there. You all know this as well as I do. The fact is, while much of it is superstition, superstition usually begins because of some truth. We know that women have gone missing around that place for decades. That's not *normal*, Mr. Tremblay. No matter how you spin it, there's too much there to chalk it up to coincidence."

Dave nodded. "Did the police ever search the castle?"

"You'd need a search warrant for that," Germaine answered.

"You couldn't get one?" Stasia frowned.

"On what grounds? That I had a gut feeling the castle had something to do with it? Same as it did with the other women throughout its history? No judge would ever issue a search warrant on something that flimsy."

"Are you saying the Tremblays weren't suspects?" Dave didn't bother to acknowledge Deacon's glare.

Cleo shrank further into her chair, glad she wasn't the focus of Germaine's attention.

"Sure they were. Squeaky clean too. Back then, it was your

grandmother and her husband living there." Germaine looked to Deacon. "Fact is, folks around Needle Creek liked your grandfather. Respected him. He was a pharmacist, known by everyone in the community. People related to him 'cause he was *normal*. Married into the Moreau-Tremblay money but came from good Needle Creek stock. Charles and Virgie cooperated with us throughout the entire investigation."

Dave looked disappointed.

Deacon appeared relieved and a tad proud.

Stasia worried her lower lip with her teeth, probably in some sort of contemplation. Cleo watched her and waited. Something was about to come out of the goth girl's mouth, and she wasn't going to chew on her thoughts for very long. Stasia proved Cleo right.

"So, the tape changes nothing really. Meredith's testimony is thrown out as not being credible and we have nothing new to go on?"

Germaine nodded. "That's how I see it. It's a cold case. Same as the other ones. We combed that property, thanks to the Tremblays, and we never found a body. Never found a sign of anyone—current or old—who'd been murdered there. No matter how coincidental something may seem, you can't make a case against a place like Castle Moreau, or the family, when there's no body stuffed into the closet."

twenty-six

"We need to find Meredith," Dave announced as they left Germaine's house and headed toward their vehicles.

"Give it a rest," Deacon snapped. "You heard what the detective had to say. There's nothing new on that tape."

"Except *someone* left it on Cleo's car," Stasia argued, digging her keys from her pocket.

"Happenstance," Deacon retorted.

"Like everything else in this case." Dave spun toward Deacon. A vein pulsated in Dave's neck. "I don't get it. I would think you'd do everything you could to find out the truth so your family name could be cleared once and for all. What is it with the Tremblays? Never wanting to talk about their precious castle and all the stuff that's gone on there. It's suspicious."

Deacon slid on his glasses and tugged his cap lower over his forehead. "Not here."

"*Not here?*" Dave asked, clearly emotional now. "Where then? When? Name it and I'll be there."

"Look." Deacon took a step closer to Dave, his index

finger pointing. *Crud.* Cleo and Stasia exchanged worried looks. Deacon jabbed at Dave's chest. "I'm sick of people trying to smear my family. The media, this town, conspiracy theorists"—he gave Stasia a sideways glance—"but my family had nothing to do with Anne Joplin's disappearance."

"What about my great-great-aunt's disappearance? Elsie Stockley?" Stasia asked quietly.

Deacon tilted his head back to the sky and groaned. "Listen, I get it. Weird stuff has happened. But that was over a hundred years ago. People need to let this stuff go. Just because my ancestor built a flipping castle in a place like Wisconsin, this is the kind of attention we get?"

"It's not the only castle in the Midwest," Cleo offered, hoping to help defuse the situation.

They stood around Stasia's car, no one getting in. Dave leaned against the trunk of his own vehicle parked ahead of Stasia's.

"No. It's not," Stasia agreed. "There's one in Ohio. Built by German immigrants. It's supposedly haunted."

"See?" Deacon stretched his hand toward Stasia. "Castles scream story, suspicion of this and that, then throw a famous name on top of it and a lot of money and *wham!* You have my family in a nutshell." He jabbed at Dave's chest again. "Leave us alone."

This time, Dave drew back from the poke. "My cousin deserves to have her killer brought to justice."

Deacon rubbed the back of his neck. "I'm sorry. Nothin' I can do about it."

"You don't care that a girl was murdered on Tremblay property?" Stasia inserted.

"I—"

Cleo interrupted Deacon. She had to. There was an obvious fact they were all ignoring. "Who said Anne is dead?"

A car passed them on the street.

A robin hopped along the yard just outside Germaine's window.

Dave stared at her.

Stasia coughed.

Deacon crossed his arms over his chest and eyed her.

Cleo regretted saying anything, while at the same time she didn't. There *were* human remains in the castle. One blaring fact that couldn't be denied but was being kept secret. "I just mean . . . no one found Anne's body. Why does everybody assume she's dead?"

"You think she was abducted?" Stasia raised her brows. "'Cause that's crossed my mind before too."

"It's been forty years. We would have heard something long ago." Dave's defeated sigh was enough to garner a bit of empathy from Deacon, who gave the man space by backing up a few feet.

"Not necessarily," Deacon suggested. He glanced at Cleo, and she didn't miss the glint in his eyes.

Mouth shut. Say no more.

Copy that.

Cleo curled into a ball under the blankets of her bed. Murphy draped his furry body over her neck, and his purring brought her some comfort. Still, she stared through the darkness toward the dresser, where the letter from her grandfather lay.

Come home.

Two words she'd sworn never to do. It wasn't safe. Not for Riley. Everything, *everything* was for Riley. She had to remember that. She had to remember why she was here. It was why she'd practiced her own vanishing act. If they couldn't find her, they couldn't be hurt. Riley would be safe. *She* would be safe. Everything would be . . .

Cleo pulled Murphy from her neck. He opened a lazy eye and readjusted on her pillow.

"You need to snuggle over here and—"

Cleo stopped.

Murphy's purring ceased.

The doorknob on her bedroom door turned one way, then the other. From her position in bed, Cleo could see it slowly move. She opened her mouth to call out a greeting, something to make whoever it was identify themselves, but she couldn't force the words past her throat.

Was it Deacon?

Or Virgie? Virgie had been very subdued this evening. Silent. Almost morose. She had gone to bed in her room, which was stacked to the ceiling with boxes and crates, her cot in the middle of them as if they were her walled fortress.

The knob stilled.

There was no sound except Cleo's breath as she tried to release it quietly. This was a different type of hiding than she was accustomed to. Staying off the grid was one thing, but feeling like a child tucked in her bed and praying the covers would be enough to protect from some unknown entity? That was new entirely, the sudden sensation that she was not alone.

Murphy scrambled into a standing position. His claws raked Cleo's arm, and she slapped her free hand over the scratches, feeling the instant beading of blood.

The cat arched his back, fixated on the bedroom door. His hiss filled the air.

"Murphy," Cleo whispered. "It's okay, boy." But her words lacked conviction.

Murphy sprang from the bed, his feet landing on the wood

floor. He darted behind some boxes, then leapt to the top, poised in a crouch as if waiting to launch himself at his prey.

The doorknob turned again.

Murphy's shrieking yowl as he vaulted toward the door matched the scream that ripped from Cleo's throat.

Deacon's heavy rapping on Cleo's door finally gave her enough courage to crawl out from beneath the covers. "Cleo! Are you all right?"

This time the knob twisted and the door opened, Deacon apparently unwilling to wait for her to answer.

Cleo sat on the edge of her bed, very aware that her long hair was messy, her legs bare as she wore knit shorts. Thankful her T-shirt was baggy and bragging a screen print of Papa Smurf on the front, she felt halfway modest, if not decent.

Deacon entered hesitantly, glancing about the bedroom but obviously not able to see much because of the towers of Virgie's boxed collections. Murphy yowled again and darted between Deacon's feet, flying out the door. Deacon swore softly and leaped aside. He pushed the door fully open, exposing the dark hallway behind him.

"Cleo, what's going on?" The concern in his voice was evident.

She couldn't help but feel as though she'd just escaped something terrifying. Her insides quivered and her breathing shuddered as she drew in oxygen to clear her mind and calm her frayed nerves.

"Hey . . ." Deacon approached her, his voice gentle. He lowered himself into a crouch in front of her. His own T-shirt had a Bible verse printed on the front. Cleo vaguely noticed it and was a bit surprised. The Bible and Deacon Tremblay didn't seem to go together. He wasn't the proverbial *godly man* she'd heard about in her churchgoing years. He was a man with quite the history—

"Cleo?"

The feel of Deacon's fingertips on her cheek startled her into awareness. She sniffed. Coughed. Blinked several times to clear her fuzzy, petrified mind that had her focusing on the weirdest and most unimportant things.

At last she focused on Deacon's face. "I'm sorry. Murphy freaked out and I screamed and . . . I didn't mean to wake you."

"I was already awake, roaming the halls and thinking about that skeleton in the wall." He dismissed her worry. "What was it that freaked you out?"

Cleo looked to the doorway and the hall beyond. She could see the edge of a frame that held a portrait of some Moreau-Tremblay ancestor. A light sconce made to look like an old-fashioned lamp jutted out from the wall, its golden electric light making the castle seem more warm and welcoming than it had been just minutes earlier.

"My doorknob . . . it was turning."

"Your doorknob," Deacon said. A statement and not a question.

"Yes." Cleo shivered. Deacon scooted closer to her on the bed and reached for her hand. She looked down at their hands. The platonic grasp was comforting. "Like someone was trying to get into my room."

"Your door wasn't locked?"

"No. It wasn't. But no one opened it." Cleo pulled her hand from his to wipe her palms on her shorts. They were damp from nervous energy. "It was like someone wanted to come in, but didn't. And then Murphy acted all suspicious. You know how cats are when they sense something? When he freaked out, that was when I screamed."

Deacon pushed off the bed, his jogging pants hiking up his shins, exposing his muscular legs. He glanced toward the door and hallway. "I didn't see anyone. Maybe it was Grand-mère. I should check on her."

"That's what I figured." Cleo made herself rise from the bed. "It had to be Virgie."

At the name, the old woman appeared in the doorway. She leaned on a cane, her curly short hair flattened on one side. Her eyes were perplexed, concern written in the wrinkles of her face. "Is everyone all right?" Virgie asked. "I heard the most ungodly scream."

"It was me," Cleo admitted.

"Did you try to open Cleo's door?" Deacon asked his grandmother.

"Me? No. I was in my bed. Sleeping—or trying to. Today was . . . well, anyway, I was in my room."

"It *did* happen," Cleo insisted, meeting Deacon's questioning gaze. "I didn't imagine it."

"I didn't say that you did." Deacon rested his hands on his hips. "I don't know what to tell you."

"Castle Moreau is haunted. Try that on for size," Virgie sassed. She adjusted her grip on the cane.

"It's not haunted." Deacon rolled his eyes, which only served to irritate Virgie further, who shot him a look.

"How would you know? You haven't lived here your entire life."

"Grand-mère—"

"Don't you 'Grand-mère' me. You didn't listen to me earlier, you barge into *my* home just because the deed is part of the family estate and you're CEO, and you assume I want the authorities here digging up bones out of my walls. I'm warning you, Deacon"—Virgie shook the end of her cane at him—"leave Castle Moreau alone."

"We can talk about that in the morning," Deacon said dismissively.

"Always later. Always in the morning." Virgie turned her shoulder to him and addressed Cleo. "All my life I have lived here. I know the rumors, the stories. My great-grandfather built this castle in 1801. My grandmother was Ora Moreau. It all began with her book, the story of *The Phantom Woman*. Our wealth and prestige grew starting then, and before long the Moreau family became a household name."

"I'm not sure I understand, but it doesn't matter. Sorry, I . . ." Cleo didn't need a history lesson tonight. She needed peace. Peace and quiet. She needed to be left alone in her room. To feel safe. To not have eyes staring at her from unseen places, or letters from the dead mailed to her private address, or the memories of her grandfather and of Riley stealing her sleep.

"You don't understand because you don't know. The woman—she's here. She's *always* been here."

"Grandmother." Deacon's voice was stern.

Virgie ignored him. "Every now and then we see her. The image of a cloaked woman. It's where Ora Moreau got the idea for her novel that launched her career and made her an American Gothic icon. She could outwrite Edgar Allan Poe with her gore and darkness. Where do you think it came from? Ora was haunted. *Haunted* by the woman with the crooked hand. People say she wrote fiction, but isn't all fiction based on truth?"

"You're saying it was a ghost—" Cleo bit off her words as the memory of the cloaked woman in the study assaulted her. She had written it off, almost forgotten it. Simply because it was ridiculous to believe in ghosts, even if she was staying in a castle with a reputation of disappearing women.

"Not just a *ghost*," Virgie breathed. "*The* ghost. *La femme fantôme*. The phantom woman. She has always roamed the halls of Castle Moreau." She leveled a definitive glare on her grandson. "And she always will."

twenty-seven

Daisy

The air outside was fresh. It was crisp. Daisy inhaled it into her senses as she hiked down the road toward Needle Creek. She didn't prefer to walk alone, not in the woods, not on the road, not anywhere. But she couldn't stay in the castle. Her mind was whirling. Confusion made it cloudy, foggy. If Daisy was superstitious, she could be sure a dark entity was playing with her senses. Making her feel nauseated. Disorienting her from reality.

She needed to clear her thoughts. Maybe try to pray. She wasn't quite sure the best way to go about it, but sometimes she just talked to God like He was a companion and she hoped He didn't mind. Now was one of those moments.

The trees arched overhead, but the sun was shining and lit the road ahead. A wagon was rolling toward her, a man and his wife perched on it. They gave her a friendly wave as they passed. Daisy could catch glimpses of the roofs of buildings in Needle Creek. It was strange how Castle Moreau seemed so isolated when the town was within walking distance. With civilization in her sights, Daisy couldn't help but feel that when she entered the castle, it was like stepping back in time. Back to the days when the castle was first built. When the United States Declaration of Independence had yet to reach its fiftieth birthday, and before the War Between the States had ripped the nation apart.

Needle Creek was a simple Midwestern town, with folks making their living off the Mississippi River, a chocolate factory, and a brewery. It was a cozy town but burgeoning with enough growth that it could become a city one day. Regardless, it wasn't the same world as Castle Moreau. The castle was its own era, undefined.

Her concern now was to figure out what to do for Elsie, and even for Hester May. When Daisy had left the castle, she'd roamed the grounds a bit, looking for Festus's house. Would she knock and meet Festus's wife if she found it? Yes. And then she would ask after Elsie. But there was no house. Just the castle outbuildings. The stables. No place that indicated Festus lived anywhere close to the castle.

Which meant they lived in Needle Creek? Or—Daisy was loath to recognize her skepticism—Festus had no wife, no house, and Elsie was not safely ensconced in a bed somewhere but had vanished. Like Hester May. Like the other women.

Daisy's feet hit the boardwalk, and she aimed toward the mercantile. What better place to learn the gossip than where the gossips gathered to spread their slander? She needed to know more about Elsie—who she was—and Hester May. Perhaps Elsie's brother, Jerry, would have returned from his work on the river? Though it'd been just a week since she had found Elsie, Daisy hoped and prayed there could be resolution.

A bell rang as she pushed the mercantile door open. Richard, the shopkeeper, looked up from his place behind the counter. His eyes sharpened, then narrowed when he saw her, a gamut of emotions playing across his face.

"You're still here!" he said as Daisy approached. "Not vanished into the bowels of the castle yet, eh?"

"No." Daisy tightened her grip on her purse so as not to show her nervousness. She would not mention Elsie's disappearance, but the surprise that Richard expressed in seeing her made Daisy question the wisdom of ever returning to Castle Moreau. To the lair of Madame Tremblay.

"Fine that you're still with us." Richard dropped a heavy eyelid in a wink. "What brings you to town?"

Daisy looked around the store, trying to find an excuse. Something to blame her presence on besides instigating a conversation that led with Elsie's condition and subsequent vanishing. Why Daisy wanted to be discreet wasn't clear to her, but when she looked into the eyes of the mercantile owner, she wasn't sure if she trusted him any more than the occupants of Castle Moreau.

"I am here for . . . buttons," she replied.

"Buttons?"

"Yes. I need several colors of them." She didn't. Nor did she have the money to buy several different colors of buttons.

Richard rounded the counter. "They're over this way." He led her to a shelf that held sets of decorative buttons attached to little cards, and then glass jars of buttons in bulk. "I'll help you find what you need." He didn't move. Daisy sensed his intent and her skin crawled.

Movement behind them caused both Daisy and Richard to turn. It was his wife, Tabitha, and she too had a wary look about her. More so because Richard stood closer than necessary to Daisy. He backed away a step.

"*I* will help you find your buttons," Tabitha advised Daisy while glaring at her husband.

He gave a slight bow toward his wife and returned to his position behind the counter. Tabitha moved to the shelf filled with buttons. "What color are you looking for?"

This was not going well. Daisy fumbled for words—a plan. She had no idea how to ask questions without being forthright, and if she were forthright, it would only create questions asked of her in return.

"You are well?" Tabitha handed her a card with six blue buttons on it.

Daisy took the card and made a pretense of examining the buttons. "I'm fine, thank you."

Tabitha glanced at her husband, whose head was bent over a book. "My husband and I have mentioned you several times. Living at Castle Moreau. I hope our conversation the other day, and with Mrs. Beacon's wagging tongue, didn't frighten you."

"Should I be frightened?" Daisy asked. This was her opportunity. Though she didn't consider herself savvy, she could manipulate a conversation if needed.

Tabitha thumbed through the cards of buttons as though Daisy had requested a certain color or style. "Hmmm, well, you know the tales. I regret to admit, they are true. But whether it is a coincidence that the castle is linked to these women or not, it leaves one to wonder. And now poor Elsie Stockley . . ." Tabitha glanced at Richard again, then lowered her voice. "She has also disappeared. Only weeks after Hester May."

Daisy swallowed hard and returned the card with the blue buttons to the shelf. "What happened?" She felt it wise to pretend to know nothing.

Tabitha kept glancing at her husband. It made Daisy

nervous, and she found herself mimicking the woman. There was something about Richard that made Daisy wonder if Tabitha's outward directness toward him might be hiding something darker they shared behind closed doors. It wasn't unlike Mrs. Greenberg, who paraded herself as a strong, dominant woman, yet Daisy remembered the bruises on the woman's arms and heard her cries when Mr. Greenberg became angry. A strong woman did not always equate with a confident, free woman.

Tabitha leaned toward Daisy, who noticed some graying hairs around the woman's temple. "Poor Elsie. She is very close to Hester May's sister, Addie. When Hester May went missing, Elsie was quite determined to help find her. Then Elsie's brother, Jerry, left town for work. She was to go live with an aunt, and we all thought she left early. Only her aunt sent an inquiry as to why Elsie had not arrived. The last anyone saw of Elsie was when she was on the road heading toward Castle Moreau."

"And how is Elsie similar to Hester May?"

Tabitha drew back with a frown. "I never said she was."

Daisy hurried to explain herself. "But if both women have disappeared, each connected with the castle, then Elsie must be similar to Hester May in some way, yes? What was Hester May like?"

Tabitha's chest rose in a heavy sigh. "Oh, she was a beauty. She was to be married to Chet Forester, the brewery owner's son. It was to be a solid marriage for her, and then one day she was seen going into the woods that lead to Castle Moreau. She never came back."

"Who saw her?" Daisy asked.

Tabitha shrugged. "I don't know. It was just . . . well, Mrs. Beacon said that the son of her neighbor said he saw Hester May in the woods."

"Why would Hester May go into the woods? Did she like the out-of-doors?" Daisy was trying to piece together any ties between Hester May's disappearance and Elsie's.

Tabitha was shaking her head. "I don't know why Hester May would have gone into the woods. I don't know why Elsie was walking on the road to Castle Moreau."

"Have you met Festus?" Daisy opted to change the subject to hear what Tabitha had to say about him.

"Festus Olson is a rogue!" A shrill voice broke into the conversation. Tabitha jumped. Daisy turned, startled. Mrs. Beacon stared at them both with opinionated eyes. "Well, you know he is. That man never speaks when he comes to town. Looks at all of us as if he's better than us just because he's employed by the Tremblays. How is that better than us? At least *we're* not helping to hide the awful secrets of that place. He knows more than he says, that he does." Mrs. Beacon tapped the brooch at her throat. "He is not a man I would trust any more than I would trust a Tremblay."

"What about his wife?" Daisy was, in a strange way, thankful Mrs. Beacon had appeared. It seemed she enjoyed the gossip in the mercantile, but more so, was full of opinions and ideas and wasn't afraid to speak of them.

"His wife?" Mrs. Beacon exchanged looks with Tabitha.

"He's not married," Richard interjected from the counter.

Tabitha stiffened.

Daisy didn't realize Richard had been listening so closely.

"The old man may have been married in his younger years," Richard continued, "but he lives above the stables at Castle Moreau. Only comes into town once every month or so."

Daisy felt the blood drain from her face. Her knees felt wobbly as she took in Richard's words. No wife. Lived on the castle grounds? But then who had been providing their food? Who had made the poultice for Elsie's wound? *Where* was Elsie? It was clear Madame Tremblay had been deceitful.

"Festus was never married," Mrs. Beacon said authoritatively. "I know because my aunt grew up with him, and she said he was hired on at a young age by Madame Tremblay. Or should I call her Madame Ora Moreau, the authoress? Regardless, I find Festus as suspicious as the madame of the castle. The two of them? Alone? It's unseemly."

Daisy opened her mouth to inquire about Lincoln, but then snapped it shut. Did the town even know of Lincoln, or did he truly not exist as Festus had said?

"And now poor Elsie . . ." Mrs. Beacon tut-tutted, and Tabitha dipped her head in agreement. "Jerry, her brother, will be heartbroken on his return."

"Unless Elsie is found," Tabitha added hopefully.

Mrs. Beacon laughed. Not a humorous laugh, but one thick with resignation. "They never find them once they've gone missing. Not since the report of that first one, who disappeared when our mothers were young. You remember them speaking of her?"

"I cannot forget." Tabitha blanched.

Mrs. Beacon leveled a serious look on Daisy. "A local farmer's wife was the first woman to disappear years ago when our mothers were still in school. Only this woman was *seen* going *inside* the castle. They found an invitation in her home sent from Madame Ora Moreau herself. The lure of a famous authoress? A castle? Of course the farmer's wife would accept the invitation. Only she never came back out."

"What did they do?" Daisy held her breath. She reached for a nearby ledge to steady herself.

"Nothing. She was a poor farmer's wife, and her husband was a drunk." Mrs. Beacon sniffed. "My mother always said if the farmer's wife had been wealthy, the vanishings at Castle Moreau would have stopped before they became an epidemic." She narrowed her eyes, and Daisy felt her slanderous but truthful words slice into her soul. "It's too late now. Castle Moreau does as it pleases. Women are wise to stay away from it."

twenty-eight

There was no denying it now. Daisy tugged her shawl around her shoulders, though it did little to ward off the chill that settled into her bones. Elsie was missing. Hester May was missing. The other nameless women were missing. And that was only this generation of women. The mystery stretched back decades—to when Madame was a young woman. How many? How many women had vanished at Castle Moreau?

It wasn't safe to return. She had no reason to return now—though an image of Lincoln flashed through her mind. Was he a prisoner there too? Beneath the cruel, sadistic mind and hands of Madame Tremblay?

She couldn't save everyone. No. And Lincoln was not in danger. He couldn't be. Brooding, yes, but he had smiled. *Smiled* when she'd inadvertently and horribly sat on his lap, embraced his neck, expecting him to save her from the evils the castle hid.

Daisy stepped onto the boardwalk and scanned the street. Carriages rolled by. A few women with skirts in bustles at their backs passed, one giving her a smile, another pushing a pram with a baby inside it. She wanted to scream at them to go home, to stay safe and avoid the awfulness of this world—the parts of it that lurked behind closed doors, behind polite smiles and the façades of those who masqueraded as *good* but in truth were wicked. The Greenbergs, Madame Tremblay, even Richard from the mercantile with his wandering eye and control over Tabitha, who pretended to be content.

Was that their lot in life, something women like them had to accept? To try to be content as violence and cruelty touched their lives? Yet God had not created them for this. Daisy chose to believe that. They said that God was good and yet there was so much evil. He did not wipe it out, and the evildoers seemed to prosper when the poor and abused simply . . . vanished from memory.

Daisy noted the church at the far end of the street. Its steeple with a cross perched on top. There was more to God than she understood, but there was hope in her heart too. She had read a Psalm once in which the author pled for vengeance against wrongdoers, and later he praised God for providing a way of escape. A refuge.

Resolved, Daisy straightened her shoulders. She must find a refuge. Answers for Elsie, for Hester May—even for Lincoln. Perhaps this was why God didn't wipe the earth clean of the wicked. He chose instead to use the weak ones, such as her, to rise up in His strength and become warriors.

Daisy turned toward the jail. Toward the place of law and order. It would be her first stop. They must know that Elsie *had* made it inside the walls of Castle Moreau, that the rumors and stories held truth.

A few steps later, a strong hand grabbed her upper arm, dragging her into an alleyway. Daisy stumbled, yelping. She reached up and slapped at the man who had seized her, halting only inches from his face when she saw his whiskers and rheumy eyes.

"Festus!"

"What are you doing!" he hissed. There was urgency on his face. Fear. His fingers bit into her arm as he shoved her into an alcove behind some barrels. For an older man, his strength was surprising. "You will ruin it all."

"Ruin what?" Daisy twisted under his grip. "Where is Elsie?"

"Shush!" Festus pulled her and she stumbled into him, causing Festus to waver on his feet. He then recovered, forcing her to walk beside him to the other end of the alley. "We are going back to the castle."

"I don't want to go!"

"You must. You're not to leave again. Do you understand?" he gritted out.

Daisy could feel him trembling. Festus wasn't furious or cruel—he was terrified. "Don't take me back there, Festus, please!" Daisy whimpered.

He urged her forward until she saw a buggy, hitched and waiting. "Get in." Festus helped her as Daisy obeyed, placing her foot on the runner and pushing herself onto the seat. She should scream. She should awaken Needle Creek to her predicament, and yet something stopped her as she watched Festus round the buggy and climb in. His shoulders hunched as he flicked the reins. They rolled toward the edge of town, Daisy gripping the edge of the seat.

"Festus, please. You have no wife. I know this." Daisy looked sideways at the old man. His hat was crammed onto his head, his eyes on the road ahead. He even lifted his hand in a friendly wave to a fellow driver rolling by.

"Don't listen to the gossips in town. They know nothing," Festus spat, flicking the reins again. The horse increased its pace.

"Then tell me. Tell me what I need to know! Where is Elsie?"

A sideways look told her Festus had no intention of answering her question.

Daisy twisted in her seat. "Where is your wife, then? Your house? Who cooks for us? Why are you so loyal to Madame Tremblay?"

That resulted in a choked laugh. "I am loyal to Lincoln."

His words silenced her. Daisy stared at the road as it led them into the forested lane out of town. "Lincoln," she mouthed.

"He wants you to return to Castle Moreau." Another snap of the reins, this time unnecessarily. "He needs you."

Festus left her at the castle entrance, the buggy wheeling its way farther down the drive toward the stables at the end of the lawn, which bordered the woods.

Entering the castle felt foolish. But now, all Daisy could consider was Lincoln. He needed her? Is that why she was here? The reason they'd hired her and brought her to the castle had yet to make sense. She was to keep up the castle duties, but there was no staff or guidance. She was to observe Madame Tremblay for Lincoln, yet he wasn't asking her to report to him. In a way, the bulk of her time here had been lost wandering until she found Elsie.

Daisy avoided the main entrance and instead crossed the lawn to the side of the castle that had a door for the servants. She entered it, unwrapping her shawl and hanging it on a peg in the stone wall. Entering the kitchen, she stood for a moment observing the cold stove. Nothing about this castle was as it should be.

She rushed up the servants' staircase, winding her way through the maze of halls on her way to her rooms. But she paused when she reached the point where she could either escape to the seclusion of her bedroom or steer toward the study and Lincoln.

God give her mercy.

Daisy turned toward Lincoln. It would do no good to hide in her room. She needed answers. She needed to find Elsie.

Outside Lincoln's study, she stopped, staring at the closed mahogany door. She had not seen him since she'd rushed to him, afraid and alone. She had not spoken to him since she had uncovered his secret. His wheelchair. The fact that the man, as far as what others would likely believe, possessed little ability to contribute to the world around him. They would pass him by. They *had* passed him by, assuming his mind was no better off than his legs. It was a wicked supposition—and one she determined not to make of him.

"Come in." His voice carried through the closed door.

She had not knocked. Her breath caught. He had known she was here merely by her presence?

Daisy opened the door, silent on its hinges.

Lincoln sat at the window, not unlike before, only this time he made no pretense to hide his chair. A beautiful chair, for what it was, Daisy thought. Sturdy, strong, and manly in its presentation.

The now-familiar brooding stare turned and rested on her. "You ran from us?" he asked.

Daisy felt a blush and was irritated at herself for it. She didn't owe Lincoln shame; he owed *her* answers.

"Where is Elsie?" She took a step forward.

Lincoln tipped his head to the side and studied her. "You went to town?"

Daisy tried to give Lincoln the same unblinking eye contact as he gave to her. "I went to find Elsie."

"Grand-mère told you where she was."

"And those at the mercantile told me Festus is unmarried. Has no wife. No woman is caring for Elsie's leg."

Lincoln smiled a little. "Elsie will be fine. I promise you."

Daisy hurried toward him, dropped to her knees beside Lincoln's chair, and gripped the rim of the wheel. "Where is she? Tell me! What are the secrets to Castle Moreau?"

Lincoln drew back, his face darkening. "You ask more than you're owed, Daisy François."

"Your grandmother frightens me," she admitted, her knuckles whitening with her grip.

Lincoln eyed her. "My grandmother *is* frightening. Have you read her stories? A glimpse into that woman's mind should frighten anyone."

"Please. Tell me," Daisy begged, not knowing how else to uncover the truth.

"Tell you?" Lincoln reached for a red curl that bobbed against her cheek.

"Why did you bring me here?" she whispered. "What am I here for, and why, even though I am free to leave, do I keep returning?"

Lincoln's finger grazed her cheek, his eyes deepening in intensity. "It is the way of Castle Moreau. Even when you are not in it, you are called to return to its walls. To the Moreau-Tremblays. It has always held me captive. The walls breathe inside me, and they are beginning to breathe inside you too. You belong to Moreau, and you were meant to belong to Moreau. To me."

"To you?" Daisy whispered.

"To me," he answered.

twenty-nine

Cleo

Cleo knee-shoved boxes out of the way of the bookshelves, eyeing the old volumes that had been left in their spots for so long that even their spines had collected dust.

"I don't know if they're here." Deacon scanned the rows of books. Volumes of Dickens, Austen, Shelley, Eliot, and others. "I would guess Ora Moreau's works would be on their own shelf. Displayed."

"Did you ask your grandmother?" Cleo ran her finger along spines, edging between boxes.

Deacon gave her a "Heck no," then added, "I'm not looking forward to what's coming."

"What do you mean?" Cleo stopped on a novel whose title was illegible on the spine. She tipped it out and then pushed it back in. Poetry was not quite in the same category as an Ora Moreau classic.

"I mean . . ." Deacon hefted a box and set it on top of

another, making room to squeeze in front of the shelf opposite the one Cleo perused. "I'm going to need to get her medically assessed. She's failing. It's obvious, just like you said. Her emotional balance isn't there anymore. And even her memories seem off."

"Where is she now?" Cleo glanced at the doors of the writing room. The grand entrance was void of life. Virgie wasn't hovering, watching them to make sure they didn't remove some of her beloved belongings.

"She's napping. Last night wore her out."

"It wore me out," Cleo muttered. It was also why they were searching for Ora Moreau's books. Specifically her first novel, *The Phantom Woman*. "I wasn't imagining the doorknob moving."

"I know." Deacon's response was matter-of-fact, which she appreciated.

"Did you"—she glanced at him—"call yet?"

He paused and met her eyes. "The authorities?"

"Yes, about the bones?"

He shook his head. "I just . . . I don't know what it's going to do to Grand-mère. I don't know if she can handle what will happen once I report it."

"But there's a risk the longer you wait," Cleo said.

Deacon shrugged. "Is there? They've been hidden in the wall for decades—according to my grandmother. What's a few more days for us to try to get to the bottom of what's going on here? I for one would like to *know* it's not Anne Joplin before I report it."

"It's not like she's wearing a nametag," Cleo retorted.

Deacon grinned, though it was tainted with reservation. "Yeah. Well, this whole thing is getting out of control. Now Grand-mère is going on about a haunting and a character from Ora Moreau's book?"

"I know," Cleo acknowledged. There wasn't much more to say. Deacon was in a tough spot with Virgie and the bones. But he couldn't stay silent too long without repercussions. Not to mention, did her own silence make her complicit somehow?

"Here they are," Deacon announced. "All of Ora's books."

"Is *The Phantom Woman* there?" Cleo climbed around some crates to get closer.

Deacon held up a maroon hardback with gold-foil stamping on the cover. "Ta-da!" He waved the book in the air. "Now we just have to read it, and it'll explain everything, right?"

Cleo gave him a halfhearted smile. More likely the work of fiction would merely open Pandora's box of unanswerable questions.

The afternoon was sunny. Cleo was perched on a camp chair on the lawn, soaking up vitamin D and skimming through Ora Moreau's tale of a phantom woman, a little girl haunted by the woman's stories, all taking place in a castle eerily like Castle Moreau.

If fiction was based in truth, as Virgie implied . . . Cleo looked up as a mail truck pulled into the driveway. She set the book aside and stood waiting as the mailman got out and approached her.

"This package didn't fit in the mailbox." He smiled and handed her the package. "And it was a good excuse to drive in and see this place. You hear all about it back in town, but no one ever gets to see it. Private property and all."

"Thank you," Cleo said, taking the package. She resisted looking at the return address.

The mailman nodded, his beard touching his chest. "You live here?"

"For now," Cleo answered.

"Don't get lost on us, okay?" He was teasing, but his words hung in the air as he strode across the lawn back to his mail truck, then sped off down the long, lonely driveway.

Cleo stared after it. At the moment, she wanted to jump into her vehicle and follow him. She could too. There was nothing keeping her here. And considering the note she'd received yesterday in her late grandpa's own hand, running was probably the wisest next move.

She looked down at the brown package in her hands. She expected to see Virgie's name written on it—probably something she'd ordered off the internet to add to the collections Cleo was supposed to be organizing but failing miserably at. Instead, Cleo's name stared up at her. The label was printed in a standard font. But it was there nonetheless and with no return address, save for the postmark of *Needle Creek, WI.*

She plopped onto the camp chair, the castle beginning to shade her spot in the lawn as the sun crept upward. If this were from Grandpa . . . but no. The postmark said Needle Creek.

Her hands shook as she ripped off the tape sealing the package. She opened the flaps of the box and dared to look inside. A frown furrowed her brow as she pulled out a cotton T-shirt. It was older, based on the print emblazoned on the front—a Journey scarab with wings. The rock band had been popular in the eighties, hadn't it? She didn't know for sure, seeing as that was a decade or so before she was born.

It made no sense. A Journey T-shirt? She searched the box. A manila folder lay at the bottom. Pulling it out, Cleo opened the folder cautiously. A photograph of a pretty young woman greeted her in black-and-white newsprint. She appeared to have long blond hair, parted down the middle and curled in waves away from her face. She smiled, and it reached her eyes that were emphasized with black eyeliner.

She wore the Journey T-shirt.

Cleo unfolded the newspaper article, knowing who it was before she even read the name.

Local girl missing after night in the woods.

Anne Joplin, 19, of Needle Creek, Wisconsin, has not been seen since Friday night, May 15th. After a group of high school students dispersed following a party that ran past midnight, it was noticed that Anne was missing.

Local authorities have initiated a countywide search, as well as received cooperation from the Tremblay family of Castle Moreau to search the surrounding woods and property. So far, nothing has been found and there are no suspects.

If anyone knows anything about this case, or has seen Anne Joplin, please contact the Needle Creek authorities at . . .

Cleo blew out a shaky breath. This package had nothing to do with *her*. It had everything to do with Anne Joplin.

Another piece of paper had been included with the newsprint. It was a handwritten poem:

> *In the darkness of night I pray*
> *that I will see the light one day.*
> *Given another world in which to live,*
> *I may find within the strength to forgive.*
> *For now I fight, I kick, I scream;*
> *to die would be better than to learn to dream.*
>
> *—Anne*

Cleo slapped the manila folder shut and looked in the box again. Nothing more there. Just the T-shirt Anne had been wearing in the photograph, which the newspaper printed with their story, and Anne's poem.

Who had sent her the package, and why? Who would possibly link Anne Joplin's disappearance in 1981 to *her*, *Cleo*? This proved the cassette tape left on her Suburban was not a coincidence. It had been planted there, the person fully aware of who Cleo was.

Someone wanted her to dig into Anne's story. All Cleo could picture were the old bones buried in the trunk behind the wall. The image of the cloaked woman in the study. Last night's fright with her doorknob turning. The woman with the crooked hand. All the stories and legends of women disappearing in and around Castle Moreau . . .

The worst part of it all was that Cleo saw the parallel. She saw the irony of how it mimicked her own fear, her own journey to escape. Her attempt to stop the cycle of terror before it seeped into the next life and poisoned it. Until it claimed her younger sister, Riley, and refused to let her go.

For Riley, Cleo could vanish and never be found. Perhaps she had, after all, come to the right place to disappear. Castle Moreau.

Cleo knew then that Anne had been here, somewhere, in Castle Moreau. That the woman with the crooked hand was likely more real than Gothic fiction readers believed. That Stasia's ancestor—Elsie Stockley?—had also disappeared here.

The ironic thing was that someone wanted it all to end. To end with Anne's story. And they hoped Cleo would be the one to bring resolution.

thirty

Cleo awoke to a new world. After she showed Deacon the package, the resolve in his eyes proved he was no longer going to procrastinate the inevitable.

Already this morning, one of his lawyers had arrived on the castle premises. A nurse had also arrived, to care for Virgie, whose stability was fragile. Deacon had apparently given up hope for keeping his presence at Castle Moreau quiet.

Cleo rounded the corner to the writing room and paused in surprise. He must have been awake all night. The room had been cleared of boxes and crates, and a folding table with metal legs and a white plastic top was moved to the center. A few folding chairs were positioned around it.

". . . so I want my grandmother to be cared for gently. This process will upset her."

"I understand." The nurse, probably in her mid-fifties, nodded. She was all business, un-enamored by Deacon's presence. "May I suggest we remove her from this place? Perhaps tell her she's taking a short vacation? There are homes for rent not far from here where she can rest. Once she's settled,

I'll help her through some medical assessments, so we can get a clearer picture of her current condition."

"I find that agreeable," another man said, who had silvery-gray hair and wore a brilliant purple tie. He must be the lawyer.

Deacon glanced up and saw Cleo. He waved her in as he answered the nurse. "I like the idea, but the trick will be getting my grandmother to cooperate. She's very attached to the castle."

The nurse dipped her head. "I understand. And frankly, we're not going to just yank her from the castle today. My recommendation is that we give her at least forty-eight hours to get used to me and then perhaps move her by the weekend."

The lawyer shook his head. "Not soon enough."

Deacon shot Cleo a look of exhaustion mixed with resignation, tossed together with a bit of desperation.

"You can't just force Virgie to leave the castle," Cleo interjected. "It will wreck her."

The nurse twisted in her chair to look at Cleo.

The lawyer looked up with a frown.

Deacon offered her a small smile of gratitude. "I agree. Nurse Jenkins's recommendation, while not great for our agenda"—he turned to his attorney—"is what's best for my grandmother. She's going to hate every moment of this, Stephen, and it must be done with her well-being taken into consideration."

The lawyer, Stephen, responded with a grimace. "Fine, but we can't wait three or four days to alert the authorities. Especially not with this box you say just arrived yesterday. No matter how old the remains are, we're holding hot coals in our hands, and the authorities have to be involved."

"I know." Deacon blew out a breath. "We don't wait. Cleo?"

"Yes?" Cleo stepped farther into the room, her heart pounding. She should have left yesterday. She was being sucked in too deep into this Castle Moreau mess.

"I need you. Will you help with my grandmother?"

I need you. She wasn't prepared for the desperation she saw in his eyes. The clinging sort that begged for her support, her friendship. Yet he had no idea what he was asking. *Who* he was asking! Need her? Riley needed her too. Grandma. Even Grandpa needed her, whose ghost had sent her a note telling her to come home. But she wouldn't go home. She couldn't. And now having Deacon Tremblay, one of the most prominent men in the nation, *needing* her? In another life, it would be an intoxicating idea, even if he didn't mean it romantically but merely from a shared sense of camaraderie. But now? This life?

Cleo winced even as she felt that familiar and uncontrollable sensation of tears. "I-I can't."

"You can't?" Deacon's jaw dropped. "I don't understand. Why?"

Stephen and Nurse Jenkins looked between Deacon and Cleo, then at each other, confusion on their faces.

Cleo chewed her bottom lip. "I'm sorry, I just . . . I need to leave."

Deacon pushed himself up from his chair. "You what?"

Cleo looked at the other two occupants in the room, wishing they weren't here. It was too messy. Too real. Too close to home. "I can't be here anymore." It was a flimsy explanation, and Stephen, the savvy lawyer, saw right through it.

"Ms. Carpenter, is it?"

Cleo nodded. Her real surname was something altogether different, but she had no desire to elaborate on that fact.

"Yes, well, I'm afraid you cannot leave. Not when a package of Anne Joplin's belongings was mailed to you. You are involved whether you wish to be or not. The police will want to speak with you."

"I don't know anything," Cleo argued, trying to ignore the myriad emotions she saw in Deacon's expression. Honestly, he looked betrayed by her abrupt announcement.

"And," Stephen continued, "I've recently become aware"—he looked with censure at Deacon—"that we've been paying you under the table. Cash. This is a violation of . . . well, the point is, the Moreau-Tremblay estate has always been aboveboard with its financials. I understand Deacon's wish was to keep private about his grandmother's . . . uh, propensity to hoard and the problem this has become. I understand his wanting to rectify it before the media turned Mrs. Tremblay and the castle into a circus. But had Deacon first spoken with the board—which includes myself—we would have advised against your sort of anonymous employment."

Cleo tried to swallow the lump in her throat. She shouldn't feel this obligated. Shouldn't feel such attachment, not only to Virgie and her persnickety ways but also to Deacon, a man she had no right to have any affection for at all. It'd only been two weeks. Just two. "You don't have to pay me anything," she said, hoping that would settle the matter.

"On the contrary. We do. For the Moreau-Tremblay estate to remain aboveboard and transparent, your employment must be legally established."

She shot Deacon a panicked look. He responded by locking eyes with her and waving his hand at Stephen. "Can you both leave us alone for a minute?"

Stephen frowned. "I have only your best interests at heart."

"I know." Deacon squeezed his eyes shut and then opened them. "But I need to talk to Cleo alone."

"Fine." Stephen pushed back his chair and rose, motioning

to Nurse Jenkins, who appeared professional and distant from the conversation.

"I will take the liberty of introducing myself to your grandmother," she inserted.

"Good luck with that," Deacon mumbled, apparently having lost the willpower to assert his authority over the situation.

With Stephen and Nurse Jenkins gone, Deacon rounded the table to approach Cleo.

Fabulous. Now he'd gone from being charming and friendly to that simmering seriousness of the first day they'd met.

"You can't leave," Deacon began.

Cleo looked away. How did one argue with a man so handsome? Gone was the initial feeling of meeting Deacon Tremblay and practically stopping breathing when he looked at her. Now she simply didn't look back at him. Couldn't look back at him. It was like saying no to Captain America or telling Aragorn of *The Lord of the Rings* she'd never see him again. No woman in her right mind would do such a thing!

But Cleo wasn't in her right mind. She never had been. She never would be. He had made her that way, Grandpa, the man whose death dogged her and kept her from going home. The man she loved more than anyone in the world besides her sister, Riley. The man who had damaged her more than anyone in the world. The man whose ghost had sent her a letter.

Deacon's palms pressed gently against either side of her face, forcing her to look him in the eyes. "I don't know what's going on with you, Cleo, but you can't leave."

"I have to. You don't understand."

"I *want* to understand you. The same way I know you want to understand what's happening here at Castle Moreau."

"I *do*," Cleo replied, hearing the whimper in her voice.

Deacon's hands felt warm against her face. Strong. "But this isn't my story. This is *your* story. Your family. Not mine." It was an excuse, and she knew it. Unveiling the truth of his family somehow demanded she unveil the truth of her own. Though not tied together by anything other than the common bond of the unknown, the truth of both stories was crying out to be told regardless, and Cleo was terrified of it.

"Then what is your story, Cleo Carpenter—if that's even your real name?" He bent his head lower, and she smelled mint on his breath. It intoxicated her. Drew her toward him. His fingers trailed down her cheek, her neck, and toyed with a strand of her hair. "What's your story, Cleo? Why are you here? Why are you hiding?"

"Please don't ask. Don't ask questions that you won't like the answers to." Cleo's whisper was silenced as Deacon lowered his mouth to hers.

His kiss was tender at first. Hesitant. Not what she would have expected from a man like Deacon Tremblay, who had probably kissed many women in his lifetime. Cultured women. Women more beautiful than her. Less broken.

"Cleo . . ." His murmur rumbled in her ear as his lips moved along her jaw. "Don't leave me. Not yet. Not now."

"But—"

He stopped her again, this time with more fervor in his caress. Cleo whimpered for a moment before giving in to him. Hands at her waist, Deacon drew her closer, his chest pressing against hers. She couldn't help lifting her hands to his shoulders, then around his neck, her fingers threading their way into his dark curls.

Deacon pulled back, then changed his mind and kissed her again before finally giving her a moment to breathe. But breathing didn't feel possible. No more was he Deacon Tremblay in the media, or Deacon Tremblay the sought-after bachelor—well, maybe he still was that a little, and if she was being honest, it gave her a thrill—but mostly he was just Deacon. Deacon who needed her. And she needed him.

Cleo was loath to admit it, though. She couldn't admit it because it would only hurt him.

"I can't let you know me, Deacon."

"That's just an excuse," he scoffed gently. "Do you think I can't relate to whatever you're running from? Have you looked at my family and the media attention? The onslaught of rumors and half-truths? Life isn't pretty, Cleo, and no one's family is without its share of scandal. Even if the world worships you because of your money, or because of . . ." Deacon stumbled, searching for the words.

"Your looks?" Cleo supplied, then felt the hot blush on her face.

Deacon's crooked smile was marked with embarrassed acceptance. He knew. He knew what the public gushed over. He gave a halfhearted shrug. "Not quite what I was looking to say, but the point remains. No one has a picture-perfect story to tell."

Cleo blinked quickly, wishing away the burning tears, her quivering chin, and all the tells that revealed the pain she was harboring inside her.

"There are no happily-ever-afters," Deacon added as he thumbed away a renegade tear from her cheek, "just endurance through the mountains and valleys."

Cleo turned away from his touch, pulled back, and faced the window. Pastel pink petals from the apple blossoms in the nearby orchard floated past on the breeze, a glimpse of beauty in the ruins of a place riddled with curses.

"My grandfather . . ." They were the only words Cleo could choke out. Her throat closed around unshed tears. She grappled for the thumbprint necklace, rubbing the imprint of Grandpa. He'd left imprints on her life, on Grandma's life, on Riley's—probably on her mother's as well.

"What about your grandfather?" Deacon stood behind her, keeping his distance now. Yet Cleo felt his warm presence in the room, which reminded her of a campfire on a chilly evening. Encouraging. Embracing.

She sensed herself being drawn into the shadows and places she didn't want to go but had little strength to resist. "He died," she said at last, "three years ago. My grandma found him in the garage. It was a heart attack."

"I'm sorry," Deacon replied.

Cleo nodded, her back still to him. She drew in a shuddering breath. "He was my best friend, but he was . . . also a monster."

Silence.

Cleo could hear Deacon breathing.

She tucked the thumbprint necklace under her T-shirt. "My parents were dysfunctional. After my mom OD'd, we went to live with our grandparents."

"We?"

Cleo didn't answer at first. She couldn't. Her throat hurt, like knives scraping the inside of it. Emotional knives. "My little sister. Riley."

"You have a sister." It was a statement of recognition, not a question.

Cleo spun around to face Deacon. Panic clawed at her. The panic that had pushed her away from her grandmother, drove her from Riley. It was what kept her running. The danger. The precipice she teetered on. "I need to leave."

"You're going to run again?" Deacon challenged.

Cleo saw the letter on her dresser upstairs in her mind. She saw her grandfather's handwriting, *Come home.* On one hand, a sentimental statement, and on the other, a threat.

"Who's chasing you?" Deacon's expression turned determined. "Are you in some sort of danger? Because I'll pay whoever they are if that will get them off your back. Are you being blackmailed or something? Did your grandfather have debts?"

Cleo laughed a watery laugh that was helpless. "I wish it were that simple."

Deacon reached for her hand. "I'm good with complex problems. You should've seen me talk my way out of an altercation at a party in LA."

Cleo dodged his hand and took a step backward. "It's not a party altercation, Deacon."

His look was contrite at his flippantness. "Okay." Deacon ignored Cleo's attempt to sidestep him as he threaded his fingers through hers, effectively capturing her. "But listen to me. You've seen the media attention my family has received—that *I* have received. It's why I avoid them at all costs. My background is no garden party. You know I have two DUIs, right?"

He did? She hadn't expected that.

Deacon's thumb stroked hers. "I had to fight off a pending lawsuit from an old girlfriend, who accused me of stuff I didn't do."

Cleo remembered reading about that a few years ago.

"Before my parents died, my dad was accused of assaulting a woman on his staff."

"Was it true?" Cleo bit her tongue. She probably shouldn't have asked.

Deacon shrugged and pursed his lips. "Only God knows. I wouldn't put it past him, though." His eyes darkened to a deep honey-gold. The black rings around his irises sparked with something intense and sincere. Cleo struggled to look away, so instead she tugged at her hand, but he didn't release it.

"What more do you want to know about me?" His question was just above a whisper, vulnerable and yet woven with strength. It reassured her that he couldn't be shocked easily. He was used to the ugly parts of life.

Cleo chewed on her lower lip. Deacon's eyes dropped to watch for a second before his serious gaze rose back to meet hers.

"If you're in danger—if that's why you're hiding—tell me. I can help you."

Cleo averted her eyes. She couldn't breathe, couldn't capture into words the swelling panic inside her. In danger? No. It wasn't she who was in danger. It was Riley. The sequined pink unicorn hat was the last piece of Riley's childhood innocence. Lost. Lost that night because of her. Because of *Cleo Clemmons*, not Cleo Carpenter.

"My sister," Cleo choked out. Yep. There came the tears that made her more predictable than well-manned waterworks.

Deacon tilted his head. "She's after you?"

"No." Cleo rejected his assumption. "No, she is fourteen. It was two years ago when I left her with our grandmother. Grandpa had died, and I was . . . a complete mess." She paused and lifted her eyes to Deacon's. "Did you know they say alcoholism is inherited?"

Deacon nodded solemnly.

Cleo sniffed. "I was driving Riley home from school. I was upset—I didn't know how to process Grandpa's death. I knew what to expect with him around. Even when he got mean. I was . . . the buffer. For Riley, for Grandma. Without him there . . ." She wiped her cheeks with the back of her hand, then coughed to clear her throat.

Deacon nodded, understanding in his eyes. "Without your grandfather there, you didn't know what your place was?"

Cleo nodded, thankful he'd figured that out. She still couldn't talk, so he supplied the next part for her.

"So you drank."

Cleo coughed again and offered a cynical laugh. "Someone had to carry on Grandpa's tradition. Anyway, I was drunk. Riley wasn't wearing her seat belt—the house was only a few miles away. There was this dog being walked by a kid. I heard Riley scream, and I swerved erratically. I took out a mailbox right before I—" She stopped. It wasn't the worst that could have happened, but it was still awful.

"You hit the kid?" Deacon asked in a whisper.

"No." Cleo hurried to redeem what little bit of herself she could. "But I hit the dog. I hit the dog and—" she gulped—"I kept going."

"Hit and run," Deacon finished.

"Yeah." Cleo sagged against the wall, the window overlooking the castle's yard to her back. She could feel the sun shining in and warming her. She didn't want it to. She deserved the ugly, a cold wind, rain and thunder.

"Did you turn yourself in?"

It was the question she most hated. Cleo shook her head. "No."

Deacon nodded. "That's why you left."

A long silence followed. Shame was hard to bear when held inside and private, yet it was especially horrible when it was in the open for others to see. No matter, for it was too late to take back her admission.

"I couldn't add charges for driving under the influence to my family's trauma. And the kid's dog?" Cleo's voice cracked. She wrapped her arms around herself, staring at the far wall. Looking at anything other than Deacon. "*I'm the villain in my story*. If I stayed there, I'd ruin Riley the same way Grandpa ruined me. My actions will influence her in a negative way, and . . . and I could have *killed* that kid, Deacon!" Cleo heard her voice rise in an agonizing confession of her worst regrets. "I could have killed Riley! She's better off with Grandma. But I know they look for me—Grandma will look out of a sense of responsibility."

"To turn you in?" Deacon asked.

Cleo shook her head and frowned. "I don't know. Maybe. She's all about doing the right thing—which isn't bad, but living with Grandpa didn't exactly endow her with a huge storehouse of grace and understanding. She hates liquor. Hates what it does. So she hates me."

"Does she, though?"

His question pierced her, causing Cleo to grimace. She didn't know. That was the problem. She assumed Grandma would hate her. Cleo certainly hated herself.

The simple truth was that genetics ran deep, generations didn't escape the curses of those who came before, and sins were likely destined to repeat themselves.

What did it matter now? Deacon knew that she was the ugly one. She was the abuser, the one who brought pain to others, who inflicted the consequences of her own mistakes on to the people she should be protecting and loving.

Yes. She would leave now, never see Deacon again, and disappear. And he would let her because he understood what it was like to have your past hunt you. He understood what it was like to want to disappear.

"I am my grandfather. His monster is my monster." Cleo dug into her pocket and pulled out a coin, pressing it into Deacon's hand. "You might as well take this. I already blew it."

She shoved past Deacon, her shoulder accidentally brushing his in her hurry to exit the room that was fast becoming a prison. She left the one-year sobriety medallion in his hand to burn his skin with the truth of the matter. She'd messed up the night Deacon had arrived, the morning after puking all over his shoes. That should have been her first clue to leave. Right then. She would always go back to the vice. The thing that had destroyed her family and would cause Riley more hurt than if Cleo left her behind. Her grandfather's alcoholism was her own demon. If left unchecked, she would pull Riley further into the darkness of the only way of life her family had ever known. And when she turned into a monster, abuse was sure to follow.

She had asked herself repeatedly if she'd made another horrible mistake by leaving Riley. But the harsh truth always brought Cleo back to the same determination: She would not be that monster to her sister.

She refused to be the villain.

The Girl

DECEMBER 1801

When a child loses a mother, every day is a struggle to carry on. When Christmas comes to visit, not even an orange in one's stocking is enough to bring a smile that fully reaches the eyes.

My papa was not celebrating the season. The birth of the Christ child was a secondary consideration, and a tree with the trimmings was a mere fragment of the imagination.

So it was on Christmas Eve that I sat in the middle of my bedroom and stared out the window that spanned the wall opposite me. Snow embraced the world outside. A harsh snow. No one came to the castle, and no one left. Papa was locked in his study, no longer willing to come out to play, to sing, or to laugh. Laughter had taken its leave the day *Maman* died. Despite all my hopes and prayers, it would not return.

But she returned, the woman with the crooked hand. Every night. On Christmas she came bearing no gifts but instead more stories that both frightened and fascinated me.

"*Joyeux Noël,*" she whispered, and then she was gone.

As the weeks passed, I would tolerate her comings and goings. I would tolerate her tales. I found no warmth in them, or in her, but in a strange way I was also not alone in the desolation of my childlike grief.

"Papa," I would insist to his bowed head, for he refused to look at me, "the woman will not go away."

"There is no woman," he would growl into his hands. Then he would raise his head and look beyond me. "There is *no* woman," he would repeat.

But there was. As I grew, and as winter turned into spring, one night I awoke to see the woman standing over my bed. Her face was hidden in the hood of her cloak. Her crooked hand was held over me like a stiff and deformed staff. I pressed my head into my pillow. If she struck me, I would scream, and yet the woman never struck me. She never touched me. One cannot touch a phantom.

"You will grow. You will believe I never came to you. Remember, a spirit watches, always. You are never alone. Even if you wish to be."

I did not take comfort in her words. No one wishes to be haunted by a phantom. And if I was, as she liked to call me, her "story girl," then she was my story demon. I would never see the story the same again. I would never know fear the same again.

And yet I was also grateful for the phantom woman. For while she spoke fearsome things, she always reminded me that somewhere, beauty existed. She would tell me that life brought terrors, and we must learn to live with them. It was why she told me such things, so that I would not be as frightened when the horror visited in real life. When grief and pain and torturous things wiped away the dreams and hopes of a child and replaced them with doubt and longing and the wish that rest could be had.

"How?" I finally asked the woman with the crooked hand. "If the world is full of terror, how can there be beauty at all?"

"*La beauté existe là où commence l'amour,*" she whispered in my ear. In the language of my mother. In the music that feared being snuffed from my soul.

In spite of my fear, I believed her.

Beauty exists where love begins.

thirty-one

Daisy

If Elsie was not with Festus and his nonexistent wife, she had to have gone somewhere. Perhaps to meet the same fate as Hester May. As the other women.

Daisy tiptoed her way through the darkness. The castle was terrifying at night, but the answers she sought could only be found in the writing room of Madame Ora Moreau-Tremblay. She was the mistress of this place, the villain behind its castle walls, luring and taking and never returning.

But Daisy needed to uncover what had happened to the missing women. If the people in Needle Creek were right, Madame had been the harbinger of evil since her younger years. While she was married? When a mother? How long had a woman here and a woman there been plucked from the branches of life and snuffed out?

To find Elsie meant Daisy had to understand Madame, the why and the how. She would not understand her from talking with Lincoln. While he seemed receptive with his dark kindness, he was vague and unwilling to provide any solid answers. He was the Rochester to Jane Eyre. Hiding his own secrets while caring deeply.

The castle was a hollow place at night with its vast rooms and endless corridors. What had inspired the original Moreau to build this place? Daisy wondered. There was no reason for a fortress here among the hills overlooking the Mississippi River. Was it pride? A show of wealth that had caused the French trapper to grow in status and lord it over his fellow settlers? Not even a century ago, though in Madame's infancy, had this place been built stone by stone.

Daisy's bare feet padded quietly as she made quick work of reaching the writing room. The double doors were closed, which she had expected, so she reached out with her free hand, the other gripping a lamp to provide her light. The door creaked open. Once inside, Daisy saw the silhouette of Madame's writing desk, also noting the wooden box on a second desk that held her dead husband's heart. She eyed the shelves of books that loomed as bulky shadows.

The window over the writing desk exposed the yard in the moonlight. Empty of life. A clock ticked the passing seconds. Daisy stood there, undecided. What was she looking for? Evidence pointing to where Elsie had vanished? A history of the previous missing women? Daisy almost laughed at the idea that Madame Tremblay would be so careless as to keep a diary or journal that could be found, one with names written in it. Surely, Madame would not create an inventory of the women who had somehow drifted away like the mist surrounding Castle Moreau.

Daisy rested the lamp on the writing desk, picking up a piece of paper inked with the cursive of Madame Tremblay.

She lofted the knife over him, soiled in her heart and with filth in her soul. Would that she might be rid of it!

Rid of the righteous fury that fueled the strength to drive the blade into his chest. Once was not enough. It must pierce him again and again.

Daisy let the paper drop onto the others. Horrid, horrid story. That Madame could write such a story meant she must know fury herself, yes? All fiction held elements of truth in it. Elements of real life.

She spun from the writing desk and approached the much larger desk in the center of the room. On it was the box with the heart of Madame's late husband. What else did this desk keep hidden? Daisy tugged open a drawer to find paper, ink pens, a slate, and a pencil. The next drawer held a stack of journals. Daisy lifted them out and thumbed through the pages of one, then another. After a long period of squinting in the lamplight as she perused the books, she determined they consisted of nothing more than the castle's financials, records of missives mailed to others, and articles of report with no mention of anything questionable.

Daisy returned the journals to the drawer. She opened a third drawer. At the bottom lay a skeleton key with a red ribbon tied to its end. Beside the key was a small box. Daisy opened it. There were four glass vials inside, all of them empty. She recalled the one Madame had filled with the flesh from Elsie's wound. Why? And where had she taken it?

She closed the box and reached for the key. Daisy knew in her soul it would open the door to the mysteries Madame Tremblay hid from the world, perhaps even from Lincoln. Closing her hand around it, Daisy slid the drawer shut. Yes, it would most likely be missed, but hopefully Madame would believe she'd misplaced it. If questioned about its where-abouts, Daisy would deny knowing it existed. She would deny everything. Every suspicion. Every fear that beneath the words Madame Tremblay penned on the page, beat the heart of a monster who made a practice of making women vanish from the halls of Castle Moreau.

With the key clutched in her hand, Daisy hurried back toward her room. She had no desire to linger in the writing room, no wish to search any longer by lamplight. The key felt warm, alive with the promise it held answers. For the first time, Daisy harbored hope that she would find Elsie. The motive for why Madame Tremblay would act so villainously still eluded Daisy, but by God's grace she would uncover that as well.

The lamp flickered as she sped to her room. This time she would avoid Lincoln's study. She knew he was there, perhaps even waiting for her. He seemed to know where she was at all times. She felt him in her soul, and a part of her sensed him calling to her. Why she was so appalled by Madame and yet so drawn to the man in the wheelchair gave her pause if she let it. A commonality seemed to stretch between her and Lincoln. Both imprisoned by life but in different ways. Castoffs by society for no other reason than her being orphaned and Lincoln having dysfunctional limbs. Both of their minds were sharp, and beyond that, their hearts, their very souls beat with the essence of life. With the ability to love. With the need for understanding, for human kindness, and for a glimpse into eternity, where God promised all would be perfection with no more cruel judgments from others, no more ostracizing and condemnation of His children.

But for now—for *now*—the indefinable call to Lincoln's side must be ignored. Daisy finally reached the corridor of her room in the north wing. She rushed past the portraits, avoiding the stares of ancestral Moreaus. Those who had hailed from France and seemed to watch to see how their family name was being upheld.

Daisy came to an abrupt halt outside her bedroom.

She had closed her door and latched it—of this she was sure. She remembered tugging and pushing on it to ensure it was sealed when she snuck away earlier that night. Should Madame Tremblay or Festus wander by for some inexplicable reason, she didn't want to have a smidgeon of suspicion she was not tucked in her bed.

Now the door stood ajar. At least six inches between it and the doorframe. A thin band of light stretched from within her room, flickering from the flame that shed it. Fear lodged in Daisy's throat. She gripped the key tighter in her free hand, raising her lamp in the other. Reaching out, Daisy pushed on the door with her fingertips, slowly. It made no sound as it drifted open, revealing first the floor, then the tall window beyond, the footboard of her bed, and then . . .

"Who are you?" Daisy breathed.

The woman's form on the other side of the bed was partially hidden in the shadows. A cloak covered her shoulders, the hood over her head concealing her face. The light from the lone candle she held illuminated her white skin, her long fingers, and a ring that was a thin band of gold. She had turned her head to the side, ensuring the hood kept her features in shadow. She did not answer.

Fear was a powerful motivator. It encouraged Daisy to flee even as it engaged her senses, urging her to explore. To ask. To seek. To uncover the truth.

"Who are you?" Daisy asked again, stepping into her room.

It was not Madame Tremblay. This she knew. The hand holding the candle was too young, the skin too smooth and void of age to belong to the authoress.

Again, the woman refused to answer. Or perhaps she could not. Had death stolen her voice?

Daisy took another step forward, straining to see the woman better. She was not a vapor or an illusion. Feet were covered by her gown, yet she appeared to stand firmly on the floor. She didn't float like a spirit. She wasn't transparent as one might imagine a ghost to be.

But her silence was horrifying.

"Please." Daisy's voice quavered as it met with the instinctual need to run from the unknown. Run from potential danger, to hide from the part of the world the normal eye could not see. The spirit world that so many believed existed. Daisy preferred to think only of God. Of His superior nature. He was safer than any spirit, or phantom, or—

"Stay silent." The woman's whisper had no tone, no voice really. It was just a breath in the night air, breaking the stillness of the room and seeping into the marrow of Daisy's bones.

Daisy opened her mouth to reply, but no sound came. Horror strangled her. The woman had spoken.

A quick movement and the woman's candle flickered out. She was shrouded in shadow as she glided across the floor in a swift motion.

Daisy felt the woman brush past her. Not a physical touch, but the sensation of the air between them being disturbed.

There was hesitation. The woman tilted her hooded face toward Daisy. Her whisper once again shredded Daisy's soul. "Leave them alone." And then the woman slipped from Daisy's room.

Seconds ticked by with Daisy hearing only the intensity of her own breaths as she gathered her wits. Then, realizing the woman had spoken, she swept toward the doorway to chase after her. To follow her as she escaped from Daisy's sight.

But she was already gone. Dissipated into the night.

The phantom woman had visited her. She had spoken.

Once again, the key Daisy had pilfered from Madame's writing room felt hot in her grasp.

Stay silent.

Leave them alone.

They were more than instructions in the phantom woman's voice. They were a plea. A sort of begging.

That had been her mantra her entire life. Through the numbing abuses administered by the Greenbergs to the tears with which she wet her pillowcase at night when wondering why she had been abandoned at birth. Why God had allowed her parents to be mere wishes in Daisy's heart but have no faces, no bodies, no memories. It was not hard to recall the bruises Mr. Greenberg had left or to feel the bitterness once again as Mrs. Greenberg's spiteful words drew blood from Daisy's heart.

Always it was "tell no one" or "leave the abuser alone." Protect them. The ones who did harm, who deserved to stand before God and receive His wrath for the atrocities they had visited on the innocent.

Stay silent? Leave them alone?

Resolution filled Daisy even as fear quickened her heartbeat. She could not. Not any longer. Not for Patty and Rose whom she'd left behind. Not for Hester May and the nameless women who had disappeared before Daisy ever came to Castle Moreau. Not for Elsie, whom Daisy prayed was somehow shielded by God's angels and could still be rescued.

And not for herself. She had stayed silent for too long. It was time that she spoke out.

thirty-two

"Where are you goin'?"

Daisy jumped at Festus's growly voice over her shoulder. Sleep had been elusive and nonexistent, and her nerves were on high alert this morning.

"I..." She floundered under his bushy-browed glare.

"You're up to no good. I can see it in your eyes."

Daisy didn't answer. She knew she wasn't good at disguising her feelings. The key in her apron pocket burned.

"There are things to be done around here," Festus grouched. "Dustin'. Spiderwebs to be taken down. Floors in need of polishin'."

It was the first time Festus had given her any instructions.

Daisy nodded. This wasn't a battle she needed to wage. When the man retreated, she would continue her search, door to door, to see which lock the key opened. If she needed to carry a rag with her under the guise of cleaning, she would.

Festus eyed her. "Well?"

She returned his stare.

"You're up to no good," he said again, then turned on his heel and headed in the direction of the kitchen.

Daisy waited, listening for his footsteps to recede. Once he was gone, she moved to a flight of stairs leading to the third floor, which wound its way to the north wing where Madame's bedroom suite was located, the room where Elsie had been sequestered.

She was quick in getting there, pausing long enough outside Madame's door to ensure the woman had not somehow skirted Daisy and returned to her bedroom. The last Daisy had seen of Madame was when the woman had entered her writing room and closed the doors behind her. It was Madame Tremblay's habit not to exit until early afternoon when she would retrieve her meal from the kitchen and then return to the writing room.

Daisy moved to the next door—Elsie's room. It was unlocked, so no key was necessary. She tried the key in the door nevertheless to see if it was a fit. It wasn't. Inside the room, there was a distinct aura of emptiness. It was as if Elsie had never been here. There wasn't much in the room besides the bed, a chair, a small desk by the window, and a wardrobe. Daisy approached the desk and tugged out its center drawer. It was barren of anything important. She closed it. Turning to the bed, Daisy drew back the spread. The sheets were clean. She hadn't changed them. Who had? With no house staff, it was remarkable how this particular wing had such clean and polished rooms.

After pulling the bedspread back in place and tucking it neatly beneath the pillows, Daisy dropped to her knees and crouched to look under the bed. The floor was clean as well, polished to a shine. Daisy sat back on her heels. The walls and furniture were free of dust. A mirror across the room with its gilded frame had no spots, no tarnishes. Daisy could see the top of her red curls in the mirror from where she sat on the floor.

Her eyes caught sight of the wardrobe, and Daisy pushed herself off the floor. It was a large wardrobe that rose over her head with beautiful scrollwork. The doors were tall, closed with a latch, and yes, there was a keyhole. Daisy tried to open the doors and stilled. They were locked.

It couldn't be this easy. This simple. Castle Moreau had many rooms to search yet. If Madame had placed Elsie in a room where the skeleton key was assigned to its wardrobe, then there must be a reason. A reason not only for this wardrobe to be here and to be locked but also for Elsie to have been moved to this specific room. Daisy did not believe in coincidence.

A scuffling sound paused her hand midway, key poised, ready to insert and try the lock. Daisy looked around her. There was no one. She remembered Elsie's worrying about staying in the servants' quarters. She had complained about the scratching on the wall. Daisy held her breath, as if the very sound of it might interrupt the repeat of the noise.

Again she heard it.

The woman from last night came to her mind. Spirits didn't materialize in the daylight, so she needn't be afraid of the ghostly apparition. And yet there it was again. The scratching. It wasn't unlike what she'd heard outside her bedroom door the other night when she ran to Lincoln's study. The sound of a woman's nails clawing at the floor, the wall, any surface as if being dragged away.

"Do you need help?" Daisy spoke into the empty room. Perhaps it was ridiculous to believe someone would answer. But she had been told to stay silent. Told to leave them—whoever *they* were—alone. This she could no longer do.

No one answered.

The scraping sound ceased.

"Hello?" Daisy called.

The room remained silent. Finally, she allowed her hand to travel the rest of the distance to the lock in the wardrobe door. The key inserted. She turned it. The lock clicked, and the wardrobe doors gave way.

It *was* that simple.

She wasn't certain what she would find, but Daisy bolstered herself in preparation for whatever she beheld. Slowly, she opened the doors all the way, and there was an instant drop of her shoulders as disappointment greeted her. Nothing but an old dress hung inside the wardrobe. It appeared to be from decades earlier. It was black, silk, a mourning dress. Moths had eaten holes in it. Evidence of mice—which might explain the scratching if Daisy was honest with herself—lay in the corners at the wardrobe's bottom. Droppings and a few crumbs of stale bread that the mice had pilfered from somewhere.

There was nothing to indicate why Madame would have stored this particular key in the desk in her writing room. Yet Daisy couldn't avoid the nagging feeling it was important. She was moving the dress to the side, attempting to see behind it, when something fluttered from its folds and landed on the floor.

Bending, Daisy retrieved it. A handkerchief with pink tatting on the edges. Its white cotton was clean and didn't appear aged at all. There were roses embroidered in one corner. Daisy turned it over . . . and gasped.

Embroidered in delicate stitches was a name. A name she'd not expected to see there, but a name that confirmed Elsie's worst fears.

Hester May.

Hester May had been in Castle Moreau. If this was her handkerchief, so fresh and new, then whose dress hung there in the wardrobe?

Daisy searched the folds and ruffles of the dress. A brooch was pinned behind a pleat, a cameo. Behind another pleat on the dress's skirt, Daisy found another kerchief with initials that matched no name she knew of but had at one point identified its owner.

She explored the sleeves of the old dress. Her fingers toyed with something tucked in the cuff of the left sleeve. She pulled on the cuff and it released. Staring at it, every sense within Daisy sharpened.

It was Elsie's lace collar. The one she had worn around her neck. A handmade lace collar that was removable and could be worn with multiple dresses and blouses. But it was Elsie's nonetheless. Daisy would have recognized it anywhere, for it was she who had first removed the collar from Elsie's feverish neck to bring the young woman relief. She had placed it on the small table by the bedside.

Someone had moved it here. Hidden in the old funeral gown, along with other mementos of owners now joining Elsie in the land of the missing. What was most awful was the realization that the dress symbolized death. And death was, most assuredly, irreversible in its power.

thirty-three

Cleo

PRESENT DAY

She tried to drown out Virgie's shouts of protest as Cleo jammed clothes into her bag. She'd have to find Murphy. The bizarre cat had decided today was the day not to curl up as usual at the foot of Cleo's bed but instead go wandering off, hiding somewhere in the castle among the many packing boxes and mounds of clothes. It was Murphy's Law. Literally.

Her bedroom door shoved open, and Deacon stood in the doorway, his body stiff and his face a mixed expression of worry and alarm. "I need you," he said.

In another life, those words would have made her heart flip. She was finished, though. Finished with imagining even the vague outline of a dream, of hope. There was no longer any reason to feel intimidated by the man's good looks, his charisma and downright vulnerable charm.

"You'll be fine without me." Cleo stuffed a hoodie sweatshirt into the bag.

"Yeah. I know," Deacon said tersely. "I need you for my

grandmother. She is freaking out on Nurse Jenkins. I can't get her to calm down."

"I won't have any effect on her. She doesn't even want me here!" Cleo snatched a T-shirt and pushed it into the bag as well. Not to mention she could see the tautness of Deacon's expression—he wasn't a fan of hers now, was he? A back-slidden alcoholic who'd offed a kid's dog and then spent the last two years avoiding law enforcement. If arrested, she was sure to be charged with animal cruelty for leaving the scene after hitting a pet. She'd looked it up online. A felony charge was possible with substantial damage to someone's personal property in a hit and run. And if she admitted to being drunk while driving? It would ruin not just Cleo, but also Grandma, and more critically, Riley.

"I need you to try." Deacon's urging broke into her thoughts of self-preservation. "I'm afraid she's going to have a stroke or something."

At his words, Cleo's humanity overtook her personal panic. She stilled and turned to Deacon, reading the truth in his eyes. "Please, just let me go."

"If you can calm my grandmother down, fine. Leave. Whatever." Deacon flicked the medallion in his fingers so she could see it, then stuffed it in his pocket. "But I didn't take you for someone who abandoned people. You think what you did was an omen or worse? How much more pain can someone cause by just abandoning the ones they love?"

Ouch. That hurt. It hurt, too, that she'd been hiding from both him and herself the last few weeks as the cravings in-tensified. She'd been thankful there was no alcohol that she knew of in the castle, but she also cursed it. She hadn't men-tioned the nights she'd stood with keys in hand, determined to go find whiskey, bourbon, anything that would drown the memories that plagued her. Sobriety was a marvelous thing when one wanted to conquer their demons. But when sobriety only reinforced your own propensity to become one, it turned into a wicked cycle. She didn't trust herself. She didn't have faith in her self-control. Oh, God gave her strength, yes, but every person walked outside of His grace. That was no secret. Her time would come, it was a family curse, and she needed to save Riley from the fallout come hell or high water. It wasn't abandonment, like Deacon claimed, it was an act of rescue. Salvation. For Riley.

"So?" Deacon pressed.

Cleo nodded. "All right." Her acquiescence was reinforced by another reverberating shout from Virgie.

Cleo left her bag on her bed and hurried to follow Deacon's long strides. He spoke to her over his shoulder as they walked.

"Nurse Jenkins moved a box, and my grandmother lost it. Completely. I don't have a clue how we're going to get her to accept Nurse Jenkins's help, let alone relocate her to a bed-and-breakfast."

"Have you called the police yet? About the . . . remains?" Cleo couldn't help the hitch in her voice at the thought of the bones hidden behind the wall.

"Yeah. Yeah, I did," Deacon answered with a tone of resignation.

"You did the right thing," Cleo said, trying to reassure him.

He gave her a sideways glance. "Maybe you should try doing that too." It wasn't meant to be cruel. Cleo could tell because of the firm but gentle expression on his face. It pierced her nonetheless.

They'd reached the wing where Virgie's suite of rooms was located. Cleo noted the wardrobe against the far wall, its ornate woodwork dulled by time. More specifically, she noted the water dripping down its doors, a pile of broken glass on the floor in front of it.

Virgie was perched on the edge of her bed, rocking back and forth, sobbing.

Nurse Jenkins hurried toward them, her eyes wide and her hair in disarray. "You weren't lying about your grandmother's state of mind. It's far worse than I imagined."

"She goes from stable to losing it," Deacon whispered.

Nurse Jenkins glanced at Cleo, then back at Deacon. "I'm not sure what to do. I'd like to administer medication to help calm her, but my presence here has spiraled her condition. She threw a glass of water at me!" The nurse looked genuinely concerned for her own personal safety.

Deacon turned to Cleo and raised his brows. "Please" was all he said.

It wouldn't do any good. She wasn't close to Virgie. Virgie saw her as the one who was rifling through her collections, forcing her to throw things away, uncovering secret human remains that Virgie for some reason protected as if it were a saint buried behind her wall.

Cleo decided to try anyway, well aware that Nurse Jenkins and Deacon watched from the doorway.

"Virgie, it's me . . . Cleo."

Virgie whipped her head up to level a glare on Cleo. "I know who you are. I'm not suffering from dementia."

"Okay. I know," Cleo reassured. She wasn't good with people. Wasn't good at defusing stressful situations. Everything in her had been trained to back down, to submit, to allow the chaos to rule. The best thing to do when in conflict was to withdraw until the conflict was over, and hopefully you came out of it unscathed.

She could not do that now.

Cleo crouched before the elderly woman, gently placing

her hands on Virgie's fragile knees. She summoned every ounce of the emotion she used to bestow on her grandfather. "Virgie, we aren't trying to hurt you."

"No?" Virgie softened her voice, but her eyes still blazed. "First it is my belongings. Then it is my treasure. Then my home, and now this . . . this *woman* says I need to leave Castle Moreau?" Virgie gestured toward the nurse.

What had happened to a gentle introduction and easing Virgie into the idea of leaving?

Car doors outside the window slammed.

Virgie stiffened. "Who's here?" she demanded.

Deacon crossed the room. "The investigators are here." He met Cleo's concerned gaze. "Stephen will greet them. I'll speak to them when I'm called."

Of course, the attorney would run interference. Regardless, it was happening. The bones would be exhumed from their place in the velvet bag, in the trunk, in the alcove of the wall. Human remains would need to be linked to someone.

"You called the police?" Virgie's shrill cry of surprise quickly turned into a whimper. "Oh no, oh no, oh no, no, no. Why did you do that? I told you not to. Leave her alone!"

"Who? Who is *she*?" Deacon moved toward his grandmother but was stopped when Nurse Jenkins held out her hand.

"It will only upset her more," she said quietly.

Virgie reached for Cleo, her eyes panic-stricken. Her fingers dug into Cleo's shoulders, her rosy, wrinkled lips trembling. "Make them go away," she pleaded.

"I can't. I'm sorry." Cleo felt tears spring to her eyes. This poor woman was tortured. In mind and body and now soul. "But I'm here," she offered. A lame attempt to comfort the woman whose entire world—entire *legacy*—was being turned upside down.

Virgie leaned into her, Cleo catching a whiff of baby powder and old perfume. Virgie's forehead rested against Cleo's shoulder. "Don't leave me," she whimpered, adjusting her grip on Cleo's shirtsleeves. "Don't leave."

Cleo didn't respond, wishing instead that she had the nerve to promise the old woman such a thing. Wishing she could stay.

Like she hadn't before.

Dave exited his car. "I heard in town that human remains have been found in the castle. We came right away."

"Of course you did," Deacon muttered, then seemed to think better of his irritation. "They're recovering the remains now," he added.

They were all standing outside, as the authorities had cordoned off the areas they needed in which to do their work. They'd allowed for Nurse Jenkins to stay with the now-sedated Virgie in her room. Stephen, Deacon's lawyer, remained just outside the cordoned-off area, careful to observe and take note that the Moreau-Tremblay estate's interests were being protected.

"Is it Anne?" Dave slammed his car door shut. He shoved the sleeves of his shirt up to his elbows. Stasia hurried from her side of the vehicle, once again looking pretty in spite of her dark clothes, facial jewelry, and black hair.

"We don't know anything," Deacon explained, holding his hand out and gripping Cleo's wrist. He'd all but forced her out of the castle. The police insisted on it, and she'd resisted. Just watching the law enforcement officers made her skin crawl. This was the beginning of the fallout. The shrapnel from the shocking news of a body in the walls of the castle. Soon the media would swarm the place, then would come the questions from detectives, the necessity to provide background information and identification, and then . . .

Deacon shot her a look Cleo couldn't quite understand. Whether he meant it to reassure her or just make certain she didn't flee, she didn't know. But his warm grip, though not painful, seared her skin. Especially when his thumb shifted and reminded her of earlier—before her confession—when he'd caressed her skin with his fingers.

"Human remains." Stasia shook her head in disbelief. "Who would have thought?"

"And you turned the package of Anne's things over to the police as well?" Dave's question was posed to Cleo, who nodded. She didn't want anything to do with that old vintage T-shirt, with Anne's poetry, or the like. "Do you have any clue who sent it to you?" he asked.

"None," Cleo mumbled.

"I don't get it," Dave huffed, clearly agitated as he tilted his head back to look up at the castle. "It *has* to be Anne."

Deacon frowned. "Do you want it to be?"

"No." Dave's chin lowered sharply and he gave Deacon a look. "I just mean . . . man, it's been forty years. My family needs closure."

A couple of police officers were posted at the front entrance of the castle, not far from where a white van was parked in the drive. A forensics team had been called in, and who knew who the other people were? Cleo was a bit surprised that Dave and Stasia had been able to drive in without being stopped. Didn't Deacon say he was going to have a security team in place? What was next? Paparazzi? Cleo glanced to the sky. No helicopters with people hanging out of them with telephoto lenses. Not yet anyway.

"There needs to be closure. I'll agree to that," Deacon acknowledged.

Dave exchanged glances with Stasia. She placed a hand on his arm to stop him from speaking. "Let me," she said before turning to Deacon and Cleo. "Deacon, we were wondering if . . . well, we feel if we could find Meredith, we might be able to get some answers. About Anne. About what happened."

"And?" Deacon rested his hands at his waist.

Stasia glanced at Cleo, who steeled her features so as not to react. "And we were wondering if you'd be able to fund a private detective?"

Deacon twisted his mouth, apparently not surprised but more like annoyed at what must be a regular thing for him—people asking him for money. "No," he said.

Dave held up a hand. "Wait. Before you say no, think about it. If Meredith listens to her own testimony, maybe she'll remember something. And if we show her Anne's shirt as well as the poem you said was with it . . . I mean, Meredith has to know more. They were best friends."

"Yeah, well, I sort of have enough on my hands as it is." Deacon jerked his thumb toward the castle.

"But—" Dave bit off his argument as Stephen strode toward them, his tailored suit looking out of place among their more casual attire.

Stephen's expression was grim, though it also carried a hint of relief.

"What is it?" Deacon asked, turning to him. Stephen glanced at Dave and Stasia. "They're fine," he said. "Go ahead."

Stephen nodded. "They'll be taking the remains, obviously. After a cursory inspection, though, they believe the bones to be old. As in decades, if not longer."

"It could be Anne, then?" Dave interjected.

Stephen gave him a stern look. "No. They believe the remains to be from around the time the castle was built. We're talking historical artifact, not local woman gone missing in the eighties."

Dave's shoulders drooped.

Stasia scrunched her mouth in disappointment.

Cleo wasn't sure how to react. Old bones meant anyone currently alive wouldn't be traumatized by the grief of confirmation that a loved one was dead. But old bones also meant the rumored legend surrounding Castle Moreau was potentially that much truer than either she or Deacon previously believed. Women went missing and were presumed dead. Here was proof of that.

"What happens next?" Deacon asked.

"Well . . ." Stephen pushed back his suit coat to rest his hands at his hips. "We also had to contact Wisconsin's State Historic Preservation Office. They'll be working in coordination with the sheriff's department. My assumption is that they will take over once it's ruled non-forensic."

"Non-forensic?" Deacon raised a brow.

"In simple terms, once it's determined the remains are not part of a crime scene."

"When will we know for sure that they're older than my cousin's case?" Dave was not letting it go, and Cleo couldn't blame him really.

Stephen shook his head. "I don't know. These things take time."

"Will we have access to the castle?" Deacon asked. "And what should I say to my grandmother?"

"They said your grandmother is fine where she's at for now. Obviously, that wing will be closed off until they clear out, which could be in a day or more depending on how long it takes to investigate."

"So, what do we do in the meantime?" It was a question posed by Deacon, but it echoed everyone's thoughts.

Stephen shrugged. "Deacon, you might start by learning the truth of the castle's past. This thing is going to bust wide open, no matter how recent or old those remains are. It's the fodder needed to reenergize every conspiracy theory out there about Castle Moreau and the Moreau-Tremblay family. You need to figure out the truth—and fast."

They gathered in the back room of Dave's store. Deacon had reluctantly included Dave and Stasia, which Cleo assumed was mostly because he wanted to keep tabs on them and try to contain the fallout as much as possible.

Dave was brewing coffee in an old coffeemaker. The room had plastic shelves against the far wall, boxes of vinyl records, cassette tapes, VHS tapes, and more, all of it collected neatly. In a way, it reminded Cleo of Virgie's collective mess back at the castle, only this was far more organized and controlled.

Stasia sat at the table with her feet propped on a spare chair. Deacon thumbed at his phone, intent on whatever he was browsing. Cleo just waited for the coffee. Waited for something—anything—to catapult the moment forward to where questions could be resolved. Murphy had been locked up in her bedroom. The castle was crawling with people investigating the bones. Police indicated they'd want to interview them soon. She was stuck here now, in Needle Creek, and her own past was dogging her every step.

"What do we know about Castle Moreau?" Stasia took charge of the conversation. She tapped a pencil against a lined, spiral notebook. "Let's get back to basics. Walk me through it, Tremblay," she stated.

Deacon looked up from his phone. He shot Cleo a look, and she wasn't quite sure how to interpret it. He looked weary already. Or wary. Maybe both.

Stasia tapped her pencil again. "Listen, I know this sucks—for all of us—but your lawyer said to get ahead of it. If you can figure out what the heck Moreau's story is, then maybe we can get to the bottom of what happened to Anne as well as my long-lost great-great-aunt Elsie."

"Fine." Deacon dropped his phone onto the table and leaned forward, drilling his gaze into Stasia. "Here's what I know: Tobias Moreau was a French trapper who, at the turn of the century, built the castle for his wife. They had a daughter named Ora. She grew up to become the famous Gothic writer whose books I've never even read. She married, and they had a son who died shortly after his own son was born. That son went on to have a daughter. Her name is Virgie, my grandmother. She kept her maiden name. Her kid was my dad, and my parents died in a plane crash when I was fifteen. It's just Virgie and me now."

Stasia was busy scribbling in her notebook. She looked up. "To summarize, then, Ora Moreau the author is Virgie's grand-mère."

"Yep." Deacon rapped his knuckles on the table.

"Which means Ora Moreau is your great-great-grandmother," Stasia concluded.

"Right." Deacon seemed unimpressed.

Cleo reached up to take the mug of coffee Dave offered her. He smiled a little, then directed his words toward Deacon.

"When did the first stories of missing women linked to Castle Moreau start?"

Deacon shrugged. "I don't know."

Stasia chimed in. "*I* know. The first woman rumored to go missing was probably around the time of Ora's marriage. So . . . the 1820s. And then roughly fifty years later, my own family had Elsie Stockley vanish, as well as another young woman, Hester May, and they say there were others too."

"The phantom woman." Once again, Cleo spoke without thinking.

"What?" Dave looked down at her.

She cast Deacon an apologetic look, but he rolled his hand in the air for her to continue. "Remember? The other night? Virgie mentioned the phantom woman—the woman with the crooked hand."

"That was a book written by Ora Moreau," Stasia said.

Cleo wasn't about to mention her visions of the woman in the castle. Instead, she replied, "But what if it is true?"

Dave's brows flew up. "That's an interesting point."

Stasia swung her legs off the chair. "You're saying maybe the book has a clue in it as to what started this entire thread and theory about the missing women?"

Cleo shrugged. Deacon locked eyes with her, and his seemed to reassure her he wouldn't share the details of her fright that night in the castle. He intercepted to spare Cleo the discomfort. "My grandmother says she haunts the castle. That she always has."

"That's just speculation. Not a real person," Stasia stated.

She was interrupted when Deacon's phone trilled. He answered it, and Cleo watched his face as he listened. Color drained, and his eyes darted to meet Cleo's even as he responded to the caller. "Mm-hmm. No, I hear you, I just . . . yeah. Yeah, I will. We're trying to get to the bottom of it. I know, Stephen. I will. Bye."

Deacon flicked his screen and slowly rested his phone on the table. No one spoke. They could tell he was unsettled. He raised his eyes after staring at his phone for a long moment as though it would somehow magically provide the answers they all sought.

Finally, Cleo asked what the others wouldn't. "What is it?"

Deacon gnawed at his lip, then sniffed, shaking his head in disbelief. "They already let Stephen know what they found."

"And?" Dave leaned on the table in anticipation.

Deacon looked over at him. "There's no news on the age of the remains yet, but the skeleton is female, and the bones of her hand—" He choked.

"Are crooked!" Stasia breathed in realization.

Silence enveloped the room.

Dave cleared his throat. "So, the bones are the woman with the crooked hand? The woman from Ora Moreau's novel—she *was* real!"

Deacon nodded. "The phantom woman."

"The very first victim at Castle Moreau," Stasia said.

thirty-four
Daisy

1871

"Thank you for coming."

Daisy stood before Lincoln as he sat looking up at her from his wheelchair. She'd had little choice. She'd been summoned by Festus, who had caught her coming from the direction of Elsie's room. What she'd seen there haunted her. She was not finished either, but the sound of Festus's footsteps had urged her from the room, and she was thankful he'd not actually caught her leaving it. Now she stared down at Lincoln, doubt more than likely etched into every crevice of her face.

"Would you have tea with me? Can we chat? Discuss books and history?"

Daisy blinked. He was sincere. Lincoln's dark eyes were fixed on her with a veiled anticipation of intelligent dialogue. Was he truly serious about wanting her companionship? Her mind was in disarray. How was she to discuss books and history when Elsie's and Hester May's very lives hinged on her staying the course to find the truth?

"Please." Lincoln pointed to the window seat just to the left of his chair. "Sit."

She stiffened. "I'd rather not."

"Oh?" Lincoln's friendliness dissipated, and he eyed her carefully. "You sound upset."

"Perhaps . . ." She tried not to reveal the fear growing inside her. A panic like none she'd felt before was welling up and making it impossible to concentrate on anything else.

"What is it?" Lincoln asked.

Daisy avoided his eyes and walked to the window, crossing her arms around herself. What should she say? Trusting Lincoln might be foolish. He had to know about the missing women. How could one live here and *not* know something was amiss?

"Daisy." Lincoln's voice was low.

She looked over her shoulder. His hand was outstretched, beckoning her. She refused to take it.

Lincoln dropped his hand to the arm of his chair. He heaved a sigh, giving her perhaps the most honest expression yet. He was agitated and allowed it to show as he worked his jaw back and forth. "You do not trust me?"

"No," she answered with equal honesty.

"Why?"

"Do you know . . . ?" Daisy halted.

"Go on."

She licked her lips and sucked in a nervous breath. "There is a woman here. In the castle. Not your grandmother, and not me. She roams the place at night. I saw her."

"You did." It was a statement of acknowledgment. He wasn't surprised.

"Yes." Daisy rejected caution and approached him, kneeling on the floor beside his chair, her hands covering his arm as it rested on the leather padded armrest. "She warned me. 'Leave them alone,' she said. Who is she? What does she want?"

Where are Elsie and Hester May? Daisy added in her mind but didn't dare speak it. Yet.

Lincoln looked beyond Daisy with a grim smile. "So you've met the phantom woman."

"Please do not try to convince me I saw a ghost."

"You saw a woman my grandmother wrote about."

"The woman with the crooked hand? I've not read the story. It sounds frightening."

Her words must have struck a small note of humor in Lincoln. His mouth twitched, flirting with a smile but not quite achieving one. "Ah, well. It's just a story."

"Based in truth?" Daisy questioned.

Lincoln leveled his dark stare on her. "You would argue that my grandmother's writing is a memoir, not fiction?"

"If it was, wouldn't the woman with the crooked hand be dead?"

"Very."

"Then it wasn't her," Daisy concluded.

"A ghost then, after all."

"I refuse to believe that."

"Why?" Lincoln smiled. Almost mocking her. Challenging her.

Daisy stiffened. "I may not be schooled in theology, but I have read the Holy Bible. There is nothing to say that when we die, we hover around the earth as unresolved spirits."

"It's heaven or hell instantly, you believe?"

Daisy grimaced. "I do not judge another's heart. Judgment is for God alone to carry out. But I *do* believe there has to be a human explanation and therefore it's not safe here in Castle

Moreau. Not with a stranger roaming the halls, threatening me. Toying with my door. Scraping at the walls. Touching my neck as I walk in the darkness." Tears sprang to Daisy's eyes, and her voice wobbled. "I am afraid. Elsie is missing. And Hester May—"

"What about Hester May?" Lincoln asked sharply.

"She, too, is missing." Daisy fought to control her tears. "I cannot lie. I found . . . belongings. She was here. And now she's gone. What is happening? Please. I want to trust you. I want to believe you are good, that you counteract the evil of your grandmother."

All warmth faded from Lincoln then as he glared at her. "My grandmother is *not* evil."

"No? But she took flesh from Elsie's leg."

"To cut away the infection," Lincoln replied through gritted teeth.

"And she saved it in a vial!"

"What else should one do with human flesh? Toss it in a bin?"

"I don't know!" Daisy sobbed. He was angry with her. She was confused. Afraid. Her confidence waned as quickly as it had risen. "I found more vials. Empty ones. And she has your grandfather's heart on her desk!"

Lincoln gave a shout of laughter. A deep, short laugh that made Daisy back away from his chair. "Good night, woman!" He chuckled darkly. "Do you have an imagination like my grandmother's? Why, yes you do!"

"She told me so!" Daisy insisted, swiping at her tears with her sleeve.

"Of course she did. She's a storyteller. Have you looked inside that box of hers?"

"No!" Daisy was appalled that he would suggest such a thing.

"Go ahead. Look inside. That wooden box contains her pen collection. There's no heart. No body parts. And her vials are for samples she collects from her walks in the woods—mushrooms, fungi, and other such things. If she was tending Elsie and removing dead skin, she probably used the vials to be safe and prevent others from contracting disease." Lincoln caught his breath after his almost hysterical laughter. "You have allowed my grandmother to play with your mind and create her tales for real and not just on the page."

"Why? Why would she be so cruel as to weave such horrific lies? The heart of her dead husband? It's dreadful, and if it's not true—"

"It's not," Lincoln interrupted.

"Why tell me so?" Daisy challenged.

Lincoln's smile was thin, implying that she should be able to see the obvious. "My grandmother writes stories of horror. She must carry on the façade in real life as well or she won't be taken seriously. As an author. As a woman."

"She frightens us with untruths outside of her novels?" Daisy could scarcely believe the boldness of such a gory lie. "Doesn't it tear at her soul to treat the memory of her dead husband in such a blithe and flippant manner?"

Lincoln rubbed his hands down his legs, which, in the daylight, appeared more withered than Daisy had first noted. He saw her watching them and raised an eyebrow.

She blushed.

Lincoln answered her question about his grandmother and also the question that lingered in her eyes about his condition. "When one is left with little, you must choose to embellish life and make it interesting or else waste away in grief and self-pity."

"She loved your grandfather?" Daisy inserted.

"True, but my grandmother doesn't shy away from the

reality of death. She sees carrying on her reputation for all things Gothic as some sort of entertainment."

"And you?" Daisy tipped her head, looking up at him. She gripped the arm of his chair, her knees still pressing against the floor beside him.

"Me?"

"Your grandmother finds morose fulfillment in mocking death. How do you find fulfillment?"

"Because of this?" He waved his arm the length of his legs. "I was born like this. It is called Little's disease, and I've known nothing else. When my parents died, I came here, as a young boy, to Castle Moreau. Most forget I even exist. That is how I find fulfillment, Daisy. By not existing."

"That makes no sense," she whispered.

Lincoln leaned toward her, and she could smell spice on his skin. "Meaningful things rarely make sense, my dear."

"Then explain it. Please, help me understand! Tell me where Elsie is, and Hester May—or show me some way to find peace within these walls!" Daisy demanded.

Lincoln did not hesitate, nor did he argue. He reached for the wheels of his chair and pushed away from her, rolling toward his desk. "My grandmother prefers this not to be seen. But since you will not be silent—nor will you heed the warnings of the phantom woman—I must show you to purchase your silence."

Daisy struggled to her feet, following him at a cautionary distance. Lincoln settled behind his desk where she'd first seen him. He removed from the desk a copy of his grandmother's novel, turning to the last page. Turning the book around, he handed it to Daisy.

In cursive, and identifiably in Madame's handwriting, she had penned the words:

To my grandson,
Remember, la femme fantôme will live on in Castle
Moreau. Always.
Respect her. Treat her with reverence. She is our past,
our present, and our future. A terror of proportions we
cannot ignore and must never forget.

Grand-mère

"This explains everything?" Daisy stared at the missive in disbelief, both at the words and the idea that Lincoln would think she might find resolution in them.

She was taken aback when Lincoln reached across the desk and gripped her hands. The book fell between them to the floor, Madame's handwriting glaring up at them. His fingers were warm, the pressure of them against her skin persistent.

"The phantom woman is the past, the present, and the future of this place, Daisy *mon amour.*"

My love.

The words quickened her heart with the ridiculous promise behind the endearment to her, a virtual stranger, and certainly not someone he loved. But it was his declaration that he believed the phantom woman to be real that made her tremble. He had alluded to her before, almost teasing as if retelling a ghost story. But now, as Daisy dared to meet his eyes, as she saw the flickering behind their depths and felt the caress of his thumbs . . . she knew.

Lincoln Tremblay believed the phantom woman was real. Had always been real. Would always be real.

As much as Daisy despised the argument that the woman in her room was a spirit of wickedness, she could deny it no longer. Not if Lincoln was telling her the truth.

And everything in his eyes said he was.

The door was closed to her, but Daisy heard the voices behind it. Lincoln. Madame Tremblay. They were arguing. Daisy held a tray with Lincoln's supper on it, but she dared not enter the study now. Not as Madame's voice rose in a harsh tone.

"You should not have!" she scolded.

Lincoln's response was a hum of unintelligible words.

Daisy shifted the tray in her hands, her head tilted toward the door. She felt no shame in eavesdropping. If Lincoln was arguing with Madame, perhaps it was to the benefit of finding Elsie. She knew Lincoln still hid the truth from her. And yet, even now, Daisy's skin crawled with the feeling of being watched. The trouble with spirits was that they lingered, invisible to the eye, and were seen only when they wished to be.

"She is not to be spoken of," Madame hissed, her words brimming with emotion.

"She is not sacred, Grand-mère." This time, Lincoln's rumbling voice could be heard.

"Speak for yourself."

Footsteps sounded, coming toward the door. Daisy backed away quickly, making a pretense as if just now approaching the door after climbing the staircase.

Madame yanked it open and stood in the doorway. Her body was erect, poised, her face troubled, but she steeled her expression on seeing Daisy.

"You've brought him dinner?"

Daisy nodded. "Yes, Madame."

"You've not done this before." The simple observation was true. She hadn't. Daisy assumed in the past that Festus had. Food brought from a cold hearth in the kitchen. She had noticed tonight an extra serving besides hers. She assumed it was for Lincoln, but for some reason Festus had not brought it to him.

"I thought—"

"You may give it to him." Madame stepped aside. It was the first time Daisy had seen her in the proximity of Lincoln. As Daisy ducked past her, she felt Madame's eyes on her back. Moving forward, she slid the tray onto the desk in front of Lincoln.

"Thank you," he responded and reached for the tray, pulling it toward him. His eyes did not leave her face. She could not read his expression, but she noted a slight tremble to his fingers as he reached for a fork.

"You may go now," Madame instructed.

Daisy met Lincoln's eyes. He offered a weak smile. "Yes. Do as my grand-mère says."

Daisy nodded once, then turned to exit the room. When she reached the doorway, Madame's voice sliced into her with thinly veiled accusation.

"I am missing a key from my desk. Do you know anything of it?"

Daisy froze, looking down at her feet. "No, Madame," she lied. Then she forced herself to lift her eyes to appear more convincing. "I don't know anything about a key."

Madame studied Daisy's face, her lips pinched together, eyes narrowed. "Are you suggesting Festus stole it from my desk?"

"No!" Daisy reacted with honest shock. "No, I'm not suggesting anything."

"So then it was Lincoln?" Madame turned to look at him.

Lincoln waved his empty fork in the air haphazardly as he chewed on a bite of his supper. "Yes, Grand-mère, it was me."

"You rolled down the stairs, did you?" she scoffed. "How did you get back up them?"

It was cruel to Daisy's ears, the taunting, but Lincoln laughed thinly and raised a dark brow. "I am quite strong, Grand-mère. I've coveted that key for months now."

He was jesting, his tone cynical. Daisy looked between them, unsure whether to excuse herself or remain where she was so as not to appear as if she were running away because of guilt.

Madame leveled her gaze back on Daisy. "I was not informed of your coming to Castle Moreau."

Daisy held her breath. She dared not respond.

Madame Tremblay ran her hand along her neck until her fingers found the black lace at her throat. She toyed with the top button of her ebony shirtwaist, which was embellished with a ruby brooch. "My grandson determined he needed you. Honestly, I've no idea why."

Daisy waited quietly, sensing any words from her right now would only inflame the woman's ire.

The authoress looked at Lincoln from the corner of her eye while he ate casually as if nothing was amiss. "On second thought," she continued, "I believe I understand why he sent for you."

Daisy noticed Lincoln didn't look their way, but he had stopped chewing. He was listening.

Madame noticed too. "My grandson is alone. He harbors no ill will toward women; rather, he fancies that he should not be alone forever. But no woman from town will engage his interest, nor he theirs. As someone who cannot stand on his own, this makes him less than—"

"That isn't true," Daisy broke in without thinking.

Madame looked taken aback.

Daisy finished, dropping the defensiveness in her voice.

"He isn't less than anything. But he could not have known I would answer the call for assistance at Castle Moreau. So I don't believe he sent for me."

Madame laughed softly. "Oh, he sent for you, my dear. He sent for a young woman who feared life enough to brave Castle Moreau. And so you came to him. And now you're here, and you question . . . everything."

Daisy swallowed.

Madame leaned closer until Daisy could feel her breath on her face and the intensity of Madame's gaze. "Don't." Her statement rang through Daisy's body. "Question nothing. This is my home. Lincoln is my guest. You are my employee. That is all you need to know. Any designs on my grandson end now. And if you continue to be untrustworthy, your employment will end as well."

With that, Madame swept from the doorway, not looking back, and turned to descend the stairs.

Daisy was unable to move.

She heard the clink of a fork against a plate. She looked to Lincoln. His face was pallid, his eyes blazing.

Daisy drew strength from somewhere inside herself. She saw vulnerability in his expression, which was unexpected.

"Don't listen to her. You are of great value," Daisy breathed.

Lincoln sniffed. "Grand-mère loves me in her way. But she tells no one I exist. She's not wrong, you know. I did seek companionship. In the end, there lies the blunt truth of it."

Daisy offered him a shaky smile. "That may be. I can hardly blame you for being lonely. But do not worry—I can be a companion without having designs on you, as your grand-mother implied."

Lincoln's brows drew together, and Daisy read his concern that she might think he'd brought her here in hopes of more than conversation, that he wished for something deeper. Love perhaps. Love to grow and prosper and shed light through the hallways of a dark place. She must reassure him that he was safe. Safe from designs she never had on him. Madame's insinuation could make things dreadfully uncomfortable and even threaten the thin line of trust that had been formed between them.

"I promise you," she said, "you can trust me. I will not try to be more than what I am. Your employee. At best, maybe a friend too."

Lincoln leaned back slowly in his chair, and his chest lifted in a deep sigh. He studied her for a long moment, the air between them thickening with a sensation Daisy didn't understand.

And then Lincoln spoke.

"Oh, but we *could* be so much more than friends, if only you would use that imagination of yours for better things than searching for lost girls."

thirty-five

Daisy fled from the study. From the depths of Lincoln's eyes. From the promises there that touched a place in her heart she'd never explored. Never believed possible, especially with a man she barely knew. Had he truly advertised for someone to offer housekeeping at Castle Moreau on faith it would be a woman he might one day love?

It was absurd. It was desperate. It was inconceivable.

Yet wasn't that the definition of Castle Moreau? For there was nothing here but absurdity, angles and twists that no one could explain, and yet the castle called with an addictive element. Beckoning. It reached into the deep places in one's soul and began to expose them for what they were. Broken pieces. Pieces only God could heal, and only others could help rescue if they simply had kindness in their hearts.

Daisy rushed through the hallways, warring with her thoughts, her heart. The castle became a maze as she fled from Lincoln, from Madame Tremblay, who seemed to know that Daisy had snooped and stolen the key. It frightened Daisy to realize that while she thought she had acted in subterfuge to find Elsie, it seemed she'd been watched the entire time. The Tremblays knew it all, despite Daisy's attempts at subtlety.

She went to where it all began with Elsie. To the servants' quarters, rooms meant for the house staff that should be occupied but were empty. When she arrived at Elsie's room, Daisy plopped onto the bed, burying her face in her hands. Prayer seemed necessary, but not enough. Hope was grasped for, but elusive.

Staring into the corner where Elsie had been so frightened, Daisy fixated on a spiderweb that clung to the wall. It was intricate, a weaving of design out of chaos. The web was empty. Abandoned by its maker and left to collect dust and trap unsuspecting bugs. There was no spider, nothing waiting to pounce. It was simply an illusion of all that had once been but was no more.

Daisy stilled. An illusion of what had once been. She startled from her position on the bed and hurried to the corner, swiping the cobweb from memory and wiping it on her dress. She felt the stones on the wall, her hands against their coolness. She recalled Elsie's fear, her insistence she heard scraping and scratching. Yes! She had heard it too, but in her room where the walls and floors were made of wood, not stone. Where someone could reason it away as a mouse or some other small animal trapped within the walls. But stone was solid. A foundation.

Unless it was an illusion . . .

Unsure what drove her, Daisy followed the mortar lines between the stones with her fingertips. The joints were solid, nothing out of the ordinary. Nothing to indicate she had stumbled upon something secretive.

Then her finger caught on a tiny hollow between stones. Daisy crouched to examine it. It was less than an inch long and appeared to be where the mortar had crumbled from between the stones. That was what age did to foundations. It threatened to crumble them, and yet, if crafted well, the foundation withstood time. As Castle Moreau had.

Still, Daisy shoved her finger into the gap as far as she could, up to the first knuckle, and felt something like cold metal. She pushed against it lightly, but it didn't budge. When she pressed harder, this time Daisy heard a small click.

The stone moved in the wall, revealing what she couldn't see before. She held her breath as she heard a series of latches release. The one she'd pushed caused more behind the stones to unlock until soon the stones began moving toward her as one solid piece of the wall. A door of stones, several inches thick, creaked open.

She stood in the opening, entranced and scared at the same time. Before her was a tunnel like a hallway, though it was too narrow really to be called one. It ran parallel to the actual corridor outside the room in which she stood. Daisy could see where it ended, but that wasn't truly an end. The tunnel merely turned, following the castle's hallway but hidden from sight.

Daisy could hear herself breathing. It echoed in the empty room. The tunnel beckoned her forward, promising answers. Promising that it would reveal Madame Tremblay's darkest secrets, expose any untruths Lincoln might yet be hiding, and most of all, help Daisy to fathom the phantom woman who haunted Castle Moreau.

With her lantern in hand, Daisy slunk down the narrow tunnel, her fingers dragging along the stone wall. For a place that would not have received much attention, it was remarkably void of webs, of dirt, of evidence of mice or other creatures that would find it a haven to hide in. As the tunnel continued, Daisy noted a flight of steps that would coincide with the larger ones on the other side of the wall. The staircase that led from the servants' quarters to the next level, twisting in the direction of the kitchen.

With no windows, it was getting darker the deeper she went. It was also getting very much more alone. Daisy eyed the stairs. There was barely enough space for her to squeeze up them. She turned a bit to allow her shoulders room. A grown man would have difficulty navigating the narrow stairway, but Daisy did so with little trouble. She could envision where she was in the castle based on the direction she was going. She became confused, though, when after reaching the top of the stairs, instead of veering to the left—which would follow the natural flow—there was a plain wood-plank door. It had no knob, just a small pull.

Daisy reached for it. Now would be a fabulous time to stop recalling the stories she'd read. *Jane Eyre* with the wild woman hidden on the upper floor. Or Poe's "The Tell-Tale Heart" with the old man's body hidden beneath the floorboards, its heart pounding so loudly that the murderer was sure the world heard it. Lincoln was correct about one thing. She *did* have an overactive imagination, but unlike Madame Tremblay, Daisy attempted to keep it in check.

Still, it was difficult not to imagine opening the door and seeing beyond it the missing dead women collected by Madame over the decades. Perhaps they would be lying on shelves, along with trays of vials that Madame kept for testing and whatnot, much like Shelley's *Frankenstein* implied.

Daisy squeezed her eyes shut and then opened them. It was just a door. More than likely what lay beyond it was only a continuation of the passageway. Assuring herself all would be well, Daisy pulled it open.

Her breath caught.

It was a small room. Inside, an old oil lamp hung from a hook in the wall. She took a moment to light it, using the matches she'd discovered on a small table. Light flickered, then illuminated the room in a soft yellow glow. The room was not crowded with the missing women. In fact, there was no sign of anyone. It was empty save for three wooden chests placed against the wall to Daisy's right, with very little space between them and the opposite wall. One could barely call this a room, and yet someone had stored the chests here. Out of sight of anyone snooping around in the castle.

Daisy moved to the chests arranged in a row. They looked to be wooden steamer trunks with rounded lids and black hinges. She knelt before one, her feet almost touching the wall behind her. A buckle in the front latched the trunk shut. She unbuckled it, trepidation seeping into her as her imagination once again took flight.

A body could be in there. An entire human being would fit inside if coerced, especially if the person were deceased.

In a hurry to disprove herself, Daisy lifted the lid. A distinct musty smell hit her nose, but there was no body inside. Thankfully. Daisy released a sigh of relief, not realizing she'd been holding her breath.

The trunk was filled with clothes: dresses, shirtwaists, stockings, as well as shoes. After a bit of inspection, Daisy saw they were of different sizes and not made for one specific woman. She rummaged through the neatly folded items and, after finding nothing more of interest, shut the lid and moved to the next trunk.

Again, the idea of a body fluttered through her mind, but she quickly dismissed it. One wouldn't store a corpse in a secret passageway . . . at least she didn't think so.

A lift of the lid proved that she was correct in assuming

her imagination had run wild. It contained nothing more than some capes, coats, shawls, gloves, and a few scarves. What an odd assortment of things to hide away in a place no one would know even existed. Instead of enlightening her, Daisy found herself more confused, and more anxious to open the third and last trunk.

Books. It was filled with books.

She lifted one out, a later title by Madame Ora Moreau. Searching further, she found more titles by Madame, including several copies of *The Phantom Woman*. It appeared that this trunk held the collection of Madame's works. Why were they hidden behind the wall? Daisy knew they were also displayed on Madame's bookshelf in her writing room. These books were no secret. They held no surprises and no mysteries that someone would wish to hide from the outside world.

Daisy noticed a copy of *The Phantom Woman* had a larger sheaf of papers stuffed into it. There was handwriting on it, faded ink, and the edges were torn and bent from use and time. She tugged the pages from the book to read them.

The true ending of the woman with the crooked hand.

Daisy glanced at the hardbound books in the trunk, then looked back to the papers in her hand. The true ending? A thrill rippled through her. There was another ending to the story that was unpublished? Madame Tremblay's readers would be delighted to know this. But there was something else that piqued her curiosity. If fiction were based in truth, then perhaps Madame had penned certain pieces of the story that were never meant to be seen by the public. Pieces that would explain the phantom woman of today and provide the answers to the mysteries of Castle Moreau . . .

Daisy leaned back against the wall, holding the pages so

she could see them in the golden light of the lantern she'd brought with her.

Growing up so desolate and alone changed me in ways no child should be changed . . .

The Girl

*G*rowing *up so desolate and alone changed me in ways no child should be changed. A young woman should have her mother present, and if not her mother, a matronly figure to guide her first steps into the larger world. At sixteen, I was a young woman now, though I understood little of the outside world—the world outside the castle walls.*

Papa was rarely at home anymore, having taken to traveling the river, exploring, trading, losing sight of his self-made wealth and returning to the roots he'd first planted in the wilds.

This left me alone. To teach myself to grow into adulthood under the watchful eyes of a cook, a housemaid, a housekeeper, and a groundskeeper.

It left me alone to spend ten years accustomed to the regular visits from the woman with the crooked hand. With time, her tales grew less terrifyingly fantasized and instead became more horrifically true.

As I aged, she regaled me with the story of her childhood as a young girl, chained in the cellar at night when her master and mistress were abed. A bond servant, she had been all but sold to her master and mistress at the age of ten, and by the time she'd reached eighteen, she had experienced the quick end of a whip, the harsh slap of her master's belt, and the back of her mistress's hand many times. On fulfillment of her obligations, she told me how she ran away with the stableman's son to begin a new life. One that would free her of the bruises and beatings she had endured for eight long years.

I remember the woman telling me more stories of atrocities she experienced at the hand of her husband. No longer the hero she had hoped he might be but instead a monster who did heinous things.

I recall her scars on her wrists and arms. She showed me the long, thick scar on the side of her face where her husband had, in a drunken state, dragged his blade across her flesh to mark her as his own.

Now I was sixteen. This castle was my own sort of prison, the darkness inside of it gentle in comparison to the life led by the woman with the crooked hand.

We had learned to exist with each other. As I grew older, she was no longer the enigma she had been when I was a child. Instead, she was simply the woman with the crooked hand who had met my own mother one day at the market. Who had taken the offer of escape when my mother had told her of the hidden rooms behind the walls of the castle, with the aid of the housekeeper whose own silence all these years resonated with me, both in anger and in gratitude. These hidden passageways my mother had designed were rooms not even my papa knew existed, for it was my mother who had given the builders instructions of what she wished the castle to be. Rooms that were meant for my own maman's escape—to be alone, out of sight.

I became very aware that my maman's absence had been sharply felt by more than just Papa and myself. I became aware that Papa may not be all I believed him to be but instead someone my maman felt she needed respite from.

Maman was a kindred spirit with this woman who hid in our walls to free herself from her abuser, who now grieved the loss of the woman who had given her refuge. On Maman's death, she took it upon herself to watch over me more closely than she had before. In payment of debt to my dead mother. Though she knew only stories of brutal life and frightening things, the woman with the crooked hand had tried to be what my maman could no longer be. A guardian.

March is a wicked month in this part of the world. When one experiences a day with the breath of warmth, followed by a day with brutal ice and snow. It was on a day such as that when I realized I had not seen the woman with the crooked hand the night before. Knowing the secrets of the castle walls, I took it upon myself for the first time to go to her.

I found her that day looking pale and ghostly, her eyes staring vacantly at the wall, her body still and hard. Perhaps it was age that had introduced her to death, or perhaps it was fear that had finally enveloped her and stolen from her the last vapor of breath.

What does one do with a dead woman the world believes does not even exist?

I left her there. On the stone floor, surrounded by stone walls. It was where she had lived for a decade, and it was where she would remain.

One day I may visit her again, to wrap her bones in something soft and warm. To hide her safely away for eternity. But for now, at sixteen, I determined to leave her there and close the walls that few knew existed.

She would no longer speak fear into my world with good intent, but instead she would leave it for me to inherit. To warn other women through story that wickedness lurks, but hidden in the words was a secret. A clue. To escape to the Castle Moreau. Each story called to the downtrodden, to the woman who had no place to find freedom. In every story the woman with the crooked hand ever told me, it always ended with the words, "Beauty is found in walls of stone, beauty where love begins."

Hidden among the travesties and nightmares of violence, all the abused must know that of this place. Only they would recognize the words for what they were. For only the broken are searching for a place to heal.

The woman with the crooked hand had left behind terrible stories that must be retold, for in them redemption could be found. She had left behind a duty to be carried on.

La femme fantôme was dead, but I was very much alive.

thirty-six

Daisy

1871

Daisy stared at the last handwritten words on the page: *La femme fantôme was dead . . .*

If what she had read was true, then Madame had left the phantom woman in these very walls when she was yet a young girl. The phantom woman would have been the first woman to vanish at Castle Moreau, stolen away from abusers by Madame's own mother. The woman with the crooked hand was not, as Madame's novel implied, evil and a harbinger of death. She was in need, and her life had given her nothing but the knowledge of horrors. Castle Moreau had given her hope.

Daisy lifted her eyes to stare at the trunks. Did the clothes inside them at one time belong to the phantom woman? They were different sizes, so they couldn't all be hers. And their styles and cuts, the fabric of many of them, were too recent to be made sixty or so years ago.

She was holding in her hands solid evidence that the

woman with the crooked hand had been real, a part of Madame Tremblay's early years. She was now most certainly dead. Was her body still behind the walls, or had Madame—as implied in her writing—returned to inter the woman's bones in a way that was more dignified, to honor her as the years progressed? Either way, Castle Moreau had become a tomb the moment the phantom woman had died.

Daisy shivered and pushed to her knees. She must put the pages back where she'd found them. That she had read them felt as though she had pried into the private diary of Madame, and yet, in her soul, she could not be angry at herself for doing so.

Daisy shut the lid on the trunk with a gentle motion. According to the writing, there were lots more passageways, a virtual maze within the castle walls. Madame's mother had made it so, fabricating a plan of mystery known only by a few, perhaps foreseeing she would one day use them to hide a desperate woman from a vicious world, and not just herself from Ora Moreau's father.

The lamplight flickered and cast eerie shadows on the walls. Daisy heard a clink, and the sound startled her from her musings. She would be missed soon if she remained here. It was time to take her leave. But she would return to this hidden place. She *must* return. Somehow she knew these passageways, these secrets of the phantom woman's life, reached into the present. Touched the lives of Hester May and Elsie, perhaps the other women as well.

Daisy hurried to the narrow door, which she had closed behind her on entering. She raised the lantern with her left hand so the light would cast ahead of her and lead the way back to the servants' quarters. The lamplight stretched before her as she pulled the door open.

There on the other side stood the phantom woman! She was cloaked and hooded, her face a flash of white.

Daisy froze, every fiber in her taut like the strings of a violin. She could utter no sound other than a high-pitched whine, shaky with fear.

"I said to leave us alone." The woman's voice was monotone, and she had no expression other than a small trace of condemnation.

Daisy stared at her. The woman looked very real and alive. Very *not* a ghost. And yet . . . Daisy glanced at the trunks. The phantom woman had died decades ago. In these walls, yes, and here she was now. How was it possible for a spirit to appear so alive?

The moment was shrouded in a sense of dread that paralyzed Daisy. She could neither move nor speak. Instead, her eyes locked with the deep pools of the phantom woman's. Pools of dark blue lined with black.

"You will ruin everything," the phantom woman said as she took a step forward, which made Daisy stumble backward into the little room.

The woman followed and shut the door behind them, and then a thin smile stretched across her face. An unfriendly smile that was laden with ill will, with wickedness.

"Welcome to the Castle Moreau, *mon chéri*. Where lonely women come to die."

thirty-seven

Cleo

PRESENT DAY

She had to get out. Cleo stumbled through the store and out the front door onto the sidewalk. A passerby gave her an odd look, but she didn't care. The reality of finding the bones of the infamous woman with the crooked hand was one shock to the system. But the other was the realization that the woman's body had lain there, encased in velvet and protected in a trunk, for generations! And no one knew who she was. Where she came from. There was nothing but the story told by Madame Ora Moreau, the writer, who had penned a tale of horror in which, in the end, the woman with the crooked hand consumed the spirit of the girl who had grown into a young woman, and the woman continued to live within her, snuffing out the memories of the girl who once was.

That was a tale Cleo identified with too closely. It was why she now found herself leaning against the building, battling tears of dread and panic.

"Cleo?" Stasia stuck her head out the door of Dave's store. "You okay?"

"Yeah. Yeah, I'm fine." Cleo tried to gather the fragments of her emotions. She wiped her hands on her jeans to dry her sweaty palms.

Stasia's dark brows drew together. "Listen, I know Dave and my search for Anne has put a lot of pressure on you. I didn't mean—"

Cleo held up a hand. "It's okay. I get it. It's difficult for family to be separated without a good explanation."

Or when the one who was missing knew *why* they were missing and also knew that the family she had left behind would feel abandoned and betrayed, never understanding the intent that by her disappearing, they were being saved from further pain and trauma.

"I'll be back," Cleo said, deciding suddenly. She needed something—a Pepsi, a Coke, even a syrupy Mountain Dew would suffice. Her mouth was dry, her hands beginning to tremble with that familiar panic that she knew how to assuage but would hate herself for later.

Stasia reached out and touched her arm. "Do you want me to come with you?"

"No," Cleo said quickly. Too quickly. Stasia frowned. Cleo tried to reassure her. "No, I'll be fine. I just . . . today has been a lot to process."

"Yeah," Stasia agreed. "There's no doubt about that!"

"I'll be back in a bit." Cleo mustered a smile. It was enough to appease Stasia, who ducked back into the store.

Cleo started down the street, walking past gift shops, a health-food store, dodging a kid on a skateboard, and turning the corner toward the downtown park. She spotted a vending machine and steered toward it.

On arriving, Cleo dug into her pocket for some quarters.

She hadn't thought to grab her purse, but she usually had change because she always stuffed it in her jeans, being too lazy to open her wallet. Sure enough, she had quarters. She slid them into the machine, scanning the rows of options. What did it matter? It would be like this forever. Any flavor, any sip, would always remind her of what she wasn't drinking. It would always remind her of Grandpa. Of why he'd died. Of her own mistakes. Of why she'd left. It would always remind her of Riley.

Cleo jabbed at a button, not caring what beverage fell out for her to crack open. The clattering of the machine releasing met her ears, the can rolling into the delivery tray.

Grape? Fine. Grape soda it was.

Cleo snagged it and stepped away from the machine, popping open the top of the can and taking a long sip. A car pulled into the parking spot directly in front of the vending machine, so Cleo moved farther down the sidewalk to give the person space to make their purchase.

"Cleo?" The voice broke into her grape-soda stupor.

Cleo faced the woman, who had stepped out of the car and half hid behind her car door. She didn't recognize her. "Yes?"

"I was wondering if I could talk with you?" She was a pretty woman. In her late fifties if Cleo's gauge on looks was correct. Her hair was wavy and shoulder-length. There wasn't any gray—she must have dyed it the color of dark brown. Her eyes matched her hair. It was her face that gave her age away. It looked tired, and there were wrinkles at the corners of her eyes.

"Okay?" Cleo didn't move from her position on the sidewalk, and the women stayed a polite distance away, behind the car door.

"Word has it around Needle Creek that the authorities

removed human remains from the castle today." Her statement sent a thousand red flags up in Cleo's mind.

"No comment." She ducked her head and started walking away. A reporter? Some nosy conspiracy theorist? Deacon was right. This thing was going to blow up in their faces.

"Wait!" the woman cried. Cleo heard the car door slam shut, followed by heels clicking rapidly on the sidewalk. "Please." She grabbed for Cleo's arm, but Cleo skirted her attempt.

"I won't talk about it." Cleo tried to sound firm, hoping the woman would get the point. Instead, tears filled her eyes. There was urgency in the way she breathed as she glanced over her shoulder. Was she looking for someone?

"Was it Anne?" she asked.

Cleo stared at her, her fingers tightening around the soda can. "Excuse me?"

"I just need to know if it was Anne."

"Who are you?" Cleo looked around them. The street had several cars parked along it, and people milled about casually. They weren't alone. They were in public. There couldn't be much danger.

"Please. Can I buy you coffee?" The woman motioned toward a coffee shop.

Cleo, still uncomfortable, shook her head. "I'm sorry, but I—"

"Just tell me if it was Anne."

"I don't know if it was." Cleo didn't know why she lied. It would have been easier to say just that the bones were old and belonged to the real-life version of Madame Ora Moreau's popular fictionalized character. But she didn't.

The woman tilted her head to look into the sky, her chin quivering. She drew in a shuddering breath, crossing her arms around herself. "I was so hoping the tape would help you."

Cleo stilled. "The what?"

The woman met her eyes. "The cassette tape. And the package I sent to you. I was hoping . . . oh, I don't know what I was hoping. I-I just need closure, you know?" she added, her voice lowered. "And when I heard you telling that girl behind the counter in the gas station that you were going to work at Castle Moreau, it was like God dropped an opportunity into my lap. I've waited forty years for answers!"

"It was you who left the tape on my car and sent me Anne's shirt and poem?" Cleo vaguely remembered the other customer in the gas station, her first day in Needle Creek.

The woman nodded. "I'd been carrying the tape around for a long time—struggling to know what to do with it. Whether I should visit Detective Germaine or . . . or Anne's family. It was my original testimony, and I've carried that copy with me for years. I never knew what to do—"

"Are you Meredith?" Cleo thought she might be putting the puzzle pieces together in her mind.

The woman bit her lip and nodded. "But, please"—she held up a hand—"no one knows I'm back in Needle Creek. I've been here just a few months. And then you came and . . . it's like a nightmare all over again."

"Why did you give me those things?" Cleo needed more explanation.

Meredith pushed hair behind her ear as she considered her answer. "I-I guess I'd hoped you could see something I couldn't. Anne's poem, her T-shirt, I've kept them for years and I'm so tired. I wasn't always honest, but I don't know what happened to Anne that night. I promise you, I don't!"

Cleo sensed Meredith was telling the truth, even if she had been sketchy in her details as a teenager. "Anne's poem.

345

Why would that be significant? Your testimony on the tape
... your stories didn't match. We talked with Detective Germaine, and—"

"I know," Meredith interrupted. "But you have to understand how afraid I was."

"Afraid?"

Meredith nodded. "Yes. Did you read her poem? Anne
wanted to die. *She* wanted to die. That night she told me she
was going to run away or she'd end up killing herself. So I
ran after her, and then she . . . vanished."

"Why was Anne so upset?" Cleo ignored the can of grape
soda growing warm in her hand. "What made her run?"

Meredith was silent for a moment. Finally, she said, "Have
you ever been afraid of someone? Been afraid to go home?
Have you ever thought it'd be safer to run away than to stay?"

Cleo couldn't answer. Didn't know how to explain that,
yes, she did understand. She understood what it was like
when Grandpa turned violent. She understood what fear was
and how it grew inside of you until running seemed the only
escape. *Was* the only escape. Especially when you knew that
one day you too could become a monster. A product of the
environment in which you'd been raised because you knew
nothing different.

"Who was Anne afraid of?" Cleo asked quietly. For her
it was Grandpa—whom she also loved immensely. It was a
wicked cycle that made no sense and yet made all the sense
in the world.

Meredith swallowed hard. "People always thought I had
a rough life, being a foster kid. But it was Anne. Anne and
her perfect family—they weren't so perfect. *He* wasn't perfect at all."

"He?" Cleo felt that familiar rolling dread in her stomach. The truth that Anne wasn't much different from her.

That while Anne was willing to run from her abuser to save herself, Cleo was running away to save her sister from any potential wounds Cleo might one day, unintentionally, inflict on her.

"Kevin . . ." Meredith finally breathed the name. "He is Anne's brother. My old boyfriend. He was not a nice guy."

Perhaps it was against her better judgment, but Cleo agreed to get into Meredith's car and guide her toward Dave's shop a few blocks away. This was beyond anything she could address alone. If Meredith was finally coming forward after all these years with more information—with a potential suspect and motive behind Anne's disappearance—Cleo needed Dave. No, she needed Deacon. She wasn't about to approach this alone. Meredith wasn't a threat. She was desperate for answers, scared to be seen and have the town come back on her for Anne's disappearance, and she was aching to have a life of normalcy that wasn't marked by violence.

Oh, could Cleo relate. She sensed an instant connection with Meredith despite their age difference, and sadly she also felt connected to Anne Joplin. Today, Cleo had been a part of the first missing woman at Castle Moreau to be found, and now she was faced with finding the last woman to go missing. Maybe this was why God had brought her here. If anyone would understand the plight of a missing woman caught up in the cycle of abuse, Cleo could.

Meredith turned the car when Cleo advised her to. "I'm grateful, Cleo, that you're not pushing me away. I should talk to Detective Germaine. I need to find closure. And if I can't find Anne, I . . . I just need to know something. More than I do now."

"Why didn't you just approach me instead of being so

secretive? Just hand me the tape, the box of things? Ask me to help?" Cleo would have. She knew she wouldn't have been able to refuse Meredith.

They pulled in front of Dave's store.

Meredith shifted the car into park and gave Cleo a small smile. "I wasn't supposed to leave Needle Creek. Not during the investigation. But later I did. It'd been awhile, but I had to leave. People . . . didn't trust me. And I waited all these years to come back. I've been gun-shy, afraid of how I'll be received."

"But it wasn't your fault Anne was in trouble."

"No, it wasn't. But I was the last one to see her alive. I didn't always tell the truth. No one was going to believe me if I said anything about Kevin—about his abuse against Anne. I'd already caused too much trouble with stories about people in high school and not being truthful. I just ran too, I guess. And coming back, it's not easy to face your past, your worst fears—yourself."

Cleo needed to get out of the car. She fumbled for the door and shoved it open.

Just as Meredith called her name, Deacon burst from the store, jamming his baseball cap onto his dark curls. "We've gotta go!" He motioned to Dave and Stasia, who were on his heels. Dave made quick work of locking up the store.

"Where?" Cleo didn't like the edge in Deacon's voice.

"The castle." His gaze leveled on Cleo, and her heart clenched at the panic in his face. "It's my grandmother. She's in hysterics. Nurse Jenkins called. She's throwing things. She hit a cop. Now she's . . . they're afraid she's having a stroke."

Cleo told Meredith to start her car. "We're leaving."

Deacon eyed Meredith cautiously but quickly. "Who's she?"

"It's a long story," Cleo answered. And it was. Longer than even she realized. It stretched way back to the beginning of

Castle Moreau. To the phantom woman she'd glimpsed in the study that night. To her own story. To the story of Anne. To the story of women who had been hurt, could be hurt, *could* hurt. A cycle of abuse that never seemed to end.

She could understand why Virgie was in hysterics. Sometimes life was just too burdensome to maintain your sanity. Sometimes you needed a refuge but finding one could be elusive. Like trying to catch a cloud.

thirty-eight

"She's in here." Nurse Jenkins led them all into a corridor that Cleo hadn't yet ventured into. It was walled in stone, and they'd gone through the old castle's kitchen to get there. A pair of rooms were on either side, both void of furniture and of any piles of Virgie's collections.

"How did she get down here?" Deacon tried to understand what had happened while they were away.

"I don't know." Nurse Jenkins shook her head, leading the charge. "I've checked her vitals and they're all normal. Blood pressure is high, of course, because she's very agitated."

"Did you call an ambulance?" Deacon asked.

"Yes." Nurse Jenkins halted in front of a doorway that led into a small room. "She has stabilized, though, so while I think it best to have her taken to the hospital to be checked out more thoroughly, I don't feel the urgency as I did when I first called you. In fact"—Nurse Jenkins looked between them, Deacon, Cleo, Meredith, Dave, and Stasia, her mouth set in a serious line—"I think this is more emotionally and mentally driven. She is very upset."

"Yeah, me too," Deacon mumbled as he pushed past the

nurse into the room. Meredith, Dave, and Stasia hung back. Cleo could see the question on Dave's and Stasia's faces, and the looks they kept shooting toward Meredith. Cleo gave Meredith a weak smile, begging for patience from a woman who had waited decades to return to the grounds of Castle Moreau.

Virgie sat on a lone chair, her delicate body swaying back and forth. She was fixated on the wall, on the stone, her lips moving in a soundless plea.

"Grand-mère." Deacon crouched beside her.

"Take me home," Virgie whispered.

"You are home." He rested a hand gently on his grandmother's arm.

She shook her head, resignation oozing from her. "No. I'm tired. I can't do it anymore. They've taken her away. And she'll be next. It's all over. Everything. It's over."

Deacon shot Cleo a look of desperation and confusion. Cleo wished she had more to offer.

Noise in the hallway alerted them to the arrival of the paramedics. Nurse Jenkins spoke softly and firmly to them, and within moments, Deacon had been urged to step aside as they began to administer medical services to Virgie.

"I'm not ill!" Virgie tried to dislodge herself from their caring grasps. "I want to go home!"

Nurse Jenkins stepped in. "Virgie, we're going to help you. We'll get you home, but first I want to have you see a doctor. To help you."

"I don't need help," Virgie spat. Her wild gaze landed on Cleo. "You! You know. You found her. Don't let them look anymore. He told me to keep my things. Don't take them away."

Nurse Jenkins motioned to a paramedic, but Cleo couldn't fight the sudden compulsion to rush to Virgie and take her hand. When she did, Virgie's fingers gripped hers so tightly it pinched her skin. "Charles told me not to move anything. *Nothing*. All these years I've collected. I've stored. For a *reason*. To keep her hidden."

"The woman with the crooked hand?" Cleo bent over Virgie's prostrate form. A paramedic was strapping her onto a gurney, another wrapping a blood-pressure cuff around her arm.

Virgie's eyes lit up. "Yes! Yes, we've guarded her all these years. Ever since my grandmother wrote about her being true. The papers. The real story—I read them years ago. I saved them. They're in the wardrobe in my bedroom, along with all the other things."

Cleo looked up at Deacon and mouthed, "Do you know what she's talking about?"

He shook his head.

The EMTs were explaining something to Nurse Jenkins. The nurse touched Cleo's arm. "We need to get her on the ambulance. Her blood pressure is higher now, and I don't feel comfortable prolonging this."

Cleo nodded. A wild sense of protectiveness flooded her as she met Virgie's eyes, so pleading, so desperate, and so confused. "Virgie," she said, bending over the old woman, "we won't get rid of anything. Not without you here."

"But they took her!" Virgie whimpered.

"Yes, but they care. They're scientists, historians—they're professionals. They will take care of her remains."

Tears trailed down Virgie's wrinkled cheeks. "But what about the other one?"

Cleo drew back a bit, studying Virgie's face. "What other one? Are there more remains here in the castle?"

Virgie's chin quivered. The paramedics released the brake on the gurney and started to move it forward. Virgie grasped wildly for Cleo's hand, and it was as if no one were in the room but them.

"Castle Moreau is filled with remains. The memories. All of it. All of them. The stories are true, you know? I must protect them."

"The missing women?" Dave's voice sliced through the moment.

Virgie startled, and then a long whimper erupted from her lips. Then the EMTs took over, pushing her through the doorway, Deacon fast on their heels, followed by Nurse Jenkins. Cleo's glare slammed into Dave, and Stasia winced beside him, knowing that Dave's anxiety over his missing cousin Anne might have shut down an opportunity. Meredith stood still and not speaking in the corner, biting the tip of her fingernail.

"Is she talking about Anne?" Dave insisted, oblivious to the irritation welling within Cleo. Irritation that his impatience, while understandable, had only added to the confusion and hadn't relieved any of the intensity.

Overwhelmed by it all, Cleo pushed past them and hurried into the corridor. She needed to think. To breathe. It was all too close to home, to her heart, and yet it was so foreign and so removed at the same time. All Cleo could think about was the tears that had streamed down Virgie's face, how they'd matched her own. The tears of women who acted as protectors over what they believed was theirs to guard, theirs to shelter. However misguided or wrong that might be, they did it out of love. And sometimes, protective love was heartbreaking.

Cleo thought of Virgie's words—*wardrobe, papers, truth*—as she wound her way through the castle, not caring whether she was supposed to be there or not. Maybe the entire place was supposed to be evacuated until the forensics team was finished. Were they planning to search the castle for more human remains? With its reputation over the decades, it wouldn't surprise her.

Still. Cleo had to go there. She had to go to Virgie's room, to the wardrobe she claimed held the truth of the woman's bones that had been found behind the castle wall. Truth of the women—whoever they were, whatever decade they were from. If it helped Dave and his obsessive search for Anne Joplin, so be it. If it gave Meredith the answers and closure she needed, that would be wonderful.

But for now, Cleo did this for herself and Virgie alone. For their broken pieces that were so raw, the world they lived in made little sense, and the worlds they'd created to build a protective fortress around them were crumbling.

She pushed open the door to Virgie's bedroom. It was quiet. Clean. Crowded with all of Virgie's things, but not filthy or even depressing to Cleo anymore. This room was Virgie's haven. With her bed surrounded by stacks of boxes, piles of books, a lamp, a pillow, and a water bottle. Cleo couldn't blame her for wanting to be boxed in by things to feel safe. The castle was vast, cold, but here? Here it felt manageable.

Cleo scanned the room and saw the wardrobe Virgie had mentioned. Climbing over some crates, she managed to get to it. The doors weren't blocked by anything, which was a bit surprising. Cleo toyed with the latch to access the wardrobe.

Unlocked, it opened easily, and she observed its strange, disconcerting contents: a moth-eaten black silk dress that had to be from the turn of the last century. A box on the floor was filled with antique brooches, handkerchiefs, and more current items like a Ronald Reagan campaign button from the 1980s and a friendship bracelet with a basketball charm hanging from it. What was all this stuff? It wasn't the sort of collection Virgie would hoard. There were no books or magazines or figurines. They were . . . Cleo's chest felt heavy with the realization of it. They were belongings—*others'* belongings. Little treasures that had been gathered as mementos. Mementos of the lives Castle Moreau had stolen.

A book lay on the wardrobe's floor. One of Madame Ora Moreau's classics, with a sheaf of old papers stuck between its pages. Cleo pulled them out carefully, the paper feeling fragile in her hand. She skimmed the words. Her heart slammed against her chest as she read the old words. Words that must have been penned by Ora Moreau herself. A story of abuse, of escape, of refuge.

Perplexed, Cleo looked around her, searching for something, anything that might bring clarity to the history of Castle Moreau. She jumped when the bedroom door closed firmly. Cleo couldn't see the door because of the stacks of boxes in the way. She clenched the story of the phantom woman in her hand.

"Deacon?"

No answer. Just a shuffling sound. Conflicting emotions roiled within her. She wanted to run, but at the same time she wondered if she hid herself in the wardrobe, maybe she would get some answers. Answers that might force a horrible truth into the light.

"Who's there?" Cleo heard the quaver in her voice. She took a tentative step forward, then froze.

More movement around the boxes. A cloak, a hooded figure, and then she was standing there. The phantom woman. The vision of the woman Cleo had seen that night in the study. Only in the daylight, she was real. She was alive. And she was very much a vision of Anne Joplin.

thirty-nine

Daisy

1871

Daisy pressed herself against the wall, into the cold stone as the hooded woman approached her. That she was real was quite evident. The woman blinked, and breathed, and eyed Daisy with a look that curled into Daisy's soul, terrifying her into a paralyzed state.

"You should not have come." Her voice grated with a controlled anger that chilled Daisy. The narrow room left only feet between them. Daisy could sense warmth emanating from the woman's body. Ghosts were not warm. This woman was as real as she was.

"I—" Daisy tried to speak but didn't know what to say.

"You were never supposed to be here. Never supposed to look in places you weren't meant to find."

"Please, I . . ." Again, Daisy tried to speak.

The hooded woman lurched forward, her fingers curling around Daisy's throat, pushing her into the wall. "Go. Away."

Daisy nodded, clawing at the woman's hand, choking as her fingers dug into her skin.

"Go away from here and never come back." The woman's breath washed over Daisy's face. Tears sprang to Daisy's eyes for lack of breath. She struggled, trying to free herself from the grip that threatened to take the very life from her body.

She was going to die? Here? Within the walls of Castle Moreau? This was how it was then. A stranger. A woman. Strangling until they were no more. That was how the women had vanished.

Daisy kicked, connecting with the woman's shin. It didn't seem to faze her. There was fear in her eyes accompanying the anger. Daisy realized then that the woman was afraid of *her*. This was not a murderous intent to kill based on a sick desire to take life from another. It was self-preservation. It was an attempt to stay alive herself, the hooded woman, and keep her existence a secret and ensure that no one threatened her ever again.

"I'm sorry," the woman whispered, pressing her lips against Daisy's ear. "I don't believe you will leave on your own." Her fingers tightened on Daisy's throat. Daisy whimpered as she dug her nails into the woman's flesh, then realized it did little to stop the woman.

Daisy's vision clouded.

She was going to die.

Here in Castle Moreau.

And then she, too, would vanish.

Cleo

No. It couldn't be Anne Joplin. The resemblance to the picture in the old newspaper clipping was uncanny, but this woman was older. Her eyes were clear and lucid, but her hair was curlier. Shorter. She wore the cloak like a blanket, trying to stay warm. There was no expression on her face to tell Cleo if she was a friend or a foe.

"It's all over." The woman sounded defeated. Accepting. Perhaps a bit relieved.

Cleo held Ora Moreau's pages to her chest as if somehow they would provide protection. "Anne?" It was impossible. But in her stunned mind, Cleo did the math and remembered Anne Joplin would no longer look like a nineteen-year-old. She would be Meredith's age. In her fifties. But if this were Anne, then Anne was not dead. Not at all.

"Is that who you think I am?"

Cleo returned her stare, stepping back a step just in case the woman decided to launch forward and assault her. She didn't feel like the woman would, but nothing in Castle Moreau was ever as it seemed.

"I don't know who you are—not for sure," Cleo said.

The woman turned to the wardrobe and stretched her arm out, pointing at the items. "All those mementos. It's appalling, isn't it? The blood, the fear . . ." The sentence hung in the air unfinished.

"W-whose are they?" Cleo stuttered. Maybe if she kept the woman talking, she could find a way to escape. To get help. Deacon was probably gone with Virgie in the ambulance. But law enforcement was still in the castle itself! Not to mention Dave and Stasia and Meredith. Just one chance, to run, to get away, to—

"Did you know many women have gone missing from Castle Moreau since the day it was built?" the woman asked, her voice holding a hint of resignation.

Cleo nodded. She saw movement behind the woman. Murphy, her cat. The long-haired feline was bristled as it came up behind the stranger. Sniffing, his whiskers twitching at the unfamiliar being in the room.

"And now? It is all over. Finally. You ended it when you found her bones."

"I'm . . . sorry?" Cleo didn't know if the woman wanted her to be sorry or not. Murphy was crouching, his backside higher than his head, the tip of his tail twitching.

The woman stared at her then. Not responding. Not answering. Her eyes took on a distant look, one that could be either growing fury or growing sadness.

Cleo didn't have time to consider for long. Murphy, in all his feline suspicion, pounced, wrapping his paws around the woman's ankle and setting his teeth in her skin. She shrieked, more from surprise than pain, but it gave Cleo the opportunity she needed.

Shoving past the woman, she yelled for help as she plunged into the hallway. It was time for the rumors of Castle Moreau to end.

Daisy

She could hear the woman breathing, but she couldn't see her anymore. Daisy felt her legs giving way as the air was cut from her throat by the deadly woman. She began to sink, her back scraping against the wall. Here is where she would meet God. Face-to-face. Oh, there were worse endings, but she'd thought she could escape life first and live a new one. Death was not something she was ready for. Not yet. Not beneath the clawlike grip of a phantom woman who was no more a phantom than Daisy was.

"Stop!" A commanding voice filled the room as the door slammed open.

Instantly, the hooded woman's hand released. Daisy sucked in air, filling her lungs again. Awareness flooded her, even while she dropped onto a trunk, too weak to remain on her feet.

"What are you doing?" The newcomer's voice filled the room and addressed the woman. "Are you mad? Will you become what you hate?"

"I'm sorry." The hooded woman's tone took on a note of submission, of regret. It trembled.

Daisy's eyes came into focus, and she gazed in shock at Madame, who stood beside the woman with a censuring glare.

"Madame?" Daisy coughed, her throat sore. She raised her hand to the base of her neck, massaging the skin that would be bruised.

Madame Tremblay looked between them and then her gaze settled on the woman. "Explain yourself."

"I merely wanted to protect the castle—"

"Protect?" Madame was shrill and furious. "Protect the very place that saved you by murdering, the very act you yourself tried to escape?"

"I didn't know. I'm sorry . . . I don't why, I-I was just afraid. That it would all come to ruin. That you, that Festus, that *I* would be found. If they find me, they'll kill me." Tears cascaded down the hooded woman's face now, the signs of wickedness and confidence erased by helpless fear.

Madame assessed her, then eyed Daisy, who watched with both fascination and terror. "Now you know," she stated baldly.

Daisy didn't know, but she remained silent.

Madame continued, "Hester May has been hiding here at Castle Moreau. She makes our meals in Festus's kitchen in his quarters behind the stables. She has not wanted to leave Castle Moreau, not like the others."

"The others?" Daisy managed.

Madame pursed her lips. "If you read my pages—which I can tell you did—you know when I was a child my mother helped a woman with a deformity escape her abusers."

Daisy nodded.

Madame narrowed her eyes, obviously displeased it had all come to this moment. "It is something I continue. There are women who need me. Who need Castle Moreau to escape to—as a refuge when no one else will come to their aid."

Realization filled Daisy with a different kind of horror. She had envisioned everything backward, and her accusations were unfounded, as the truth was based in goodness, not evil. She lifted her gaze to her would-be strangler. "You're Hester May?"

Elsie would be so relieved!

Daisy spun her attention back to Madame. "Where is Elsie?"

Madame pursed her lips as if she didn't owe Daisy an explanation but knew she must give one anyway. "She is with her aunt as originally intended. When you brought her here wounded, Hester May determined to help her friend heal. We then contacted her aunt, who arranged transport for Elsie."

"Why not tell me?" Daisy tried to comprehend.

Hester May managed to speak. "We did not want you to know I was here. Elsie needed . . . her aunt is safe, but her brother—it is better for her to be with her aunt. Safely. Quietly. Needle Creek will believe Elsie disappeared. Her brother will believe Elsie disappeared. Her aunt will never tell and will make sure Elsie is safe."

Madame broke into Hester May's explanation. "Elsie was in the trap in the woods after her brother left her there. He wanted her to die there. That's why he went away on the river. He won't be back. But when you found Elsie, she was terrified. Terrified to tell you the truth, and since she didn't know the truth about Castle Moreau, or of Hester May already taking refuge here from her abusers, this place frightened Elsie."

Daisy meditated on the information. Elsie was safe. She was where she'd wanted to go. She was . . . Daisy jerked her attention to Hester May. "And you remain here?"

"Yes," Hester May answered. "I help aid Madame Tremblay and the women who read her words and the clues in her story and flee here—to Castle Moreau—for a way of escape. Of hope. I'm sorry, I was overcome with . . . I was afraid you would ruin it all. That Castle Moreau would no longer be a refuge for women wishing to escape their lives. There is no place for women like us, no safe place. Not unless you have Castle Moreau and the Moreau-Tremblay family to aid you to a new life. I couldn't let you . . ." Hester May broke off in a sob, her fingers pressing against her mouth. She was pale at the thought of what her instinct had caused her to do.

Madame warily looked between them. "It is known now.

Hester May, you must control the demons inside you that make you lash out. It is all you knew, but it is not what you should become."

Hester May nodded.

Madame leveled a look on Daisy. "And you—you must decide. Will you keep the secret of Castle Moreau?"

Cleo

She flew to the balcony, to the stairs. Officers below alerted to her screams. Dave, Stasia, and Meredith looked up startled as Cleo raced down the stairs. She caught a glimpse of Deacon—who apparently had not gone with his grandmother—rushing toward her. He grabbed her arms as Cleo wildly flung hers to point behind her. She was out of breath, and her words came in gasps.

"A woman—upstairs—in the east wing!"

"What are you talking about?" Deacon frowned.

"Tell us what happened." An officer was by her side, his concern evident.

"There's a woman upstairs!" was all she could say.

Confusion reigned for a moment, and then Meredith let out a wild shout from the bottom of the stairs. "Anne!"

The entire vast room fell silent as eyes turned to the woman on the balcony.

"Anne?" It was Meredith again, this time questioning, doubting what she was seeing.

Anne removed the hood from her head, allowing it to fall back onto her shoulders. A sad smile stretched across her face.

Dave rushed forward, then stopped, as if surprise kept him from being able to move.

"Now you know," Anne said, looking and sounding weary. "I'm the secret of Castle Moreau."

forty

It was true. Anne Joplin had been at Castle Moreau since the night she'd disappeared. It had been part of her plan, she explained, as they gathered on the lawn outside the castle. She had met Virgie's husband when he tended her at the medical clinic, filling prescriptions for her. When the abuse from her brother came to light, it was then he had offered Anne a way out. Through Castle Moreau. Through the tried-and-true system that had made the castle a place of refuge for the abused, but a place of mystery and darkness for those who didn't know.

"I didn't intend for you to be a part of it, Meredith." Anne's look toward her friend was apologetic. "When you followed me into the woods that night, I had to . . . to vanish. To leave you behind."

Meredith's face expressed sadness and understanding simultaneously.

Anne swung her head around to address the rest of the group. "And then Virgie insisted I stay, as I had nowhere else to go. I became a part of Virgie and Charles's lives. They had no family"—she glanced at Deacon—"no family who visited anyway. I grew to love them—as parents, and when Charles was passing away, he encouraged Virgie to keep collections. I promised to stay with her. To care for her and to continue the legacy of Castle Moreau. All of Virgie's hoarding, well . . . the more that was in the castle, the less likely people would look, dig around, try to uncover the past. It wasn't until you came, Cleo, that I went back to hiding in the secret passage-ways. I've tended to Virgie all these years. Virgie is—" Anne paused, collecting herself before continuing—"everything to me. You may think it lonely that I've stayed at Castle Moreau all these years, but the peace here, the hope, the belonging . . . it's everything I ever wanted," Anne finished with a choked sob.

"But why not tell me?" Meredith wiped tears from her face, having shared a long embrace but now understandably hurt. "I loved you. I *ran* with you, thinking I was helping, and you just disappeared."

Anne's face fell in a regretful expression. "I know. But if I reached out, it would only unveil Castle Moreau. For over a century, it has protected women. And the madame of the castle has protected the women. I couldn't risk show-ing myself. On occasion a woman will reach out to us. She will have met someone from years before—even before me— who was saved by Castle Moreau. Virgie and I have helped several escape their abusers—we are a place of hope. Even some secretive agencies who assist women know of Castle Moreau. As it is, now that it's known . . . the story of Castle Moreau ends."

"But does it have to?" Deacon asked. There was amaze-ment in his voice, perhaps from the understanding that the history of the castle was more precious than anyone had ever imagined. That the perceived evil was merely a façade for a place of rescue.

"What do you mean?" Anne raised her eyes to meet his.

Deacon gave a broad smile. "We may not be able to help women in secret anymore, but we can partner with the organizations who do that. We can open the doors of Castle Moreau to women who need refuge. A place to start again. A place to find freedom."

Hope spread across Anne's face. She grabbed Meredith's hand, reaching also for Dave's.

Stasia stared at them and whispered, "My relative, Elsie Stockley—she must have been one of Castle Moreau's rescued women." The story had not evolved in a way any of them had fathomed.

Cleo held her arms around herself, standing off to the side. Deacon's vision for Castle Moreau was so beautiful, it brought tears to her eyes. Yet all she could see was her grandfather's message to "come home." Still, she knew with stark reality that he was dead. There was nothing mysterious in the note. Not really. Only one person could have forged it. One person who knew Cleo wouldn't be able to ignore her grandfather's request for her to return home.

It had to be Riley.

"I can't do it." Cleo pressed her phone into Deacon's hand. It had been a week since the reveal of Castle Moreau. A week since Anne had been discovered. Virgie had returned home, her mood more peaceful and content. A plan was already in motion for Anne to help Virgie go through her things. Deacon had engaged Stephen regarding the Moreau-Tremblay estate's interest in converting Castle Moreau into a safe haven for battered and abused women and their children.

There was only one thing left on Deacon's list of things to do. Cleo cast him a desperate look. "I can't."

"You know Riley sent you that letter."

Cleo nodded in admission.

Deacon tugged on her hand and pulled her into a warm embrace. She hadn't expected this bond to form between them. It was a fairy-tale dream if she stepped back and viewed it from the outside. But for now, she rested there.

Deacon nestled his chin on top of her head. She could feel the vibration in the rumble of his voice as he spoke. "You're past the statute of limitations on a hit and run. You can't be charged any longer. My lawyer said if there is anything that comes up, we'll get it taken care of."

"But the dog—"

Deacon's sigh silenced her. "It was a dog. Heartbreaking, yes, but be thankful it wasn't the child." He pulled away and placed his palms on her cheeks, urging her to look into his golden gaze. "You are not your grandfather, Cleo."

"I don't want to be," she whispered hoarsely, "but I'm frightened."

"You won't be alone in your struggle." There was promise in Deacon's words. "I'm not going anywhere." He swept his lips over her forehead. "We'll get you what you need professionally to gain healing and confidence. God didn't bring you here by accident, Cleo. It's so obvious this was meant to be your place of refuge too."

"But how . . . how did Riley ever find me?" Deacon had already, with Cleo's permission, paved the way and reached out to Riley and her grandmother. Now it was her turn.

Cleo inhaled the scent of Deacon Tremblay. She'd never imagined in her wildest dreams that such a man would hold her in his embrace. But more than that, she'd never imagined that hope could absolve a lifetime of disappointment.

Deacon answered her question. "Riley saw a photo of us online. The paparazzi snuck in the woods and snapped our picture. She knew it was you. She believed the only way to get you to come back to her was to make it look like your grandfather was calling for you."

"That's so Riley." Cleo gave a watery chuckle. "She's all imagination and intrigue."

"Well, it worked."

Cleo looked up at Deacon. "I don't want to ruin her life. I-I don't trust myself. I don't trust that what I know won't be my instinct."

"We weren't ever meant to trust ourselves. That's a lie, as evidenced by my own life and my own past. It is only by God's grace that we maneuver through this frightening world." Deacon reached up and tucked her hair behind her ear, his fingers warm and comforting. "Call your sister. Start your life anew. Fresh. I'll be here. I'm not going anywhere. Neither is Castle Moreau."

For the first time since—well, since forever—Cleo felt the relief that she wasn't alone wash through her. There were no promises she'd not make mistakes. But now there was support. Deacon's lips pressed against her forehead. She closed her eyes and reached for her phone. She would call Riley. She would find healing. *They* would find healing.

There was hope. There was a future. And there was Castle Moreau.

Daisy

What more could she do or say?

Daisy approached Lincoln, who was sitting by the window. He didn't look at her, but his words sliced through the thick air between them.

"So you know." It was a statement.

Daisy nodded.

He turned, his eyes filled with apology. "I have lived here many years. I have watched Grand-mère protecting women while crafting herself to look like a villain."

"Why?" Daisy asked in earnest.

Lincoln smiled a bit sadly. "Because the more monsters there are to scare people away from Castle Moreau, the safer we will be."

"And you were afraid I would not keep it safe?" Daisy breathed.

Lincoln looked torn. His jaw worked back and forth before he answered. "Sitting in this chair, sometimes I feel as though . . . well, the truth is, we cannot do this alone. My grandmother needs help. I was praying whoever answered my advertisement would be a woman of empathy, someone who would understand, who would *feel* the pain and the need to rescue others."

"I do." Daisy nodded as she reached for his hand.

Lincoln took her hand and pulled her ever so gently toward him, and she came, lowering herself into his lap in an act of boldness. Surprise spread across his face. Surprise and also delight.

Daisy leaned in, lifting her hand to his face. "You are a hero to your grandmother—to these women. You guard the castle."

"Guard it with me. We can continue here under the shroud of Castle Moreau. It can be our refuge in the world." He drew her face toward his. There was pleasure in his eyes, the kind that spoke of need, of loneliness, of a tie between them. A purpose. A shared brokenness. A unified hope in a holy fight against evil. Against fear.

"Guard Castle Moreau with me," he whispered against her lips.

Daisy could breathe only one word. One promise. One conviction she now held with her whole soul. "Always."

The Girl

I'm an old woman now. There are many things I've done in life I am not proud of. One would think I would look back and be honored by the acclaim, proud of my success, and raise my chin with confidence.

But all of it is nothing compared to what the woman with the crooked hand taught me. She taught me that fear will always be a part of us. Sometimes we will glory in it because it heightens our senses, engages our emotions, and entertains our imaginations. Mostly, though, we will seek to avoid it at all costs, and pray it never touches our lives.

Fear is never-ending. It will always be there. But as the woman with the crooked hand showed me, we can also learn to live in spite of it. Love in spite of it.

I would be nothing without her. A motherless child with no one to watch over her. She was not ideal, nor was she schooled in mothering. She did her best, and in doing so, protected me, just as my mother protected her.

It is what, as women, God has designed us to do—to watch out and care for one another. A sisterhood that is greater than fear, and a holy strength that conquers evil.

I learned this because of her.

La femme fantôme.

Author's Note

Words fall short when I consider the abuses suffered in the world since the beginning of time. This story is for the ones whose hearts are breaking. There is a refuge. Reach for it. Begin your journey of escape. Be brave, dear hearts, and find courage in the mighty power of God.

National Domestic Violence Hotline: 800-799-7233

Questions for Discussion

1. With Dave's vintage store of old electronic devices, the reader visited the days of cassette tapes and static recordings. What's the oldest type of device you've ever used to access music? What were your favorite recordings on that device?

2. Before reading *The Vanishing at Castle Moreau*, when someone mentioned a castle, what aspects of such a building would you have thought of? In what ways would your answer change because of this novel?

3. What about Castle Moreau suggested it was a dangerous place? Did your view of it change as you read the story?

4. Both heroines, Cleo and Daisy, had questionable backgrounds that led them to the doors of Castle Moreau. How did Cleo's and Daisy's lives and their spiritual journeys parallel? How were they different?

5. Did you relate more to Cleo or Daisy? Why?

6. As you read about the woman with the disfigured

hand, who did you think she might be? How did you believe she would influence the ending?

7. In what ways were the two grandsons alike? In what ways were they different from each other?

8. What did the two grandmothers' responses to life teach you about the repercussions of the choices each of us makes?

9. Why do you think one of them became a writer? Why did the other hoard?

10. What was the main spiritual insight you gained from *The Vanishing at Castle Moreau*?

Acknowledgments

There are always too many people to list who make these stories possible. Imagine trying to accomplish anything in life by yourself, and then surround yourself with experts, friends, people who love you, geniuses, savvy-minded individuals, creatives, and consider the outcome when you have that tribe behind you.

To name just a few of my "tribe," so many thanks go to my peeps at Bethany House and Baker Publishing Group. To say you're "involved" in the process is a wild understatement. To my editors, Rochelle Gloege and Luke Hinrichs, you both take my brain dump of a muddle story, mix around, create rainbows (somehow), and then *voilà*, we have a book that's readable! To my marketing team, Raela Schoenherr (also known as my prior editor because that girl can wear all the hats!), Anne Van Solkema, Joyce Perez, Rachael Wing, you ladies are "Jaime's Angels"—only without the feathery bangs and seventies-style go-go boots, 'cause . . . yeah, no. To my agent, Janet Kobobel Grant, who weathers my lapses of communication and then my onslaught tsunami of updates and questions when I come up for air.

On the home front, as usual, the humans I live with declare their allegiance daily, as evidenced by burnt eggs and bacon, overly watery soup, and the all-time favorite fallback: cold cereal. Also, a very special shout-out to CoCo and Peter Pan, who have perfected the eye-rolls and exasperated sighs when I snap back, "What? I'm trying to write!" to their incessant preteen questions. Homeschooling has been an adventure. Apologies in advance if you master creative writing and nothing else.

As for friends, so many have come and gone, but there are those who stick closer than a brother—that's biblical, folks. Tracee Chu, fine, you can be first, that way you'll stop asking if you're the most important. Sue Poll, because you're pretty much on text speed dial. And Tim, who, while he isn't really part of the conversation, still has to deal with me as the significant other in his wife's life. Natalie Walters, Anne Love, Jessica Patch, Pepper Basham, Christen Krumm, and all my other writing pals spread across the nation like a glorious plague of words and imagination.

And finally, a special note to my writing sister, Kara Isaac. How would I have navigated grief without you? I'd rather not have shared this journey, but since it's the one chosen for us, I'm grateful you've been there.

Jaime Jo Wright is a winner of the Christy, Daphne du Maurier, and INSPY Awards and is a Carol Award finalist. She's also the *Publishers Weekly* and ECPA bestselling author of three novellas. Jaime lives in Wisconsin with her cat named Foo; her husband, Cap'n Hook; and their littles, Peter Pan and CoCo. Visit her at jaimewrightbooks.com.

Look for Jaime Jo Wright's next book
in the fall of 2023!

The Lost Boys
of Barlowe Theater

Keep up to date with all of Jaime's releases
at jaimewrightbooks.com
and on Facebook, Instagram, and Twitter.

Sign Up for
Jaime's Newsletter

Keep up to date with
Jaime's latest news on book releases
and events by signing up for her email
list at jaimewrightbooks.com.

FOLLOW JAIME ON SOCIAL MEDIA!

Jaime Jo Wright   @jaimejowright   @jaimejowright

More from Jaime Jo Wright

In 1910, rural healer Perliett Van Hilton is targeted by a superstitious killer and must rely on the local doctor and an intriguing newcomer for help. Over a century later, Molly Wasziak is pulled into a web of deception surrounding an old farmhouse. Will these women's voices be heard, or will time silence their truths forever?

The Premonition at Withers Farm

Wren Blythe enjoys life in the Northwoods, but when a girl goes missing, her search leads to a shocking discovery shrouded in the lore of the murderess Ava Coons. Decades earlier, the real Ava struggles with the mystery of her past—all clues point to murder. Both will find that, to save the innocent, they must face an insidious evil.

The Souls of Lost Lake

In search of her father's lost goods, Adria encounters an eccentric old woman who has filled Foxglove Manor with dangerous secrets that may cost Adria her life. Centuries later, when the senior residents of Foxglove under her care start sharing chilling stories of the past, Kailey will have to risk it all to banish the past's demons, including her own.

On the Cliffs of Foxglove Manor

You May Also Like . . .

In 1911, Europe's strongest woman, Mabel MacGinnis, loses everything she's ever known and sets off for America in hopes of finding the mother she's just discovered is still alive. When circus aerialist Isabella Moreau's daughter suddenly appears, she is forced to face the truth of where, and in what, she derives her worth.

The Weight of Air by Kimberly Duffy
kimberlyduffy.com

Popular podcaster and ex-reporter Faith Byrne has made a name for herself telling stories of greatness after tragedy—but her real life does not mirror the stories she tells. When she's asked to spotlight her childhood best friend's missing-person case on her podcast, she uncovers desperate secrets and must face the truth before she can move forward.

What Happens Next by Christina Suzann Nelson
christinasuzannnelson.com

After Ingrid Erikson jeopardizes her career, she fears her future will remain irrevocably broken. But when the man who shattered her belief in happily-ever-afters offers her a sealed envelope from her late best friend, Ingrid is sent on a hunt for a hidden manuscript and must confront her past before she can find the healing she's been searching for.

The Words We Lost by Nicole Deese
A Fog Harbor Romance
nicoledeese.com

BETHANYHOUSE